ONCE UPON A TIME IN THE MYSTICAL NORTH

JOHN LUDDEN

Copyright© 2023 John Ludden
All Rights Reserved.
No part of this book may be reproduced, stored in a retrieval system, or transmitted, in any form or by any means, electronic, mechanical, photocopying, recording or otherwise without permission in writing from the copyright owner.

INTRODUCTION:
DRAGONFLY
1963: ONCE UPON A TIME IN MANCHESTER
SEND IN THE CLOWNS
THE TALE OF FRANKIE ANGELS
STARMAN
SMALL FACES
MADONNA AND MR WILSON
THE SEA ALWAYS WINS
GOOD AFTERNOON MR TURING
JFK: GRANADA CALLING

INTRODUCTION
ONCE UPON A TIME IN THE MYSTICAL NORTH

(All written in three acts)

A collection of ten of my favourite stories with a life of their own. All together in an anthology for the first time. 500 pages of sheer unadulterated, mind-bending madness. I loved writing all of them. Imagination off the scale, some may say round the bend, but you live once and what you leave behind, be it in life or on a page is totally down to you. Wishing upon a crazed Mancunian moon, ladies and gents, I give you the mystical North.

DRAGONFLY tells the story of two young British soldiers. Tommy Conlon and Colin Lindsay. On the day of the Manchester bombing back in 1996, the two boys are 10 years-old and playing in Bogart Hole Clough. They are being observed by a strange looking Dragonfly. Suddenly, Colin catches the insect off guard and grabs it. He gently holds for a second then let's go. The Dragonfly remains unharmed and is grateful. It decides to stay with the two boys until their very end. 2008. Twelve years later, now both Paratroopers, Colin and Tommy are supposedly killed in Afghanistan. However, at the same time they are seen in Manchester. Tommy at the birth of his baby daughter, Colin having a drink with his dad in a local pub.

2014. Six years on, famous novelist James Pearson receives a visit off a former Sergeant-Major who relates to him this extraordinary, poignant tale.

1963: ONCE UPON A TIME IN MANCHESTER tells of the notorious Kray twins visit to Manchester, in the late November of 1963. There has been a thousand tales, all the stuff of legend and myths. This simply a take on what is one of the most fascinating and controversial gangster fables of our time. A story filled with colourful characters lighting up what was deemed a miserable, former ''Cottonopolis'' of the North. A city still recovering from World War two, its infrastructure a landscape of debris and broken buildings flattened by the Luftwaffe, but one teeming with intrigue and gangsters looking to stake a claim. A world still reeling from the JFK assassination, strange, worrying if electrifying times. Then came the Krays with an eye on taking over and raining blood on the rainy city. Only to find despite their reputation as legendary gangland figures, in Manchester this mattered nothing at all.

SEND IN THE CLOWNS is a story that takes place over one Manchester evening back in 1970. During a mysterious time before dawn breaks when George Best, a clown, a Priest, a hitman, a hooker and a dwarf actor walked the late night, early-shift on the canal paths of Manchester, and traipsed over a drawer-bridge, to unknowingly enter a nightclub, that was a world apart. Where the eternal drinkers gathered. A sea of wine, whiskey and pills. Of lovers, dreamers and poets. Scum, lowlifes and those who simply wanted to do nothing more than drink until the sun once more rose over the River Irwell the following morning. A magical, bewitching, but also a dangerous place. Over the rainbow and under a Mancunian moon. Where lives changed forever, where mermaids swam, Red Indians held sway, gangsters played cards under the Devil's eyes and the Grim Reaper often came to collect. The last time where George could have walked down a different road. A once in a lifetime chance of ruin or redemption. This place had a name but it was more of a time. They called it Oz and I'd like to take you all back down that cobbled canal path. A yellow brick road. Because of the wonderful things he did George was given one last chance, but would he take it?

THE TALE OF FRANKIE ANGELS
is set in the Northern English city of Mancunia on Christmas Eve. The assassin Frankie Angels has to deliver one last bullet. Against a constant backdrop of a blistering snowstorm and Sinatra songs, Frankie's Tale unfurls. A story laced with characters good, bad, lost and sheer evil. A city in fear, seething with corruption. Ruled mercilessly since time immortal by the crime syndicate, The Foundation, it finally comes down to a holy man of the cloth who has been handed the power to bring the whole thing tumbling down. It can't be allowed. A call is made. Step forward Frankie Angels. Ordered to save the bosses from this turbulent priest, Frankie is forced over one festive evening to confront past demons and in a city that simply can't sleep, free it forever from chains with one final Christmas hit.

STARMAN
tells the story of two worlds. 9 year-old Charlie Baker from Manchester. A young boy obsessed with the stars and the Moon. And Yuri Gagarin, who on Wednesday 12th April 1961, became the first man in Space. Charlie's and Yuri's worlds become inextricably linked when the Russian cosmonaut tours England, only three months since travelling around the Earth. Theirs' is a short meeting, before they return to separate lives. Charlie's, a life under Northern Mancunian Stars, a gentle existence, whilst for Yuri, the Kremlin's insistence that he never be allowed to fly again, because of his importance as a symbol of Soviet power, breaking his heart inside. Also, underlying the entire story of Starman, what did Yuri Gagarin witness during his short time above the heavens? Why were powerful men in the Russian Politburo panic stricken? To the point where one in particular ensured Yuri, when it appeared set to happen, would

never be allowed to walk on the Moon. A tall tale of our dreams to conquer the stars.

SMALL FACES

It is the winter of 1927, and 40 year-old Laurence Stephen Lowry is sat on a wall overlooking Bolton Wanderer's Football ground, Burnden Park. He's watching as thousands of people make their way from all directions into the ground. Slowly, Lowry starts to sketch what he sees before him. Unbeknown to Lowry, a young boy is staring up toward him. A curious, mischievous 11 year-old called Charlie Riley. Charlie is fascinated by Lowry's Matchstalk figure. So begins a remarkable short period as the two become friends, until events take a tragic turn.

MADONNA AND MR. WILSON

Anthony H Wilson was once famously quoted as saying, when forced to pick between truth and legend, print the legend. What is true is way back in the midst of time, Madonna performed, albeit miming, two songs at the Hacienda. The rest of this story, well? Print the legend! We're going to take you on a mystery tour of late-night, early eighties Manchester with Tony Wilson as your guide, and a star-struck Madonna listening on to his every hyperbole. For one night only Anthony H is back! A love story about a city.

THE SEA ALWAYS WINS

In the midst of a legendary, ferocious storm on September 23 1973, five fishermen off Ireland's West coast trapped a mermaid in their nets. What happened that night unleashed a power and vengeance beyond human comprehension. One so powerful that sixty-one years previously it had wreaked revenge on the ship they said was unsinkable. The magnificent, grandiose RMS Titanic. As the fishermen voted whether to keep or throw the mermaid back, she shed a tear, closed her eyes and passed away. For this heinous sin against the sea those involved paid an unholy price.

Terrible losses and tragedy befell. Poisoned waters and broken hearts. They say the sea always wins and the boys from Drunamere found this to their cost. As Van Morrison sang about a "Moondance" on a Manchester juke box, the story begins to unravel.

GOOD AFTERNOON MR TURING

On the last day before his death, Alan Turing takes a walk in his local park, and comes face to face with the Tall Man. The ghost of his life. The date is Monday 6th June 1954, just nine years after World War two ended, and a dark-suited, solemn faced, 41 year-old Alan Turing is sat on a Wilmslow park bench. He appears nervous and upset. A Tall Man in a similar dark suit, wearing a trilby low down on his face, and clutching a small brief case approaches him. He's smiling. 'Mr Turing sir, I do believe you have been expecting me?'

JFK: GRANADA CALLING

On Friday 22nd November 1963, in Dalla Texas, the 35th President of the United States John F Kennedy was gunned down in Dealey Plaza. An assassination occurring at 12.30.pm in Dallas, 6.30.pm in Manchester, England. This story tells the fascinating tale of how Granada television was the first to break the dreadful news across the country from America, that Kennedy had first been shot at, and then shortly afterwards was indeed dead. It also touches on many of the characters involved on a never to be forgotten day when the world wept.

...BORN IN THE NORTH...

DRAGONFLY

"A Dragonfly to remind me even though we are apart. Your spirit is always with me, forever in my heart."
                    Unknown

PROLOGUE
THE RETREAT FROM AFGHANISTAN. 1842.

In the year of our Lord,
   Thursday 13th January 1842.
 A gravely wounded British assistant army surgeon, 30 year-old Scot William Brydon reaches the British sentry post at Jalalabad, Afghanistan. He's crying out for water. Although part of his skull has been sheared off by a sword, Brydon ultimately survives because he had placed in his hat a magazine that deflected the blow. Brydon is the lone survivor of a 16,000 strong Anglo-Indian expeditionary force that has been slaughtered like cattle in a disastrous retreat from Kabul.

A dying cavalryman told the badly wounded Brydon to take his pony and he rode off into the darkness alone.

The entire force of 690 British soldiers, 2,840 Indian soldiers and 12,000 civilians killed, or in very rare cases taken prisoner. The vast majority of the camp followers, men women and children struck down mercilessly by both Afghan rifle and blade. When later questioned Brydon spoke in terrible detail of the massacre in the Khyber Pass where the Afghans gave no quarter.

For several nights, lights were raised on the gates of Jalalabad and bugles were sounded from the walls in the hope of guiding any further survivors to safety, but none came. The retreat from Kabul was later described as *"The worst British military disaster until the fall of Singapore by the Japanese in World War two exactly a century later."* Initially, it was a sharp-eyed young officer on the walls of Jalalabad who saw Brydon first slowly riding a bedraggled and exhausted pony towards them. When a rescue party reached him, they found a shadow of a man, his head sliced open and a ripped, tattered uniform heavily bloodstained. Brydon appeared more dead than alive. ''Where is the rest of the army?' he was asked.

'I am the Army,' replied Brydon. The young officer offered him a canteen of water which he gulped down. 'How on earth did you escape?' The surgeon looks up towards him and wipes his mouth clear. 'I'm not sure I have as yet,' answers Brydon.

'You see, there was this Dragonfly…'

ACT ONE

THE CAPTAIN

London.
 Soho. 2015.
I think it's best I begin by introducing myself.

   My name is James Michael Pearson. I'm 42 years-old and a former Captain in the British Paratroopers. I saw plenty of action in Bosnia, Kosovo, two tours in Iraq and finally Afghanistan. It was there I came so close to being killed. A Taliban sniper shot me in the chest out on operations, but I was saved by a quick-thinking Sergeant-Major who stemmed the wound, and the swift arrival of a chinook that flew me out of there and back to Camp Bastion. To this day every breath I take pains a little. I can still feel the choking dust and grime of that wretched place. Thankfully, the flashbacks are rare now, though they still strike when least expected. I do tend to drink more, but that's my choice. I do thank my blessings and I never moan because I'm still alive. I'm still here. There are many other soldiers I served with that simply don't have such a luxury.
 I left the army in 2004.
   After resigning my commission I took up a first love of writing. Something I've always been told I had a real talent for. In no time many novels followed. I became an overnight success would you believe, the Daily Mail's flavour of the month with my boy's own tales of the so-called war on terror. Made all the more glorious by changing names and incidents, and increasing the enemy death toll,

and upping the ante by making our lads even more heroic in print than in reality. All done to help increase book sales and by god did it work because I've made an absolute fortune.

 For I had a plan. I was going to be the next big thing in the publishing world. A male JK Rowling but with British soldiers, machine guns and knives, not witches wizards and fucking wands. Established fellow authors in my field wouldn't see me coming and they didn't. I cleaned up. But then something happened.

 I was contacted by a former fellow Paratrooper who informed me of the most extraordinary tale. One which is now told in this book. It's a story of two young soldiers who lost their lives in Afghanistan, but before doing so experienced out in the midst of battle an incident so strange, it left senior officials in the British army seriously contemplating mystical forces were at work in that place.

 A cemetery for the greatest military powers the world has ever seen. Alexander the Great discovered an unconquerable army of Afghan devils in his conquest there. We the English twice, the Russians, the Americans, all have been handed our backsides in Afghanistan and ultimately sent packing. But there was something else out in the killing "poppy" fields and the white mountains of that tortured but beautiful country. Not just the Taliban, but another force, a neutral one possessing a power so beyond our understanding, so profane, the reality of having to deal with it left hardened soldiers on both sides that thought they had witnessed all the horrors of war as broken men. For this thing gave a last fleeting peace in death, and the chance to love a final time before the lights went out, and you travelled on to another place. What am I talking about you may ask?

 I am talking about Dragonfly.

THE SERGEANT-MAJOR

London.
 Soho café. 2015.
  It was a mysterious invitation the type us authors simply just can't resist. An email from an unnamed source who claimed to have the story of the century and that it would make a magnificent book. We shall see, meanwhile I order my usual coffee and watch the door for strangers. There's the usual assortment of bohemian characters in here. Actors preening at their reflections in mirrors and windows. Wanting, praying to be noticed. Writers typing away on laptops. Some pretending to be famous and desperate to finish their epic. Others just desperate to be asked what they are working on so they can ruffle their hair and demand to be fucking left alone. Then there are the chancers who are putting a once in a lifetime pitch to a movie director who is smiling at them and nodding approvingly whilst secretly thinking: "Please just leave me alone and get the fuck out of here!" Other wannabee out of work showbusiness types, though currently collecting glasses in bars or on production lines, whilst chasing the dream. Still clinging onto the outside of a world that has absolutely no inclination of granting their wish to be invited inside. These now are the assorted cast of characters in this next act of the story of my life. As you might have already guessed people watching is a terribly, cruel habit of mine. It's what I do between writing books. In my spare time, I head here and silently take the piss out of this shower of clowns and dreamers. I live nearby in my ridiculously, expensive Soho flat that's paid for by the many thousands of war novels that I sell with the ease a young child devours an ice cream. A public that can't get enough of easy to read stories as my heroic Paratrooper and SAS heroes wipe the desert floor with those evil, Islamic Militants. The Jihadi lunatics bless their fucking, suicide belts

provide perfect fodder as the bad guys. The more horrific they are these days, the more books and kindles I shift. I'm always surprised they don't fucking bother me for royalties.

Hollywood is also beckoning with my agent saying: "You James have a talent for printing money." I've actually made it to the top of my literature mountain, but then why is it I feel so damned empty and miserable all the time? Isn't it obvious, it's because I so miss the army. My ex-family. The camaraderie. This thing what I do now is pretend. It's make-believe. If I'm going to write I want a real story. One that touches both my heart and soul and makes me feel alive again. One to see if I really am as good as the countless five-star reviews on Amazon claim me to be. I go to book signings and I'm feted. At dinner parties I'm the centre of attention, the gossip columns, the Daily Mail constantly write about my latest conquest. It's all fucking bullshit and false. I need a reality back in my life for this isn't who I really am.

Then I see my mystery guy...

It's obviously him because he's like a fish out of water amongst the normal, everyday Soho regulars. I catch his eye, he nods back and heads over towards me.

'Excuse me are you Captain James Pearson?'

'I am.' We shake hands.

'My name is Roy Taylor, I'm like yourself sir, an ex-Paratrooper.'

I point to the chair facing me. 'Please sit down Mr Taylor.'

'Thank you.' He does so. A pretty, dark-haired waitress comes across to serve. 'What would you like?' My guess is a Latvian accent. I've become quite the expert on Eastern European accents since living in Soho. Especially the female ones.

'A coffee black with three sugars please my love.' Her startled expression as she writes it down makes me smile, and Taylor's broad Brummie accent is awakening memories for me of lads I served with years ago, before that Taliban sniper took aim and put me on a different life path. 'You'll be the talk of the kitchen with that order Mr Taylor! Not much call for sugar around here. Soho is full of health freaks you see who believe they're going to live forever.'

'With all due respect they can fuck right off sir. Three sugars in my coffee has never done me any harm. Besides, who the fuck wants to live forever?'

'Absolutely,' I reply. 'I couldn't agree more. They can fuck off!'

I look at his face, the magnificently, groomed moustache. This man could easily pass as Colour Sergeant Frank Bourne out of the movie Zulu. These kind of men haven't changed in hundreds of years.

'It doesn't really take a Sherlock Holmes to work out you were an RSM whilst serving?'

He smiles. 'A lifer sir, but even that wasn't long enough. The army has been very good to me, it's been my family since I was sixteen years old, and I'll be fucked if I know what I'm going to do next. I'm a bit lost to tell you the truth. Pissing in the wind so to speak.'

'I know it's an obvious route but surely security is something for a man of your considerable prowess to go down? I've no doubt someone of your vast experience would be snapped up immediately. I have contacts in this particular world and would be more than happy to put a word forward for you. Not that I believe you'd need it.'

'Much obliged sir, that's very good of you. I've already been offered lots if I'm honest. There are plenty of jobs going in the Middle East for bodyguards. I've security firms ringing and emailing me all the time. The pay is out of this fucking world. More so than ever now we have this bunch of beheading freaks that are all the rage. They've been great for hourly rates. Got the civilians working over there running fucking scared of their own shadows. Especially the Yanks.'

'Those lunatics help in my line of work also. They make splendid villains. Well, the offer is there Mr Taylor. Now then down to business. Why are you here in Soho, what can I do for you Sergeant-Major?'

'Please call me Roy sir.'

'Please call me James.' I reply smiling.

'Oh, fuck no I prefer to call you sir if you don't mind. Force of habit you see. That'll never change.'

Old school doesn't do this man justice.

'Let me get straight to the point, I think I've a bestseller for you. And with all great respect sir it's on a different level to the usual pulp that you serve up. I've read some of it. This is a true story of two young Paras from Manchester that were killed during Operation "Snake Pit" back in 2008. They were bloody good lads and people need to know about how what happened to them.'
'What did happen to them Sergeant-Major?'
'They died sir. Sadly.'
'I see.'
 I'm trying hard to hide my deep disappointment from his pulp comment, I know now I'm going to disappoint the Sergeant-Major with my answer. 'I'm sure they were great boys. The best, but every British soldier killed over there were heroes in my eyes. I'd love to do a book on them all, but I'm afraid I could never get it past my agent. Not to mention the publisher. Not unless there's a truly, unusual angle to their stories.'

   He smiles. 'Fucking hell, you writers sir! Oh, I have an angle for you.' The waitress arrives back with his coffee.
'Thanks love.'
The Sergeant-Major stirs his coffee in between staring at me. It feels like he's trying to see behind my eyes. A dangerous place that. Finally, he finishes and takes a sip.
'Not bad for the Cockneys,' his summing up! 'I've had worse I suppose,' he adds with rather a touch of disdain.
   I really like this man.
   'Sir, I need you to look into my eyes.'
I do so. 'What's the reason for this Sergeant-Major?'
'It's so you know that I'm completely serious about what I'm about to tell you, and not fucking round the bend sir.'
 'I think I can safely say I by no means think you're round the bend. Please go on.'
'Very good sir, I hope you're sitting comfortably because what I'm about to tell you is going to rock your fucking world and everything in it…'

My initial coffee with former Sergeant-Major Roy Taylor turned into a twelve-hour drunken sojourn around the bars and pubs of Soho, that ended with me quite literally having to put him on his train home back to Birmingham, with the help of a couple of young Brummie squaddies. Happily, they told me they'd look after him and make sure he was okay. The man had drunk twice as much as me that evening, this I believe to pluck up the Dutch courage to tell me his tale, and I after listening, shook his hand and promised to write it. What he's told me with tears falling down his face at times is so ridiculously outrageous. It simply sounded like pure, drunken madness, and I honestly can't, don't want to believe a word of it. But such was the Sergeant-Major's sincerity on the subject, I feel duty bound to check it out. Soldiers coming back from the dead, magical dragonflies and strange coloured mists descending down upon battlefields? And he'd the nerve to call my stuff ''Pulp?''
We shall see.

Once back home in the flat I open my whiskey for a last nightcap, and looked through the small list of names Roy wants me to contact. One of them in particular stands out, and will involve a journey back to Afghanistan that hopefully will help bury a few ghosts for me. A former Taliban commander called Abu Ramzi who has reinvented himself as a mover and shaker in the shadowy world of Afghan politics. Before though I have to check out the names on these shores, and it looks like first on the agenda is a trip North to Manchester. I've also been entrusted with a photograph of the two soldiers at the centre of this quite, absurd tale. It was taken at Camp Bastion and has a smiling Colin Lindsay and Tommy Conlon together with their arms around each other. Conlon has a guitar strung around his neck.
''A pair of fucking rascals'' were Roy's words to describe the lads, however as he spoke about them choking up. ''But they were good soldiers'' he added. ''Good lads that didn't deserve what happened to them.'' That was enough to hook me in, I intend to give it my best shot to figure out just what went on over there? It's the least I can do for like me they were Paratroopers. My moustachioed friend from

Birmingham also alarmed me slightly with his insistence that I be careful and to watch my back at all times.

"There are people out there who will not want this to get out. High ranking figures in the establishment, both military and government that buried this when it happened. Men that will do anything to keep this information from the public sir. And I do mean anything."

As pitches go it was truly original,

and it's worked!

MEETING NORTHERN GHOSTS

Manchester. Moston. 2015.

I arrange to meet Rachael Conlon in a huge park called Bogart Hole Clough set in North Manchester. A beautiful May afternoon and we are walking around a circular lake with a small island at it's very heart. The blond-haired, blue-eyed Rachael is pushing her sleeping 7 year old daughter Jessica in a pram. She only agreed to talk after I mentioned the word. At first Rachael never even bothered to answer my emails and putting the phone down on me twice, before I finally managed to stay on the line long enough to say…

''Dragonfly''.

That changed everything.

Rachael points across to the island. 'When they were kids the lads used to hang out over there. Colin used to enjoy scaring Tommy half to death with stories of little horned creatures called Bogarts, that he claimed lived in the trees all around here. She smiles. 'Tommy was a right, gullible sod. They were inseparable and I mean joined at the hip. Colin was Tommy's best man when we got married. Every wedding picture has got the three of us on it. Colin is even on the one where me and Tommy cut the cake! Rachael goes quiet for a moment choosing instead to just stare once more across at the island.

'I'm just glad they were together when, well you know at the end.'

'A man came to see me in London Rachael. A Sergeant-Major Roy Taylor. He knew the lads and told me some outlandish story involving Tommy and Colin. He wants me to write a book about it and even gave me a title. Dragonfly.'

Rachael turns to stare at me. 'When Jessica was born Tommy came to see me in the hospital. He was talking crazy about already being with the angels. At first I thought he was drunk but then later in the day, my mum and dad came to tell me Tommy had been killed in

Afghanistan at just gone two o'clock that same afternoon. I told them that wasn't impossible because he was with me in the hospital, thirty-minutes later? I remember going hysterical. Nothing made sense, none of it. I thought I was going mad Mr Pearson.'

I listen on in quiet disbelief. She's confirming everything Roy said to me. 'What exactly did the army tell you Rachael?'

'They said there'd been a terrible mix up. That Tommy was actually AWOL, but you know as well as I do they were lying, otherwise, you wouldn't be here today. Would you? Besides, there's more. Colin was spotted the same day as well. He was chatting to his dad in a local pub not a ten minute walk from here. It was packed as well so there was loads of witnesses who saw him. I can't explain how this all happened Mr Pearson, I really can't but I know what I saw. I swear on my Jessica's life, Tommy was with me that day and he was no ghost. And I can prove it.'

'How?' I ask.

Rachael hands me her mobile phone. 'Look for yourself.'

I find myself staring at two pictures of Rachael, Tommy and the baby in the hospital. Another one shows just him and Jessica.

'You can check the time and the date on them Mr Pearson. 2.27.pm, on 17th March 2008. Twenty minutes after my husband was said to have been killed. I also have a DVD at home of the hospital CCTV, showing Tommy walking down a hospital corridor. My friend's fiancé worked on security. He sent it to me. Now how can you explain all that away?'

'I can't Rachael, I just can't, but to every riddle there's usually an explanation no matter how strange. I promise you I'll try and find out what happened, but you still haven't mentioned the Dragonfly, why's that?' Rachael smiles and reaches down towards Jessica in the pram to gently lift her hand up. 'Look at this.' She shows me a small birthmark in the shape of a Dragonfly on the little girl's palm.

'I still don't understand Rachael?' She stands back up and stares again at the island. 'When Tommy's and Colin's bodies were finally recovered in Afghanistan, it was found they both had similar

Dragonfly tattoos on their right arms that were the same as my Jessica's.' Suddenly, a chill goes down my spine. Rachael wipes away a tear. 'I don't care what anybody else says the boys came back Mr Pearson.

They returned home to say a last goodbye.'

Later that same day,

I enter The *Mowers Arms* pub on Moston lane, looking for Colin Lindsay's dad, Derek. Rachael had said to me: "You can't miss him. He'll be sat under the window doing the Daily Mirror crossword with a pint of bitter and a whiskey chaser."

True to her description there he was. 60 years-old and sadly looking twenty-years older. Rachael also told me he'd never got over the loss of his wife Helen from cancer, and that combined with Colin's death has left him a broken man. To the point she's convinced that these days he's simply content to drink himself to death.

It's a small vault room.

Apart from Derek, two older men sit at the table next to him playing cards, whilst another man, middle-aged, and clearly the worst for wear is watching the horse racing on a television fixed high in the corner wall. On the jukebox, Andy Williams is singing *The Impossible Dream*. I buy myself a pint of lager from the bar and approach him.

'Mr Lindsay, I'm sorry to disturb your crossword, but do you mind if I had a quick chat with you?' He puts down his paper and stares up towards me. 'Just who the bloody hell are you?'

'My name is James Pearson sir. I'm an author, but in a previous life I was a Captain in the Paras. I'm researching a book on the death of your son and his friend Tommy Conlon. I wondered if I could possibly buy you a drink and maybe half an hour of your time?'

'I already have a drink thank you Mr Pearson. Two drinks. I don't want or need another one. At least not as charity off a stranger.'

'Oh, it's most definitely not an act of charity Mr Lindsay. I would consider it an honour to buy the father of a fallen Para a beer.'

Derek starts to look annoyed. 'Like I said I'm fine. Just how did you find me here anyway?'

'I've spent the afternoon with Rachael Conlon. She sends her love and said you'd be in here.' Derek takes a drink of his pint. He smiles, but it's by no means a happy one. 'I bet she did. How does my granddaughter look?'

'She a beautiful little girl with blond hair and big blue eyes,' I reply. He smiles. 'Obviously takes after her mum. Rachael hasn't been near since what went on, but mind you I can't say I blame her. It's too painful for all of us. Anyway, I suppose you want to know about Colin coming to see me that day?'

I nod and can clearly see the hurt in Derek's eyes. I think best to just let him talk.

'It was a Monday. The 17th March 2008. The day my boy was supposed to have been killed in Afghanistan, but that was absolute bollocks. Colin was sat where you are now. The army later told me a cock and bull story he and Tommy had gone AWOL. That's after firstly informing me he'd been killed in action in Helmand Province. Then shortly after that they put the blame down to a mix up. A clerical error. I ask you, the British Army not knowing whether one of their own was dead or AWOL? Then seen within minutes on both sides of the world? Believe me they had no idea what was going on. None of us did. But now over the years and given time to think. All the lies and the deceit. Well my own eyes don't tell me lies Mr Pearson. My boy was here with me. Living and breathing, and I'll say that to the day I go to the grave.'

'Mr Lindsay, I'm not here to pretend I have all the answers. The truth is I simply don't have a clue what's gone on. There's a part of me thinks this whole thing is crazy. It could've been some kind of mass psychosis caused by grief, but I'm no psychologist. After speaking to you and Rachael and the things you've both told me. Well everything about this is just completely insane?' Derek takes another swig of his pint then finishes the whiskey chaser in a single go. He slams the glass down on the table making the old men playing cards jump and look across. 'Insane?' he says quietly. 'The fact that a son comes to say goodbye to his dad thirty minutes after he's been reported killed on a battlefield ten thousand miles away. And he asks to have one last pint with me before we go to visit his mum's grave a final time. Well yes Mr Pearson, you're right it is insane. Insane and true. It's what happened and no representative of her Majesty's government, a high ranking Colonel, even a military psychologist they sent to see me claiming, like you say, it was all a hallucination brought on by grief can fuck off! Every single one of them.'

He takes a photograph out of his pocket that shows himself and Colin sat at this very same table. 'That was taken at 2-35.pm, on the Monday afternoon. Ask Karen over there behind the bar because she took the picture.' Derek points across to the landlady, a smart well dressed and attractive lady in her mid-forties. She's wiping glasses clean, but has clearly been listening in on our conversation. Karen smiles. 'Yes I took the picture!' she shouts across. 'Colin was in here for an hour before he and Derek left for the cemetery. I loved that lad. Someone's not telling the truth of what happened that day, it's not bloody fair, and I don't care who knows it.'

I look again at Derek. 'About that beer? I insist.'

'Go on then,' he finally relents. Before I can stand to go and get them Karen is stood at the table with two beers. She smiles wide.

'On the house gents. For Colin and Tommy.'

'For Colin and Tommy!' shout the two old men in unison raising their own glasses high. The lone man watching the racing also lifts his drink up in Derek's direction. 'To Colin and Tommy!' he calls out. …'Wherever the fuckin' hell they are?'

Later that night on the train back to London, my mind races with all I've been told. The notion of the Dragonfly tattoos on the soldiers and baby weighs heavy on me. As does Rachael's and Derek's utter insistence that all this is true and really happened. How do you explain the photographs? There really can be no logical explanation. Which brings me to the inevitable conclusion that I'm now in the territory of the unknown? A place and a notion that disturbs though undoubtedly is where the answer to this riddle lies. That the Ministry of Defence lied to Rachael and Derek is beyond doubt. Both were given some whimsical, official cover version of the soldiers going AWOL. That was just nonsense. Everything appeared to rapidly change when rumours leaked from Afghanistan back to Manchester that all hell had kicked off over there regarding the times of their death. As I don't remember it going viral at the time or even ever being reported, the authorities must have worked extremely fast to slam the door shut on this thing. I've no doubt also the Official Secrets Act was shoved down the throats of people who were aware of these events. The oldest trick in the book. What better way to stop witnesses talking than to threaten them with being taken away from their families for years on end? Sergeant Major Taylor was correct, this has rocked my fucking world. So, onto the next name on my list. Yet another ex-Para. Major James Reilly. Taylor couldn't speak highly enough of this man, and when an RSM is so gushing in praise of a superior, a "Rupert" as they scathingly refer to us officer types. Then he really must be worth a call and a chat. Maybe Major Reilly will have some answers to this madness?

THE MAJOR

London. Pall Mall.
The Army and Navy club.
 Originally formed in 1837, the Army and Navy club is known in affectionate terms as "The Rag" by its esteemed members. An oasis for ex-service types whom wish to do nothing more than pass the hours away with old colleagues disappearing back into the sanctity of being amongst their own. No words or conversations required just company, safe from the alien existence of everyday civilian life. Here's where I've arranged to meet Major James Reilly.
I enter into a very large and richly furnished oak-panelled long room. Clearly no expense has been spared, the entire place smells of history and tradition. You can hear the bugles and roar of battle from bygone eras in the air. On the walls sit huge painting of famous battles fought throughout the centuries. There are various gentlemen present bunched together in groups, but I spot Reilly sat alone in a leather armchair in front of a roaring log fire. He's reading The *Times* Newspaper and drinking what I can only guess is some damned, good Scottish whiskey. I simply can't imagine the cheap stuff being served in here. I walk across and he immediately smiles and stands to greet me. 'Captain James Pearson, I recognise you from your file photograph. You're a Paratrooper. One of our own. As you can see I've done some research of my own.'
 I shake his hand. 'Thank you for agreeing to meet me at such short notice Major Reilly.'
'No problem whatsoever. I'm always up for helping out a former Para. How are you now after being shot? It was a close run thing by all accounts.'
 I laugh. 'It hurts only when I breathe or when I laugh! But it does serve to remind me how lucky I am to be alive. And more importantly how grateful I should be.'

Reilly nods in agreement. 'I must say I'm a huge fan of your books. They're so easy to read.' Now there's a back-handed comment if I've ever heard one.

'Thank you. Hopefully Major, with your blessing, you'll play a huge part in my next one.' Again, he smiles but not with quite so much warmth. I sense a real sadness in this man. A great loss.

'Quite. I know what you wish to speak of James. Although you never mentioned it in your letter of introduction, a mutual friend informed me you'd be getting in touch.'

'Does this friend have a Brummie accent and possess the ability the scare the hell out of every officer from Lieutenant rank upwards?'

Reilly laughs loud. 'The very same. Roy told me of your meeting in London. That you were a man to be trusted. A higher recommendation you could not possibly receive. You should be honoured.'

'I truly am. Sergeant-Major Taylor made quite an impression.'

A waiter arrives. A distinguished gentleman waiter with hair as silver as the platter in his arms arrives. He's holding a bottle of the finest Scottish Grouse whiskey.

'Ah, George thank you,' smiles Reilly. 'Leave the bottle with me and my friend here and a spare glass also. Save your legs going backwards and forwards.'

'Thank you, sir,' replies George. Clearly happy to be relieved of the workload, for he's undoubtedly a veteran of seeing how much alcohol can be consumed when two soldiers of the same Regiment meet up to reminisce of times past. It can get messy and especially with the Paras. Reilly fills my glass before his own. 'I take and hope you are a whiskey man?'

'Only before church and after.'

'Good man,' he smiles.

'I hope you realise James this is damned hard for me to talk about.'

'You mean the Official Secret Acts? Major, I wouldn't expect…'

'Good grief, no not that,' replies Reilly. 'They never got to me. Obviously thought I wasn't the type to go telling tall stories of angels and ghosts. I come from their world you see James. I belong to the right clubs. I was born into the right family. The right side of the road. A good sort you might say.'

'You mean the establishment?'

'I mean those who really hold the reins of power in this country James. For generations upon generations these people have made the decisions that shape our lives and the vast majority of the kingdom. They place their puppets in Ten Downing Street. They decide when we go to war and no one is too big, too popular or too powerful to defy them. Remember a tunnel in Paris? They are all knowing and utterly ruthless when challenged. It's these people who killed the story almost immediately regarding Lindsay and Conlon. For this incident scared them rigid. You can't bully or intimidate a force above life and death. They realised something extraordinarily occurred that day back in March 2008, and they got spooked.'

'And yet despite all this Major. The possible, dreadful consequences for yourself and your family. You remain willing to go out on a limb and tell me all that you know about what occurred. Maybe later even go public?'

'I am, I just want to do what's right James. They were my boys and my responsibility. Lindsay and Conlon were part of a recce platoon that was to be amongst the first on the ground in Operation Snakebite. The Paras job was to lure the Taliban out of Musa Qaleh and into an open firefight. Then when hooked the American 82nd Airborne would sweep in like the Seventh Cavalry and together we'd wipe the floor with them. However, the best made plans as they say. All went to hell because things went wrong from the very off. As the first chinook came in to land it suffered massive, small arms and rocket fire. Sheer bad luck struck when the doors that had already been opened in preparation to unload the paras jammed tight. As the chinook took evasive action to escape being shot down, Private Lindsay lost his balance and fell out. Immediately, Conlon jumped after his best mate. Such was the ferocity of incoming the decision was made to evacuate and call for air cover for the two soldiers. Unfortunately, the lads had lost most of their equipment in the fall and it was impossible to locate them before the Afghans did.'

Reilly takes a drink of the whiskey. He appears deep in thought. Lost, even. 'I don't believe the memories of these paratroopers and the bravery they shown in the face of overwhelming odd has ever been truly recognised. It was buried James and it stinks to high heaven. They showed as we say uncommon valour in the face of a fearsome foe fighting on their home ground. It was a remarkable display of sheer guts. An American drone recorded their last moments as the enemy moved in for the kill. The boys had held out for over five hours against three hundred Taliban with just small arms and a handful of grenades and knives. Their courage even impressed the Taliban. I received a letter from the local commander, a man called Abu Ramzi, who claimed the boys would have been taken prisoner but never shown any interest in surrendering. As for what happened next?'

Again, he goes quiet. The name Ramzi given to me by Taylor now makes sense. I look at Reilly's face. It's like he's back in Afghanistan. 'The Drone also picked up footage that even though I've seen it with my own eyes I still find hard to believe. Once the soldiers had been overrun, hordes of Taliban are seen bolting from the scene. Something or somebody had reduced them to blind panic. Now, I need to ask that you take a huge leap of faith with me here James. Lindsay's and Conlon's lifeless bodies are shown to move.'

Reilly finishes his whiskey in one slug then looks me straight in the eyes. 'I'm not mad I assure you. Despite how all this may sound. I'm prepared to stand up in a civilian or military court of law and repeat everything what I've told you here today.'

'I don't think you're mad Major, far from it and I can't thank you enough for speaking to me. But there's another thing I must ask. What do you know about the Dragonfly?' Reilly pours himself another drink and then me. 'Did you know James that in ancient Afghan folklore, the Dragonfly is said to weigh people souls in order to decide if they are worthy enough to enter heaven.'

Reilly raises his glass and chinks mine.

'I think that maybe is the answer you're looking for, and I wish you the best of luck in finding it.'
'Thank you Major.'
'Also James, give me the address of where you live. Tomorrow I will arrange for something to be dropped off for you.'
'What is it?'
Reilly smiles. 'Best you see for yourself.'

WAR OF CIVILISATIONS

It's way past midnight when I finally return home to the flat. I'm exhausted and my brain is struggling to take in everything Reilly's told me. I switch on the light before placing my jacket on the door hanger. 'Good evening Mr Pearson. Please excuse me I let myself in.' I hear this, then see him. He's in his early forties. Six-feet tall, slim and with eyes that dart around a room giving me no doubt as to this man's true occupation. A spook and to make matters worse he's busy helping himself to my whiskey. The man smiles and raises his glass towards me.

'You've very fine tastes in firewater Mr Pearson. Jack Daniels. It says a lot about a man's character. Slainte!'

I detect the slightest hint of an Irish accent. Northern. 'Is it worth the time threatening you with breaking and entering and calling the Police?'

'I am the police James. I am the army, I am the wind, the rain and the fucking sun so far as you're concerned.'

I go to pour myself a drink. 'What do you want from me?'

'What were you doing in Manchester talking to Rachael Conlon and Derek Lindsay. And today your meeting with James Reilly?'

'You're MI6, you work it out.'

Again, he smiles. 'James, James. You've absolutely no idea what you're getting yourself into here. You need to step back and listen very carefully to what I'm about to say. Now, I'm here tonight as a friend and to say you're being taken for a fool by people who are simply out to make money. They look at you and see nothing but a cash cow. The two soldiers were killed in battle and that's the truth. Anything else, all you've been told is false. It's a set up simple as that. Am I making myself clear here?'

'What are you afraid of Mr, I'm sorry do you have a name?'

The man smiles and shakes his head. 'I'm the man with no name James. I'm the man who lurks in the shadows. I'm a simple spook in a wheel keeping this Sceptre Isle of ours free from slipping into the hands of the unclean and the ungodly. You may not have noticed but we're on the verge of a holy war. Christian against Moslem and there's absolutely no guarantee that we're going to win it. This Dragonfly nonsense. Do you really believe the world is ready for that? Another religion for fuck's sake? More mad bastards in suicide belts blowing themselves up on the tube for some god forsaken cause?'

'Hold on, only a moment ago you told me the entire thing is a fabrication. A money-making scam? Make your mind up spook.'

The MI6 man takes another drink and leans back in the chair. His eyes never leaving mine. 'Are you a religious man James?'

'No.' He shakes his head and appears disappointed in my answer. 'I can never understand that in a man. Especially one who has experienced war. Someone like yourself who so nearly died. I always believed that would bring someone closer to the almighty?'

'I was the opposite. What I saw on the battlefield was enough to make me turn away from religion. Everlasting life, purgatory, white pearly gates and the devils horns? Not for me I'm afraid.'

The spook shakes his head. 'We all need a reason to believe James. The shutting of a coffin lid and being dropped in a freshly dug grave, or vanishing behind the black velvet curtain to be burnt to a cinder in a crematorium. That can't just be the finishing credits. It simply can't. be. So there must be a heaven and a hell James. Otherwise, what's the fucking point of anything?'

'I don't agree, I believe it's all hocus pocus.'

He's clearly not happy with me. 'Oh James, James, there's nothing quite so soul sapping as trying to convince a non-believer, so I'm not going to even bother. Tell me do you have any great purpose in your life?'

I shake my head. 'I'm not sure,' I reply. Again, he appears annoyed with my answer. 'Well I believe we're all here for a purpose. Mine? Well it's to keep the status quo. To be ready for the war of civilisations when the Islamic hordes strike and to ensure we blow their world to fucking kingdom come. And believe me we are prepared and willing to do just that. As for you, I think after your close brush with death in Afghanistan, it's unnecessary to now go and be a crusader. Let me tell you it's a foolish, dangerous wish to be seen as the man who paved the way for a new belief. A third testament for a new God. Do you realise just how dangerous a man like that is to the people I represent James? More so than Hitler, Stalin, the Princess of broken hearts or Bin Laden. Do you know what lengths we'd go to ensure such a scenario never comes to pass? We would unleash Armageddon on such a false idol. Everything in our power. It would never be allowed to happen. Never. Now, please think on what we've spoken about this evening. I urge you one last time forget all you've heard about Dragonfly. Believe me James and I don't say this lightly, I really don't. You would do well to heed my words before it's all too late.' The spook stands up and heads for the door. He then turns to face me and smiles wide. 'Oh, one last thing get the locks changed on this fucking door. I could've been a bad guy.' With that he steps out to leave me alone with my thoughts.

So, Reilly was correct they really are spooked. My next move? Well there's one name left on the list of contacts given to me by Roy Taylor. That of the former Taliban commander Abu Ramzi. It means returning to a place where I so nearly lost my life thirteen-years ago. Where I was twice given the last rites by an Army Chaplin, who I remember the second time looked a little cheated that his God had been denied by me refusing to die. My imagination maybe, well tough, fucking luck, I'm still here. I do believe now my life does have a kind of a purpose despite what I claimed to the spook, because nothing or no one is going to stop me telling this story. It's time to pack my suitcase and bury a few ghosts whilst hopefully discovering new ones.

It's time to go back to Afghanistan.

ACT TWO

CHASING DRAGONFLIES

Kabul.
 Soon, as the doors to the airplane swing open the hot air gushes wildly into my face. The blazing heat momentarily stifles me. I find it hard to breathe but this soon passes. The smells and the sweat, the magnificent red sunsets, the orange dawns and breath-taking starry nights. An extraordinary country that has splashes of beauty etched onto its blood-soaked, canvas. No other nation in the world has had its every rock, crevice, mountain and mud hut fought over for so long and at such cost to life. I'm back in Afghanistan and somehow it feels like I've never been away.
 I pull up in a ramshackle taxi outside a rundown café,
 on the side of a packed kerb. Walking past me are Afghan women in full black burkas and long-bearded men with mistrusting eyes all staring at me like I'm an alien. I must be a rare sight around here these days and I feel like a sheep surrounded by wolves. I step out of the cab with a suitcase and sling a white jacket over my shoulder. I motion for the taxi to go, I take a deep breath and head inside the cafe. This is where I've arranged to meet Abu Ramzi. It's crammed tight with customers, but I spot one empty table in the corner so head over and sit down. All heads turn and take an interest in the blond-haired European amongst them. They whisper amongst themselves. Some no doubt already plotting the worst. What the fuck am I doing here, I must be mad? Since the British Army have now all but pulled out of Afghanistan, general opinion must be either I'm fucking mad or just stupid. Most likely both. I have to agree being honest. I attempt a

rather, pathetic friendly smile at a gruesome looking gang of four Afghans on a nearby table, whom simply stare back at me in derision. Big mistake. From my jacket I take out a notepad, a pen and start to scribble in order to try and appear a little relaxed. When in truth I'm anything but. Suddenly a large, impressive man in a white flowing gown appears at my table. It has to be him. This is 45 year-old Abu Ramzi. Warrior features. Hugely bearded with haggard but sparkling lived-in eyes that look like they've seen and been through the gates of hell and back.

Ramzi smiles. 'So, it is true. The man who chases dragonflies has come to Afghanistan! Welcome my friend. My name is Abu Ramzi. I believe you may need me to help finish your book?' Ramzi offers me his hand and we shake. He sit's himself down opposite. Ramzi is Taliban and should hate my guts, but I've been assured by Taylor he's the man to talk too. The man who can tie up all the loose ends in this crazy story. I notice three men positioning close by. Their eyes all over the café and me. They're clearly armed and undoubtedly are Ramzi's bodyguards. One hardly bothers to hide his Kalashnikov beneath a long sheep coat. I pray they're also not my hit squad.

'I received your email Mr Pearson. It made for very interesting reading. 'Is it true then you are a former British army officer?'

'Yes, the Paratroopers. I was stationed here back in 2002/2003.' He smiles. 'Ah a very, bloody year for my country if I remember right, and is it not also true that you were nearly killed by one of our snipers?'

I smile. 'You've done your homework, I'm impressed. Your boys nearly got me, but not quite. I was airlifted out by a Chinook helicopter just in time back to Camp Bastion. But it was a close call.'

Ramzi nods. 'That pleases me. Then, the other side of your rainbow Mr Pearson. You left the army and became a writer?'

'I put words together,' I laugh. 'But not necessarily always in the right order.'

'Do not be too hard on yourself Mr Pearson. What man can say that he possesses both the heart of a warrior and the soul of a poet?'

'You obviously haven't read any of my books Mr Ramzi.'

Ramzi laughs out loud. 'I think you would be very surprised what I have read. And I shall definitely be reading your next book. Maybe we shall win in that one?'
'I doubt it.'
Ramzi again bursts out laughing. He produces from his pocket a small photograph and places it on the table in front of me. A tattoo of a Dragonfly on an Afghan man's arm. I pick it up. For a moment I'm shocked, but this is the reason I've come to Afghanistan. To solve the riddle. I take from the centre of my notebook two more photographs and hand them to Ramzi. They too are of the same Dragonfly.
'Both Lindsay and Conlon were found with a similar tattoo when they died.' Now it's Ramzi's turn to go ashen-faced. He can't take his eyes off them. 'So, it is true then the legend is correct. The English soldiers were truly saved by angels.'
'Not angels, Mr Ramzi. Well, not as we know them in the Bible or the Koran.'
'Then what?'
I put the three photographs alongside each other on the table.
'I have a theory. Totally crazy maybe but I'm close to proving it. Have the Taliban agreed to meet me?'
'Yes but with many reservations, luckily they were willing to go off my recommendation. The order was to kill you if I did not like what I heard or found.'
'And?' I reply. Hoping I'm not going to regret asking such a stupid, fucking question. Happily Ramzi smiles once more. 'I think I like you already Mr Pearson. You are completely safe in my protection. I shall make the arrangements. Meanwhile, it is not safe for you to be alone in Kabul at the moment. There are many here with vendettas and very long memories. I invite you to be my guest. Come and stay with me at my home tonight, and tomorrow we shall travel up into the mountains?'
'Thank you that's very generous.'
'Not at all. I indeed have selfish reasons, for I wish to know all about these two English boys who refused to die.'

'Oh, but they did die Mr Ramzi, just not at their decreed time.'
He looks at me like a 5 year-old child who has just been told there's no Father Christmas. 'I think I have a lot to learn yet about that day Mr Pearson.'

Abu Ramzi's home.

It's night time in Kabul and the black skies are glittering with stars. This sight one of the few things about Afghanistan that I've missed. Ramzi and I are sat at a small table on a balcony high overlooking the huge city. We've just finished a meal. Both of us are smoking and looking out at the view. There are few lights. Power cuts regularly reduce Kabul to darkness. 'I notice no ring on your finger Mr Pearson. Are you not married?'

'Divorced.'

'I'm sorry to hear that. No children?'

'No,' I smile. 'I'm afraid my being shot in the chest and leaving the army was not in the plans of my upwardly, mobile Suzanne. Being in a wheelchair for twelve months and acquiring a sudden taste for the strong stuff to quench the pain interrupted her forward momentum in life. And to be brutally honest, I wasn't a good person to be around back in those days. I remember one memorable occasion taking great delight whilst drunk in pouring my colostomy bag over the floor at her Parents fiftieth wedding anniversary. I'm afraid there's no coming back after that particular party trick.'

'Hardly,' smiles Ramzi. 'I suppose it is true. Women and war do not make good bed fellows. Would you care for, as you say, a drop of the hard stuff now?' I'm shocked after convincing myself Afghanistan would be liquor free. But also genuinely happy to hear this because I could murder a fucking drink!

'What, you have alcohol?'

'I am what you may call an open minded man Mr Pearson. I have been fighting and killing for so long as I can remember. The Prophet, peace be upon him will forgive a lot worse. For I have more than earned a place by his side with my deeds when the time truly comes.'

Ramzi stands and heads inside. He returns with an unopened bottle of Jack Daniels. A laughing Ramzi shows it to me. 'Does this, as the saying goes, float your ship?'

'I think you'll find its float your boat. And yes Mr Ramzi, it most certainly does! My favourite actually.' Ramzi pours the whiskey into two glasses. He hands one to me then raises his for a toast.

'To our Dragonfly!'

I smile and we drink.

'Are you married yourself?'

'Mr Pearson, I lost my wife and two daughters in a rocket attack on our village seven years ago. The Americans in their ungodly rush to target me decided to wipe out the entire village. They did so, but unfortunately for them I wasn't there. Sadly, my family were. As ever their information outdated and incorrect. I ask you? How can the greatest power the world has ever seen be so wrong so many times?'

'I'm so very sorry.'

Ramzi smiles. 'Please it is okay. We all have as it says in your holy book, our crosses to bear Mr Pearson. That I am afraid is mine and mine alone. I bear no malice towards you or the British. As for the Americans? History dictates they will come back in force here one day. Then I shall settle this matter with them.'

For a moment we go quiet. 'So, then,' our silence happily finally broken by Ramzi. 'The two soldiers. Please tell me their names and where they were from?' Ramzi swiftly refills both his and my glass.

'Their names were Colin Lindsay and Thomas Conlon from an English city called Manchester.'

'Manchester United?'

'Yes,' I reply smiling, the very same.'

'What were they like?'

'Well it appears they were the best of friends from childhood. Both joined the army together. Both served in Iraq, then came to Afghanistan in 2008, and in Helmand Province on March 17, they were cut off from their platoon, South of Musa Qala. Surrounded by the Taliban in a poppy field, overrun and killed. Then, well, that's where our story really begins.'

'The Dragonfly took them away yes?'

I smile and take a large slug of my whiskey before answering Ramzi, because I think I'm going to need it. 'We've incredible American drone footage of a strange mist coming down on the poppy field as the Taliban were closing in for the kill. As for what happened next, who the hell really knows?'

Ramzi shakes his in disagreement, 'No, no Mr Pearson. I can tell you now there can be no argument about what happened next because my people saw it. They witnessed the Dragonfly over the soldiers. We believe it was a miracle. An act of God.'

I shrug my shoulders. 'That, I don't know. I can't tell you.'

A surprised Ramzi appears taken a back at my answer.

'How then do you explain what happened over the following days?'

'I can't,' I reply. 'I'm an atheist. I can't believe a so-called, all-knowing super-being could ever have in his heart to save a pair of young soldiers in these circumstances, when allowing for so much other senseless bloodshed to happen elsewhere. What was it, a minor blip of conscience on his part? I don't think so. Whatever happened to Lindsay and Conlon was indeed unearthly, but I don't believe for a moment it was the act of some God. That for me simply doesn't add up. Anyone can do the maths. Just look around the damn world at the moment, because it's hardly heaven right here on Earth is it?'

Ramzi is clearly shocked at my comments, but smiles and again refills our glasses. 'Yours is a much-needed voice in the wilderness Mr Pearson. But I strongly recommend that whilst in my country you do not ever repeat such comments. Heartfelt as they may be because otherwise one of my countrymen is likely to take your fucking head off!' Immediately, I realise I've overstepped the mark.

'I'm sorry. I didn't intend to offend your hospitality. I do tend to get a little carried away on matters of heaven and earth when it comes to this particular subject. But I promise not to mention this again.'

'Please do not apologise. As you can see Mr Pearson, I am not your archetypal Afghan male who screams Allah Akbar at the mere mention of a so-called slur on the Prophet. May peace be upon him. I come from a wealthy background. I was educated in England and as you are finding out have a fondness for the finer things in life. What happened with the Dragonfly has only increased my bewilderment at how we give up our lives so willingly for a God who gives us so little back. It is not as if I am losing my religion, just questioning his wisdom sometimes? I too have to be careful because like you, I could quite easily lose my head at times!'

I stare at Ramzi and can't help but smile. 'I have to say, you sound remarkably like me!'

Ramzi laughs. 'Perhaps. Ah, it must be the whiskey! We kick the hell out of every army they ever send against us, so instead of bombs and missiles, you foreigners now change tact and poison our minds through Mr Jack Daniels here.' Abu Ramzi is definitely not what I expected, for that I'm truly grateful.

THE FIFTH SEASON

The next morning we're in Abu Ramzi's battle worn, broken-down open truck travelling along a high ribbon road in the Afghan hills. Ramzi is driving whilst I'm staring out at the never-ending vast Mountain ranges. 'These mountains Mr Pearson. These mountains are stained with the blood of hundreds of thousands. The shepherds and goat herders claim at night the ghosts of the fallen scream out in many different languages. But mainly Macedonian, Russian and English.'

I smile at this. 'I was so nearly one of them.'

'I understand that but you my friend was spared for a reason,' replies Ramzi. 'To write the book and bring this story of the Dragonfly to the entire world.'

I turn to stare at Ramzi. 'I want everyone to know what happened to those two soldiers. And when the establishment tries to dismiss it as the rantings of a madman because they will. I need men from both sides of the war whom were present that day to admit what they saw. This is why today is so important.'

Ramzi's arm grips tight onto mine. 'I promise you Mr Pearson, the effect on the Taliban fighters that day was equally as it was on the British soldiers. As you will very well hear and see for yourself soon enough.' After a further two hours of travelling on death, defying twisting mountain ridges, masquerading as roads, we finally arrive at the Taliban camp. Fifty tents and more litter the landscape. Now all pitched out in the open with the fear of air attacks ceased. It's set between a mountain crevasse and is a hive of activity. A huddle of armed men gathers around Ramzi's truck as we enter. It's clear he's a warrior of huge respect. Many greet him with friendly waves and knowing nods which he returns. Fighters high upon the mountainside raise their rifles in recognition. This man it appears is truly a hero amongst his people. As for me? There's clearly a feeling of great unease. I feel like I'm being viewed once more like a surrounded single sheep being made ready to have its throat cut. Ramzi puts a much needed, reassuring arm around my shoulder. 'Do not worry. During your time in Afghanistan, the British were viewed as worthy opponents, now you are our guest. These men around who stare with what you think is hatred in their eyes also have respect for your presence amongst them. 'Relax,' he smiles. 'The war between us has finished Mr Pearson. For now! Besides, they have probably heard the rumours that you come with news of the Dragonfly?'

The camp leader, 40 year-old Rahid Khan approaches.

Slim, wiry and long bearded, he strides through the crowds with arms outstretched to greet one of his oldest friends. Ramzi sees him and steps out the truck. He walks towards Rahid Khan as a path opens up between the fighters for them to come together. They embrace. Khan puts an arm on Ramzi's shoulder and smiles wide.

'You are truly a sight for sore eyes. My dear brother, how are things in Kabul? Now that your business is politics and to wine and dine with politicians and businessmen.'

'Maybe that is true but it is not my world Rahid Khan. My place is here in the mountains alongside you brother.'

Khan starts to laugh. 'But there is no one left to fight anymore, we have beaten them all!' Ramzi nods in recognition of his friend's words, but remains unconvinced. 'Someone else will come along. They always do. Keep our Kalashnikovs oiled well my friend. We Afghans, whilst the rest of the world have four seasons in Winter, Spring, Summer and Autumn have a fifth. War!'

Both men laugh.

'Come,' says Ramzi, 'I have someone I wish you to meet.'

Abu Ramzi and Rahid Khan come walking across towards me.

'Rahid Khan, may I introduce you as my oldest friend to my newest. The Englishman here Mr James Pearson.'

Khan warmly shakes my hand. 'Welcome to my camp Mr Pearson. Mullah Talwasa has agreed to meet you shortly. This is a great honour for it is rare these days he shows his face amongst us. You are truly an important man. I am led to believe you are a former officer in the

British army. Is this true?'

'Yes, it is. I was a Captain with the Paratroopers back in 2002-2003.'

'We have great respect for the British soldier. One of the reasons you have been allowed to meet with the Mullah today is that we see a little of ourselves in you. You are, despite your million-pound helicopters, planes and surveillance drones, a warrior race and a worthy opponent. Twice you have attacked Afghanistan, I pray now you have learned your lesson and do not come back looking for a fight a third time.'

I smile and look around the camp. 'The world has moved on. I fear we maybe marching further South. A new enemy has shown itself. I don't think you will have to worry about us coming again any time soon.'

Khan starts to laugh. 'Oh, we won't worry, I can promise you that! Come, let us go eat and drink before business.'

Khan walks between myself and Ramzi with a hand on both our shoulders. Like Ramzi he's a highly impressive man. ''A worthy opponent'' indeed. From someone like Khan, I'm not sure there can be a finer compliment.

THE WITNESS

Taliban camp. Afghanistan. 2014.
  Sitting cross-legged, hundreds of Taliban fighters watch on as the ageless Mullah Talwasa makes his entrance. His beard now pure white and down by his midriff giving him the nickname of the "Snow King." A living legend amongst Afghans, he's led them in the wars against all the great powers. The Russians, the Americans and the British. Talwasa will sit in judgement about what exactly occurred on that day back in Helmand Province, 2008.
Sat opposite him are Abu Ramzi, myself and Rahid Khan.
  Nearby is a witness from the day. A veteran Taliban fighter by the name of Hafiz, who is claiming he killed one of the English soldiers in a knife fight. Hafiz is staring across at me and I return the stare. At times old feelings are hard to disguise, and there's still a part of me that would love five minutes alone with this man so I could rip his fucking head off. I feel Ramzi tug my arm.
  'I shall translate everything you need to hear. First they will hear the testimony of Hafiz. There were many others present in the camp, but only he has volunteered to speak. They are scared of coming forward. When Talwasa has finished with Hafiz, he will call for you. But my friend and this I beg of you. You must show great respect. Do not repeat what we talked about last night. Our snow king over there with the white beard will not take kindly to the Koran being reduced to the literary status of a Harry Potter novel. If you do so we could both easily lose our heads.'
  'Don't worry,' I reply. 'I promise no mention of wands or magic spells.' Ramzi looks at me like I'm mad but then smiles.
  'Thank you. I promise my new English friend if we survive this another bottle of Jack Daniels awaits us on returning back to Kabul. There Mr Pearson we shall drink to a successful end to our task. Agreed?'
  'Please call me James.'
  Ramzi smiles again. 'Then James it shall be!'

This is insane and just for a moment I wish I was back in the safety of my boring Soho café watching the actors and players go through their daily routine. But it's only for a moment. I need to see this through now to the end no matter what the cost.

   Mullah Talwasa motions to Hafiz and he stands to approach. Hafiz anxiously looks around at a thousand pairs of eyes upon him. Including mine. 'Speak honestly of what you saw that day,' orders Talwasa. Hafiz is clearly a bag of nerves.

  'I am not wise or educated my chief. I cannot read, I am but a poor man of the mountains. I fight only for God and to feed my family, but I know what I saw that day was not of this world. I, I also have to speak of the bravery by the young English soldiers as we set upon them. Even as we shot and stabbed their bodies they clung to each other like true brothers. They fought side by side until the very end and were a fine enemy. But it was as they lay dead and we wiped our knives clean of their blood that strange things began to happen.'

  I find myself feeling sick.

 Hafiz suddenly appears to chokes on his words and he stares up towards the sky. As if asking for guidance. A large murmur goes around the camp. Something tells me Ramzi was right, there are most definitely many others amongst this lot whom know what's coming next. Hafiz appears a most unlikely spokesman. I ponder his reason for coming forward.

'On with your story!' snaps Talwasa.

 Hafiz nods and rubs his eyes as if to fight off a tear. 'Time suddenly seemed to slow down. It was like being in a hazy fog. Then I saw the Dragonfly. It hovered over the English soldier's bodies. I couldn't take my eyes off it. Nobody could.' Again, Hafiz stumbles on his words. I doubt he's going to be able to carry on.

  'You must keep talking!' roars out an impatient Talwasa. 'Be a man about all this. Go on.' Hafiz nods after being admonished.

  'I saw the soldier's eyes open.'

   A rumble of shock and incomprehension echoes loud over the crowd. Finally, Mullah Talwasa recovers and glares angrily at Hafiz, 'What you say is impossible. You have already stated that these two

men had been killed. To use your own words. "Stabbed and shot."
So, how can this be? How can they come back from the dead?'
'I can only tell you what I saw my chief. I swear in the eyes of God, I am telling the truth. Why should I lie about such things? Their eyes opened and they were dead. My own blade ended the life of one of them. I watched the light disappear from his eyes and then when I saw the Dragonfly hovering over them...'

'You mention the Dragonfly again,' interrupts Talwasa. 'Why is it so important in this story? The mountains are full of insects. Of many kinds of Dragonflies. Why do you keep talking of this nonsense?'
'Because ever since that day I have seen the Dragonfly in my dreams.
It will not go away. I believe that it brought the two soldiers back to life.'

'Enough!' erupts Talwasa who has clearly heard too much. 'You are dismissed. One more word of heresy from your mouth and I will have your tongue cut out.' Hafiz bows his head as if praying for forgiveness. He returns to the crowd and sits back down. Mullah Talwasa points towards me. Abu Ramzi grabs my arm and we both stand. 'Come James, as they say in the movies. Time to rock and roll.' Where is Ramzi finding these lines?

We walk to face our inquisitor. Talwasa eyes me like I'm shit on his shoes. 'So, Abu Ramzi, you have decided to speak for the Englishman?'
Ramzi nods. 'I have my chief. This is a good man and I trust his word.'

'I will be the judge of this infidel's story. Tell him to tread carefully, I will not have this foreigner insult the Prophet by dragging his name into matters of witchcraft. He is a guest and we shall respect this, but let him understand there is a line he must not cross.'

Ramzi translates to me Talwasa's words and I smile on hearing. 'Tell him he's going to hear the truth. Witchcraft or not. Also ask him if he's sitting comfortably because it's a long, fucking story.'

A worried looking Ramzi shakes his head towards me.
'You bloody, stubborn Englishman. I will happily translate the second part, but not the first, because I like my head where it is. On

my shoulders.'
　I begin, with Ramzi translating...

NO TOMORROW

Camp Bastion. Afghanistan.
 Sunday 16th March 2008.
 It's late afternoon,
   as 37 year-old Major James Reilly of the British Parachute Infantry Regiment is in his tent stood up before a crowd of RSM's and junior officers. All are listening intently on as Reilly prepares to brief them on an upcoming mission.
'Well, gentleman, let me tell you, after our recent short period of inactivity events around here are going to liven up very shortly.'
  He points to a large hanging map and places his finger on a specific reference point. 'At first light tomorrow we shall be air-lifted by chinooks here. East of the Taliban stronghold at Musa Qaleh to begin Operation Snake Pit. Our task is to flush the enemy out of the town and into an open fight. Yes, we're going there to stay and boys, I do believe we're going to wipe the floor with them.'
  Across the tent there are many smiles. Reilly is hugely popular with his men and has vowed to himself that he'll be always on the front line alongside them during their tour of duty. 'Now, we know Terry Taliban are around a thousand strength in Musa Qaleh and won't be able to resist having a pop at us, but let me reassure you, once we're engaged and they are hooked then our US cousins, the 82nd Airborne will be on hand to help. This is no hit and run, we're in there to seek and destroy the bastards. It will be destruction, not reconstruction. Hearts and minds are being put aside for the moment as tomorrow the Paras do what we do best. We go face to face, eye to eye, with the enemy and we fucking nail them.'
  Suddenly, a feeling of excitement sweeps over all present. This is what they've been waiting for. 'So, just to sum it all up, we're the hare, the Taliban are the dogs and the Americans as usual are the

bookies that will undoubtedly clean up and take home the winnings. Which, gentleman, is Musa Qaleh and 23,000 miles of Helmand Province. An area half the size of England. We take the town and the enemy are finished around there. Now, any questions?'

38 year-old, Sergeant-Major Roy Taylor stands to speak. Taylor is a battle hardened veteran of Northern Ireland, Bosnia and two Middle-Eastern wars. He's highly respected by all present. A tough, no-nonsense Brummie never afraid to speak his mind even to superior officers. 'Sir, in regards of how we lure the rag heads out of the town? May I suggest my magnificent rendition of Tom Jones' Delilah?' Laughter erupts across the tent including Reilly, who's smiling wide. 'Thank you Sergeant-Major, I shall keep that in mind, but I don't really think it'll be necessary. I believe four hundred paratroopers screaming blue murder will prove sufficient to entice them into our grasp. But very much appreciated anyway Roy!'

Sergeant-Major Taylor salutes and sits back down.

'Okay then, to wrap up. Tell the boys to get a good night's rest for tomorrow we finally get to make our mark on this whole, sorry mess. And I want us to ensure it's a positive one. Thank you, that's all gentlemen. Let's get this done.'

They all stand, salute and filter slowly out.

'Roy, can I have a moment please?' calls out Reilly, to Sergeant-Major Taylor. Taylor heads across to the Major.

'Sir?'

'I just wanted to say that if I should get hit tomorrow, I need you at the very top of your game. My younger officers will turn to you for advice, so don't be afraid to kick backsides and hand out a few rollicking's on my behalf. Is that understood?'

'Crystal sir. But if you don't mind me saying you're talking fucking rubbish, because no rag head would dare to shoot you, on the grounds that I would rip his head off and shove it up his fucking backside. With all due respect sir.'

Major Reilly smiles. He expected nothing less from this man.

'Thanks Roy. You're on the first chopper in. When we arrive shortly after, I expect a nice cup of hot tea waiting with two sugars. Carry on

Sergeant-Major.' Taylor salutes one last time before turning and stepping out of the tent, leaving Reilly staring alone at the map. Something in him is nagging and he can't put his finger on it. Afghanistan never fails to surprise in a bad way and Reilly is worried. 'This damn, fucking country,' he mutters quietly under his breath.

  Nearby, in another tent housing paratroopers, two squaddies from Manchester are sat lounging around. They are 22 year-olds, Colin Lindsay and Tommy Conlon. Lifelong friends, they enlisted in the Regiment together. Tommy sit's strumming on a guitar. A fanatical Oasis fan, he's currently serenading anyone who dares to listen with a tuneless version of Oasis's *Wonderwall*. Lost in his own world, Tommy is oblivious to all.
... "Backstreet, the word is on the street, that the fire in your heart is out. I'm sure you've heard it all before..."
 Colin has had and heard enough, 'Oi, Tommy mate. Give it a rest eh. Don't you think it's bad enough being in this dump without having to listen to you murdering one of the greatest songs ever written?'
Tommy stops strumming and looks across at Colin. 'I've got feelings you know. There's no fuckin' need for that!' Around the tent other soldiers watch with increasing amusement. Suddenly, Sergeant-Major Taylor enters the tent and all the paratroopers jump up standing to attention. 'At ease ladies. I've some news. At 0700 hours, tomorrow morning we're being airlifted by chinook to make life hell for the Taliban. Now, we've been itching for a good scrap since we got here and gentlemen. I can certainly guarantee when we drop right on top of their heads we're going to find one. So, rest up, make sure your kit is in full working order, oh and Conlon.'
Tommy stands back to attention.
  'No need for you to take your rifle into battle tomorrow son. Just bring that guitar along and when you start playing, Terry Taliban will plead for fucking mercy and surrender. Do you not agree Private?'
 'A little harsh Sergeant-Major, but if you say so, then yes, I do.' Laughter erupts around the tent. Conlon too smiles, as does Taylor.

'Good lad. Now carry on and enjoy your evening.'
He steps out the tent and Tommy turns to face the rest of the Paras, whom are all still smiling at him. 'That man has absolutely no taste in music. The fuckin' nerve of him. I heard he was a Tom Jones fan.'
'Oi Conlon!' shouts back Taylor from outside the tent listening in. 'One more bad word about Tom and I'll personally shove that guitar of yours up where the sun never shines. Is that fuckin' understood?'
'Yes, Sergeant-Major!' replies Tommy. After what is gauged to be a safe amount of time for their RSM to be out of earshot, the Paras again all breathe easy. 'You idiot,' smiles Colin. 'You should know better Tommy. RSM'S are real life Bogarts.'
'Bloody hell, you and your Bogarts mate,' laughs Tommy.
He puts an arm around the shoulders of his best friend. 'Tomorrow,' says Colin, 'You stay in my shadow okay.'
'Is that an order?'
'Yes, it is. None fucking negotiable. I promised your Rachael I'd bring you home in one piece to her and your new arrival. So, no heroics. You stick close do you hear?'
Tommy smiles. 'Yes sir.'
'Good lad, you know it makes sense. Moron!'
Later that evening, Colin and Tommy are chatting whilst taking a stroll around Camp Bastion. 'Look at this place,' says Colin. 'Pizza huts, cafes, no wonder they call it fuckin' Butlins.'
'Are you nervous about tomorrow?' asks Tommy.
'No, not at all, I'm looking forward to it. Why, are you?'
'Something just doesn't feel right Col. Maybe it's because with Rach and the baby due any day now.'
Colin stops walking and faces Tommy. 'Listen, tomorrow when the bullets start flying, I know it isn't going to be easy, but you have to put Rachael and the baby out of your head okay. I'll be watching your back, but you need to be switched on mate. This isn't Iraq and Basra, we're not fighting fuckin' amateurs. This is the Taliban. They've booted us out once before and sent the fuckin' Russians and American packing. The RSM rates them as amongst the best soldiers in the

world at close combat and we're on their patch. Their territory. So, promise me you'll get your fucking head straight.'

Tommy says nothing. He just stares into space. An angry Colin slaps him. 'Hey, fuckin' listen to me!'

A shocked Tommy holds his cheek. 'What was that for?'

'Because you wasn't listening dickhead!'

Tommy rubs his cheek. 'I heard every word Col. I was just thinking that's all.'

'What about?'

'It's five years ago tomorrow that your mum died.'

'I know, I e-mailed for some flowers to be placed on the grave.'

'What about your dad? Did you speak to him before we were shipped over?'

'What's the point? We just ran out of things to say when mum passed away. The well has run dry mate. No tears or jokes left anymore. I'm exhausted trying to get through to the old bastard. Besides, if I ever change my mind he's not too hard to find.'

Tommy smiles. 'Derek Lindsay. Sat beneath the window in The *Mowers Arms* vault, struggling with a crossword and his pint of bitter, and the ever faithful whiskey chaser close by.'

'Part of the furniture,' replies Colin. 'He's in there that often they have his face on the beer mats!' Both laugh.

'You should make the effort. He's not a bad bloke, he just couldn't handle it when your mum died. He does loves you Col. This thing we do. It's not really the job for putting off today what can be done tomorrow. With this line of work there can easily be no tomorrow.'

'When did you get so fuckin' wise Einstein?'

'I'm not sure to be honest, it must've been that slap you gave me.' Colin smiles wide. 'Maybe I should do it more often. Keep your brain in motion?'

'Just you try it Lindsay!' laughs Tommy. The two start to have a mock fight and end up wrestling and rolling around on the floor.

'What in God's name is going on here?' Suddenly, they hear a familiar voice. Sergeant-Major Taylor.

'Are you two fucking or fighting, I can't tell?'

Colin and Tommy immediately spring to their feet and attention. 'What is it with you Mancs? Haven't you got enough with the Taliban on your hands, and you still want to fight with each other as well? Anyway, I thought you two were best of mates?'
'We are Sergeant-Major,' both Colin and Tommy reply in unison.
'Then why are you rolling around the floor like a pair of fucking Welsh tarts?'
'Well, Sergeant-Major,' replies Tommy, trying desperately not to laugh. 'It's like this. We were arguing over what is Tom Jones' best ever record. I said *Delilah*, but Col here insisted on *It's Not Unusual*. Maybe you'd do us both a favour and like, settle the argument?'
'Are you taking the piss Conlon, cos if you are, so help me I'll...'
'He's not Sergeant-Major! Honest,' replies Colin, also having to bite his lip not to laugh. 'For some reason I expected a little more from you Lindsay.'
'Sergeant-Major?'
'*It's not Unusual*? Come on lad. A decent record, but not in the same class as *Delilah* is it?'
Colin smiles. 'Not if you say so Sergeant-Major.'
'Good choice Conlon, now you and your Manc mucker here head off back to the barracks. Go on now, fuck off out of my sight.'
'Yes, Sergeant-Major,' again, Lindsay and Conlon reply in unison, before walking off. 'Oh, and lads,' Taylor calls out after them, as they both turn around hearing to face him. 'Look after each other tomorrow eh. We do our jobs and everybody comes home together.' That said, Sergeant-Major Taylor strides off into the darkness. Colin and Tommy watch him go. 'Not a bad old twat really is he?' says Tommy. 'He's almost even human at times.'
'I fucking heard that Conlon!' roars back Taylor!
A laughing Colin and Tommy jog back to barracks.
'That slap really hurt Col.'
'Stop moaning soft arse.'

THE FALL

Next morning,
  into a blazing red sky above Camp Bastion, a Chinook helicopter takes off carrying the first British Paratroopers into battle with the Taliban. Two rows of soldiers sit in lines. Amongst them Colin Lindsay and Tommy Conlon. They find themselves next to the doors. Around them men normally laughing and joking are deadly serious. They're to be the first on the ground. A Recce platoon to pave the way for the forthcoming assault. On board commanding is Sergeant-Major Taylor and he has to shout loud to be heard over the helicopter blades and engine. 'Alright, listen up lads! No long speeches just basic, fuckin' common sense. You keep your eyes open, you watch your mate's back and remember your training. Do this and everything will click in automatically once we hit the ground. You then gather around me and wait for my command. I don't want no John fuckin' Wayne antics, do I make myself clear?'
They all nod. 'Okay, good. We secure the landing zone and wait for the rest of our boys to arrive. We stay together, we stay alive and get this job done. That's all ladies. Good luck.'
  Thirty minutes later the Chinook arrives over its target. Inside, where the Paras are situated a red light goes on to indicate it's time to prepare. As the Chinook begins its descent, Colin, who's nearest to the exit stands to do a last check on his equipment. Slowly, the doors start to open when suddenly from the ground strafing gun fire erupts and an emergency siren starts to blare out! Chaos erupts as bullets and tracers strike inside the Chinook. Explosions deafen!
They're just twenty-feet above the ground.
    A hand-held missile fired from nearby woodlands misses the cockpit by inches. 'Fuck this!' exclaims the pilot to his flight Lieutenant. 'We're getting out of here. Those lads won't stand a

chance down there with what's waiting for them.' The pilot turns to his intercom to address the Paras. Back amongst them it's hellish as the Taliban firepower continues to rip though the jammed open doors. 'Hold tight chaps we're postponing the drop,' announces the voice over the intercom. As the pilot's message resonates loud, Colin is struck on the arm by a bullet, loses his balance and falls backwards out of the Chinook doors.

'Col no!' screams out Tommy on seeing this.

Without thinking he immediately jumps out after his friend. Watching on in horror is Sergeant-Major Taylor. He rushes to the door and sees that both men are on the ground and moving. A machine gun burst causes Taylor to duck and as the Chinook starts a rapid ascent upwards, he makes his way back towards the cockpit. Once there Taylor grabs hold of the pilot. 'Two of my men are on the ground. Turn this thing around we're going back!'

'I can't do that Sergeant-Major!' exclaims the pilot. 'I'm sorry but it would be suicide for all on board. We'd be a sitting target and the rest of your men would be massacred. I cannot allow it. I'll ring through the co-ordinates for air support straight away. It's their best hope.' Knowing this is true a devastated Taylor returns to his men. All are staring in his direction and pangs of guilt sweep over him.

The radio operator is desperately trying to contact Colin and Tommy, but with little success. 'Nothing, Sergeant-Major, just static.'

Then suddenly voices and gunfire starts to cackle through on the transmitter and as Taylor and his men listen in, it becomes clear that the two stranded Paras are already in a fight to the death with the Taliban.

THE LETTER

Taliban Camp. 2014.
 I continue speaking to Mullah Talwasa.
 'Later that day, just after 2-07pm in the afternoon, British Paratroopers Colin Lindsay and Tommy Conlon following a five-hour running battle with the hunting Taliban were finally trapped and surrounded, South of Musa Qala. Once out of ammunition they fought to the end with knives, until eventually both were overpowered and killed. Yet instead of this being the end of the story it's only actually the beginning, because moments after their death, something truly extraordinary occurred.'
 Talwasa points towards me, but speaks to my translator Abu Ramzi.
 'Ramzi, remember what we spoke of before. Warn your English friend to be careful. I will not listen to any talk of heresy. I refuse to have the Prophet mocked.'
 'But surely my chief he must be allowed to tell the whole story. Otherwise what is the point of all this? We must know the truth about what happened.'
 Talwasa waves his hands in consternation. 'Very well then. Tell him to get on with this fairytale…'

Helmand Province.
Tuesday 18th March 2008. 2.15.pm.
 Led by Major Reilly and Sergeant-Major Taylor, a hundred Paras spread out across a red poppy field to retrieve their fallen comrades, Private Colin Lindsay and Tommy Conlon. Above two Chinook helicopters keep a close eye out for Taliban, but they appear to have fled. On reaching the two soldier's lifeless bodies Reilly removes his helmet, whilst Taylor goes down onto one knee. Both appear utterly devastated. Taylor motions for body bags to be brought forward and

very gently Colin and Tommy's bodies are lifted into them. Just before this is done Taylor notices on both their arms newly drawn tattoos. 'Wait lads,' he calls out, before the bags are fully zipped. Taylor takes a closer look at what appear to be matching Dragonflies. Reilly catches his Sergeant-Major's eyes. 'What is it Roy?'

'I'm not sure sir.' He motions to the Para to carry on putting the bodies on the helicopter. 'This doesn't ring true, where are the fuckin' Taliban? They would have known we were coming for the bodies, so why no waiting committee? It's not in their nature to turn down a fight.' Reilly stares out across the wide-open expanses of the poppy field. There's total silence. Not even insects can be heard. They watch as Colin and Tommy are readied to be evacuated. A Para radio operator approaches and salutes Reilly. 'A message for you from Camp Bastion Major. High priority.'

He takes the phone. 'Major Reilly here.'

Reilly listens and replies with what appears ever increasing anger and frustration. Finally, the conversation ends and he walks back across to Taylor. 'The whole thing is a bloody disaster. It's just come through that the operation has been cancelled due to political pressure from London. Apparently, Whitehall is concerned about possible heavy casualties. We're trying to win a damn war here and suddenly the politicians develop a fucking conscience?'

'With all due respect sir, that's utter bollocks they're telling you. There's no chance London would have overruled the top brass on this. It's a cover story. Something else has gone on.'

The Chinook lands and the dead Paras bodies are placed on board. 'You may think this is mad,' says Taylor. 'But I noticed on the lad's arms they both had what appeared like matching, new tattoos.'

'Nothing against army regulations in that,' replies Reilly. 'Why do you mention it?' Taylor can't take his eyes off the chinook as it hovers, then swiftly gathers speed and sweeps off over the nearby mountains. Until appearing as just a speck in the distant Afghan sky.

He turns to his commanding officer. 'It's not important sir. Just been a rotten day at the office that's all. We've lost two good lads today

and I'm sick to the fuckin' bones about it. Bring on another dawn I say when we can have some payback against the bastards.'
  Major Reilly realises his Sergeant-Major is suffering badly after not being allowed to go back in the Chinook and attempt to rescue Colin and Tommy earlier that day. 'Don't do this to yourself Roy, it wasn't your fault. A rescue mission was never an option. If it had been attempted I would have lost an entire platoon and the finest Sergeant- Major in the Regiment.' Reilly offers Taylor a cigarette which he accepts. 'Thank you, sir.'
  'I think we should get the men organised and out of here Sergeant- Major before things do turn nasty.'
  The two men head back.

FROM THE HEAVENS

London. Ten Downing Street.
Tuesday 18th March 2008. The evening.
 British Prime Minister Gordon Brown is sat behind his desk at Ten Downing Street, when there's a quick rasp of knuckles on the door, and entering is his smiling, Foreign Secretary David Milliband.
 'Hello Gordon, you may need a drink for what I'm about to tell you.'
 Brown looks up, 'Go on, you pour David,' he replies.
 Milliband pours them both a large whiskey from a nearby drink's cabinet. He passes one to the Prime Minister and sits down opposite him. 'There's been an incident in Afghanistan out on operations.'
 'What kind of incident?'
 Milliband takes a gulp of his whiskey. 'Do you remember the story from the First World War about the Angel of Mons?
 'Of course,' replies a quizzical Brown. 'An old soldier's fable where it was claimed an angel of God appeared on a cloud above the battlefield at Mons and saved an infantry regiment from certain death. David,' asks Brown. 'Why the hell are we talking about this?'
 Milliband points to the Prime Minister's whiskey. 'Drink up.'
 Brown does so then puts down his glass. 'Now go on.'
 Milliband takes a deep breath. 'Yesterday in Helmand province, two paratroopers Private's Colin Lindsay and Thomas Connor were cut off by the Taliban and surrounded in a poppy field. It was open ground, the lads were sitting ducks for the enemy.' Milliband stops, seemingly unable to believe his own words. He takes from a suit pocket a mobile phone and sets it to video before handing over to Brown. 'Take a look at this.'

Afghanistan. Camp Bastion.
 Wednesday 19th March 2008.

Major Reilly is pacing up and down in his tent when enters Sergeant-Major Taylor. He salutes. Reilly smiles. 'Sergeant-Major please sit down, take a seat.'
'Thank you sir.'
Taylor pulls up a chair and sits opposite Reilly. 'I've received the following letter off the Taliban commander who was present at Lindsay's and Conlon's death. It's quite extraordinary. I would like you to listen whilst I read it.'

"Dear Major Reilly

I write this letter across the battlefield to salute the two young soldiers of your regiment that were killed. Their courage made an impression on me in a manner I never thought possible in this conflict that exists between us. I would like you to know that they were given an option to surrender but declined. On this matter I give my word. In the end they stood together and died as true soldiers and brothers in arms. I must confess to you that in the immediate aftermath of their passing we experienced something very strange. Whether you are aware of these events I am not sure, but if so, then I consider you blessed also. Our two worlds have collided here in Afghanistan with cruel and bloody results. I speak as one soldier to another that in the light of this miracle maybe there is hope, if not for this generation. Then, I pray the next.
Yours sincerely,
Abu Ramzi"

Reilly puts down the letter.
'What the bloody hell is going on Roy? I feel like I'm in an episode of the bloody Twilight zone. Fighting the Taliban I can handle, it's what we trained for. But this? There's nothing in the rulebook that tells you how to handle fucking ghosts.'
Taylor nods his head in agreement. 'To be honest I've heard some strange gossip sir. I've put guards on the coffins. The local Afghans are spreading rumours about evil spirits, so no point in taking any chances. The boys are already spooked and upset. Lindsay and

Conlon were good lads. I spoke to them the night before we went in. I told them to watch each other's backs. A pair of comedians, but excellent soldiers. They didn't deserve what happened and all this going on now? It's a fuckin' insult to their memories.'

Taylor appears choked.

'There's more Roy. I'm going to show you something, but you must never reveal the nature of it to anyone. Am I understood?'

'Of course sir,' replies Taylor. Reilly positions his laptop so both can view it. 'Watch this. The footage is taken from an American drone of the moment, Lindsay and Conlon were killed.'

The screen shows 2-07.pm, in the top right-hand corner.

…It begins. Black and white footage from overhead of Afghan fighters moving in for the kill and the struggle that ensues. Finally, the British soldiers are overpowered and we see them being killed. Colin is stabbed repeatedly whilst being held down and Tommy is shot from close range by a lone fighter. He falls to his knees and dies at the feet of his friend. Then, a strange mist appears and through it we see the Taliban fighters run away and the bodies of the two soldiers rise to their feet…The picture then cuts out.

Taylor puts his head down and is clearly devastated at what he's just witnessed. 'Sir, we saw the bodies, they were cut up bad. What we just watched? It's not fuckin' real. It can't be?'

'It doesn't stop with this Sergeant-Major. Lindsay's headcam on his helmet stayed operational for another seven minutes. It picked up everything. Including Lindsay's and Conlon's last moments and the strange mist coming down. The boys coming around and the Taliban fleeing. And then…' Reilly's hands are shaking. He takes a cigarette from a pack on his desk but struggles to light it. Finally, he succeeds.

'Sir, what?' asks Taylor.

'Before it packed in Lindsay mentioned a Dragonfly. He spoke about a debt being paid from when they were kids. About being given a last chance to put things right and to say goodbye.'

'Where's this footage now sir?'

'When I enquired I was told it's been shipped back to London.'

'I'm not surprised. No doubt the top brass will want to bury this, whatever this is, soon as possible.'

Reilly inhales on his cigarette. 'I'm afraid it's a little too late for that. Do you remember you said to me about those newly done tattoos on their arms, and you felt something didn't ring true?'

Taylor nods.

'Well, it appears Lindsay and Conlon went on a final journey.'

'I'm afraid once more you've lost me sir.'

'No shame in that these days Sergeant-Major,' smiles Reilly.

'You see, only twenty minutes after the boys were reported killed, they were seen in Manchester. I believe your favourite Mancs went home one last time Roy.'

ACT THREE

THE LAST GOODBYES

North Manchester General Hospital.
Monday 17th March 2008. 2-27pm.
22 year-old Rachael Conlon is lay in a side-ward hospital bed. She's cuddling her new born baby girl Jessica, when the door opens, and to her utter shock it's her husband Tommy.

'Tommy! What the hell are you doing here, you're supposed to be in Afghanistan?' exclaims a joyful Rachael. He races over to the bed and hugs both her and the baby. A tearful Tommy is reluctant to let go of his young family and they stay that way for a full minute. Finally, Rachael hands him the baby. Tommy holds Jessica gently in his arms. 'Hello little lady, I'm your Dad. We haven't got long, so I best keep this short.' Rachael watches on with tears falling down her cheeks. She has so many questions but is too upset to ask Tommy anything. Instead, she just listens on.

'I feel like I'm dreaming, but when I look into your eyes and feel your skin my angel, I know this is real. I've been blessed to be allowed this moment.' Tommy gently kisses Jessica on the forehead. He goes to lift her fingers, only to be shocked at finding a tiny birthmark shaped into a Dragonfly on the palm of her hand. He smiles and hands Jessica back to Rachael. He sits on the bed and strokes his wife's hair and wipes a tear from her eye.

'Tommy, why didn't you ring and say you were coming home?'
'Everything all happened rather fast Rach. It's hard to explain, all I can tell you is that I have to go away again very soon. And…'
Tommy goes quiet.

'What's going on? Tommy, tell me what's happening here? Are you on the run? Please don't tell me you've gone AWOL?'
'Not exactly,' he smiles. Tommy is fighting so hard to control his emotions. How does he tell Rachael holding their new born daughter that he's dead, and by some miracle the Dragonfly has allowed them a last goodbye?
'Rachael, you're going to hear stories. Strange stories about me, but all you need to know is that I was here for you and our daughter, and that you've both made me the happiest and proudest man on this earth. But now I have to go and won't be coming back.'
'Tommy, you're scaring me, I don't understand. What are you saying?'
'I'm already with the angels Rach.'
 Tommy hugs Rachael tight. He spots her mobile phone on the side cabinet, picks it up and sets to camera. Again, he dries the tears from his wife's face. Tommy laughs. 'Come on now Rach, I want a big smile. Our little girl is going to inherit this and I want her to see us at our best.' Rachael is scared to ask, but feels she has to.
 'Tommy, are you a ghost?'
 He simply smiles at her and snaps the picture of the three of them. Rachael then takes the phone off him and hands the baby back into his arms. 'Here, let me take one of just you and Jessica.'
 Rachael takes a picture of Tommy cradling Jessica in his arms. He then hands her back. 'I have to go now.'
Rachael starts to sob loud. 'Tommy, no!'
'I've no choice. The angels are calling Rachael. Remember Oasis. Remember our song *Wonderwall*. Mine and yours. You make sure it becomes Jessica's. That she knows every line. You make sure when she sings it that she has me in mind. You tell her what I was like. What a pain in the arse I was! How we'd argue like cat and dog, then make up by watching the sun come up over Moston with two bottles

of wine and a huge joint. Then again, best you don't mention the joint, and I'll say nothing to the angels.' Rachael laughs, then cries,

close to despairing. 'Oh, Tommy, please! Don't go!'
'I love you Rachael.' He kisses his wife and daughter once more then steps out of the room shutting the door behind him. Tommy races off down the hospital corridor so he can't hear Rachael's screams.

Manchester. The *Mowers Arms* Pub/Moston Cemetery.
Monday 17th March 2008. 2-10.pm.
'Hello Dad.'
   Colin Lindsay stands above his Dad who's sat in the normal spot, and as ever working on a crossword and struggling badly.
'Hello son,' replies a shocked Derek, looking like he's seen a ghost.
'When did you get home?'
   Colin smiles. 'Just now, I'm going to the bar. Can I get you another beer?'
'Love one lad. A bitter please.'
Colin points to his empty whiskey glass. 'What about your chaser?'
'No, I'm good,' says Derek. Inside he wants to scream and shout in joy that his boy is home! Around the room people swiftly realise who has come back into their midst. The returning war hero! Immediately, a host of old friends and well-wishers have surrounded Colin.
''Welcome home Col!''
''Did you kill anyone Col?''
''Can I buy you a drink Col?''
 Trapped in a barrage of goodwill, backslapping, kisses and hugs, finally Colin is saved by the landlady Karen. 'Right, you lot, get off him! Let the boy breathe.' Not daring to risk the wrath of their big-hearted but fearsome landlady, the regulars release Colin from their grasps. 'Thanks Karen,' says Colin, as she hugs him tight whilst whispering into his ear. 'Welcome home son, now go and spend time with your dad, and I'll bring the drinks over.'
 'Karen, can I ask you a favour?'
'Of course you can, anything.'
'I'm not going to be around long. There's stuff going on that I can't really talk about. I was wondering if you'd keep an eye on the old man for me. You know, talk him out of the chasers. Water down his

pint, stuff like that. Help him with the crosswords when he's getting wound up with them.' Karen wipes away a tear falling down Colin's cheek. 'I promise you, I'll be his bloody guardian angel, but what's going on Col, are you in trouble?'

Colin shakes his head and smiles. 'No, not anymore.'
He kisses Karen on the cheek and goes to sit down next to his dad.

'How are you getting on with that crossword?' asks Colin.
Derek smiles. 'I've never finished one in twenty years son. I'm close today, but for the life of me I don't know the answer to this last clue.'
'Go on then, what is it, let me see if I can finally put you out of your misery?' Derek stares at Colin and tries hard to keep a straight face. It feels so good to have his boy alongside him.

'Okay then smartarse, insect, nine letters?'

'Dragonfly,' replies a smiling Colin.
'Yes!' exclaims a beaming Derek. 'Thanks son.'
 He puts out his hand for him to shake, but instead Colin stands up. 'Give me a hug instead eh Dad. It's been a long time.'
 Taken aback Derek is not sure how to react. He looks around the room, clearly a little embarrassed. 'Sit down Colin, eh lad, you're not a kid anymore. Just shake my hand.' Colin does so and is relieved to see Karen arrive with their drinks. She passes them over.

'There you go, my two favourite men in the world. Derek, give me your phone, I want to take a picture of the two of you together.'

'Oh, Karen, I can't be...'
'Arsed? Stop your bloody moaning Lindsay and hand over your phone now!' Reluctantly Derek does as he's told. Colin moves to sit next to his dad as Karen snaps the photo. On it both have attempted, forced smiles. 'Not bad you miserable looking sods!' laughs Karen, handing him his phone back. Once she's returned to the bar, Colin suddenly realises time is running out. 'Dad, how about we have this pint, then go and visit Mum?'
'Fine by me Son,' replies Derek, sounding pretty abrupt and picking up his newspaper once more. Colin feels the coldness in his dad's voice back again, but he's not giving up. 'I think it would be nice for the three of us to be together.' His dad doesn't reply, so Colin takes a

huge gulp of his pint then puts it down. 'I hope they sell this where I'm going.'
'And where's that then?' asks Derek, without even looking up.
 Colin can't help but smile. 'Oh, it's out of this world dad!'

 Derek and Colin enter through the gates of Moston Cemetery. Neither has said a word since making the ten minute walk from The *Mowers Arms* down Moston Lane. Colin looks at his Dad. He can clearly see that distant glint in his eye again. 'It's this way,' remarks Derek, with a real air of sarcasm, much to Colin's distaste. An obvious arrow to his heart. 'Dad, if it was possible I'd have visited Mum more. I'm in the army. It's not bloody easy to get away.'
'Watch your language!' snaps Derek. 'Show some respect for the dead.' At this comment Colin can feel the anger boiling over, but still he manages to keep calm. Given this once chance to make things right there's no point rising to the bait. Finally, following behind a silent Derek, they arrive at his mum's graveside. Derek goes to tidy the plastic flowers that have fallen out of a vase. He bends down and straightens it, before rolling a hand over his wife's inscribed name.
 Helen.
 'Someone else is here to see you today love. Our Colin is home and has come to say hello. He looks well. He helped me finish my first crossword. The first one I've completed in years! He's a good lad, I don't tell him often enough I suppose.' His voice quivers. Colin fights hard to hold back the tears. It's almost time for him to leave.
 'Dad, there's something I have to tell you.'
Derek looks up. He sees real sadness in Colin's eyes.
 'What's up son. Tell me what's going on?'
 'I've got to go away and I won't be coming back. I just needed you to know that I love you, and I'm really sorry for not being around after mum died.' Standing up, Derek approaches his son and hugs him tight. The years of sadness melting away. This small act of kindness causes Colin to break down crying. The two stay this way for a full minute. Finally, they come apart. Colin kisses his dad on the cheek. He smiles through the tears. 'Now, I'm complete. You take care dad.'

Derek looks puzzled as Colin walks away.

'Colin, where are you going, Colin! Where are you going son?'

He doesn't turn around.

Waiting at the cemetery gate for Colin stands Tommy. He smiles on seeing his best friend. 'One more thing to do Col. Are you ready for your tattoo?'

'A Dragonfly?'

'What else?' smiles Tommy. 'What a fuckin' day eh!

Come on mate.'

THE VERDICT

Afghanistan. Taliban camp. 2014.
I go quiet whilst waiting for Abu Ramzi's translation of Tommy's and Colin's last meetings with Rachael and Derek. A collective intake of breath and the instant rumble of chatter greets Ramzi's summing up. For a moment nothing happens. Then Mullah Talwasa stands. He's clearly shaken after listening to what occurred.

'Abu Ramzi, ask the Englishman what proof he has of these so-called meetings after death?' Ramzi relates this to me and I go into my shirt-sleeve pocket handing him over a small envelope.

'Show him these.'

Ramzi hands the envelope to Talwasa. He quickly rips it open and is staring at the two Polaroid's taken in Rachael's hospital room twenty minutes after Tommy's supposed death. Also Derek's picture of him and Colin taken by Karen in the Mowers Arms.

Talwasa looks up to address Ramzi. 'These could have been taken anytime. How can I trust this man?' Guessing correctly that Talwasa is highly dubious, I jump in. 'Ask how could these pictures be faked if the baby was born after Conlon was killed? Tell him I have other evidence. More than enough to prove my point. Including American drone footage of that day.' Ramzi turns towards me and appears shaken with what I've just revealed. He again starts to translate.

I catch the eye of the Taliban witness Hazif, I can't help myself and point towards him. 'And if Talwasa still doesn't believe me, ask his man over there why he and the others ran away that day when the soldiers were killed?' Immediately, Ramzi stops and glares angrily over towards me. 'You're going too far James.'

'This meeting will adjourn for a short period whilst I make my decision.' Still unaware of my comments Talwasa has intervened. He stands and the entire camp rises up with him. Ramzi grabs hold of my arm and pulls me aside. 'You simply cannot say such things James.

This is Afghanistan. Even to suggest men are cowards and ran away will get you your throat cut.'

'But it happened. I've seen the footage. Something spooked them.'

'You do not have to convince me James.'

'How do you mean?'

'I was there my friend. I was one of those who ran away. Why do you think I brought you here and agreed to help? I saw the soldier's eye's open and I saw the Dragonfly. There is something I need you to see.' Ramzi lifts up his sleeve and shows me a tattoo of the Dragonfly on his arm. 'It was my arm in the photograph and the Dragonfly is in my dreams every night. The events of that day remain to torture my soul.'

I listen on open-mouthed. 'Why didn't you tell me this before?'

'I knew you were aware that I was Taliban, but I was not sure how you would feel knowing I maybe played a part in the soldier's deaths.'

'Well, did you?'

Ramzi goes quiet for a moment. He stares at the sky and the ground beneath him before looking me straight in the eyes. 'Right up to the end I gave them both the chance to surrender, but they refused leaving me with no choice...

It was me who killed Lindsay, James.'

Suddenly, I feel faint. All the goodwill I felt towards this man has now vanished. I've met Lindsay's and Conlon's family and here at this very moment the two men who killed them are both within my touching distance. 'What did you expect me to do James? It was war. Are you honestly suggesting that in my situation you would have done different? If two of my soldiers refused to give in how would you have dealt with it? Let me tell you the British army would have blasted them into oblivion, so, please. I beg you. Do not let this revelation destroy our friendship.'

Abu Ramzi is right, I would've done exactly the same. The world has changed since 2008. I came to Afghanistan not just to try and explain the unexplainable, but also to help bury the demons of that sniper's bullet back in 2002. It's now time to move on. I hold my hand out for Ramzi to shake and he does so.

'Thank you James. They say to forgive your former enemies is infinitely harder than to continue hating them.'

'You're not an easy man to hate Abu Ramzi.'

He smiles. Suddenly, we hear a commotion amongst the fighters. Mullah Talwasa has returned and it's time to hear his verdict. I have on my mobile phone one last piece of evidence that will certainly prove my case here today, though to show it may cost me so much more. Ramzi grabs my arm. 'Come James, let us go and hear what the old crow has decreed.'

All the camp have gathered to sit and watch. Each one I can feel their eyes upon me. Talwasa rises from his seat.

'Englishman, I have listened to all you have had to say today, and to the witness who was present. I have been told by farmers who work in those poppy fields that sometimes they can give off hallucinations. Strange visions. And this is what I have decided. My verdict is you are of good character Englishman, but wrong in your opinion of what occurred that day.'

I can't have this. We've come too far, seen and witnessed too much just to be dismissed in this manner. I take out my mobile phone and start to walk over to Talwasa. I set it to video, 'Ramzi, please translate my every word. I implore you don't leave anything out.'

'Be very careful what you show him James. It will be a death sentence if he takes it as an insult.'

I hand it to Talwasa and switch on the American drone footage which was supplied to me by James Reilly. Talwasa watches transfixed on the mobile as the events unfold. I have to make him change his mind. 'What you are seeing is the truth Mullah Talwasa. It was no hallucination, this actually happened. I know this is hard for you to believe, but with great respect only a stupid and arrogant man would not believe what his own eyes are telling him.'

I notice Ramzi's translation slow down. 'Tell him, tell him everything!'

Ramzi reluctantly nods and continues on with the full translation.

'I have no answers chief, I have no magic wand to solve this. I have no God to turn to or blame. All I have is what you're seeing now, and

the word of family members who swear they were with these men after they'd been killed.' The footage ends and for a second Talwasa appears deep in thought. Suddenly, he throws the phone to the floor and starts to scream into my face! 'You have gone too far Englishman. I won't tolerate this act of defilement against the Prophet. You must pay for this!' Abu Ramzi appears horrified as he looks towards me. I can guess what is happening.
 'James, what have you done?'
  Talwasa calls out to his two bodyguards. They grab me and I'm pushed to my knees. So, thirteen years after escaping an Afghan bullet all is set to end here today back in the same dirt and dust. I hear the click of the Kalashnikov being branded and can feel the cold steel in the back of my neck.
'This is wrong!' shouts out Abu Ramzi to Talwasa. 'You have no right to kill him!'
 'You dare to oppose my word Abu Ramzi? You forget in bringing this man to us you are equally guilty. Be quiet and hold your tongue or you will face the same penalty.'
 'I will not allow this,' replies Ramzi. 'You are nothing but a foolish old man. The Englishman came to us in good faith, he will leave equally so and alive.' Rahid Khan moves to stand alongside Abu Ramzi. 'Do not worry my friend. I think the time has come to melt the fucking snow king.' He calls out to his fighters and they all rise as one. Each start to raise a sleeve and I watch on in disbelief as every Taliban soldier present in the camp shows off the Dragonfly tattoo on their right arm. Rahid Khan steps towards a bewildered looking Mullah Talwasa displaying also the Dragonfly on his arm.
'These are different times. Your day has gone old man, I think you should leave now.' A fearful Talwasa motions for his two bodyguards, and with them either side of him he swiftly vanishes. Ramzi comes across to me. 'The power of the Dragonfly Captain James Pearson has today saved your life.'
I'm in a state of shock. 'I had no idea that so many of your fighters were affected by what happened back then.'

'Afghanistan is a country of myths and legends James. There were too many witnesses that day for it to simply disappear. It has become part of our heritage. The Dragonfly now stands for hope.

The witness Hafiz approaches Ramzi. 'Will you translate to the Englishman for me?'

He nods.

'I am sorry for taking the life of the British soldier called Conlon. I felt I had to speak today in honour of his memory. I hope you find somewhere in your heart to forgive me?'

I smile. 'Tell him the war is over.'

Ramzi does so and Hafiz bows his head before walking away.

'So, my friend,' asks a smiling Abu Ramzi. 'Do you finally now have the ending for your book?'

'The book will be written I promise you that, and I pray I live to see it published. As for its ending, I think the best place to finish would be at the beginning. On a magical little island in the middle of a Manchester lake.'

LIVE FOREVER

Manchester. Moston. Bogart Hole Clough.
 Saturday 15th June 1996.
 Oasis are singing *Live Forever* on a small transistor radio.
 The sky is a crystal, sparkling blue. It's a June day, a sun-drenched morning and best friends 10 year-old Colin Lindsay and Tommy Conlon are in Bogart Hole Clough. In the centre of the Clough there's a lake with at it's very heart a mysterious circular island, only reachable by rowing boat. Here the two boys have made their den, and all the time they are being watched from the branch of a nearby tree by a Dragonfly.
 'Do you believe in Bogarts?' asks Colin.
Tommy nods. 'Kevin Turner in year seven claims he saw one whilst doing cross country in here.'
  'Give over Tommy,' smiles Colin. 'Kevin Turner has magic mushrooms for his breakfast every day. Since when did you believe him about anything? Is it just since you fancied his sister Rachael?'
 An indignant Tommy goes all defensive. 'I do not.' He's obviously embarrassed by his friend's gentle teasing, but Colin is not letting him off the hook. 'Of course you do. She's in our science class remember. You spend the entire lesson staring at her. It's true love!'
 He puts an arm around a red-faced Tommy's shoulders who shrugs him off, desperate to change the subject because his friend is right. Tommy is head over heels in love with the pretty, blond haired, blue eyed Rachael Turner. 'I thought we were talking about Bogarts?'
  Colin turns down the radio playing Oasis and continues his storytelling. 'The Bogarts are evil fairies condemned to live forever on earth because heaven and even hell won't take them in. They're only happy when causing trouble. A bit like me and you! They can turn milk sour and make dogs lose their bark and go lame. Bogarts will follow you to the end of the world if they want to own your soul.

Wherever you try and run they'll find you.'
Colin's voice is now a whisper. He's enjoying himself teasing Tommy. 'They do say hanging a horseshoe on the door of a house keeps the Bogarts away. Tommy doesn't appear happy at hearing this. 'Oh, that's just great. Where are you going to find a horseshoe in Moston?'

Colin smiles at this. 'They say Bogarts live under that bridge over there and love to sneak up on people to scare them, and when in a really bad mood they're far, far worse.'

'What do they look like Col?'

Tommy looks up and sees the bridge they have to cross to get out of the Clough. Suddenly, he's really afraid.

'Terrifying,' replies Colin. 'The Bogarts are described as being squat and hairy with horns and a tail.'

A scared Tommy has heard enough. 'Right, leave it now! There's no such thing as Bogarts. You Colin Lindsay are just trying to scare me.' Secretly, Tommy isn't so sure because his best friend has given such a chilling portrait of the beasts. Then something makes him look up to see a Dragonfly watching them both on a low tree branch. He points. 'Col, look!' Colin also gazes upwards and without really thinking grasps the Dragonfly, and catches it off guard holding it ever so carefully in the palm of his hand. The Dragonfly is stricken with fear. This young boy could if he desired end its existence with just a gentle tightening of a fist, but Colin is never going to do such a thing. He slowly opens his hand and smiles wide as the Dragonfly escapes to fly away. It's wings swiftly taking flight.

The boys stare as it hovers over them. Almost as if stopping to thank Colin. Tommy shakes his head. 'You're so soft mate. Why did you let it go?' Colin is still unable to take his eyes off the Dragonfly.

He smiles. 'Because it asked me too.'

The Dragonfly soars high across Bogart Hole Clough towards Manchester city centre. It's still a beautiful, summer's late morning, and below the city is now fully awake as thousands of people are on the move by car, tram and bus. It's the day before Father's Day,

Manchester is bound to be busy. Packed to the rafters with shoppers.

The Dragonfly starts to descend and lands upon the top of a red post box on Corporation Street. But something is wrong for the streets are deserted. An alarm siren blaring the only noise to be heard. The Dragonfly cocks it's head up looking around, curious. Then, the explosion! Blazing fire and leaping flames! Blinding smoke and choking dust. A mushroom cloud reaches high into the sky...
It's the Manchester bomb.

All around the post box on which the dragonfly sit's lies devastation. Huge mounds of debris flies around its head, but the Dragonfly and the post box remain undamaged, like they're both protected by a magical force field. Again, once more the Dragonfly takes flight and returns to the Clough. The once, blue skies so prevalent before have become black with dirt and grime. It rushes to be back amongst the two young humans. Still both unaware as to what's gone on, but the explosion shaking the ground beneath them. The Dragonfly believes their friendship and lust for life gives hope for the future. The Dragonfly has decided it will guide their path in this life doing all in its power to deliver the boys from harm. Or at least give them safe passage from this world to the next.

TESTAMENT

Afghanistan. Helmand Province.
Monday 17th March 2008.
 As bullets thud and spatter around their heads,
 22 year-old Paratroopers Colin Lindsay and Tommy Conlon find themselves alone and exposed in a poppy field, surrounded by Taliban. Slowly emerging from cover dozens of Afghan fighters start to advance towards them with Kalashnikovs blazing. Knowing well the outgunned British soldiers are out of ammunition, encircled, and all but done for.
 At the mercy of their knives.
Both know the situation is hopeless. Colin throws himself on Tommy, as a grenade explodes only yards from them. The shouts and taunts from the encroaching Afghans grow ever louder as they're now only yards away closing in for the kill. Colin desperately searches for his rifle, but can't find it as Tommy is left with just a knife.
 'I can't find my rifle Tommy, are you okay, stay close! You hear me. You stay close!'
 'Use your knife Col, don't let them take you alive. You've heard the stories, it's not going to happen. I'll kill you myself before that!'
 'Until we see the colour of their eyes Tommy!' shouts Colin.
The boys lie waiting with knives in hand for the approaching Taliban fighters. They hear them shouting in Afghan.
 'You have shown your bravery,' then the voice of Abu Ramzi cries out in English. 'Surrender now and we shall let you live.'
 'No way, I don't believe them,' whispers Colin into Tommy's ear. 'Wait until they are right on top of us, then go for their guns okay?'
 Tommy nods and grabs Colin's hand. Both are sweating profusely and bleeding from face wounds. 'I'm not going gently into that light Col. We're going to live. Bring these fuckin' Bogarts on.'

'When they come don't take your eyes off me Tommy Conlon, Do you hear? Don't take your eyes off me. Don't take your...'

'Allah Akbar!..'

Screams ring out as the shadows of the Afghans are on them and a fight to the death begins.

But it's not the end...

1963: ONCE UPON A TIME IN MANCHESTER

1963...

From Liverpool the Beatles erupt to release their first album *Please Please Me* in the United Kingdom, and the world went mad!

Alfred Hitchcock's film The Birds was let loose in the United States. The 35th Academy Awards ceremony were held with Lawrence of Arabia winning the Best Picture.

The 35th US President John F. Kennedy told the world: 'Ich bin ein Berliner' during a speech in West Berlin, Germany.

16 year-old Pauline Reade was abducted by Ian Brady and Myra Hindley in Manchester. The first victim of the Moors murders.

The Great Train Robbery took place in Buckinghamshire, England. The Queen's coin.

Martin Luther King Jr. delivered his "I Have a Dream" speech on the steps of the Lincoln Memorial to an audience of at least 250,000, during the March on Washington.

Christine Keeler was arrested for perjury in the Profumo affair and sentenced to nine months in prison, as the British Government rocked and panicked.

Sam Cooke and his band were arrested after trying to register at a "Whites Only" motel in Louisiana. In the months that followed, Cooke recorded *A Change Is Gonna Come*.

U.S. President John F. Kennedy was assassinated in Dallas, Texas. Upon Kennedy's murder, Vice President Lyndon B. Johnson was sworn in to become the 36th President of the United States, and JFK's wife Jackie stood behind him on the plane as the ceremony took place, still covered in her husband's blood.

12 year-old John Kilbride was abducted by Ian Brady and Myra Hindley in the North of England. The horrors on the Moors continuing on.

The alleged assassin of JFK, Lee Harvey Oswald was gunned down by Jack Ruby in Dallas, in an event shown live on national television. Oswald was led out to be killed in front of the cameras like a sacrificial lamb.

The State funeral of the President took place buried at Arlington National Cemetery. His small son applauded and a watching world wept. Lee Harvey Oswald was buried the same day, but nobody cared. Nobody wept.

The Beatles' *I Want to Hold Your Hand* and *I Saw Her Standing There* were released in the United States, marking the beginning of Beatlemania.

Meanwhile, in Manchester, something was brewing and it wasn't the tea!

PROLOGUE: today: (Part One)

We begin in the present day.
  Manchester. Just after 2.00.pm, on a rainy, miserable and windswept Sunday afternoon, a white transit van turns left off Deansgate in the city centre and heads across the Blackfriars bridge over the River Irwell, into neighbouring Salford. The van radio is playing Arabic music. It comes to a halt opposite a run-down pub with boarded up windows and graffiti covered walls. Inside, music can be heard.
The Smiths are playing on a juke box.
  There is a light that never goes out.
The pub is the Brass Tap.
  Across the road,
a mass of wasteland filled with burnt out cars and twisted metal. Concrete over run with grass weeds. Needles and beer cans strewn all around. Empty wine and whisky bottles lie dumped, as two small dogs are scampering around for scraps. A smashed up bus shelter nearby with the letters *MUFC* lovingly scrawled across it.
  A little further on over the River Irwell is Salford's big brother.
  Manchester.
  A grey, Northern Mancunian skyline covets the horizon, whilst the distant rattle of a Metrolink tram trudging south over Castlefield's railway bridge echoes in the wind.
  The van driver is 40 year-old Azil Aturak. A veteran of the drugs business. Born in Istanbul, now living in Longsight. He's working with a newly, arrived Syrian criminal gang from London, looking to make their mark on the Manchester cocaine trade. The Syrians have a simple, bloodcurdling policy. Eliminate the opposition, take over their business and first on the hit list is Salford.
  Originally from the war-torn city of Mosul, the feelings amongst them is this will be like stealing sweets off children.
  Onwards they drive into the dirty old town.

Azil's task is to deliver the cargo, nothing more. Once the job is done the cargo is on its own. They are deemed expendable for the pool of hired guns arriving daily from an exploding Middle-East is never-ending. He goes to open the van's back doors, letting out the two young boys carrying Uzi machine pistols with hoodies covering their faces. 16 year-old's Hassan Sharim and Ali Khalil. Both have come over on the small boats across the English channel, and are desperate to get their families to the United Kingdom also. The price they have to pay for such golden tickets awaits in blood through the doors of the Brass Tap pub. They have been ordered to kill all in there. Azil faces them. 'My boss wants their fucking blood. We have your families waiting in Damascus, and if you want them brought to this country make sure he gets his wish. There can be no excuses. You leave nobody alive, then you make your way to the meeting spot where I'll be waiting. From there we'll get you to safety and start preparations to bring over your loved ones. Do you both understand me, no fuck ups?' Looking apprehensive the boys nod and clutch tight on their weapons. Both are sweating. Azil attempts to offer them a reassuring smile, but it appears more like a grimace. 'It is time, may God be with you. Now, go!' He points towards the pub and pushes them onwards. 'Go! Think only of your families when you press the trigger. Of your mothers and your sisters. Kill every infidel in there!' Then with an unholy haste to save his own skin Azil races back to the van, starts the engine and screeches off back towards the direction of Manchester. There's no guilty conscience, just relief that the first part of the job is done. Whether the boys succeed or fail matters little, the war has begun and Hassan and Ali's fate is already sealed. Azil has orders to kill them both if they return.

"To die by your side!
Is such a heavenly way to die!"

Inside, the Brass Tap pub is relatively quiet. The same faces, the usual, small collection of Sunday afternoon drinkers are gathered in a tattered, nondescript vault. In one corner of the room three elderly men sit playing dominoes. They're arguing amongst themselves and

77 year-old Tommy Keenan is the loudest amongst them. The other two are the same age. Eddie Hopkins and Eric Taylor.
However, Tommy's still film star looks, silver, grey hair and sparkling blue eyes give him the look of a man fifteen years younger.

A smiling Tommy loves teasing his friends. Both whom he has known for over fifty years. 'Right, you pair of cheating Collyhurst bastards, this is where I take your pensions and your false teeth off you but I'll let you keep your walking sticks!'

'We shall see big mouth,' grins Eddie.

'More front than bloody Blackpool prom Tommy Keenan. Always have had,' adds Eric.

At the bar are four younger men, whilst another two across the room play darts. All members of Salford's most notorious crime gang. Amongst them is their boss, a dark-haired, lean handsome figure.
33 year-old Paul Brady. He appears laid back with a quick smile, but in manners of family business, like his father and uncle before him, when required, Brady is ruthless. A murderous individual who has inherited a natural air of leadership,

Paul Michael Brady rules Salford with an iron fist in a velvet glove.

Suddenly, the gentle demeanour of a Sunday afternoon drinking session is violently interrupted, as the Syrian shooters charge through the door screaming with guns blazing! Hassan fires towards the lads drinking at the bar, but misses wildly, succeeding only in putting two bullets into a juke box silencing Morrissey.

Ali fire into the ceiling, and he's swiftly jumped upon and dragged to the floor. As the madness ensues, Tommy, Eddie and Eric are grabbed hold of and quite literally thrown under the table. A young gang member covers their bodies with his own. The others rush to overpower Hassan, and he too is disarmed. Once the two shooters are flat on their faces, a calm Brady motions with his hands for silence. He leans down towards them. 'Where the fuck do you think you are, Baghdad? That was some entrance. You've seen too many movies lads. Right, who are you working for?' Hassan starts to plead for his life in Arabic. Brady's best friend and second in command,

31 year-old Shaun Barlow points at the terrified Hassan.
'What the fuck are you saying lad? Stop gibbering on, speak English!' Still, Hassan continues on in his native tongue. Ali joins in, and it's obvious to all they're both pleading for their lives.
Brady shakes his head: 'I just can't have this,' he says under his breath. 'Not here, not this close to home. Not in Salford.'
Brady stares across to Barlow, who with one glance knows what his boss wants him to do. He turns to two other members of the gang, 26 year-old, Salford born, Stephen Marshall, and 20 year-old Tony Rea. Ancoats born, a tough kid of Italian descent. 'Stephen, Tony, go and get the van. I don't want to see their fuckin' ugly faces again. Do you understand me?' Initially, both Marshall and Rea appear shocked. They look over to Brady who nods in their direction and only then does it become crystal clear what's expected of them. Marshall smiles at Rea: 'Okay Tony mate, looks like we've got work to do.' They haul the Syrians to their feet and drag them out of the pub. 'Come on Laurel and Hardy,' says Rea.
'We're going for a last little ride.'

Paul Brady goes across to the three old men who have been watching and listening on with an air of quiet disbelief.
'No broken bones I hope gents?' asks a smiling Brady, as he bends down to pick all the Domino pieces off the floor placing them back on the table. He sits down. 'Sorry about ruining your game. To make up for it let me buy you all a few drinks.'
'Buy us a drink?' exclaims Tommy, 'I was winning that last bloody game.'
Brady leans across. 'Nobody saw anything right gents?'
Tommy looks him straight in the eyes. 'What, from hiding under the table? Don't be silly son, I'm just glad they took Morrissey out and shut him up. Miserable sod.' Brady laughs, whilst the other two shake their heads at Tommy's typically cool reply. He's never changed.
'Nothing we haven't seen before Paul,' replies Eric, with a shrug of his shoulders.

'You can say that again,' laughs Eddie. Both men are hardly strangers to what just occurred. Like Tommy, they're colourful
veterans of Manchester's past gangland. Another era maybe, but equally grim at times with never any medals handed out for valour. Just blood scars and hidden graves.
'This used to be a normal Saturday night around here back in the sixties,' adds Tommy.

Paul Brady glances through the window to see Marshall and Rea leading the two tied-up shooters over towards a black transit van at gunpoint. They push and shove them through the rear doors and drive away.

Brady stands and walks back to the bar where a smiling Barlow passes him a beer. 'I think we're going to war Paul.'

'You don't fuckin' say!' smiles Brady.

Inside the van, which is speeding down a Salford back road, the Syrians are still crying and begging for mercy. Marshall turns and stares at them from the passenger seat in utter disdain. They try desperate to make eye contact. 'You should have thought of this before acting like a fuckin,' drunken Butch and Sundance. What do you expect us to do? There's a price to pay for what you've just done. You're fucked boys.'

Rea looks across to Marshall. 'We'll take them to Brennan's warehouse and do it there, okay?'

Marshall is cocking the barrel on his pistol. 'Perfect.'

Still Hassan and Ali plead, but their words fall on deaf ears. Rea turns on the radio and the Stone Roses: *I am the Resurrection* is playing loud. 'I fuckin' love this tune!' he shouts, whilst turning up the volume and singing along.

Back in the Brass Tap, the damage has more or less been cleared up. A bullet riddled juke box apart, it has escaped relatively unscathed. An uneasy sense of normality has returned.

Paul Brady goes back across to Tommy, whose now sat alone after Eric and Eddie have headed home after experiencing enough excitement for one day. 'Do you mind if I sit down Tommy?'

'Be my guest son.'

Brady looks around. 'Where've your mates gone?'

'Scuttled home to recharge their pacemakers and watch Countryfile. There's been far too much excitement for those two old farts today.'

Brady grins wide and takes a large swig from a beer bottle. He then checks his mobile phone for messages before placing it on the table. Tommy watches Paul Brady intently. This is a young man who so reminds him of his father-Michael Brady.

'Have you got problems lad?' A smiling Brady is amused at Tommy's sarcastic tone. 'A bit of hassle, but nothing I can't handle.'

'Oh, I don't doubt that for a minute.'

Brady stares at him lighting up a cigarette. 'Shouldn't you be doing that outside?'

Tommy inhales, before smiling wide. 'What are you going to do, shoot me?' A laughing Brady checks his mobile again.

'It's bad for your health Tommy. I'm only concerned about you. You knew my old man really well didn't you?'

'Back in the day we did a lot of business together. Both with your dad and your uncle Paul. They were good blokes, I miss them.'

'Me too,' replies Brady, his mask momentarily dropping.

'Every fuckin' day. I remember my uncle Paul saying you was a top man back then. A real gentleman. An old fashioned gangster. I've been told by so many people you're touched by greatness, that there's a real sprinkling of Manchester gold dust about you Tommy Keenan.'

'I was never no gangster Paul. I just made a living that's all.

A bit like your good self.'

Brady smiles wide. 'Touché! Come on then Tommy, cards on the tables. Tell me what happened back in 1963, when the Krays came to Manchester? What really went down? My old man nearly opened up one night just before he died. He was from the same old school as you. Never said much and in the end he took it to the grave. But you? Your name popped up one too many times. Even from Dad's lips. You know the score, and you know who sent them home.'

Tommy inhales again on his cigarette: 'It was all nothing to do with me son, that story is all myth and legend. Everybody has added their own salt and vinegar over the years. I've no idea what really happened.'

Brady shakes his head in disbelief and laughs. 'You old timers. It's like Omerta on that subject. This isn't Sicily, it's not even fuckin' Ancoats! My God, all these years and still you won't speak about it?'

He checks his phone once more, but still nothing. 'Hurry up lads,' says Brady, very quietly. 'Get it done.'

The van arrives at Brennan's Carpets. An abandoned warehouse sat in a Salford Industrial wasteland. Around them is nothing but deserted/boarded up buildings and burnt out cars. Rea and Marshall drag the Syrians out of the van and take them kicking and screaming into the building. Inside it resembles a vast, deserted airplane hangar. Still, Hassan and Ali are begging for their lives, but it appears just wasted breath as they are pushed to the floor. 'Say a prayer boys,' smiles Rea, before along with Marshall, he takes out a pistol and together they let fly a hail of bullets into the stricken Syrians. It all goes quiet and Marshall starts to film the blood stained bodies with his mobile phone. 'Stephen, what the fuck are you doing?' asks Rea.

'For my book,' Marshall declares smiling wide.

'My life in the Manchester gangland!'

Rea laughs. 'You're one sick bastard. You best text Paul and tell him our unexpected visitors have decided to get their heads down. It's done.'

Brady's phone buzzes loud.

He looks at the message from Marshall and smiles. 'Well done lads. So, it all begins. let me buy you that drink Tommy.'

'No thanks.'

'Why not? It's not as if you're going anywhere. You practically live in here.'

'Because the truth is I haven't got the money to buy you one back lad,' a clearly embarrassed Tommy replies. Brady appears a little taken aback by this. He already really likes Tommy. 'Let me help you out old timer,' Brady starts to take out his wallet. 'Will a couple of hundred do to bide you over? If you need more just…'
'Blimey, I don't want your bloody money lad!' replies a shocked Tommy. 'But thanks anyway. It's a nice gesture and much appreciated.'
Brady smiles and puts away his wallet. 'Okay then, let's cut a deal. I buy us a few drinks, and you tell me the truth about the Krays. We both have a little time, so let's finally have the story off you. What do you say Tommy?'
  'I've a tale, but whether you chose to believe? It's been a long time Paul. Even I find it difficult now to distinguish between the truth of what happened and the myth. The stories people say.'
Brady slaps Tommy on the arm. 'Don't you move! Stay here or I'll shoot you!' He laughs whilst Tommy just smiles and shakes his head. 'Kids,' he mutters quietly. Why the hell not tell Paul Brady what went on back then? Tommy thinks he hasn't got anything else to do, or anywhere else to go. Besides, the boy could be dead tomorrow. He deserves to know. It's his heritage after all. Brady returns with the beers and sits back down. He looks across to Tommy. 'Come on then legend, from the beginning.' Tommy inhales and puts his cigarette in the ashtray. He takes a drink, his mind racing back to events what feel like a lifetime ago. They were quality days.
  'Once upon a time...'

ACT ONE

LONDON CALLING

The East End.
The snooker club. The Regal.
London's East end, Bethnal green. Gangland bosses, 33 year-old twins, Reggie and Ronnie are playing whilst discussing business. The club is closed, nobody else is around.
A radio is on with the talk all about the assassination of President Kennedy. A world seemingly knocked off its axis by JFK's murder.
'He wasn't killed by a lone gunman Ron, they've fuckin done him from inside, I can smell it.'
'Not our business Reg, we've got enough going on.'
Top of the twins agenda is expanding a criminal empire across the entire country. The Kray's burning desire to rule nationwide is matched only by a ruthlessness to make it so, and together they make plans. 'What do you think then Reg, fancy a short holiday and getting your hands dirty?'
'About going up to Manchester? I say yes. I was reading the other day if the Germans had won the war then Hitler was going to make the Midland hotel there his main headquarters for the North. Don't you think that's just fuckin' amazing Ron? We have to stay there. If it was good enough for Adolf, then it is for me. Besides, I'm a Colonel, he was just a fuckin' Corporal.'
Reg smiles and takes his shot. 'So what are you getting at Ron. Are you really comparing us to the Germans? Don't let Mum hear you say that for fuck's sake.'

Ron laughs. 'I'm just saying that's all. There has to be more to that city than chimneys, cloth caps, pigeons and George fuckin' Best.'
'Who do we know up there?' asks Reg.
'There's Paddy Mullen. Paddy owns the Cromford club, the best in Manchester. He's a smart operator who goes under the radar, not like the other bosses in that city. Paddy is easily somebody we can work with. Then there's Paddy's main boy Tommy Keenan. We worked with Tommy last year. Another good lad, for a fuckin' Northerner that is. Tommy helped us shift those American cigarettes from the docks to make a tidy sum.'
Reg puts down his cue. 'Like you say, Paddy is somebody we can do business with. As for Tommy? He's just small fry. A spoke in a wheel. But who's up there we can actually fuckin' hit?'
Ron also stops playing. 'From what I'm told there are four main gangs. Salford, North, South Manchester, and some run-down dump called Moss side. The city is divided between them, but it's not London, Reg. These are just a few Northern grease monkeys with lump hammers and chains. No class. We could put it all to bed in a single night.'
Reg grins. 'Just me and you. What do you think?'
Ron smells blood. 'let's do it Reg. Let's take the train up and surprise them. Educate the savages. We can book into the Midland, have a good drink then go and pay their top boys a visit. Shake the tramps up a bit, break a few heads. Lay down some fuckin' ground rules.'
Reg nods, he loves the idea. 'Two new sheriffs in town. The Krays. Men against boys. We'll show them how we do things in the big city.'
Ron is already planning ahead. 'Manchester, Liverpool, Leeds, Newcastle, even Glasgow. Invade Scotland and put the Jocks in their fuckin' place. We'll make the Mafia look small time.'
Reg is laughing. 'Steady on, they're fuckin' savages in kilts that far North. First of all we deal with Manchester, Ron. One at a time eh.'
Suddenly, Ron's eyes glaze over. 'Manchester. They call it the Rainy city, don't they? Well, it'll be raining fuckin' blood by the time we've finished with it.'

Ten Downing Street

  Sir Peter Dowling,
  a senior member of the government and close personal friend of the Prime Minister Harold Macmillan, is sat in his office reading a classified document on the Kray twins. The 61 year-old Tory peer takes off his glasses and rubs both eyes. Dowling is mortified on what's in front of him. The Krays have become monsters out of control. Their influence is like a viper's hiss, it's poisonous and stinking out the corridors of power. Whitehall is infected with a plague of blackmailing and corruption. The Conservative government in power have already been badly rocked by the Profumo affair. His resignation hasn't eased the pressure on men like Dowling, whose job it is to basically make any problems that may hurt the party vanish. But the Krays can't be banished. They're ghouls and have become a huge danger to the establishment. The people who run the country from the dark shadows for the privileged few, going back generations upon generations. Dowling considers John Profumo nothing more than a fucking idiot who got unlucky, but the twins? Alongside the KGB, Ronnie and Reggie Kray now sit with equal standing as enemies of the state.
  From the highest echelons of power the word has come down to Dowling. ''Whatever means necessary to bring them down.''
  It has fallen for him to make this happen.
  The gloves have come off in the battle against this pair of East end villains, whose power now reaches into the inner sanctums of the Houses of Parliament. A number of Dowling's fellow politicians, friends have been far too over keen to enjoy the services of rent boys and other minors provided by the Krays at secret parties, and whom are now being made to dance on a gangster's string for their perverted actions. Caught on camera, photographed and in some situations filmed. Two in particular, one a member of the cabinet and another of

royal blood in pictures so horrific, that if ever made public could not just bring down the government, they would topple the monarchy and have them all, politicians and royals hanging from London town lamp posts.

Even more worrying for Dowling, he's amongst the many worried band of brothers of who the twins have polaroid's. Scenes that would end his career in an eye blink, with a jail sentence a certainty to follow if they ever came to light. A man of Dowling's standing in years simply wouldn't be able to endure such an ordeal. So, this is more than personal for Dowling, it is a matter of life and death. His own. The Krays have to fucking go.

Dowling hears a knock on his door.

Entering is head of C11, 58 year-old Charles Worthing. A close ally of Dowling, they are former Eton boys and long-standing friends for many years. C11 are an elite, highly secretive branch of Scotland Yard, whom operate beyond where the normal arm of British justice isn't allowed to reach. A law unto themselves. A smiling Worthing walks across to Dowling who stands to shake his hand.

'Good to see you again Peter. No guesses for why you have sent for me?'

Dowling goes to his drinks cabinet and makes them both a large gin and tonic. He hands Worthing a glass. 'It appears our mutual friend has given us the red light. I assume you have the necessary people suitable to carry this kind of mission out Charles?'

Worthing nods. 'The very best. And I believe something has just arose that could help us reach our goal far quicker than we originally planned for. All is a little unexpected, and we shall have to work fast, but it is doable Charles. Very doable.'

'Go on,' answers Dowling.

'Well, we have received word from our operative within the Kray's organisation that they are planning on making a surprise trip up North to Manchester, this coming Monday. It appears our worse fears of them planning to expand their empire have come to fruition. But there is some good news, for this has opened up a door of opportunity, one which just may be the solution to our two problems.'

'You have my undivided attention Charles,' smiles Dowling. Worthing grins wide. 'It is all quite simple really. We end this farce in the North. I have already briefed our Northern brethren to warn them the Krays are heading up. I spoke to their best man up there. A Detective inspector George Collins. He shall be our liaison. With your permission, I would like to expand on what just may occur when those two vermin step foot off the train in Manchester.'
Dowling raises his glass. 'So long as they do not get back on it, you have a free hand to do whatever is required to rid us of this pestilence.' Worthing joins Dowling in the toast.

He smiles. 'Then we have an understanding. The Krays do not leave Manchester alive?' Dowling nods and the two men chink their glasses. 'End this fucking nightmare Charles.

End it!'

THE GATHERING OF THE CLANS

November 1963.
It's night time in the North.
From across a darkened Manchester, cars carrying the city's leading gangsters head towards the Portland hotel in Piccadilly. All have been summoned to a mystery meeting on the understanding it's in their very best interest to attend.

From across the river in Salford comes 38 year-old Michael Brady. Tall with black hair and sparkling blue eyes. A studious, deep thinking man, but also a ruthless individual. Sat alongside him his younger brother, 34 year-old Paul. Medium build with choir boy looks that hide like Michael, a ferocious, fearful temper when roused.

From the North of the city, the 'Irishman'. 57 year-old, Mayo born John Flannery. Short of stocky build. A large forehead, with fading curly hair and Irish, green smiling eyes. Outwardly mild mannered, but he also possesses a murderous nature when pushed too far.

From Moss side, comes the Jamaican. 32 year-old Jimmy Da Silva. A huge, tall man with cold eyes, but a quick winning smile. He's full of life, an extrovert. Da Silva is wearing a ridiculously, expensive sheepskin coat, with diamond rings on both hands. Da Silva is feared and respected throughout Manchester.

Arriving from the South of the city. 46 year-old Harry Taylor. A dashing figure with a rounded but handsome face, lively eyes, slicked back hair and a permanent cigarette in his mouth. A smooth operator whose calm persona and likeable personality also hides the capacity when required to wreak blood and carnage on his enemies.
All are Mancunian crime royalty.

Outside the Portland hotel, stand two smartly dressed concierges chatting idly at the main entrance. They are 23 year-old local lads from nearby Ancoats. Peter Coates and Brian Ashley. Their attention

is suddenly taken by a Rolls Royce pulling up. 'Here we go again,' says Coates, as they both leap into action. Ashley strides up to greet the guest. He opens the car door. 'Good evening Sir.'
'How are you two doing tonight son?' The man takes out his wallet and hands Ashley a five pound note. He then walks over to Coates, who nods in acknowledgement, and is given the same amount. The man smiles. 'Very impressive. Keep up the good work boys.' Coates and Ashley stand and stare at each other in shock, clutching their tips as he disappears through the lobby.
  'Was that who I think it was?' asks Coates.
  Ashley grins wide. 'It certainly was mate! Bloody hell what's going on in there? We've got every fuckin' major villain in the city inside!'
  The man in question and last to arrive is Manchester's most famous gangster, Harry Taylor. He swaggers into the hotel with all eyes upon him. Staff stop in their tracks what they're doing, whilst paying guests stand and stare at this larger than life character who never seems to be out of the newspapers. Taylor makes his way over to the reception desk. An attractive blond-haired, 21 year-old receptionist, Sara O'Farrell watches him approach. Sara knew he was due and has been looking forward to meeting the charismatic Taylor. She gives him her best glowing smile. 'Good evening Mr Taylor, we've been expecting you. Please will you follow me.' She leads Taylor into the lift and presses the button. The door shuts. Taylor smiles and offers her a cigarette. Sara shakes her head. 'No thank you, I'm on duty sadly sir. But I do get off at two?'
He moves towards her. 'Hopefully I'll see you later then?'
  Sara grins wide. 'Maybe?'
  'You never know your luck in a big city girl.' Taylor leans in to kiss Sara just as the lift doors open. She smiles and motions with her hand towards the long corridor in front of them. 'Saved by the bell! Please follow me sir.' Both step out of the lift with Sara in front, and a seemingly, mesmerised Taylor watching her walk off down the corridor. They stop halfway down. She points to a door where inside voices can be heard. Sara turns to Taylor. 'Well, have a nice evening sir.'

Taylor winks at her. 'Hopefully later?'
'Hopefully. You never know your luck in a big city Mr Taylor,' replies a smiling Sara, before heading off back to the lift. Very pleased with herself!

   Inside,
 and glaring at him soon as he opens the door are the rest of the night's invited guests. Taylor grins wide towards them. 'Hello lads, no show without punch as they say. Does anyone know what the bloody hell all this is about?'
   'Hey Harry,' replies Flannery. 'Welcome to our little party!'
'It's Errol fuckin' Flynn!' laughs Da Silva. 'Harry man, good to see you.'
The Brady brothers eye Taylor with a little suspicion due to a recent clash over the ownership of a popular pub on the city limits of the Salford and Stretford territory. Settled finally, but leaving a little bad blood and a few bruised bodies. Taylor stares across to the Brady brothers. 'Michael, Paul, it is good to see you lads. No hard feelings I hope?'
Michael smiles. 'None at all. Water under the Irwell Harry.'
'Ancient history Harry,' adds Paul. 'All in the past.'
   The Brady's walk over towards Taylor and they shake hands. He offers out cigarettes and glances around the lavish suite and especially at a long serving table filled with huge plates of sandwiches and bottles of wine and beer laid out. 'Someone has gone to a lot of trouble to arrange this little get together,' he says. 'Best get stuck in lads until we figure out what's going on. If it's a hit we might as well go out on a full stomach.'
'No one would have the guts,' replies Paul Brady.
   Suddenly, the suite door opens and the host of the evening arrives.
   Stood before them is 54 year-old, Police Detective-Inspector George Collins. A small, stocky figure with a world-weary face. He's smiling wide. Collins takes off his trilby and looks around at the sea of shocked faces before him. 'The gathering of the Mancunian clans. Gentlemen how nice it is to see you all getting along so well. Such a

pleasant sight as this moves even my very black stone heart. He pulls out his pockets. 'Look, no handcuffs, so nobody panic!'
Flannery doesn't appear impressed on seeing Collins. 'George, I'm a fuckin' busy man. What's going on here?'
'It's a fair kop George, I'll come quietly,' says an ice cool Taylor, who laughs whilst putting both hands in the air.
'I've a hot date tonight George,' grins Da Silva. 'I don't want my lady going cold, if you know what I mean.'

The Brady brothers appear the most tense of all present at Collins' sudden appearance into their midst. He notices this. 'Don't worry lads, I've come here on a white horse. A truce. I've come in peace.' Collins points across to a long table with chairs already set out. 'Shall we go and be seated over there, you'll want to hear what I have to say. I promise you.'

They all sit down with Collins at the head of the table.

'Please, I hope this isn't about you retiring George?' laughs Flannery. 'You'll break my big Mayo heart.'
'Unfortunately for you I'm going nowhere John. How can I possibly consider retirement when you undesirables are still walking about on the Manchester streets? I'd never sleep at night. Besides,' he says smiling. 'I'd miss you all far too much. Right, enough sweet talk, down to fuckin' business. Listen up. In just three days' time on Monday morning, those cockney reprobates Ronald and Reginald Kray will be departing on the 8-20 from Euston station London heading our way. This is no social call. Their aim is to stake a claim up here in the North. Their preference, I've reliably been told by my London contact is us. Manchester.'

For a second there's a stunned silence in the room.

'You can't be fuckin' serious George?' Michael Brady replies. 'I have it on good authority those two psychopaths never move out from the East end.'

'Too far away from their mum,' Paul adds. 'Fuckin' mummies boys. One is a fag as well by all accounts. They wouldn't dare come up here causing trouble George. No, I think your information is way off.'

Collins shakes his head. 'I don't know whose giving you boys your information, but its wide off the mark. Trust me, this is the gospel according to George Collins. I'm telling you. The Krays are coming. They're power mad and see themselves as kings of this realm. A criminal empire stretching from Land's End to John O'Groats that takes in all points North, far as Newcastle. Maybe even Glasgow. Yes, the fuckin' Jocks. But you gentlemen, we, are set to be their first port of call.'

'Why are you telling us this George?' asks Taylor. 'The last time I looked me and you were on different sides of the law.'

'Because, because we can't stop them coming Harry, for despite my better judgement on the matter, England remains a free country. So, my hands are tied, but yours are not. You lot here tonight can do something about it. What I need is for you to put your considerable immoral brains together, and come up with a viable solution to keep these lunatics out. Believe me, I'm open to all suggestions. Mad, bad and the utterly, fuckin' outrageous.'

'Do your job for you George,' remarks Flannery. 'Is that what this is all about?'

Collins sighs heavily. 'Look, Manchester isn't the big smoke. We're not London. The politics and practicalities of fighting crime is different up here. Shall we say it suits all parties if everyone just keeps their heads down and gets along. Now, you all know me, I'm a hard-faced bastard, but I'm Manchester's hard-faced bastard. I'm your hard-faced bastard. Nothing would give me greater pleasure in life than nicking you lot and throwing away the key in Strangeways. Look, Gentlemen, I love this fuckin' city. Hitler tried to bomb us back into the dark ages, but we survived, and I'll be damned if two cockney wide boys with their sharp suits, razors and rotten fuckin' accents are going to turn the streets of Manchester red with blood in a gang war.

No chance. Not on George Collins' watch. Myself and those I'm here to represent are willing to do whatever necessary to ensure such a scenario doesn't occur. Let's just say there exists from this moment on an unofficial truce whilst the matter is resolved. And I've been told to inform you if all goes well, we'll be looking, shall we say a little more favourably on all your business interests. But on the other hand if this doesn't work out as we require, then the heavens will fall on everyone here like a fuckin' ton of bricks.'

'What happens if they don't want to listen to reason George?' asks Da Silva. All eyes intently fall on Collins.

'Like I said,' he replies. 'This comes from the highest authority. Higher than fuckin' god in our world.'

'Are the Krays coming alone?' inquires Taylor.

'Of course, Harry,' smiles Collins. 'These two think they're bullet proof, believing it's divine providence allowing them to throw their weight around. But, let me assure you that despite the rumours coming from the smoke, they're flesh and blood, and bleed red like everybody else.'

'I heard a story the twins have half the coppers in the Met on their payroll?' asks Paul Brady.

'Only half?' quips Collins. Everybody laughs.

'Meet them at the station. Find someone you trust and agree on to explain in no uncertain terms that the Mancunian air is bad for their health. Too much smog and smoke gets on their soft southern chests. Tell them you can't buy jellied fuckin' eels in this city.'

'And, you promise,' says Flannery. 'That if it gets bloody, no comebacks? No retribution and twenty year sentences?'

Collins nods. 'You have my word and everybody here knows I'm good for it.' There's a stoney silence. Flannery looks around at the faces of the other bosses. One by one they nod towards him.

'Of course it is. That's enough for us George,' says Flannery. Collins claps his hands together. 'Right gentlemen, give me some names to get this done?'

'There's only one,' replies Taylor.

'Tommy Keenan,' says Da Silva. Taylor nods in agreement.

'Agreed,' adds Flannery. 'Tommy can handle this pair of freaks.'

Michael Brady smiles. 'Me too, I go along with old Irish here. Tommy is the man.'

'No contest,' adds his brother Paul. 'The only problem I see is if the Krays cut up rough. Maybe this particular job requires a more persuasive character of lunatic substance? Paddy Costigan maybe?'
 All present stare at Paul Brady like he's mad.
 'Come off it Paul,' says Collins. 'Paddy's idea of gentle persuasion would be to blow up the fuckin' train as it arrives in Manchester.'
They all laugh, but Collins is a hundred percent serious.
 'Paul has a point George,' adds Da Silva. 'If events take a turn for the worst and these London boys don't play ball, it'll be people like Paddy who settle this. Let's be realistic, the Krays won't go quietly.'
 'Preferably with a sawn off in his hand,' says Michael Brady.
 'Calm down now Michael,' replies Collins. 'Let me be clear. For the next few days I see no evil, I hear no evil, so, I never fuckin' heard that. Right then, I'm going to leave you thieves, rascal and vagabonds alone. Eat and drink and be merry courtesy of the Manchester Police. A last word before I depart this den of Mancunian inequity. Sort this out lads. Do a good job for me. This is our city.
 Don't let Manchester become just an extension of the Kray's empire. The twins are rotten bad fellows. They're vile, they're poison and they corrupt. Most importantly for you lot they're bad for business. On that note I'll bid you all goodnight. Oh, one last thing, no one blows up that fuckin' train.'
They all smile and nod.
Collins tips his hat towards the bosses and leaves the room.
 Taylor watches as Collins shuts the door behind him. He turns to the others. 'Collins is right about one thing, if the Krays get their foot in the door we'll never get rid of them. This has to be nipped in the bud.'
 'I agree,' says Flannery. 'They obviously think we're a soft touch. If not the case why don't they move first on Liverpool, Leeds or Newcastle. Glasgow even? No, they really fancy their chances here.'
Michael Brady nods in agreement. 'I say we hit them so hard that they wake up on the Old Kent road looking for their fuckin' fingernails. Make a statement of intent so that no one from London

ever dares contemplates trying it on again. We've got to stand our ground. Stay tight. Give them two choices, get back on the train or a first-class ticket to the fuckin' graveyard.'
'By the way,' says a smiling Flannery. 'Talking of Paddy Costigan, I have him waiting in the hotel bar for me.' Everybody stares in annoyance and shock at Flannery. He simply shrugs his shoulders. 'Well you never know, I thought maybe one of you was planning some kind of a hit. Let's be honest we've all had our past moments here lads.'
'Oh, come on John,' says Da Silva.
'That man is an animal,' says Taylor. 'A wild dog John. You've heard the stories like the rest of. I don't know how you can tolerate having him around.'
'Don't play the saint with me Harry Taylor!' snaps Flannery. 'What are you a priest? What does Billy Tarr do for you, the fuckin' cleaning up? Men like Costigan are worth their weight in gold. In our line of business even wild dogs, as you say have their worth.'
Taylor shakes his head. 'I draw the line with scum like Costigan.'
'Will you two just leave it!' jumps in Da Silva. 'If Costigan is here let's use him to go and pick up Tommy. It's Friday night, so he shouldn't be too hard to find.'
'He'll be on the roulette tables at Paddy Mullen's place, the Cromford club,' smiles Paul Brady. 'He practically lives in there.'
'Don't you think it makes more sense if one of us goes to pick him up?' asks Taylor. 'No need to attract attention, and if Costigan causes grief with the doormen or Mullen's clientele, it could spell unwanted trouble. Paddy isn't someone we want to upset. Especially at the minute with the balloon set to go up.'
'No, let's just send Costigan,' says Michael Brady. 'Have a real good word with him John, make sure he behaves. No fuckin' scenes.'
'I just had a thought,' adds Da Silva. 'Why isn't Mullen here?'
'Paddy keeps his own council,' replies Taylor. 'He's done business in the past with the Krays and wouldn't hesitate to shut this madness down straight away. Paddy wouldn't put up with this. That's why Collins probably thought he couldn't trust him?'

Flannery shakes his head. 'No Harry, I don't think so. More likely Collins doesn't want to lose his table at the Cromford club. If we're all agreed, I'll go and tell Costigan to pick up Keenan?'
 'Go tell him fetch,' says Taylor, in a sarcastic tone, before smiling and winking at the Irishman. Flannery eyes Taylor angrily before leaving the suite.
 'Don't needle him too much Harry,' says a laughing Paul Brady. 'The Paddies are naturally paranoid. It's their fucked up history. They blame us for everything. Besides, we've a couple of tooled up lads in the next room!'
 'Me too!' adds a grinning Da Silva.
Taylor shakes his head in disbelief. 'I don't fuckin' believe it. Whatever happened to good old fashion traits like honesty and trust? Anyone would think we were common criminals.'
After a second they all laugh. Even Taylor. 'Right then,' he says. 'If you boys will excuse me for a moment, there's a young lady in reception who I need to have a quick word with for later on.'
' Da Silva shakes his head, smiling. 'Errol Flynn is at it again man.'

  Sat nursing a large glass of whisky at the hotel bar is 31 year-old Paddy Costigan. A brute of a man, huge in size with a bulldog, pug-nosed, badly-scarred face. A dark, nasty aura surrounds him. Costigan gives off a stench of violence. A young couple sat quietly in the corner of the room can't help but stare at him. Costigan catches their eyes and they both swiftly look away in mortal fear.
  John Flannery appears in the bar and approaches him. 'How you doing Paddy son, terrible news about our boy in Dallas don't you think?'
'Who is that then Mr Flannery?'
'Kennedy of course?'
'Never heard of him.'
Flannery thinks it's not worth wasting his time, so decides to get on with business. 'I've a small job for you tonight. One that involves a little delicacy.'
Costigan is listening intently. 'Whatever you say Mr Flannery.'

'I need you to find Tommy Keenan at the Cromford club and bring him back here. Tell him it's a matter of urgency. But, and I cannot stress this enough Paddy, there must be no trouble. No violence. Do you understand me? I can't afford to be made to look bad in this matter.'
Flannery is still rather unsure whether his message is getting through. 'Tommy is a good friend of mine, as is Mr Mullen the owner. Be firm, but be very polite. Don't insult or hit anybody. No trouble.'
  Costigan nods. 'Yes Mr Flannery, no trouble. Just bring Keenan back here in one piece and smiling. No broken bones Paddy. No blood on the pavement am I clear?'
'No Mr Flannery, no broken bones or blood on the pavement.'
'Good lad,' Flannery smiles. 'Now away with you son.'
Costigan stands to go. He heads out of the hotel and pushes the two concierges out of his path as he leaves! Both end up in a huddle on the floor. 'Get out of the fuckin' way!' growls Costigan, as he storms off like a wild bull into the Manchester night muttering. 'No broken bones, no blood on the pavement…'
'What's his problem?' asks Ashley. As he gets back up brushing himself down. 'I don't know,' replies Coates. 'But I fuckin' hope and pray it's never me mate.'

THE CROMFORD CLUB

Paddy Costigan makes his way through Piccadilly gardens towards the Cromford club. Here gangsters, priests, movie stars, famous singers, footballers and politicians mix happily. Nobody bothered them. It's a Mancunian oasis of class and calm. Entrance is by invitation only, and the fearful sight of Costigan walking menacingly towards them has the Cromford's three burly doormen twitching. 'What the hell does this lunatic want?' whispers one, still well out of Costigan's earshot. 'Who's going to tell this fuckin' ogre he can't come in?' replies another.
'Just calm down lads!' exclaims the third and senior doorman. 35 year-old ex-boxer Jimmy Toolan. 'He's probably just here on business. Leave it to me, I'll deal with him.'
Costigan approaches the doormen. 'Evening boys, how are you doing?' Remembering his boss Flannery's warning, Costigan attempts a friendly smile, but it only helps to makes him appear even more ominous! 'Evening Paddy. Look, no offence mate, we don't want any trouble, but you know Mr Mullen's strict door policy? Guests only on a Friday, absolutely no exceptions.'
'I'm not here because I want a drink, I'm working. I have an urgent message for Tommy Keenan,' says Costigan. A smiling Toolan relaxes and steps out towards Costigan from the door.
'Come with me then Paddy.' He escorts Costigan into the club-foyer where the powerful, if rousing, magnificent voice of a woman singing can be heard coming from the next room. Shirley Bassey. The guests present in the foyer stare rather worryingly at Costigan.
'Paddy please stay here for a minute whilst I go and find Mr Mullen.'
Costigan hands Toolan a murderous stare. 'Hurry up I haven't got all fuckin' night!'

Toolan is no shrinking violet and can seriously take care of himself, but Costigan is well known as a proper maniac. He walks over towards him. 'Just stay calm yeah Paddy? I'll be back before you know it.' That said Toolan steps through an entrance into the luxurious inner sanctum of the Cromford club.

Costigan catches a slight glimpse through a half open door.

What he sees is a lavish room bedecked out in the finest surroundings. Dimly lit, shrouded in cigarette smoke, a mysterious other world. Tables are evenly scattered around where diners and drinkers sit gossiping and laughing. Others deep in business talk. On the stage the aspiring young Welsh lady singer Shirley Bassey is bringing the house down.

This is the Cromford club.

Manchester's classiest joint.

Sat on one of the side tables is the owner, 54 year old Paddy Mullen. A tall, impressive man. Elegantly suited and clearly a much-respected figure. Mullen is in conversation with two of his best friends. The owner of a Mancunian gambling empire, 44 year-old, Lenny Foyle, and the Manchester United manager, 53 year-old, Matt Busby. Both are equally sartorially dressed as Mullen and also kings of their domains.

Toolan approaches Mullen's table. 'Excuse me Mr Mullen, can I have a moment.'

'Course Jimmy, what's up son?'

He leans down and whispers into his boss's ear. Mullen appears a little shaken on being told of Costigan's presence and request. Just the thought of having him on the premises makes his skin crawl.

'Get that damn Costigan out of the foyer and away from the punters Jimmy. Take him to my office. I'll be with you shortly.'

'Yes sir.'

Busby notices his friend's sudden change of mood. 'Is everything okay Paddy?'

'I'm not sure yet Matt. Will you lads excuse me for a couple of minutes?'

Mullen stands to go. 'Of course,' replies Busby.

'No worries Pat,' smiles Foyle. A man who operates in the same world as Mullen, and knows immediately something isn't right.
  'Paddy has a problem Matt,' he says. 'I 've seen that look before.' They watch on as Mullen starts to make his way through the dining room, but is immediately pulled up by several punters. He stops to take the time to chat. 'Look at him Matt' says a smiling Foyle. 'They all love our Paddy, but he's definitely got a bug under his skin. He's rattled.'

  Mullen finally reaches his office. On entering, stood waiting for him is Paddy Costigan. The two shake hands. Mullen smiles, but he feels uneasy. 'Patrick it's so good to see you again. How are the family?' Costigan shrugs his shoulders. 'I'm not sure, the last I heard they all wanted me dead Mr Mullen.'
  For a moment Mullen is stuck for words!
  'Well that's a real shame. Now what's all this about Tommy Keenan? What do you want with him? I'm sure you and Mr Flannery are well aware he's a very good friend of mine?'
  'There's no problem Mr Mullen. None at all. Mr Flannery and the other bosses just need to have a little chat with him.'
  Mullen lights up a cigarette. 'You know of my reputation Patrick?'
  'Yes sir.'
  'Regarding this chat, I wouldn't be happy if anything unfortunate was to happen to Tommy. Not a scratch, a broken nose, or an unlucky bang on his head. Do we understand each other here?'
  'We do Mr Mullen. I'd never lie to you.'
  Mullen smiles. 'Good lad.'
  He picks up his phone.
  'Have Tommy come up to my office.'

  27 year-old Tommy Keenan, man about town, a fixer, a gangster. Black hair with striking blue eyes and movie star looks is enjoying himself on the Blackjack tables. Swamped by a crowd of admirers Tommy is on a winning run and the chips are piled high in front of him. Suddenly, a croupier taps Tommy on the shoulder and

whispers into his ear. 'Tommy, the boss wants you upstairs in his office straight away.'

He stares at his mountain of chips. 'Cash me in please Charlie.' He hands Charlie a handful of chips then turns to walk back through the large crowd of backslappers. Tommy heads towards his girlfriend. A young blond lady, 24 year-old Alison Jones. Waif-like beauty.
'I have to go and see Paddy. I shouldn't be too long.'
'What does he want?' asks Alison.
'Oh, he probably just wants to know if I have any good tips for the horses.'

Alison kisses Tommy on the cheek. 'Of course he does. I love you Tommy Keenan.'

He smiles. 'Then I'm the luckiest man in the world.'

Tommy knocks on Mullen's office door, enters and his smiling face turns to stone when he sees Paddy Costigan standing staring at him.
'Hello Paddy, how's your luck?'

Costigan totally ignores him.

Paddy Mullen is sat behind his desk. 'It appears young Keenan, your presence is required elsewhere and quickly.' Tommy points towards Costigan. 'With him?'

Mullen nods.

'John Flannery and the other bosses would like a chat about a subject I know nothing of, but Paddy here has given me his word he'll look after you, making sure you don't end up being found dead, eaten up by the Irwell fishes in the canal.' Mullen stares daggers at Costigan. A look that unnerves even him. 'He has indeed been kind enough to guarantee his own good health upon the fact. Paddy could you wait downstairs now please? Tommy will be with you shortly when we've finished.'

'But Mr Mullen...I'

'Paddy Costigan, this is my club, my rules now get out.'

Mullen's tone is quiet, firm but measured with just a hint of a threat. Costigan reluctantly turns to leave the room and glares angrily at

Tommy on the way, who is relieved to see him go. The door shuts behind Costigan. 'Oh great, cheers Paddy, you've gone and upset him now.' An exasperated Mullen stands up from his chair.

'Tommy what's going on here?'

He shrugs his shoulders. 'I was hoping you'd know. You're the oracle around these parts Paddy.'

Mullen appears genuinely worried. 'Nothing ever happens in this city without my knowledge, but I have to admit I'm out of the loop on this one, and that makes me very nervous. Something is up and I don't know what. Have you been behaving yourself lad?'

Tommy smiles and sits down on Mullen's desk. 'You know me, I've done bits and pieces, but nothing dangerous. Just the day job.'

'Are you working on anything that might have put somebody's nose out of joint?'

'Even you can't blame the JFK hit on me?'

Tommy's attempt at black humour with Mullen fails badly as his look only hardens. He shakes his head. 'Nothing Paddy, nothing that would rattle Flannery or the others.'

'Are you totally sure about this Tommy?'

'Come on Paddy,' replies a smiling Tommy. 'Would I lie to you?'

'Right lad, listen up. Go to the meeting. They all know you're under my protection, so you'll be safe enough. Then I want you to come straight back later on and fill me in. I can smell trouble here son and I don't like it.'

Tommy stands to leave. 'Paddy, one other thing, I've left Alison alone downstairs at the tables.'

Mullen smiles. 'Don't worry I'll invite her to sit with me, Lenny and Matt until you get back. We've some of the United lads calling by later on as well, so I'll ensure they make a big fuss of her. She'll be treated like a princess.'

Tommy sighs. 'Oh great, whilst I'm about to disappear into the night with the craziest mick ever to come out of Ireland, my girlfriend is being serenaded by a bunch of randy footballers.'

Mullen laughs. 'I'll keep a good eye, now get going before Costigan starts tearing my bloody doormen apart limb by limb.'

A foul mood Paddy Costigan with Tommy Keenan walking behind him leave the Cromford club. Tommy smiles at the doormen. 'If I'm not back in a week call the police boys!' He looks around him.
'Hey Paddy, where've you parked your car?'
'It's only ten minutes by foot you lazy bastard,' scowls Costigan.
'So, come on Paddy, what's going on?' Costigan ignores him and just keeps on walking in front.
'Oh, come on Paddy,' pleads Tommy.
'I haven't got a clue. I was told to just come and pick you up and that's it.'
'Am I in trouble?'
Costigan smiles, but it resembles more of a grimace. 'You're always in fuckin' trouble. Too much to say for yourself. Always have had. A big fuckin' mouth you Keenan.'
Tommy laughs. 'You don't like me do you Paddy?'
An irritated Costigan grunts. 'I don't like anybody, now just shut up and walk.'
But Tommy can't resist winding him up. 'Well I like you Paddy,' he says with a huge grin. Suddenly, Costigan snaps and in a fit of rage has Tommy by the lapels on his suit. 'You mouthy bastard! You just don't know when to shut up do you? You're going to talk yourself into an early grave Keenan. Luckily for you I'm under orders, now for the last time just fuckin' walk and don't even breathe loud! Otherwise, so, fuckin' help me God...'
Costigan let's go of Tommy and strides off. Shrugging himself down, Tommy straightens his tie and thinks best to stay quiet.
    The concierges are still on duty outside the Portland hotel when the bulky figure of Paddy Costigan comes into view hurtling towards them. He does nothing more than push both of them aside.
'Get out of my way!'
'Evening lads, I feel your pain,' says a smiling Tommy, following close behind. Costigan leads him into the hotel and up in the lift towards the suite. They both stand outside the door. Costigan knocks on, and opens it just enough for Tommy to walk through.
'In you go smart mouth, I'll see you later.'

'Not if I see you first,' replies Tommy, hastily walking inside before a mad-eyed Costigan has his chance to grab him!

FOR THE ANGELS

A nervous looking Tommy Keenan enters and all eyes are upon him. A smiling John Flannery approaches. 'Tommy Keenan, thank you so much for coming.' Flannery puts an arm around Tommy's shoulders and leads him over to a table where they're all sat. Obviously still pensive, Tommy takes in all the faces staring back at him. It's a greatest hits of the Manchester underworld.
 'Good evening gent's, Can someone please explain what am I doing here?' Harry Taylor offers Tommy a cigarette and he accepts. 'Cheers Harry.'
 'Tommy, last year you did some work for the Krays in London. Is that right?'
 'I did, what about it?'
 'What did you make of them?'
 Tommy shrugs his shoulders. 'They were good lads, I had no problems with them. The job got done, it got done well. We shock hands and they paid up. That's about it. No dramas.'
 'What Harry is getting at Tommy, is should we fear them?' asks Michael Brady.
 'Whose this we Michael?' replies Tommy.
 'Manchester, Tommy boy,' adds a smiling Da Silva.
  Tommy appears confused. 'You've lost me. What exactly is going down here lads?' Michael Brady passes Tommy a glass of wine. 'On Monday morning they're coming up from London with the intention of taking over. Got it in their heads we're all soft up here and ripe for plucking. That we'll just give in at the sight of their fuckin' Savile Row suits.'
 'Walk all over us,' says Flannery.
 'We can't have it Tommy,' jumps in Da Silva again. 'We just can't have it.' Tommy goes to light the cigarette, but his lighter isn't

working. Taylor strikes a match and offers to light it for him. He does so. 'We need you to have a little chat with them. Explain discreetly, but firmly that they should just get back on the train and go home. The weather here is rough. We wouldn't want them to catch a cold. Let's call it Northern hospitality.'

'How exactly do I go about this?' asks Tommy.

Taylor smiles. 'Come on Tommy, you've a silver tongue mate, you can charm the birds out of the trees.'

'It will be better coming from you,' adds Flannery. 'A friendly face, someone they know and have done business with before. But most importantly someone who they trust.'

'What if they refuse to listen?'

'Well then it becomes our problem Tommy,' replies Michael Brady. A shocked Tommy can't believe what he's hearing. 'You seriously can't be contemplating hitting the Krays?'

Taylor shakes his head. 'Tommy, Tommy, you really surprise me. Don't be so naïve son. You've been around long enough to know anybody can be got rid of, if the will is there to achieve it. Kings and Queens, Prime Ministers. Hell, somebody managed to hammer a couple of bullets through Kennedy's skull a few days ago. The President of the fuckin' United States was put down. So, who on this earth is going to give a moment's grief about those two lunatics? Nobody will care, I promise you. Apart from their mother of course, who I'm told is a lovely lady and we'll send her some flowers.'

But Tommy has major doubts. He's convinced they're all mad to even contemplate this. 'Lads, I've worked down there. I know, I've seen it. They control the entire East End and huge swathes of club land over across the city. This is such a huge call that I'd urge you all to think again. The twins have great influence in London that even extends into Parliament. Politicians, bent coppers high in the Met who dance to their tune. They collect dirt on the establishment like a schoolboy collects stamps. They love it and they bloody well use it.'

Taylor listens intently, but clearly isn't impressed. 'That's true Tommy, but if the Krays go down they'll all run for cover. The twins pollute everything and everyone they come into contact with. Trust me, no one will care Tommy. Indeed, we'll be doing the country a fuckin' favour.'

Tommy remains unsure. 'People call them crazy Harry, but I'm telling you they've got a sixth sense. The twins can smell trouble and if it does turn nasty, you're going to have to cut their heads off to stop them coming after you.'

'Like we said before Tommy,' replies Da Silva, in a rather ominous tone. 'Our problem.'

'They're staying at the Midland,' says Flannery. 'You turn up and switch on the charm and then none of this has to come to pass.'

'You've forgotten one thing, what about Paddy?' asks Tommy.

Flannery looks nervously towards the others. 'This isn't Mullen's problem Tommy. He's no need to know because it'll only complicate matters. Best for him, us, and you in particular that he's kept in the dark until we can sort this problem out.'

Tommy stares long and hard at Taylor. 'Okay, so the worse scenario I fail to get them to go home. What happens then?'

Flannery looks around, and they all nod back at him. 'If that happens then this is how it'll all go down. We'll have four shooters within spitting distance of the room. Depending on how it goes the twins either walk out of the hotel and back to the train station breathing in one piece.'

'Or they leave in body bags,' adds Paul Brady. 'With rivers of blood staining their fuckin' Savile Row suits.'

Taylor notices Tommy's deep concerns. 'But, hopefully Tommy, with you whispering sweet nothings in their cockney ears we'll never have to make that call.'

'It's all down to you Tommy boy,' says a smiling Da Silva. 'The Angels have decided this beautiful city of ours is in your hands.'

Flannery laughs. 'The Man who saved us from the Krays. You'll go down in folklore son. A legend.'

Tommy can't help but smile. 'So, I'm doing this for the angels. I'm filling up. One thing more, do I actually have a choice in this?'

'All life is a choice Tommy boy,' replies a smiling Flannery. 'We need you for this, we need you to come through for us.'

Taylor pats Tommy on the back and refills his wine glass.
 'Get working on your speech son.' Tommy looks around the table and lights another cigarette. He inhales deeply, puts his head back and sighs. Absolutely convinced everyone else in the room apart from him have gone insane. The night has suddenly taken a turn for the unexpected and the worse.

THE BOY WITH NO SHOES

Tommy Keenan enters back into the packed Cromford dining room and walks over towards Paddy Mullen's table. Sat with Mullen are also now Manchester United footballers Denis Law and Paddy Crerand. A smiling Keenan nods to acknowledge their presence and sits down next to Mullen. 'Well, how'd it all go?' he asks.
'It was nothing,' replies Tommy. 'Flannery has got hold of some bootleg whisky from home. He wants me to spread the word.'
Mullen eyes Tommy and doesn't look too convinced. 'That's it, all this fuss for Bootleg whisky?'
'That's about it,' replies Tommy. 'Not worth worrying about. The stuff is only one step up from potcheen at best.'
Mullen smiles. 'You can't take the boy out of Mayo eh?'
Tommy laughs. He lights up a cigarette. 'Still a farmer's boy at heart is our John. In his head he's never left Belcarra.'
Mullen stares long and hard at Tommy. So much it unnerves him. 'What?' he says, appearing ruffled.
'And the others?'
'They just wanted a nosebag on the deal. That's it?'
'Nothing?'
'Nothing, I swear!' answers Tommy. Inside his heart is racing. He's never ever before lied to Mullen about anything, and had no intention of doing so. Until now. Mullen's granite features suddenly break into a smile, and he points towards the dance floor. On there is Matt Busby dancing with Tommy's girlfriend Alison. 'Matt has kept your girl busy,' says a now, seemingly more relaxed and smiling Mullen. 'He thinks he's Fred bloody Astaire and she's Ginger Rogers! Another ten minutes and they'll run off together.'
Busby leads a beaming Alison by the hand back over to the table. Everybody stands up to greet them. 'You're a lucky man Thomas Keenan. You take good care of this lassie.'
Tommy smiles. 'I intend to, thank you Mr Busby.'

Busby kisses Alison's hand before passing it over to Tommy.
 'Now go and dance this beautiful lady's feet off lad.'
 Tommy and Alison return to the dance floor and Mullen and Foyle watch them go. 'Is everything sorted now Paddy?' he asks.
 Mullen's eyes are locked on Tommy. 'I hope so Len,' he says. 'I truly hope so.'
 Tommy holds a smiling Alison close. 'So, what was so important that you had to leave me in the charming arms of the most famous man in Manchester?'
 He laughs. 'The usual stuff. Curing lepers and blind kids. All sorted now though. I'm all yours.'
 'Tommy, why don't you ever tell me what you do for a living?'
 He grins wide. 'I just told you I cure...'
 Alison puts her hand gently over Keenan's mouth to stop him talking. 'Please Just dance Saint Thomas, Just dance!'
 Tommy kisses Alison, then goes to whisper into her ear.
 'I love you.'

 The next morning Tommy Keenan jumps off the back of a double decker bus on Deansgate, Manchester, and heads into a large cafe. The Noble. It's crammed packed. *All my Loving* by the Beatles is playing on the radio. The smell of sizzling bacon drifts through the air. Tommy spots Paddy Mullen already sat down with his breakfast and goes over to join him.
 'Morning Paddy.'
 'Are you thirsty?' asks Mullen.
 'Excuse me?' answers a surprised Tommy.
 'Here, have my coffee.' He slides his cup of coffee over to Tommy.
 'Are you hungry?' continues Mullen. He then picks up his full breakfast plate and throws it across the table!
 'How about my wallet, do you want my money?'
 Mullen takes out a large bundle of notes and slams then down on the table. Suddenly, Tommy realises what's going on. 'Paddy, please, let me explain?'

But an angry Mullen is seething. 'How about the clothes off my back? Here's my tie!' He rips it off and throws it in Tommy's face.

'Go on, put it on.' Tommy goes to pick it up only for Mullen to snatch it back off him. 'You lied to me boy!'

Tommy's head is down. 'I'm sorry.'

'Look at me!' insists Mullen. Tommy stares towards his boss. He's never seen him this angry. 'I'm going to tell you a story lad and you'd do well to listen to it.'

'There was this kid from Collyhurst.

He was 12 years-old. Eight stone wet through. His father would knock him around like a spinning top. His mother was a drunk who only ever cared where the next drink was coming from. So, this poor kid, one day I'm out and about in town and I see him sat on a bench in Piccadilly. He's crying, so I go up to him and ask what's wrong? He points to his shoes, both of them have big holes in the soles. He tells me with tears falling down his face that if he went home with his shoes in this state, his father would take the belt to him. So, I take him into Manchester's finest shoe shop and pick him out the best pair of shoes they had. And then this kid smiled. We said our goodbyes and he went home.

The next day I'm in town again and I see this same kid, sat on the same bench. Wearing the same old shoes. Again, he's crying. He tells me that he'd gone home and his father had accused him of stealing the new shoes. To teach the kid a lesson he then kicked him around the house and slashed him with a buckle belt. Then he threw the new shoes into the fire. This kid was badly bruised. A black eye, busted lip. Well, I got mad then see. But first I bought him another pair of shoes before making him take me to his house. The kid was terrified when we knocked on the door. His father appeared, a big ugly brute of a man, but a bully. You know the type, only picked on women and kids. I told the boy to go inside whilst I spoke to his old man. I asked him if he knew who I was and he nodded. I told him that if he ever even shouted at the kid again, I'd personally break every bone in his body. And do you know what happened?'

'He never touched the kid again,' answered Tommy.

His eyes firmly fixed on Mullen and close to tears.

'Correct,' continues Mullen. 'That same kid when he was sixteen came knocking at my door looking for a job. He began by running errands and sweeping up around the club. I always told him to watch what goes on. Listen and learn. To always show respect. To keep his nose clean, and I'd look after him. The kid graduated and I grew to love him like a son. He spread his wings, he flew the nest. He became a man, respected. I had a father's pride in how he treated people and did business. I only ever had one rule. An eleventh commandment. Never lie to me. And last night Thomas Keenan, you broke it that rule.'

'Paddy, I'd no choice. It was for your own good. I didn't want you involved in this madness. They've all gone crazy!'

'So you did lie to me then?' replies Mullen.

Tommy appears shell-shocked. 'You tricked me?'

Mullen leans over to Tommy. 'I'll ask you this one last time Tommy. Tell me what the hell is going on?'

Tommy knows he's left with little choice. 'Okay then. They're going to hit the Krays.'

'Say that again?' utters a stunned Mullen.

'On Monday morning the Krays are arriving from London. They have it in their thick heads to take over Manchester. Flannery, the Brady brothers, Da Silva and Taylor have been given the all clear by the Old Bill to deal with it. I've been given this one chance to reason with the twins, and send them home. If that doesn't work. Well, Paddy, if that doesn't work they're both dead men.'

'Shooters?' asks Mullen.

'The best we have. If I can't get them back on the train, five minutes after I leave their hotel room the balloon goes up and they go down.'

'Why you? Why can't they use one of their own people?'

Tommy shrugs his shoulders. 'I've no idea. Look, Paddy, nobody wants you involved because this isn't your problem. Please, this one time, for me. Just keep your distance. I don't want you mixed up in this.'

'So, my Mancunian brothers in arms don't trust me? Is that it?' Tommy shakes his head. 'No, it's not that, they're just businessmen playing the odds. To them you're an outsider. You operate in a different world. They didn't want to cause you the hassle.'

Mullen appears hardly convinced. 'I'll tell you why the others didn't want me involved, it's because I'd have told them straight off this is sheer, bloody stupidity, and I'd have ended it before it began.'

'Paddy, you're not listening. This came from the police, it's political. If I fail the gangs have been given the red light to do their dirty work for them. It's a rubber-stamped hit. An assassination. Stay out of it. Please, I can do this thing. I can end it peacefully with no bloodshed. I can get them back on the train.'

'The kid with the holes in his shoes,' laughs Mullen. 'This kid who was scared of his own shadow is going to make everything right?'

'I'm not a kid anymore. I've listened and learnt from the best. I can do this.' Mullen stares hard at Keenan. In his eyes he still sees the same scared young kid beaten to a pulp by his father. Finally, he smiles. 'Pass me back my wallet.'

Tommy hands it over.

'And my breakfast.' Tommy laughs and passes the plate back.

'I want to know everything you know, and if it satisfies me you just might leave this café in one piece.'

'Yes sir,' says a smiling Tommy, as he lights up a cigarette.

'And another thing,' says Mullen. Suddenly, he slaps Tommy around the head, and snatches the cigarette out of his mouth throwing it to the floor. 'He glares at a shamefaced Tommy. 'You ever lie to me again young man, I'll put you back on that bench in Piccadilly Gardens where I found you. Now, what are you having for breakfast?' Tommy feels it safe to smile again and catches the merest glimpse of forgiveness in Mullen's eyes. But one thing is certain.

He'll never ever lie to him again.

Paddy and Tommy are walking along the banks of the River Irwell. Nearby are the docks with huge freight ships from all over the world loading and unloading their cargos.

The two stop for a moment and stare over the water.
'They sail here from all over world Tommy,' says Mullen.
'The United States, China, Africa, Australia, Japan, Russia, and never one bit of hassle. Yet, two mouthy cockneys with delusions of grandeur and a mother fixation from London's East End can cause us such grief. So, tell me son, what are you going to say to them?'
Tommy appears transfixed by the ships. He turns to look at Mullen. 'Well it isn't Shakespeare, I can tell you that. I've a speech in mind Paddy, but I feel I only have it in me to deliver once. Do you know what I mean?'
Mullen smiles. 'I hear it from the theatre types the entire time. It'll be alright on the night? I pray for your sakes you don't get tongue tied, because those two crazy bastards will cut it out.'
Mullen clenches his fist. 'The Krays respect only one thing Tommy. Power. Real power. Oh, they'll have done their homework with the result being they consider Manchester ripe for the taking. Your words have to resonate loud with them that they are set to make the biggest mistake of their lives. Leave a lasting impression, not just to get them on the train, but to ensure they never come back. No half measures. Anything else, if you come across in any way weak or unsure they'll see through you, the game will be over, the shooting will begin.'
Tommy hasn't taken his eyes off Mullen. 'Paddy you have to promise whatever happens you won't step in?'
Mullen shakes his head. He's disgusted with himself for not being able to help this boy, who is his son in all but blood. 'This thing is already in motion Tommy. Even if I wanted to I couldn't stop it now. No, it's down to you. You have to kill them with words.' Mullen stops and puts his hand on Tommy's shoulder. 'Send them home lad.' The two men continue to look out across at the docks. It feels like the gentle calm before a raging storm. No more words are necessary.

THE HITMEN

Welcome to Salford.
Saturday Afternoon.
The Brady brothers, Michael and Paul drive through the gates of Monroe's scrapyard on the borders of Salford and Manchester. Around them huge mounds of old cars reach high.
A crane is busy flattening scrap metal. The workers whom they drive past all nod in acknowledgement, but the Brady's ignore them. Michael suddenly spots the owner, 56 year-old, fat, balding and permanently in a bad mood, Eric Monroe.
Michael motions for Paul to pull over.
Wearing a white hard hat Monroe is deep in conversation with his foreman. He's raging. 'Sack the idiot, this is his second day off sick in a year. I'm not a fuckin' charity!' Monroe notices the brothers walking towards him. 'Oh no, what the fuckin' hell do these two clowns want?' Monroe smiles wide as they draw closer.
'Michael, Paul, it's good to see you. What brings you both down here on a Saturday afternoon when United are at home?'
'We're looking for Damien Quinn,' replies Paul. 'Is he around?'
Monroe points up towards the crane. 'He's up there.'
'Well fuckin' go and get him down here then!' snaps Michael.
A shaken Monroe motions to his foreman to go and fetch Quinn.
'Your payments are late Monroe.' says Paul.
'Things are a bit tight at the moment Paul. No bugger is paying up. You know what they're like around here.'
Michael smiles and shakes his head. 'Come on Eric, you're working on a Saturday afternoon for Christ's sake. You must be rolling in it, so don't fuck us around. I want two grand by Friday, otherwise you'll find yourself at the bottom of one of these fuckin' piles. Do you understand me?'
Monroe nods his head.

The foreman returns with 23 year-old Damien Quinn.
A Salford lad. Slim build with cropped black hair and sparkling, blue eyes. Cool, scared of nothing and a devil may care attitude. However, where Quinn differs is in his ability to handle a shotgun and kill for money. Paul Brady turns towards Monroe and his foreman.
'Fuck off.'
The two men shuffle away quickly leaving Quinn alone with the Brady brothers. 'How are you keeping Damien?' asks Michael.
'Fine thanks Mr Brady. It's good to see you both.'
'We've a job for you,' says Paul. 'It'll pay well, but it may mean you having to leave the city for a while and lie low.'
Quinn laughs and looks around at the scrapyard. 'You mean having to leave all this behind? No problem, I'm in.'
Michael smiles. 'Good lad, we'll pick you up tomorrow at three and explain more then. Be ready.'
Paul Brady winks at Quinn. 'Nice to be working together again Damian.'
'Likewise,' he replies.
The brothers get back in the car and drive off. Quinn is watching them go, when suddenly Monroe walks back over, until only inches from his face. 'Eh, Quinn, I don't pay you to stand around. Now get back up there and to fuckin' work soft lad.'
Quinn eyes Monroe, as if sizing him up for a future target, before simply smiling. 'Anything you say Mr Monroe.'
One day soon Quinn has just decided he's going to kill Monroe.

Welcome to Moss Side.
Saturday night.
With bodyguards on either side of him Jimmy Da Silva, steps out of his car opposite the Nile Club. He stares with disdain at the run-down building. Situated on the first floor, the main entrance is blocked by two burly, black doormen. They swiftly move aside as he goes upstairs. On entering Da Silva can hardly see through the thick swirling Marijuana and tobacco smoke. A saxophone player is

performing live and the dance floor is packed. He clicks his fingers and a pretty young girl from behind the bar in a mini skirt and beehive haircut comes over. Da Silva talks into her ear and the girl points a finger to pick out a table through the haze.

Sat holding court is 28 year-old Leon 'Pearly' Spence. Dressed immaculate in a tailor-made suit and handmade shoes, Spence's devilish good looks and charm is currently being used on three female admirers hanging onto his every word. Spence is Da Silva's most deadly hired hand. A born killer. He only uses him sparingly because of his disturbing nature and the fact Spence actually appears to enjoy killing. A smiling Da Silva approaches his table. 'Leon my man!'
He leans down and shakes a beaming Spence's hand. 'What are you doing in here Jimmy?' replies Spence. 'This isn't your scene.'
'We need to talk,' says Da Silva. 'But not in here, let's go outside?'
'Sure,' he replies. Both men head out of the club followed down the stairs by Da Silva's bodyguards. He offers Spence a cigarette.
'We have to go to work on Monday, Leon. I need you at your best for this is huge. We can't afford any mistakes.'
'Who is it?' inquires Spence.
'They're two brothers. Twins. You'll be working with three other men. Locals.'
'Twins? It's not the fuckin' Krays, is it?' laughs an excited Spence.
Da Silva stares back at him saying nothing but everything.
'Fuckin' Hell Jimmy, it is! JFK and the Krays in the same month. What's going on man?'
'It's not a certainty Leon. They have one chance to get back on the train, if not, well you and the others blast them into the next life to meet their cockney ancestors.'
'Guns? That's disappointing. I was hoping I'd get the chance to carve them up.' Da Silva suddenly remembers why Spence turns his stomach so much. 'Stay by your phone tomorrow. I'll be in touch. Now go on back up those stairs and back to your ladies.'
'Hey man.' Smiles Spence. 'I can smell blood, it excites me. They could get lucky tonight!' As Spence heads back upstairs Da Silva

watches him go. His face clear to what he thinks of Spence. Da Silva turns to his bodyguards. 'That bastard makes my skin crawl. Come on, let's get out of here. I need a drink.'

Welcome to Collyhurst.
 Billy Green's Pub.
 Paddy Costigan is sat at the bar drinking whisky when in through the door walks his boss John Flannery. The place is in a state of absolute mayhem! An Irish fiddle and accordion band is playing The *Fields of Athenry*. Every table is packed. A fist fight breaks out! Pint pots and bottles hurtle through the air before it's swiftly broken up and taken outside. Rousing sing songs are in full flow drowning out any brave efforts of the band to be heard. At Costigan's feet a dog is licking clean a bowl of beer gifted to it by the locals. It's Saturday night in Billy Green's and you can't get a seat to save your life!
   A smiling Flannery sidles up to an unsuspecting Costigan. 'How are you Patrick, are you up for a large one?' Flannery motions the barmaid over towards them. 'Two large Irish whiskies please my dear.'
   Costigan nods in gratitude. 'Thank you Mr Flannery.'
   The barmaid hands both men their drinks. Flannery clutches his glass and smiles at Costigan. 'Who shall we drink to Patrick?'
   'I'm not too sure.'
   'How about to our friendship?'
   Costigan raises his glass. 'To our friendship.' The two men clink glasses and down their whiskies in one gulp. Flannery leans close in to Costigan. 'Patrick, I need you. I need a friend, someone I can completely trust to perform a difficult task for me.'
   'Anything Mr Flannery. You know that.'
 'It may mean you'll have to leave England for a while and go back home for a while until I give you the all clear to come back.'
   'Aye, that'd be grand, Mr Flannery. I've a few things I need to fix at home anyway. I left in a hurry, a small family problem see that turned a little messy.' Suddenly, Flannery is intrigued. He knows nothing of Costigan's background. The man is a complete mystery to him.

'Tell me what happened then Patrick?'
'Well, I lost my temper and crippled my cousin.'
 A shocked Flannery stares open mouthed. 'How in god's name, how the fuck did that happen?'
'He owed me money and was refusing to pay, so, I put a kitchen knife through his hand. He was a writer, a good one as well they say, but he had to give it up after that.'
'Could he not just write with the other hand Patrick?' asks Flannery.
'Not really,' replies Costigan. 'He only had the one. He lost the other when a tractor went over it as a kid.' Flannery is stuck for words. He tugs the passing barmaid's arm. 'Two more large Irish please love. And I mean large.' Flannery hands Paddy his drink and offers up a toast. 'To families, fuck em!'
Costigan raises his glass. 'Fuck em!'

 Welcome to Ancoats.
 Rea's funeral Parlour.
 Paddy Mullen enters into the office of 55 year-old Salvatore Rea. A large, bulky figure with fierce Sicilian features. Piercing eyes, a large moustache and greased back oily hair. Rea and Mullen are dear friends who share a close bond. Brothers in all but blood they embrace and both are smiling. 'How is the funeral business doing Salvatore?'
'Thriving Patrick. People keep dying for luckily God in his divine wisdom forbids us to live forever. I soothe my soul by commiserating with the crying widows and daughters. I serve them good wine and pay due respect. I must be honest, I grow a little richer with every loss. A sad but true fact of life. But that is me, how goes the way of things in your world?'
 Paddy sighs. 'Complicated.'
Salvatore can immediately sense his friend has the weight of the world on his shoulders. 'Something is wrong, what is it, tell me?'
'There's a storm coming my friend. One that could destroy us all if things go wrong.'

Salvatore puts his arm on Paddy's shoulder. 'How long have we known each other, thirty years? If you have a problem it becomes my problem. Our families have shared births, marriages and loss. Great days and bad days. We survived a war. You looked after my wife and children when your government felt it wise to intern me. This whilst I had two sons fighting in their army. The windows on our houses was smashed on the day that clown Mussolini declared an alliance with the Germans. And you, what did you Patrick Mullen? You went and boarded up the broken windows and stood outside my home all night armed with an iron bar. Nobody dared come near again. I do not forget this. We are brothers Patrick. Now, tell me what is wrong?'

'Let's just say that if events over the next few days spill out like I think they might then your profits are set to soar.'

Salvatore stiffens his stance. He stands tall and straightens his braces, 'There is going to be a war? If you are in trouble I shall stand by your side. You know my true nature Patrick Mullen. I bring much more to the table than hugging old widows and wiping away their tears. We have large numbers. We have guns and much ammunition. Not only in Ancoats, but across the city and elsewhere. I can have a small army at your disposal. You just have to give me the word and we shall smash this enemy and send them to hell.'

'If it comes to a war Salvatore, there's no one more I'd have stood by me than you, a brave son of Sicily. But in this particular matter I think a little of that famous Sicilian cunning maybe more called for.'

Rea nods and smiles wide. 'Very well. Then I shall go and bring us a bottle of my island's finest red and we shall talk long into the night.'

Welcome to Stretford.

Harry Taylor is on the touchline watching his 12 year-old son play football. Alongside him are other Dads either shouting advice or abusing the referee! Stood next to Taylor, watching his son play also is 46 year-old William 'Billy' Tarr. Balding with glasses, an unremarkable appearance, but a Victoria Cross holder earned during D-day, when Tarr took out an entire German bunker on his own killing all inside. He's also one of Manchester's most feared henchmen. An old wartime pal, Tarr is recognised as Taylor's second in command, and whilst he's the respected public face of their business, Tarr is the General in the field. When required the assassin. He also shows unswerving loyalty to Taylor. This stemming from a time when he saved his life in the retreat to Dunkirk. They're discussing whom from their firm to use as the hitman in the Kray job.

'So, who do you think?' asks Taylor. 'Who do we give this golden ticket to?'

'Harry, we've gone through all the lads and the one person perfect for this you haven't even mentioned.'

A quizzical Taylor stares at his old friend. 'Who?'

'Me.'

'You must be fuckin' joking!'

'What do you mean?' replies Tarr.

'There's no way in the world you're getting this one Bill. You're my oldest mate. So, forget it and just watch our boys play football eh. And if this referee doesn't pull his finger out maybe you can go and see him off.'

'But Harry there's nobody else up to it. You know this as well as I do.' Taylor remains quiet and keeps his eyes focused on the pitch. He knows Tarr is right but doesn't want to admit it. 'What happened at Dunkirk is irrelevant Harry, because you'd have done the same for me. No, this is strictly business. And I have to say on this matter you're simply not thinking straight boss.'

This comment irks Taylor, he doesn't want his friend involved for he fears events are set to soon spiral out of control and there could well be carnage. 'You do realise Bill, if Tommy can't talk those lunatics round, then your lad out there on the pitch and mine also will probably be forced to grow up without their Dads? Once we hit the Krays a firestorm is going to blow up the likes we haven't seen since the fuckin' Luftwaffe filled their boots with Manchester. I trust Collins, but who is it that's behind him? No doubt they'll be London Met, you can guarantee that. Probably even higher up to make a call like this. MI5, or some other secret organisation that we don't know

of. Who is to say these people won't decide to get rid of those doing their dirty work? Me, you and everyone involved else in this fuckin' madness? No, something stinks. This is a hornet's nest Billy, and if you shake it hard enough, god knows what'll fall out. This isn't the country we fought for mate. We'd come home to a nation fit for heroes the establishment promised us? What a fuckin' joke that was.
 England is now nothing more than a fuckin' banana republic.'

Tarr shakes his head. He hears Taylor, but remains steadfast in his opinion. 'All you say I agree with, but still it makes no odds. Face it, I'm your man Harry. We've nobody else good enough for a hit like this. Deep down you know it, so let's just do this thing and get back to normal.'

Taylor offers a resigned smile. 'I should have left you in that fuckin' ditch in France, you hard headed bastard.'

'Always been your trouble Harry,' laughs Tarr. 'A heart bigger than your brain.' The two continue to watch the football in silence. Taylor watches Tarr out of the corner of his eye, he clearly isn't happy and fears greatly for his best friend.

ACT TWO

CONFESSION

Sunday evening.

Tommy Keenan enters the huge doors of Saint Patrick's church in Collyhurst, on Livesey Street. He was expecting it to be empty, but instead notices the Irish parish priest, 68 year-old Father John Kelly lighting the candles. A small man, slim with a mischievous, friendly, wizened face. A smiling Tommy makes his way towards him. 'I hope you're lighting one of them for me Father?'

Father Kelly turns around. 'I'll need more than one candle to save your soul Thomas Keenan.'

He approaches Tommy, then breaks into a huge smile and shakes his hand warmly. 'How long has it been my son? Are you still performing the devil's work for that Patrick Mullen?'

'Come on Father,' Tommy grins. 'You know my heart is pure and intentions mostly honourable. At least that's what the judge said.'

'What brings you here today Thomas? You're a little too old and wise in unworldly ways to resume your role as an altar boy. I'm not sure I can sell that one to the Bishop of Manchester.'

Tommy laughs and looks around at the church. He appears deep in thought. 'I just wanted to see the old place.'

'Are you going away?' says Father Kelly. His dry sense of humour never failing to amuse a smiling Tommy.

'Father, can I ask you a favour?'

'You can ask Thomas but I have sufficient Communion wine and enough cigarettes for myself. As for women, sadly it's a vice I'm not allowed.'

An exasperated Tommy knows he has met his match. 'Father please!'
'I'm teasing Thomas, ask away.'
'Will you hear my confession?'
A surprised Father Kelly is taken aback. 'Of course, but...'
Tommy points to the confessional box. 'We can talk better in there.' Both men make their way. Tommy climbs in with Father Kelly behind the veil. 'Father forgive me, it's been at least ten...'
'Fifteen,' replies the priest.
A smiling Tommy shakes his head. 'It's been at least fifteen years since my last confession. I've pulled a few strokes in my time. Not all exactly legal. In fact most of them not. I've broken the odd nose, but only if they've had it coming to them. I've stolen, swindled, I've fooled around. I've drunk and swore. But I never told lies Father. Well apart from this one time and that was only meant with good intentions.'

Father Kelly listens on. 'Small mercies Thomas. I'm glad to hear it.'
'You see,' continues Tommy, 'I'm in a dangerous profession, and sadly my vocation, my calling in life takes me down roads I'm sure you'd never approve of. But I've never hurt anyone who didn't have it coming, and I've only ever stole off those who could afford it.'

The priest smiles wide. 'Ah, the angel of Collyhurst has granted me with his blessed presence!' Tommy goes quiet for moment.

He takes a deep breath. 'Father have you heard of the Kray twins?' I'm a priest Thomas, not a monk. What about them?'
'Okay then, here goes. Cards on the table. Tomorrow morning they're coming to Manchester with the intention of taking over, but Flannery and the other gangs are not backing down. There's going to be hell to pay. Unless?'

'Unless what?' asks Father Kelly. 'Please don't tell me you're involved in this?'

Tommy smiles. 'In this one Father, believe it or not I'm the cowboy in the white hat. There's, shall we say a window of opportunity where

I've been given one chance to talk them around and put the twins back on the train alive. Otherwise, otherwise they never go home.'

Father Kelly listens on in both astonishment and horror. 'You could go to the police?'

'No chance Father, they're the ones loading the bullets.'

'Christ have mercy!' exclaims the priest. 'This is bloody Manchester not Chicago. Is Patrick involved?'

Tommy shakes his head. 'He knows nothing about it.'

'Don't lie to me Thomas. I've known you since you were 5 years-old. Something tells me he knows, but is against it, and hates the idea of you having anything to do with this madness.'

'Paddy's hands are tied. Things have moved too fast, he can't stop it without making matters worse. I was hoping in the unlikely event of an unhappy ending, you might have a word? I owe everything to him. This little talk we are having here is I suppose my last will and testament. I need you to prevent him from going crazy. He'll listen to you. Please?'

'Hold on a minute, you think that because I'm a man of God, I may have some hold over a man like Patrick Mullen? All the saints and angels in heaven won't be able to stop him should you be killed. I can promise you now, such would be his retribution, the devil would fear to allow him entry into hell.'

The two go quiet for a moment.

'Knowing such what I've told you today Father, can you still give me full absolution of my sins? Not that I deserve it mind, but perhaps maybe for old time's sake?'

Father Kelly heaves a deep sigh of disbelief. 'Ten Our Fathers and ten Hail Marys. In their entirety I might add and he'll be listening, so no cheating Keenan.'

Tommy is shocked. 'Is that it?'

'Consider yourself lucky Thomas, God is in a good mood today.'

'Thank you Father, you take care of yourself.'

Tommy stands and steps out of the confessional box. He makes the sign of the cross then turns to go. 'And Thomas, I'll light a candle or two for you in the morning,' says Father Kelly. Unaware he's already left.

'Thomas, are you still there?'

Suddenly, the Priest hears Tommy's departing footsteps.

'Go with God Thomas Keenan...'

GREETINGS FROM THE BIG SMOKE

178 Vallance Road.
Bethnal Green.
London.
　The Kray twins are at home in a bedroom preparing their suitcases for the trip to Manchester. Reg pulls out two hand guns hidden in the back of a wardrobe and shows them to Ron. He smiles. 'Which one do you want?'
'No guns,' replies Ron.
'Are you fuckin' serious?'
'You said it yourself Reg, Northern monkeys.'
'Pack some bananas instead yeah?' laughs Reg. 'Nothing but grease monkeys with fuckin' bows and arrows!'
　The Krays crack up with laughter whilst carrying on packing.

Bootle Street Police Station,
Late Sunday evening,
　Inspector George Collins is sat in his office reading an intelligence report on the Kray's imminent arrival in Manchester. There's a knock on the door and in walks C11 officer, 41 year-old Charles Lewis. A tall, imposing figure. A snobbish individual, proud of his Eton background and feeling like he's slumming it up North here in Manchester. Alongside him is his partner, 43 year-old Robert Flynn. A streetwise, short burly figure with an unhealthy view of everything and everyone outside London.
'You working late George?' asks Lewis.
Flynn smiles as George looks up. 'We really have appreciated all your help in this matter. I know it couldn't have been easy. These types of jobs never are. But remember you're on the side of the good guys. No matter what happens tomorrow Manchester wins.'

In the short time he has known them Collins already can't stand either of the two men. 'What you really mean is London wins. We're simply doing your dirty work. Let the boys from the provinces soil their hands with this filth. Well it doesn't sit right with me. Never has done.'

'A little late to develop a conscience don't you think?' says Lewis.

'These are big boy's games now,' adds Flynn. 'Not your normal mickey mouse policing, dealing with small town hoods and nicking ferret shaggers. If you can't handle it go home and put on your fuckin' carpet slippers.'

Collins looks at Flynn in utter disgust. 'You patronising, fuckin' cockney wide-boys. Let me tell you something. You think you can come up here with your flash Harry suits and arrogant manner, and strut around and tell me how to run my city? All this has nothing to do with policing, this is politics, pure and dirty politics. The Krays have got too powerful for you. You can't fuckin' handle them. They have pictures and film of powerful men in power sleeping with rent boys and abusing kids. Some so high up that if it ever got out this government would fall. And God knows what other dirt they have? The Met, C11? Fuck me if you lot were any more bent down there you'd be ringing bells and shagging Esmeralda!

Now, I bit my tongue before. If the Krays have to go then so be it. They're scum so blow those two bastards to kingdom come. They hurt people, I can swallow it. But tomorrow is not the end of it for us, because if Keenan can't talk them back on the train and it gets bloody, we'll be cleaning up this mess for years. Long after you two have gone back to whatever London gutter you crawled out of.

So, a little advice gentlemen, if you want to keep your teeth don't ever look down on me or my home town again, because I won't have it. This is still my watch, my city and my fuckin' Manchester!'

Flynn claps his hands in mocking style. 'A nice speech George. It has brought a tear to my ear. You should run for sheriff in this town. We all know your man has not got a prayer in hell of succeeding. The Krays are going to slit him ear to ear and enjoy doing it before he has a chance to open his mouth. Personally, I hope the twins do slot

Keenan and the shooters go in. For me then it's case closed, we can go home to civilisation, and it's then, like you say.
Your fucking problem.'
   Collins shakes his head. His heart is filled with hate for this man. 'You boys from the big smoke? We fought a war against bastards like you.'
'You just don't understand George,' says Lewis. 'Dealing with the Krays is a new type of war. There are no rules, and you are right it is political. Am I comfortable with that? No not really, but they are evil, and they are out of control. A new type of villain. They'll have to be dealt with, if not tomorrow then on another day.'
   'Go home George,' adds Flynn. 'Go home, you are so out of your league it's embarrassing.'
Collins smiles. 'Go home? I am fuckin' home. To say I'm out of my league? Jesus H Christ, you look so far down your noses at us that you can't see what's in front of you up here.'
   He laughs. 'You really do have no idea who you're dealing with do you? There are forces out there not a stone throw from where we are speaking now who could eat you fuckers for breakfast. But anyway, like you say, I'm out of my league. So, I bid you goodnight, and us good luck tomorrow gentlemen. For I fear we're going to need it.'
   'It'll have nothing to do with luck,' says a smiling Lewis.
Collins looks puzzled. 'What are you trying to say? Has something changed that I don't know about?'
Lewis sports a huge grin. 'Goodnight George, sleep the dream of the good copper. We'll speak tomorrow.'
   Then the penny drops with Collins. He says nothing more just stands from the desk, puts on his overcoat and hat, and steps out the office. Lewis and Flynn watch him go.
'Can he be trusted?' asks Lewis.
'Ignore him,' answers Flynn. 'He's upset but can be dealt with if needed. Nothing but cowboys this far North, fucking cowboys.'
   'And our insurance is arranged?'
Flynn smiles. 'No one gets out of there alive. No matter what.'

OLD MAN KABEL

George Collins is ringing Paddy Mullen from a public phone box on a quiet, deserted Deansgate.
'Hello Paddy, George Collins. We need to talk.'
Mullen is in his office at the Cromford club. 'You've got some nerve George. The normal spot in an hour,' he replies and hangs up.
George Collins pulls up in a black taxi cab on the Old Trafford forecourt of Manchester United Football club. It's late, there's not a soul around. He pays and steps out the cab before walking through a side entrance left unlocked for him to go inside.
Collins heads up the tunnel.
The floodlights have been switched on.
He glances around the empty grandstands then onto the pitch.
Paddy Mullen stands waiting for him in the centre circle.
He walks across...
'Sorry to drag you away from the club at this late hour Paddy.'
'Something on your mind George? Something like the Kray twins?'
Collins offers a wry smile. 'When did it all get so complicated Pat? When we were both younger it was just good and bad guys. Black and white, no shades of grey. Today, everything, all of it is fuckin' grey. I'm struggling to tell the difference anymore.'
'This was your choice,' says Mullen. 'Nobody forced you to go along with this crazy charade.'
'I could never have the Krays in this city Paddy. Never. The consequences of those two psychopaths let loose on the people of Manchester. I heard a story. A true story from one of the boys at the Met. How they crucified a punter in one of their clubs because they claimed he didn't show enough respect. All the poor soul did was nudge one of them at the bar for Christ sake and didn't apologise, so they put nails through his fuckin' hands. Our lot are angels, fallen

maybe compared to that. But there's a line, a difference between simple villainy and sheer evil. Those two operate as if even God's laws don't exist, and I couldn't have that here. Whatever the cost to my career or my conscience. I just couldn't stomach it.'

Mullen is clearly not impressed. 'I think you need to speak to a priest George. I can't help you with this I'm afraid. Maybe he'll grant you absolution with penance. A bunch of Our Fathers and Hail Marys from the confession box to make you feel better.'

'I want your word Paddy that if it all goes wrong, if Tommy goes down then you won't retaliate.'

Mullen lights a cigarette and inhales. 'You've already set fire to the rain George. Now you expect me to let my own blood be sacrificed. For what, so some faceless perverted bastards in London can sleep a little easier at night? You know me better than that. Tommy is my son in all but name. He comes out of this alive or else you lot think the Krays are your biggest nightmare? You've no idea. If this kid gets hurt I won't rest until...'

'I thought so.' A smiling Collins cuts him short.

'Do you remember the old Jew guy who owned the pawn shop on Nelson street? Ronnie Kabel? That time when the Salford boys came across the river looking for easy pickings?'

'What about it?' replies Mullen. 'That was all a long time ago.'

'How old was you Paddy, sixteen, seventeen? You waited for them as they came across the swing bridge. You were on your own. No knife, nothing. I followed you but never let you see me because I didn't have your guts to stand up to them. But I saw what happened. The entire gang walked up to you and whatever you said made them turn around. And they never, they never, ever came back across that bridge again to bother old man Kabel. You put the fear of God into them. One ragtag kid from Collyhurst against ten.

What was it Paddy, what did you say?'

Mullen smiles at the memory. 'Old man Kabel was always good to my family. My Mother went in the shop once and tried to pawn her wedding ring because we had no food on the table. Do you know what the old man did, bless him? He refused to take it and gave my Mother ten pounds from his own pocket. He told her she was a good woman and not to worry about ever paying it back. She came home with two bagsful of groceries and wept at the kitchen table. I never forgot that, so I picked out the biggest lad and told him I was the old man's son, and they'd have to kill me to get at him. But before that happened, I'd kill one of them. They looked at each other like I was crazy, but I was deadly serious. I was ready to kill. They obviously never fancied finding out, and so they turned around and went back home.'

'They did the right thing,' says Collins. 'You were crazy back then.'

'I don't like bullies George, I never have, I never will. I've always looked after my own. And Tommy is my own.'

Collins gazes around the stadium. In the distance there's the rattle of freight trains roaring past Trafford Park into the night.

'I'm a blue myself, but of course you know that,' he says.

'I love Matt, but I never could abide this place.'

'I know,' smiles Mullen. 'That's why I always arrange to meet you here!'

'What would Matt make of this mess Paddy?'

Mullen shakes his head. 'A parallel universe. I'd not dare mention it, and he has too much class to ask me.'

'So, tomorrow then is in the hands of our fallen angels,' says Collins. 'I pray Tommy can pull this off.'

'The path to hell is paved with bad intentions George. I pray so too because I'd hate us to fall out.'

Suddenly, Collins realises he can lie no longer. 'Okay then, fuck the knighthood. I've a confession to make Paddy, but one not to be heard by a priest or anyone in a fuckin' uniform. Listen up old friend, I'm going to tell you a story…'

COMING NORTH

It's early Monday morning and the city has come to life. At the Midland Hotel's staff entrance a black transit van pulls up. The driver steps out and goes to open the back doors. Four men jump out each carrying bags under their arms.
The hitmen.
Damien Quinn.
Leon 'Pearly' Spence.
Paddy Costigan
William 'Billy' Tarr.
 The four are swiftly ushered inside by a man wearing a waiter's uniform.

In his Altrincham home Tommy Keenan climbs out of bed and as he does so stares back at the still, sleeping Alison. Tommy leans back over and gently kisses her on the forehead, before heading into the bathroom. He starts to shave, but stops for a moment looking long and hard at his reflection in the mirror. A pensive Tommy breaks into a resigned smile. 'You've one chance Keenan,' he says to himself. 'Don't mess it up.'

London.
Euston Railway Station,
The Kray twins dressed in matching suits are strutting down the platform carrying small suitcases. A path opens up for them from the star-struck fellow passengers, one that they stride purposely through. Fully aware every eye is upon them. A smiling Reg ruffles the head of a young boy no older than ten who hands him a pen and piece of paper for an autograph which he signs.

In the railway carriage the twins both have their backs to the door as they load the suitcases onto compartments above the seats. Two other men enter. Both talking and laughing loud. Young and cocky teddy

boys. Ron clocks them. 'Not in here eh. Find yourselves another carriage boys. Me and my brother want some peace and quiet.'
'We paid for these seats so we'll sit where we want,' answers back one of the teddy boys. 'Besides, who the fuck are you to tell us what to do?' The teddy boy is totally unaware of who he's speaking to. Then Reg turns to confront them also, and seeing the two Krays side by side, both realise how much trouble they're now in.
Reg appears ready to explode. 'Fuck off now whilst you can still walk!' The frightened teddy boys pick up their suitcases and shuffle back towards the door. Scared stiff, shocked and full of remorse. One turns around to Reg. 'I'm so sorry Mr Kray. We'd no idea who you were.' Reg says nothing and they swiftly scramble out of the carriage into the corridor.
'You bloody idiot! You could have got us fuckin' killed!'
'Shut up and just keep walking,' says the other, as they head far away as possible from the Krays!
The twins smile and sit down in their carriage facing each other.
'I've never been this far North,' remarks Reg.
Ron laughs. 'We should've had fuckin' jabs. Do you remember when we were kids? We used to think the West End was a foreign country.'
'It is Ron. So, they definitely don't know we're coming?'
Ron shakes his head. 'They haven't got a fuckin' clue. We'll be a great surprise for our Northern brethren. We hit their top people hard, smash a few heads and make our mark. Show these amateurs just what real power means.'
A smiling Reg likes the sound of this. 'The Krays will reign in the rainy city.'
Ron gazes long and hard out of the train window appearing lost in his thoughts. 'We'll drown them in their own blood,' he says quietly to himself.

A fully dressed Tommy Keenan is in his kitchen just finishing off a cup of coffee preparing to leave, when in walks Alison.
'Where are you going?' she asks him. 'Why didn't you bother to wake me?'

Tommy smiles. 'You looked so peaceful I didn't want to disturb you. I thought I'd let you sleep.'

Alison is worried. 'Tommy, what's going on, please tell me?'

He motions for her to sit down. She takes one seat, him the other. Tommy holds Alison's hand. 'There's absolutely nothing for you to worry about,' he says.

Alison looks into his eyes and instantly knows he's lying. 'Thomas Keenan. you are the worse liar in the world.'

Tommy sighs. 'So I've been finding out lately.'

'Whatever you are up to just be careful Tommy, and promise me you'll be home later.' Tommy can't look Alison in the eye.

'Promise me Tommy?'

'I can't,' he replies.

'Fine then!' she says, now angry. 'If you'd rather stay out drinking with your friends then you can make your own tea!' Alison jumps up, storms out of the kitchen and back up the stairs. From the top of the stairway she turns around. 'And don't forget your key!'

The bedroom door bangs shut. This sound makes Tommy jump. He smiles and lights up a cigarette.

If only life was always this simple...

ACT THREE

DOUBLE CROSS

The Midland Hotel cellar.
the hitmen are sat around smoking and drinking coffee. It's a dark and grimy room lit up only by candle light. Entering comes their handler, 42 year-old Frankie 'the horse' Johnson. A gangly figure with a long face and mistrustful eyes. He's watched intently by the four men as they wait eagerly for news. Johnson claps his hands for attention. 'All right, listen up! The Krays are due to arrive in Manchester around an hour's time. From the station they'll come to the hotel where Keenan will go to see them in their hotel room. When he comes out he gives me the nod to go or cancel. If it's go, I come down, fetch you lot, and you blow those two cockney bastards to kingdom come. Straight in and straight out, we have other people in place to move the bodies. When done you come back down here where there'll be a van waiting. One thing, be certain. Head shots. Under no circumstances can either be allowed to live. Finish them off.' Tarr is concerned. It sounds to him as if it's already been decided that the Krays are dead men walking. 'And if it turns out a no go?' he asks. 'If Tommy succeeds and talks them back onto the train, what then?'

Johnson smiles. 'Let's fuckin' hope so eh Billy. Same applies. I come down and tell you, and we all go home. And everybody still gets paid the full rate.'

Spence starts to laugh. 'Come on Billy, you being a war hero and all that. Don't you miss the killing man? The smell of blood. A chance like this to make history. Maybe they might even give you another medal?'

'I was fighting for my country Spence,' replies an angry Tarr. 'For my family and friends. I was defending our freedom against tyranny. The notion of patriotism is something you could never understand. You probably couldn't even fuckin' spell it.'

'So, why do you do this shit now? The war is over Billy man. You beat the Germans. The Nazis are gone, Adolf Hitler is fuckin' dead.'

An irritated Spence doesn't take kindly to be spoken down to by who he considers an old man. 'Me, I think you missed the taste of blood. We're the same you and I, you just hide it better.'

'That's enough Spence!' shouts Johnson.

'I don't mind Frank,' says Tarr. 'The kid is an idiot. It's water off a duck's back for me.'

He turns to Spence. 'Anyone I've ever clipped had it coming to them. I'm a professional, I work for one man. Someone tries to hurt us, I hurt them. It's always been purely business. Whereas you? The stories I've heard. You get off on it, you're sick in the fuckin' head. That's the difference. You my boy are not right in the fuckin' head.'

An outraged Spence springs up and attempts to lunge at Tarr, only for Damien Quinn and Paddy Costigan to grab him. Johnson stands in front of Tarr, who's staring at Spence in utter contempt. 'You wait Tarr!' screams Spence. 'When this is over we'll see who's the better man.'

Tarr simply smiles. 'Anytime lad, I'm not going anywhere.'

An irate Johnson comes between them with the help of Quinn and Costigan. Order is finally restored and both men sit back down, whilst continuing to give each other the evil eye.

'Enough!' shouts a sweating Johnson.

He wipes his brow. 'Fuckin' calm down. We need clear heads. Now you don't have to like each other, but you have to work together, so, this bullshit ends now. Peace in our fuckin' time, okay? You're supposed to be professionals, so damn well act like it!' Johnson glares at both Spence and Tarr who both nod back in acknowledgement.

'Good.' He breathes a huge sigh of relief. 'Right I'm off. Next time

you hear from me will be to say whether we have the red light or not. So, please do me a favour gents. Until then please try and refrain from killing each other.' Johnson exits the cellar door, slamming it shut behind him.
Quinn smiles. 'Lads, why do they call him the 'horse?'
'Because he's got a fuckin' long face,' replies Costigan.
Spence, then Tarr starts to laugh, before they all join in!

On Peter Street, opposite the Midland Hotel front entrance, sat in an unmarked police car are Charles Lewis and Robert Flynn. They're waiting for the Kray's to arrive. From the hotel foyer a suited man appears. A C11 officer. He nods over to the car.
'All our chaps are in place,' says Lewis. 'Two doors down from the Kray's room. On word they go in.'
'They are clear on their orders?' asks Flynn.
'Absolutely, extreme prejudice. These are the best we have. They take out the twins and Keenan.'
'And the shooters in the cellar?'
Lewis looks at his watch. 'Johnson goes in five minutes. We tell them something has gone wrong, so they have to leave the city for a short while.'
Flynn laughs. 'It never fails to amaze me how men like Johnson become so easy to turn. These Northerners. Put a few pound in their bank balance, they'd sell their own fucking kids. No morals up here. Johnson goes as well yes?'
Lewis nods. 'All of them. No exceptions, we clean everything up in one go.'
'Excellent,' smiles Flynn. 'Then we can go home and leave this miserable, God forsaken city for good.'

Tarr, Spence, Quinn and Costigan are sitting quietly when the cellar door bursts open. A frantic looking Frank Johnson appears!
'Something's gone badly wrong, we have to move now and fast. Get all your stuff together, there's a van waiting outside. It'll take you to a safe house in North Wales. Just for a day or so until things calm

down.' The four stand and head out of the door. Paddy Costigan is last and turns to face Johnson. 'I still want fuckin' paying.'
Johnson smiles. 'No worries Paddy, you're going to get everything that is due to you. I promise.'
  Costigan grunts and leaves the cellar.
  A worried Johnson watches him go.

  The clock is ticking as the hitmen jump into the back of the van. The C11 man is waiting and slams the door shut before walking back to the driver's seat. He smiles at his fellow officer. 'The animals are in the cage.' The van roars out onto Peter Street, past Lewis and Flynn. Neither take much notice of the one following shortly behind it.
 'Hi ho! Off to the slaughterhouse they go,' says a smiling Flynn. Lewis checks his watch. 'The Krays should be arriving any time now.' As they both stare towards the Midland, Tommy Keenan is entering inside. Lewis smiles. 'This is coming together like child's play. It's all just too fucking easy.'
  Tommy walks into the foyer and is met by Frank Johnson. They shake and a smiling Johnson hands Tommy a note with the room number in which the C11 hitmen are hiding. He heads into the hotel restaurant area whilst Johnson walks up to the reception handing another piece of paper to a good looking, young man stood behind it in a smart black suit. Dark hair, striking eyes, perfectly groomed, clearly of Italian decent. He's Antonio Rea. Assistant manager of the Midland and nephew of Salvatore Rea. The two exchange glances, then Johnson leaves whilst Rea glances at the paper and smiles. He puts it in his pocket and picks up the phone. 'We have the room number. Get the boys ready.'

  An announcement comes over the Piccadilly railway station tannoy.
  "The 8.20 From Euston station has just arrives on Platform nine"
  The platform is packed as the doors to the train open and passengers start to step off the carriages. The Kray twins amongst them. As ever, around the twins there's a flurry of excitement. All eyes upon them. A pretty, young blond girl in her early twenties smiles at Reggie, who

winks back at her. The Krays walk business-like down the platform with small suitcases in hand. Nearby, a policeman stands seemingly unaware of their presence. However, in reality across the entire station a small army of undercover detectives are monitoring their every step.
A man in a bowler hat sitting on a bench reading a newspaper. Two porters unloading baggage and the young girl who previously smiled at Reggie. All police officers.
On an early December morning they step out of Piccadilly station into daylight. It begins to rain.

Reg puts his hand out to catch the raindrops whilst staring up at the dark, miserable Mancunian skies. Black clouds are gathered. He smiles and looks at Ronnie. The telepathy between the twins easy to read as Ron begins to laugh.
Easy pickings.
It's a new day in the North.
…The Kray twins have come to Manchester.

The three assassins are sat quietly smoking in their hotel room, when suddenly there's a knock on the door, and one stands to answer it. Their guns are on the bed hidden under pillows and newspapers. On opening a waiter is stood with a large food trolley.
He smiles. 'Good morning sir, Just a little welcome to Manchester.' Suddenly, four men dressed all in black, wearing balaclavas and armed with baseball bats rush past him to swiftly overpower the three assassins. They're disarmed, gagged and tied up. The alleged waiter grins wide. 'Be good and be quiet now lads. It would be rude to disturb the twins and Tommy whilst they're talking don't you think?'
In the hotel restaurant Tommy is sat at a window table drinking a cup of coffee looking out onto the busy road. He turns to see Antonio Rea approaching him. Rea leans down to whispers into his ear. 'We've got the shooters. Good luck Tommy. Send them home.'
Meanwhile, a black cab is pulling up and out of it steps the Kray Twins. Ron leans back into the driver's window and passes him the fare and a generous tip. 'Much obliged,' says the driver. He has a

puzzled look on his face. 'Don't I know you gentlemen from somewhere?' The twins appear genuinely amused at this comment.

'Are you in the movies?'

They smile at each other and stride purposefully into the hotel foyer.

Tommy watches them enter from behind a newspaper at his table. The twins book in at the main desk where a pretty young receptionist smiles wide at them, whilst handing the Krays their room key. A concierge goes to pick up the suitcases, but Ronnie puts his hand up to stop him. He smiles. 'No need son, we'll carry our own luggage.' Reg hands the concierge £10. 'Thank you sir,' he replies, appearing in shock as to who has just entered his normal, humdrum daily existence.

Once in the room the twins are unpacking when there's a knock at the door. They stiffen on hearing it. Reg goes to answer and stood there is Tommy Keenan. He laughs. 'Well, I'll be, look what the fuckin' Manchester cat has dragged in!'

Ron watches on. He looks surprised. Tommy steps inside and shakes Reg's hand. A suspicious Ron does similar. 'Nice to see you Tommy. But how did you know we were coming?'

Tommy smiles whilst lighting up a cigarette. 'Come on Ron. The Kray twins coming to Manchester? You can't keep something like that quiet even if you wanted. It's like a visit from the Royal family, Elvis even.'

'Are you our welcoming committee?' asks Ron.

'In a manner of speaking.' He points towards the suitcases. 'I've been sent to inform you not to bother unpacking.'

Tommy looks at his watch. 'There's another train back to London in an hour. I recommend you best both be on it.'

'Careful Tommy,' says Ron. 'This isn't your game. Choose your next words very carefully boy.'

The Krays appear froze in mid-rage, both ready to tear Tommy's head off of his shoulders at any given second. He takes a deep breath. 'Let me explain. Things have gone a little crazy lately with news of your visit. People talk both here and in London. News has got out about what you've in mind. It's caused many powerful noses to have been put out of joint. I don't think you two realise how many enemies on both sides of the fence want you dead. But, luckily,' he grins wide. 'You've got yourself a guardian angel.'

'I don't believe in angels Tommy,' says Reg.

'Me neither,' adds Ron.

'Well you both better believe in this one. He's called Paddy Mullen. Two doors down from here we've three London police shooters tied and gagged. They were set to do the three of us, but Paddy got word off the last good cop in the city who luckily developed a guilty conscience. Whoever you two had have upset, they were ready to pull the trigger on you. And me, which I have to tell you, I'm not too happy about.'

Ron is smiling, but doesn't appear convinced. 'Tommy, you know me. If you're lying about all this, even though I like you, I'll have no qualms about cutting your fuckin' throat. Are you following all this Reg?'

He nods. 'I am. Keep talking Tommy. It's what you're really good at.' An unsure Tommy thinks this could still go either way. He remembers Paddy's words about making his words resonate loud, so that they stayed with them. 'It's a lot more dangerous here than you two think. Believe me they protect what's theirs, and even if the Met had not decided to end you it would only have been a matter of time before one of our lot had a pop, and you ended up food for the fishes in the canal. Go home, you don't need this. Stay in your own manor. In London you're kings, up here you're just a pain in the arse. No offence but it's true. It's a different country in the North, reputations mean nothing. Especially those with an East End post code. Believe me Reg, Ronnie. You're on a hiding to nothing.'

Tommy motions towards the door. 'Come with me I want to show you something.' The three men step out and led by Tommy they walk down the corridor towards the assassin's room. Two burly, looking guards stand outside. 'You alright Tommy?' one asks.

He smiles. 'I'm Fine Eric, let us in mate.' Eric Taylor opens the bedroom door and stands aside. Tommy and the Krays enter seeing the three assassins bound and gagged on the floor. Sat nearby are their

Mancunian assailants. Now appearing remarkably relaxed, minus the balaclavas, sat chatting and playing cards.

'It's good to see you Tommy,' one shouts over. A good friend of his by the name of Eddie Hopkins. 'Hello Eddie,' Tommy replies. 'Let me introduce you to a pair of living legends. This is Reg and Ronnie Kray.' A smiling Eddie stands and goes to shakes the twin's hands. 'A real pleasure gentlemen. Any friend of Tommy's is a mate of mine. Welcome to Manchester.'
'Much obliged,' replies Ron.
'Thanks for all your help,' adds Reg.
'No problem Mr Kray,' answers Eddie. 'Glad to have been of service. We all are, you two have a safe journey back to London eh?' Ron turns to look at Reg who can't help but smile. They both glare at Tommy. 'I think we've seen enough,' says Ron.
Reg looks around the room at the faces of the other assailants and the assassin's guns on the bed. 'Thanks again for everything lads. If you are ever in London look us up.' The assailants wave back in acknowledgement and return to their game of cards.

Tommy winks at his Mancunian brothers in arms and returns to the twin's bedroom. He stands nervously near the door, whilst the Krays discuss in whispered tones at the window. He watches them closely. They finish their chatter and both stare across at him with features set in stone. For a second nothing is said, then, whilst Reg looks out of the window, Ron heads across. 'Looks like we have a train to catch.' Tommy's smile is one of relief.

Reg then walks over. 'Just one thing I need to know?' he asks.
'Go ahead Reg.'
'No lies now Tommy, because I'll fuckin' know.'
He sighs hard. 'After this weekend, I'll never lie again.'
'Those lads of yours down the hall. Something tells me there's more to all this than meets the eye?'
'What was it Tommy?' inquires Ron.
He sits down on the bed, lights up another cigarette and stares up at the twins. 'I suppose you both deserve to know. The original plan was

before the Met shown up, if I couldn't talk you back onto the train, then you were never going home.'

Ron's face has turned purple. 'Let me get this straight. If you couldn't sweet talk us back to London, then we were going to be hit right here. In this fuckin' room?'

Tommy nods. 'I wasn't happy about it, but business is business. It would have stuck in my throat. You know I really like you two.'

'Much appreciated,' says Ron. Utterly dumbstruck.

The twins stare at each other in disbelief. Secretly they admire the sheer nerve of what has gone down. 'It's like the fuckin' wild west,' says Reg.

Ron appears in a state in shock. 'Tell me Tommy, Just what would happens now if we change our minds and decide to stay?'

'After all we've done for you?' smiles Tommy.

'We should kill you,' whispers Reg. With what appears real intent. His eyes suddenly void of colour. 'But we owe you instead,' he adds. Much to Tommy's relief.

'You're one cool bastard Keenan,' Reg continues. 'I have to grant you that.' Tommy stands from the bed and stubs his cigarette out in a nearby ashtray. 'I had a good teacher. The best there is. Now go home eh. It's bad for your health up here. Far too much cold in the air, it gets in the bones.'

The twins look at each other and smile. 'Tell Paddy we are in his debt,' says Ron. 'If he ever needs anything. Just ask.'

'Reg ruffles Tommy hair. 'That goes for you too. You ever get bored of living in the sticks playing cowboys and Indians, come down to civilisation, and work for a proper firm.'

'I'll keep that in mind! Be lucky boys. Have a safe journey and give my regards to your mum.'

ENDGAME

The van carrying the four Manchester shooters is heading towards North Wales, when from nowhere a large haulage truck cuts across its path forcing them to swerve off the road. From out of the truck a large group of black clad men in balaclavas appear. They drag the C11 operatives out of their seats and tie them up on the road side. Inside the back of the van the shooters have been flung onto the floor, when the back doors are wrenched open. Stood there with their balaclavas removed and smiling wide are Harry Taylor, Paul Brady and Jimmy Da Silva. 'Sorry about this lads,' says Taylor. 'A change of plan. I'll explain on the way home.' The four hitmen look on in shock as they are helped out of the van. Paddy Costigan shakes himself down and approaches the three men. They all stand wary.

'Hey Paddy man,' says Da Silva. 'We saved your skin. You were being taken away to be killed.' Costigan points over to the C11 operatives. 'What happens to those two?'

'They go back to London Paddy,' replies Paul Brady. 'They go back in one fuckin' piece. No missing ears or fingernails I'm afraid. Out of bounds. Paddy Mullen's orders.'

Costigan grunts in disgust and walks away. Taylor goes across to talk to Tarr. He's sat nursing a cut head and wrenched arm. 'You alright Billy?'

Tarr smiles. 'I'm getting too bloody old for this!'

Taylor helps his friend to his feet. 'Come on, I'll buy you a drink and tell you all about it.' An animated Paul Brady starts clapping to get everyone's attention. 'Right, come on, job done! Let's get the fuck out of here!'

Outside the Midland hotel,
a waiter appears dressed in white shirt and black trousers, with a tray carrying two glasses of champagne. He crosses towards the car

containing Lewis and Flynn. The two men watch in astonishment as the waiter approaches them. 'What the fuck is this?' asks Flynn. The waiter knocks on the window. Lewis winds it down and the waiter leans in. 'Courtesy of Manchester sir.'

Lewis takes the tray and passes the drinks to Flynn. He notices a small note on the tray. After reading it Lewis goes ashen faced.
'What's up?' says Flynn. 'What does it say?'
'There is something that belongs to you in room 213.'

Flynn and Lewis go crashing through the door to find the three assassins still gagged and bound. Their guns on the bed in full view with a note pinned reading. …GO HOME…

Flynn has the look of a man who knows he is beaten.
'The game's up,' he says. 'I don't know how but the bastards have done us over. This fucking city.'

At that moment, the Kray twins step out the Midland hotel and enter into a waiting black cab. Watching them go from the other side of Peter Street is Tommy Keenan. As the cab disappears in the direction of Piccadilly, Tommy lights a cigarette and smiles. 'Goodbye lads, don't rush back.' Tommy walks away.

Job done.

Paddy Mullen is sat at his desk in the Cromford club when the phone rings. He picks it up. 'Paddy Mullen.'
'Hello Paddy, George Collins. It's gone like clockwork. Tommy was superb. He's safe and the Krays are on their way home. As for Johnson, he played his double bluff to perfection and is on a plane to Spain as we speak with an extra £500 in his pocket and a huge grin on his face. Speak soon.'
'Thanks George.'

Collins put down the phone and the line goes dead.
Mullen smiles and replaces the handle.

The Kray twins are boarding their train back to London. As they step on, Ron turns around and takes a last gasp of Mancunian air. Reg watches his twin take a final look. 'Well, so long you smog, ridden hellhole.' He turns to Reg and smiles. 'Fuckin' miserable place anyway. I don't think we'll bother coming back. Let's go home Reg.'

Ten Downing Street. News of what's occurred in Manchester has just reached the ears of Sir Peter Dowling from the head of C11, Charles Worthing. 'What the fuck went wrong Charles, why are those two monster on a train back here?'
'As I've just tried to explain, it was a whole series of unfortunate events my men simply failed to get to grips with.'
'In other words they were played?'
'Yes Peter, we most certainly were played I'm afraid. I had my best people working on this and well, yes. Played is the best way to describe it.'
 'Outsmarted by a bunch of Northern mobsters. Charles, I have to be honest with you, this is not fucking good. What do I tell the Prime Minister? This is abject humiliation. He may well ask for a scapegoat.'
'And do you intend to offer me up as your sacrificial lamb, is that really wise?'
'What do you mean?'
'Thrown to the wolves so to speak, because I can assure you, I shall take others down with me. This was always a risky operation, one you slipped into my jurisdiction from MI5.'
Worthing smiles. 'No need to worry. Macmillan will insist someone pays a price, heads will roll, but it won't be you. Somebody lower down the food chain. Lewis or Flynn. Maybe both, but you are part of the club. For now concentrate all your resources on the Krays. Use everything at your disposal, rain hell down upon their cursed heads.'
'What about our friends in the North?'
'Stay away from them Charles. I don't need the fucking hassle.'

Manchester. That same evening.
 At the Cromford Club, the victorious bosses Harry Taylor, Tom Flannery, Michael and Paul Brady and Jimmy Da Silva are sat with Paddy Mullen. All are celebrating the day's events.

The atmosphere is one of euphoria.
 'A toast lads! Manchester 1 London 0!' declares Harry Taylor, loud enough for the entire club to hear. Into the room comes Tommy Keenan linking his girlfriend Alison. They're immediately spotted by Paddy Mullen, who goes across to greet them. 'Alison, how are you my dear?' Mullen leans down and kisses her hand.
 'I'm fine thank you Mr Mullen,' she replies, smiling wide.
 Alison turns to Tommy. 'I'll see you at the bar.'
 Tommy kisses Alison and she walks off. He and Mullen watch her go.
 'You best marry that girl lad.'
 Tommy laughs. 'Is that an order?'
 'Yes! By the way Mr Keenan, I had a phone call from Ronnie Kray thanking me but I had no idea what for. He was singing your praises though. The twins want you in London, but my advice is stay here. After what's gone on they're on borrowed time.'
 Mullen puts his arm around Tommy's shoulders and points across to the table where all the gang leaders are sat. 'Come on, let's go and have a quick word. Get it over with.'
  They head over to the table. First to spot Tommy is a cigar chomping Harry Taylor. 'Here he is, Tommy Keenan. The man who saved Manchester!'
  The other men all applaud and cheer as Tommy and Mullen come close. John Flannery shakes Tommy's hand. 'In years to come they'll talk about when the Krays came to Manchester, and about how you, Tommy Keenan.' Flannery points his finger at Tommy.
 'How you put them back on the train.'
 'You're a hero Tommy boy,' says a smiling Da Silva. 'A true fuckin' shining light in the North.'
 'One thing though Tommy,' adds Michael Brady.
  'I don't want to rain on your parade, but no one will ever get to know what really happened. It'll be changed so much. The truth will get lost in the myth. It'll become urban legend. Once upon a time in Manchester. A Mancunian fairytale. But you'll know and we'll know.'

'Hey Tommy,' calls across Paul Brady. 'Never mind how you done it, my question is why? You could have cut and run from that room and just let the boys get on with it. But you stayed. Why?'
All eyes are upon him as they wait for his answer.
'Why?' he replies. Tommy lights a cigarette and gazes across the table. He stares at Mullen who has the look of a proud father. A smiling Tommy catches his eye. 'I did it for the angels.'

ENCORE. TODAY. (Part Two)

The Brass Handles Pub.
Present Day.
Paul Brady has sat open-mouthed listening to Tommy Keenan's wild, but magnificent tale. 'And so you all lived happily ever after then?' he asks. Tommy Keenan lights up a cigarette. 'Not really, over the years Manchester went crazy. Too much blood. No class. The old boys moved aside or were taken out. It was carnage. I got away before the decision was taken for me.'
'How's Mrs Keenan. She still keeping well these days?'
Tommy take a long drag on his cigarette. 'I lost her last year. Cancer. That's why I all but live in here with you reprobates. An empty house is not a home.'
'I'm really sorry Tommy, I had no idea. She sounded like a beautiful lady.'
'The best,' he replies. 'The very best.'
'Tommy, I've a favour to ask. There's war in the air and Manchester is going to explode like never before. There's going to be a fuckin' eruption. The Syrians, Russians, Ukrainians, Albanians. Nigerians, the Chinese? Christ, not even counting our own.
We, Salford are outmanned and outgunned. It's already begun with today's events. You've been there and done it. Worked with and against the best. I could really do with your help as a consigliore. What do you say? For old time's sakes.'
Tommy shakes his head. 'I'm afraid I'm far too old lad. Besides, I always did my bit to prevent trouble. I'd be no good to you. My one piece of advice. Don't go looking for a war, but do anything you can to prevent one. There's nothing cowardly about trying to keep the peace. Paddy Mullen taught me that.'
Brady smiles, but it's one more out of sadness. 'Too late, it's kill or be killed for us now. We're in this up to our necks.'

Shaun Barlow comes over to their table. 'Paul it's time to go mate. We've a name and address in Longsight. A Syrian fuck called Azil Aturak.'

'Longsight, my God. Allah's country,' smiles Brady. He puts out his hand and Tommy accepts it. 'Thank you Thomas Keenan, it's been an honour and a privilege to have listened to your story. Hopefully if I live long enough we'll talk again.'

'Much obliged for the drink,' says Tommy. 'Mind how you go son.'

Brady puts on his jacket as Barlow and two bodyguards stand waiting. Finally, they head for the door only for Brady to turn around and look back at Tommy one last time. 'Just one thing. You talked about angels in your story. Maybe once upon a time, but in this city today, no one is clean. Everybody takes Tommy. Even the angels have dirt under their wings.

Be lucky old man.'

Brady leaves the pub.

Tommy checks in his pocket for loose change and has enough for a last half. He accidentally pulls out a picture of Alison, taken when she was shining beautiful in her mid-twenties. So full of life and stood alongside him at the Cromford club back in 1963. Tommy stares for a moment and smiles before gently putting it back in his pocket.

'Fallen angels,' he says quietly…

As a tear falls from Tommy's eye.

SEND IN THE CLOWNS

"A heart is not judged by how much you love; but by how much you are loved by others."
  The Wizard of Oz

ACT ONE

LAST ORDERS (Part One)

West London. Chelsea. Cromwell Hospital.
Wednesday 25th November 2010.
I may not be able to open my eyes but I can hear them talking. They're saying I'm not long for this world now. That my time is drawing near well I feel no pain so I guess you could call that a result. I often wondered about this moment when it finally came around. I've been warned many times it was coming but somehow I was always able to drop a shoulder, race clear and accelerate to leave the Grim

Reaper in my wake. But as the drinking wore on and got even worse he was always in sight. Watching. Peeping from behind a street corner or through a pub window. Hiding in disguise. Towards the end I felt him next to me as I sat minding my own business drinking wine and soda and reading a newspaper in the local boozer.
I spotted his staff amidst the scum paparazzi that lived in my face. That flashed and fought and tugged and screamed abuse at those who I loved and loved me. But it was all just a matter of time. In my mind, I knew the bastard one day would tap on my shoulder, I'd turn around and he'd be there. All knowing.
'Nowhere to run now George,' he would say. Well tonight I can feel him in the room. I'm in injury time, I know that and I'm ready to finish the dregs and move on. I so often was asked the same question, 'Why George, why didn't you cut out the booze?'
The simple reason I didn't want to. I have to admit though it would've been nice to reach 60 years-old just for the celebration, and the fact I could say 'Fuck you' to all those people who claimed I wouldn't make it. So many memories, lost nights, the booze and the girls. The drinking and the fucking. Friends? Not so many as you may think. Oh, I laughed, drank and fucked with the best of them. I partied with the great, the good, the bad, the evil, the wonderful and fucking downright ugly. I'm talking about those rotten on the inside.
A fool many times with my money. I loved, I hated also but when it came to genuine honest to good people I could trust? I can count them on one hand. The greatest night, the most memorable night? Well, there was one. A rare occasion where I sobered up enough to remember and it's stayed in my memory ever since. It wasn't one where I drank with rock stars or footballers, Miss World's even. It was five people, Charlie, Father Finn, Frank, Mary Rose and Trevor. Lost souls and dear friends, if only for one night, that even to this day I wonder what became of them? A clown, a Priest, a hitman, a prostitute and an actor. That mysterious time before dawn breaks. It was back in 1970, when we walked the late night, early-shift on the canal paths of Manchester and traipsed over a drawer-bridge to unknowingly enter a world apart. Where the drinkers gathered. A sea

of wine, whiskey and pills. Of lovers and poets. Scum, lowlifes and those who simply wanted to do nothing more than drink until the sun once more rose over the Irwell the following morning.

 A magical, bewitching but also dangerous place.

Over the rainbow and under a Mancunian moon. Once read you'll understand. That was the last night where I could've walked another road. A once in a lifetime chance of ruin or redemption. This place had a name but it was more a time. They called it Oz and before I sign off to cross over, I'd like to take you all back down my cobbled canal path. My yellow brick road…

THE BROWN BULL

Saturday 7th February 1970.
Northampton Town 2-8 Manchester United. FA Cup Fourth Round.
The first goal as Kiddo crosses it, I shout for Willie to leave and I head in at the far post.
The second, I slide around the keeper and fire home into the corner.
The third, Kiddo again crosses and with three on the line my first shot is blocked before it bounces back, and I lash a rebound high into the top corner.
The fourth, Kiddo with yet another cross, this time onto my head and I flash it low past the keeper into the corner.
The fifth, I soar through the middle chased by white shirts. As the keeper comes out I roll the ball past him.
The sixth, Paddy crosses low, I beat one, two, three, before going around the keeper, scoring and resting my head on the goal post.
 The crowd go mad!
I break the record for most goals in an FA cup match. The chants from the crowd. 'Georgie, Georgie!' from both United and Northampton fans. But for me, it's all a distant hum because I'm totally fucked and so need a drink!

Manchester. The Brown Bull.
 Saturday evening.
I'm on the bed with this gorgeous blond girl. I'm trying so hard but it isn't happening. Pints of vodka and lemonade do that to you. I finally give up. She smiles and kisses me on the lips.
 'No worries, your secret is safe with me George. You were great lover boy, wait till I tell my mates I fucked Georgie Best and he was the best I've ever had!' Then she's gone leaving me alone with my thoughts. Never a good thing. But hey! Why tell the truth when you

can print the legend right? Because I'm Georgie fucking Best and I'm pissed again. The night is still young and Manchester is my heaven!

I walk back down the stairs to the pub vault and a huge cheer goes up from my corner. A smoky, dim-lit paradise. A table full of glasses, of filled up ash trays, lighters and cigarette packs. My friends. Waggy, Parky and George QC. Waggy is laughing. 'Bloody hell George that was quick!'

Parky also. 'Christ George, are you on bloody piecework?'

'One more for the bed notch dear boy!' calls out George QC.

I smile wide and sit down. My drink stares back at me. A third full, down it goes and then an empty pint glass.

'Fucking hell George!' says Waggy. 'That's vodka and lemonade. You're going to be on the moon at this rate tonight.'

'With very little lemonade if I recall,' adds Parky.

He himself putting the whiskey away like the end of the world is at hand. 'But fuck it George,' smiles Parky, as he raises his glass. 'Here's to you! The finest footballer I've ever seen who doesn't come Barnsley!'

George laughs. 'Thanks Michael that's some compliment!'

Waggy taps me on the shoulder and points towards the door.

'Look what the cat has just dragged in George.'

The Manchester City manager Malcom Alison. He's got the usual cigar in his mouth, wearing a fedora hat, fur coat and has two dolly birds, one on each arm. Our eyes meet across the room and he smiles and waves across. I do similar. Oh, fuck he's coming over. I know Mal hates me because I've fucked too many girls who wouldn't give him the time of day. The feeling is mutual, the big headed fucker but for show we act like old pals in public.

'George my old son, well done today against that bunch of shoe cobblers.'

'Thanks Mal, I'm sure you mean it.'

'I never believed what I read in the papers that you were finished. Might be a little harder against a decent team though like City!'

'Give your two ladies my best regards Malcom, I know them both intimately. Nice girls.'

'That's your trouble see George.' Malcom points to my glass, 'One day soon you'll wake up and it'll all be over. Night George, enjoy it whilst you can. You're a waster son.'
'Sloppy seconds Malcom!'
Malcom goes to leave. He grabs both girls by their arms and hustles them back out of the door. Good fucking riddance. George QC is past drunk, his tie is around the back of his neck, he has bright red cheeks and is desperately trying to light a cigarette. God help whoever he's defending in court on Monday morning. We'll be here again tomorrow boozing, they may as well head straight for fucking Strangeways and tell them to throw away the key.
'I don't fucking like him George. Six goals in one game? Even if it was only fucking Northampton that still deserves a damn good drink. You're back sir and back with a bloody vengeance.'
George QC is right, it has been a good day. A very good day. Back from a six week suspension and the whole world saying I was finished. Every hack and his fucking dog turned up at the County Ground there today to write my obituary.
Hack one. 'George's last chance'.
Hack two. 'R.I.P Bestie'.
Hack three. 'The magic is gone'.
Hack four. 'Best is a busted fucking flush'.
Not so now though since I gave them six fucking good reasons to go shove it up their fat arses. One minute I'm placed amongst the stars, they worship at my feet, the next their pens scribble I'm lower than a snake's belly. Well tonight I'm back in that place where nothing or nobody can get to me. I'm playing the legend, not the man. Roll the cameras, let the crowd applaud because I'm entering stage right. I'm going to be the person they think I am and want me to be. Getting to that place means I'm going to need more, for its not somewhere you reach by car, bus or plane…
'Here you go George,' says Waggy.
Another pint of vodka and lemonade is placed before me. It lands on my beer mat like a life jacket being placed on a drowning man in a

raging, sea storm, and now once drunk again, well, the curtains will roll back and I'll be centre stage.
 I'll be in Manchester fucking Valhalla. Bring it on!

MEETING CHARLIE THE CLOWN

I must have dozed off.
I look at my watch and it's just turned half past one. I'm still nursing a drink that's a quarter full. There's nobody left the regulars have staggered, danced and stumbled out the pub door. All have disappeared into the Mancunian night. Some home, others to party on. The landlord Billy is busy drying glasses. He looks across towards me. 'Welcome back Bestie. One for the road or do you want to get your head down upstairs?'
I have my own bedroom that's seen more action than a whorehouse in a sailor's port. 'Will do, thanks Billy but first I'm going to get some air. I've the set of keys you gave me so I'll just let myself back in if that's okay?'
'Anytime George. I'll pour you a last one and leave it on the bar. On the house this one. A good customer you George. A good lad.'
'On the fucking house?' So it should be. This place was a broken-down old shithole on the corner of Chapel Street before I started coming in here. It rattled when the trains on the Railway bridge alongside roared past. Nobody bothered with it, nobody went in. Not anymore. To the spit and dust I've added a touch of class. Now it's my place. George's place. The in place. Anybody who matters comes here. Everybody comes. From the nearby Granada studios the Coronation Street mob, the actors, the drop-dead gorgeous starlets and I fuck them all or try. The writers and the poets so full of angst and eager to drink to forget or find inspiration. Rock stars, models, footballers, boxers and gangsters. The Quality boys. All down to me, So too fucking right it should be on the house!
'Thanks again Billy,' I say this through gritted teeth and a painted smile. 'You're one of the good ones.'

I walk out. It's a freezing cold Manchester evening, but as I look above there's a clear black sky littered with a million bright shining stars, a backdrop to take your breath away. The kind of setting and night where you believe anything could happen. I pull up the collar on my jacket. I won't be out long just a blast of air, another drink then bed on my own. Tomorrow will be a hair of the dog day, a grand afternoon session with the Sunday boys where we'll get the newspaper full of me and it'll all be good again. I'm back!
Six fucking goals and fuck you big Mal, the Belfast boy is flying once more!
I'm walking over Blackfriars Bridge that joins Manchester to Salford, where beneath is the River Irwell. Her black hidden depths the keeper of secrets I guess few can only imagine. Maybe best not to know I suppose, because there's nowhere better to dump problems. Then I see him. A plump figure of a man in front of me stood on the bridge wall and seemingly getting ready to jump. When I look closer I can't believe it, he's dressed as a circus clown! The full bloody costume. I can hear his theme tune starting up in my head. A curly, yellow-haired wig, a floppy hat, a red nose, a polka-dot outfit and ridiculously large feet. 'What the fuck! Get off there you mad bastard!'
The clown turns to look at me and has tears in his eyes with the make-up running. 'Piss off! Leave me alone!'
I'm only yards away from him now. If he jumps then no chance because if the fall doesn't kill him then the chemicals in the water surely will. He'll go in a clown and be dragged out a fucking zombie. 'Come on pal. Nothing can be bad enough to make you want to do this?' The clown turns around, I'm sure he recognises me.
He looks at me closer straining his eyes. 'Hang on I know you. George fucking Best!'
'Aye, I am. Last time I looked anyway.'
'Well no offence but fuck off George, I'm a blue and this is nothing to do with you! I just want to end it all. Blow the whistle and call it full time.'
'End what Mr clown?'

'Life! Everything. The fact that I'm not fucking funny anymore!'
'Oh, no, you can't be serious. That's not funny.'
'I fucking know George that's why Billy sacked me!'
For some reason, whether it's the pints of vodka and lemonade I've been knocking back but I just start to laugh. The clown stares at me like I'm going mad. Maybe he's right, I can't help myself. The clown climbs back off the wall, his large feet landing on the floor like small skies and starts to walk across towards me.
'Tell me what's so hilarious George?'
'You. You're funny.'
'I'm funny, how?'
'You, you're just so funny! You make me laugh.'
'Yeah well much appreciated legend, but sadly this isn't part of my act. What kind of a clown am I if the only way I can make people laugh is threatening to jump off the Blackfriars Bridge every fucking Saturday night, Sunday morning?'
'Aye true not really got many legs has it Mr clown, but maybe you could get a parachute and blow your horn on the way down?'
This makes the clown laugh. He puts out his hand and we shake.
'Now that's funny George! No more Mr clown, the name's Charlie Canzone. Ex, I say again ex-professional clown, I was formerly of Billy Smart's big top but was sacked today and all but fired out of the circus like the fucking human cannonball.
'Wow, is that how you've ended up here then Charlie, fired by a cannon? I'm glad you had a safe landing!'
'Now come on George don't be silly that would be ridiculous. I got the 52 bus from Belle Vue, bought myself a bottle of whiskey, had a few blobs in Yates to drum up more courage, then wobbled down here to finish it all.'
'Bloody hell Charlie, didn't you stand out a little in the pub dressed like that?'
'Fuck me George, when was the last time you was in Yates? Compared to those around me I looked positively normal!'

'Aye, you got a point. Listen Charlie how do you fancy taking a walk with me to get some fresh air? I think we both could do with clearing our heads a little. What do you think?'

'I'd love to George, besides I've nowhere else to go anyway. There's a suitcase back at the circus with an old suit in it for funerals and weddings. That apart what I'm wearing here is all I have in the world. But even dressed like this George, if I'm with you I might still be able to get a much needed leg over. What do you think, I could be your wing-man? Wing commander Canzone at your service sir!'

The clown salutes!

'To be honest I wouldn't hold your breath Charlie but I'm willing to give it a go!' We're both laughing loud, me and Charlie the clown on Blackfriars Bridge at two on a Sunday morning. So, it all begins my after hours. Isn't it rich how, aren't we a pair Charlie lad. Time to send in the clowns. Me and Charlie walking and talking we must've cut a strange sight.

MEETING FATHER FINN

Under a starlit night, George Best and a clown strolling down a deserted Deansgate. This time of the evening a Mancunian haven for me. An invisible cloak away from the madness where the silence and our chat broken only by a far off police siren or a black taxi-cab, racing past us to god knows where. Charlie looks over towards me.

'I got told in Yates' earlier you had a half decent game yesterday George?' Charlie kicks an imaginary goal with his huge feet and raising his hands high in a salute.

'Half decent you say? Not too bad Charlie, we won 8-2, I got six and should've scored ten! I just got knackered towards the end.'

'Maybe so George, but it's only Northampton, it isn't City. We'd have sorted you out? The best team in Manchester we are. Big Mal's blue army!'

I'm smiling. 'Typical blue! I have to ask Charlie do all the City fans dress like you?'

'Oi Bestie! I'm the one with the big red nose and the funny feet. I do the jokes!' As we laugh I notice an all-black dressed figure sat on his haunches in a pet shop door entrance.

He looks up towards us. 'Well would you bless all the angels and the saints in heaven!' I recognise immediately a fellow Irishman far from home and more so with a Belfast accent. 'If it isn't the great George Best and Coco the clown!' The man stands up, he's in his early forties, bearded and obviously has been drinking because there's beer bottles surrounding him. 'The name is Charlie Canzone mate, not fucking Coco.'

The man steps out of the shadows and I notice a dog collar. He's only a Priest! 'Let me introduce myself I'm Father Michael Finn and I meant no offence Charlie, but all clowns look the same to me.'

'None taken Father. Although I could say the same about those in your profession. If you don't mind me asking what are you doing sat in a pet shop door entrance at half past two in the morning drinking?' The Priest smiles wide. 'Isn't it obvious Charlie, I'm talking to the animals! They're all God's creatures and we've had a good talk tonight.' He points towards the window. 'Especially with the parrot over there.' It's clear to me the Priest is pissed out of his brains. 'Come on Father, a man of the cloth in your state? What would the bishop and your congregation think?'
'I think they'd like Mr parrot George.'
'Come on now, where's your church?' The Priest makes a grand sweeping gesture with his hands. 'The world is my congregation Georgie boy, and everybody in it. How are you my son? I've a good offer on saving souls tonight. Two for the price of one. You and Charlie here, the sad-eyed clown. It only costs Three Hail Marys and two Our Fathers. How about it?' The Priest bows in dramatic manner towards us. This guy is three sheets to the wind. Charlie shakes his head. 'Father, please get up you look ridiculous.'
'Says the man with the big red shoes and the floppy hat!' laughs the Priest. 'Seriously Father,' I say. 'You can't stay here. Listen why don't you come for a walk with me and Charlie here. Give you time to sober up a little and when a taxi appears I'll flag it down and we'll get you home.'
'I'm afraid I've no money left George. It's all vanished on the beer.'
'Ah, no bother, I'll pay the fare, you need to get yourself home to bed.'
'My George,' smiles the priest. 'My George. You're an angel off the pitch as well as on it, but I can't accept your generosity my son. You asked where my church is, well I no longer have one. You could light a thousand candles for me but it wouldn't make any difference. The damage has been done. I can't be saved, my soul is already destined for hell.'
What's he talking about? 'I'm sorry, I don't understand Father?'
'I pray you never do George. You're a good lad. A miracle boy from the back streets of Cregah. With all the shite our people have had to

put up with, our troubled city gave birth to you, so at least we got something right. An absolute credit to Belfast you are George and to your ma and da.'
 'Father, come on, you're amongst friends here, what's going on with you?'
'George is right Father,' adds Charlie, 'A problem shared is one halved and all that.'
'You're good lads,' smiles the Priest. 'I can tell you this much, I made the problem of being human do for me today. In the eyes of the Lord I did a good deed, but in the eyes of my church I've crossed a line from which there's no return. The pain of losing my religion and the weight of this so called sin committed is something I must deal with alone. So, thank you but that's enough about my shite. Where exactly are you two maniacs heading at this late hour?'
'Nowhere really Father,' replies Charlie. 'Wherever we end up. Up until today my home was Billy Smart's circus, but they don't want me anymore. I got fired so I'm with George tonight for as long as he wants. He's been good to me. How many others would take the time and understanding to help soothe the messed up, troubled soul of a suicidal clown?'
'And you George? What finds you here tonight under these curious Mancunian stars. You're a long way from your world son. The roar of the Stretford End. An adoring audience. The champagne and ladies. What's going on with you?'
'Ah, it's not all it's cracked up to be Father. Sometimes I feel like I'm drowning, I just needed some fresh air with my friend Charlie here.' All thoughts of going back to the Brown Bull anytime soon have long since disappeared. I don't even feel like I need another drink. Maybe the amount I've poured down my mouth earlier is still in effect, but it feels strange. I feel sober. My head is clear and I can think straight for the first time in ages.'
'I'm with Charlie here Father. Where he goes in his big floppy feet, I'm following. Unless he falls in the canal then he's fucked because I'm not going in there after him!'
Charlie bursts out laughing. ' 'Oi Bestie! A typical red you!'

'Well lads if it's okay with you I'd be honoured if you'd let a still, drunken Priest tag along for a while on your late night journey. Let's have a chat about the meaning of life and see where it gets us.'
This makes me smile, 'Oh, Father. Bless you but the meaning of life is in the bottom of a glass and the trick is getting there as fast as you can!'
'I don't agree with you there George,' replies the Priest.
'The meaning of life for me is just what's around the next corner. So let's go and find out eh? God works in very mysterious ways my son. I've a feeling there's many a strange tale will unfold here tonight and many an adventure will be had.'

ACT TWO

THE CIRCUS

'You can't help but warm to this likeable if I'm sure a very troubled Priest. So now there was three of us! Lost souls in a sleeping city. The distant rattling hum of trains, a dog barking, a police siren. Where we are heading I've no idea, frankly I don't fucking care. It's after hours and I feel alive. Charlie and the Priest are already getting on famously chatting away. Me, I'm just content to listen and smile. I've always done that because I'm alone in a crowd unless pissed out of my brains that is, then I'm the other George. But not tonight happily. Not tonight.
'Tell me then Charlie boy,' asks Father Finn. 'How old was you when you first joined the big top?'
I was fifteen Father. I ran away from a children's home. Well to be honest there was no need to run that fast because nobody ever bothered coming after me.'
'Was you always raised in children homes?'
Charlie smiles but even on his painted face it's easy to recognise one beneath tinged with sadness. 'I'd been in care since I was 8 years-old Father. My mum was of gypsy blood you see. She was a beautiful looking lady. I loved her very, very much. She was always joking and singing. She used to say to me. 'Smile my beautiful Charlie boy and the world smiles with you!' To earn money she told people's fortunes for half a crown. She did palm readings, read tea leaves from cups. We even had a crystal ball in our back room that I thought was the most magical thing in the world! This cost a little more and mum even

dressed up for those readings. As a kid I thought the constant comings and goings of gentlemen, and the odd looking lady in our house was people eager to see what their future held.'
Charlie stops and pulls out a fag packet from his polka dot costume pocket and lights a cigarette. He inhales…
'One day in my bedroom I heard a scream, so I ran downstairs and found my mum with her throat cut and a man standing with a blood soaked razorblade stood over her. Turns out she was a prostitute and this mad bastard murdered her because mum went for him after he refused to pay. There was never any palm readings or tea leaves, even the fucking crystal ball was made out of plastic and covered in silver wrapping paper.' Me and the Priest listen on in utter shock. Charlie wipes a tear from his eye. 'Smile and the world smiles with you,' she said. So when I was old enough I took her advice and ran off to join the circus.
I started from the bottom up.
I cleaned out the lion's and elephant's cages every morning and night.
I'd top up Marco the blind knife throwers' whiskey with water.
I'd ignite Fergus the fire eater's torch and stand right back.
I'd pad myself up whilst the world's strongest man, the magnificent Mickey Muscles from deepest Mongolia, or so they claimed launched me through the air. His thick scouse accent always made me a little sceptical though.
I'd trim the bearded lady's beard.
I'd wait with buckets of water in case the human cannonball blew himself up.
I'd stay by the safety net as brother and sister Ivan and Isla of the legendary Kazimov trapeze family, hurtled through the air at death defying speed. Nobody knowing except me that every time Isla went up she was trying to fucking kill him!
I would tango with the shackled, dancing bear. I swear I saw a tear drop from his eye one day.
 I'd help out the one-armed juggler right until he got hit on the head by Ivan Kazimov. His sister finally succeeding in killing him and sadly the juggler by accident! RIP gents.

Then onto my heroes…
The reason I'm stood here before you two tonight. They were the most miserable bunch of bastards you could ever wish to meet.
Da, da, da, da, da, da, da! I give you the clowns! I swear you had to pay them to fucking smile. There was Ollie the pint pot, so called for obvious reasons.
Rags, not so obvious as he was the most smartly turned out clown you could ever wish to see. Rags would sleep in a dickie bow.
Last and least, charming Eddie. So named because he was the rudest man on the planet. But despite all this when these three were performing in the Big Top, I'd watch enthralled and laugh louder than any paying child in the audience. The difference being between me and them I was learning that the magic came in the timing. Their routine over the years tuned to perfection. The falling off the bikes and ladders, the hooting horns, the custard flams, the buckets of water jokes. I practiced until by the time I was nineteen I'd be trusted to stand in if one of them was ill. Or too pissed.
One day, the all-powerful Ring Master and king of our world Billy Smart pulled me into his caravan.
'It's your time Charlie boy!' he said. 'Go and get your red nose son and light up the big top!'
It turned out Charming Eddie had finally burnt too many bridges. One night after he was caught in a drunken and embarrassing position with pants around his ankles behind one of the show ponies, it wasn't the first time let me tell you, Billy fucked him off with the immortal words. 'I employ clowns to make people laugh not shag my fucking ponies! Now fuck off!'
So, cue the blaring trumpets!
Charlie Canzone was the new clown in town. Everybody loved me and I loved them. I'd taken mum's advice and behind a mask, my painted smile and a false red nose I'd finally found some peace. But just a short time ago the laughing from the audience stopped. In its place came the other cheek of a clown's arse. The boos, the jeering and today those immortal dreadful words no self-respecting clown can ever bear to hear. 'You're not fucking funny!'

A hush went around the circus ring. Grumbles and whispers. Mocking smiles and shaking of heads. Billy Smart sighed, he clocked this and took note.
The bearded woman stroked her beard.
Mickey Muscles shed a tear.
The shackled bear rattled his chain in despair.
The human cannonball jumped in his cannon and fired himself off in a last post tribute. He was a good lad. Luckily, they found him safe after landing on a load of elephant shit in Belle Vue circus. But for me it was all over. Billy took me in his office this afternoon and told me straight. 'They're not laughing at you anymore Charlie. I'm going to have to let you go. Here's a few quid now fuck off and leave your horn and your bicycle in the caravan!'
Charlie turns towards me and the Priest. We've both been listening on in total silence. I've been dying to laugh at times but dare not for Charlie's tears are real. He's had his life turned upside down today. He smiles. 'So here I am tonight with my broken clown's heart and two new friends.'

THE GANGSTER

'What a load of absolute self-pitying bollocks!'
A voice calls out.
By this time we'd made our way down to the canal path under the railway bridge, where a tall figure in a long overcoat and trilby had stepped towards us out of the darkness. The moon shining bright upon the stranger's fearful features. Unsmiling eyes and a razor scar that zig-zags down a left cheek from his forehead.
 'Good evening my son,' said Father Finn. 'It appears we've come across another lost soul tonight for our small flock who has no wish to go home.'
The stranger stares at the three of us and shakes his head.
'A clown, a Priest and George fucking Best. Christ! I thought my night couldn't get any weirder. And all this without a drink.
'I know the feeling,' I reply.
'Me and you have met before George.'
'Have we, I'm sorry I don't recall.'
'It was through mutual acquaintances at a party in Whalley Range for when the boys got back in town. I believe we nodded in passing.'
Not wanting to be rude and a little wary I decide to take a calculated guess. 'Of course, I remember. Philomena's place for Jimmy and the lads.'
The stranger smiles wide. 'Exactly, quality George but me I'm freelance.' Thank fuck for that it seems my shot in the dark worked!
'My name is Frank Collins and you clown boy! Frank points a finger at Charlie. 'I caught most of your sob story and it's time to wise up son. You can't hide behind that shit forever. Time to throw away the face paint, get rid of the fucking floppy shoes and stand on your own two feet.'
Charlie appears livid. 'I hear your words squire but who the fuck are you to give me advice?' Our new friend walks toward Charlie and just for a moment I think he's going to hit him. Happily, Frank does

nothing of the sort but offers Charlie his hand to shake. He accepts it, if a little worryingly and half-heartedly.
'The name is Charlie Canzone, it's good to meet you Frank.'
'Likewise Charlie.'
'What brings you down here at this time Frank?' asks Father Finn.
'I tend to work nights Father.'
The Priest smiles. 'Ah, I see. A night owl. You find your way by the stars. Good man.'
The two men's eyes lock. For a moment neither speak.
'No offence but you don't look like the type of bloke who grafts in a factory on night's Frank lad. What's your line of work then?'
The silence broken not surprisingly by our reliable chatterbox Charlie. Frank produces a cigarette and a silver lighter from his inside suit pocket. He inhales and stares back at Charlie. 'I'm in pest control.'
'Oh, that's interesting, 'replies Father Finn. 'Any of god's creatures in particular?'
'Rats mostly,' says Frank, whilst glaring daggers at the Priest.
'Well you're welcome to tag along with us Frank,' adds Charlie, helping to ease what was a tense atmosphere between Frank and the Priest. 'Why would I want to go anywhere with you lot? Nothing personal George but this is all a little weird. I mean a clown, a Priest and you down on the canal way past midnight? If I didn't know and hadn't witnessed you in action with the ladies I'd be even more sceptical. But I'm telling you here and now you won't find many birds around these parts. Not live ones anyway.'
'I'm not looking for skirt Frank, this is all just circumstance.'
'If you don't mind me saying Frank,' jumps in Charlie again.
'You really do look like you could do with a little company.'
'Thanks clown I'll keep that in mind. Just where are you all off then?'
Father Finn points down towards the path that stretches forever into the darkness along the canal. Huge black warehouse reach high in the night sky on both sides. 'We're going that way Frank.'
Frank looks at his watch. 'Why not, I've got a few hours to pass until my next job.'
'What's that then Frank?' asks Charlie.

'Somebody who kept asking me the wrong questions Charlie.' Charlie finally goes quiet because I think the penny dropped he was getting on Frank's nerves! I'm walking alongside Frank whilst Charlie and the Priest are ahead. We start to lag behind a little, purposefully I think because Frank wishes to say something for my ears only. 'You're a clever lad George. I guess you've figured out what I do for a living?'
'It's none of my business what you do to make money Frank.'
'You don't have to be coy with me George. You can say it, I'm a hitman. I kill people. But I only kill those in my business who have it coming to them. I kill bad people never civilians like you and the clown up there.' He points forward to Charlie who's chatting away with the Priest. 'It's a living,' I reply smiling. I'm trying hard to keep this mad conversation relatively normal.
'Until tomorrow that is,' says Frank. We stop walking and I turn to stare at Frank. 'Why what happens tomorrow?'
'Well come first light George lad my soul goes straight to hell. I have to kill somebody whose only crime was to do the right thing and now? Well he's got to go for it.'
'Can't you just warn them Frank? Tell whoever it is to disappear?'
'I'm afraid not George, this man's evidence has seen some very important people in Manchester get arrested tonight. They were friends of my client. Judges, lawyers, senior policemen. Even a fucking Bishop. He's under pressure to make this problem go away. If I don't do it, they'll do me as well. They're the rules. I've been given the silver bullet. I took their money up front with more to follow. It's our bible see George. The rules of the game. Our eleventh commandment, I break the contract and I get clipped.'
'These people you talk about Frank. These men of power. Can you tell me what they've done?'
'I see no reason why not. The worst things you could imagine. Kids.'
'Jesus Christ, Frank! You need to do the right thing here. That's just fucking awful.'
'When I took this job it was just a name. If it was down to me I'd do the bloody lot of them but this is the twisted game I'm in George. The

old adage if I knew then what I know now, well? Things would be different.'

'This man whoever he is who spoke up doesn't deserve to die. He's a fucking hero Frank. At least you have to consider it?'

'It was his choice George. He's grassed and now must pay the price. Always remember everybody dies it's just a question of when and how. What'll happen in the morning is nothing unusual. This sick world will still fucking turn.'

'You can't kill him for this surely? It'll haunt you forever more Frank.'

'We all have our crosses to bear George. I best not say anymore son. God, I could do with a fucking drink. Do you fancy one?'

What a question to ask me! Especially after what I've just heard.

'I'd murder one Frank, if you'll forgive the pun! But there's nothing around here. We could go back to the Brown Bull I suppose, I've got the keys in my pocket.'

Franks starts laughing. 'No need, I know a place close by.'

'Oi, you two!' Shouts Frank to Charlie and Father Finn. They both turn around. 'Do you fancy a drink? I know a place not far from here.' Father Finn's and Charlie's faces are lit by moonlight.

'Frank you was indeed sent by god!' replies the Priest.

'Too right Frank!' adds Charlie. 'This clown really needs a beer!'

'So, where and what is this place Frank?' I ask him. 'I thought I knew everywhere but I've never heard nothing about a place down here.'

'They call it Oz George after the film, The Wizard of Oz. Anything goes in there and I mean anything. It's crawling with fucking weirdos. Hippies with pills that'll take you up, down and fucking sideways. Absolute freaks some of them. You'll love it in there Charlie!'

'Thanks Frank,' replies Charlie, not realising straight away he's been insulted! I smile and look at the Priest and Charlie with his big clown feet plodding along! 'We should all fit right in don't you think Frank?' We both laugh and it echoes loud in the Mancunian night air.

MEETING THE DWARF AND THE LADY OF THE NIGHT

Suddenly, there's the noise of shouting and screaming going on in front of us. A man and woman's voice. Me and Frank catch up with the Priest and Charlie, and can just about make out two figures arguing further up on the canal path.
'You horrible little tramp! Don't you dare talk to me like that!' How dare you more like! 'You're paying for a fuck not to treat me like dirt!'
'Oh, excuse me for all the tea in China!' replies the man's voice. 'I never realised I was dealing with the queen of fucking Sheba!'
'I'll have you know,' continues the woman. 'The Queen of Sheba is a Biblical figure. The tale of her visit to King Solomon has undergone extensive Jewish and Arabian elaborations and has become the subject of one of the most widespread legends in the Orient. Would you like me to continue? You little fucking shit!'
'What, oh lady of the night!' he fires back. 'Have you swallowed a history book? As well as other things!'
'Just give me my money dwarf!' she screams, 'And f…'
'Oi! What's going on here?' interrupts Frank.
The sight greeting us before our eyes. A very pretty, tall blond lady wearing knee length boots, a mini skirt, a white jacket with a twiggy style cap on her head. The man's voice coming from a dwarf. Smart attire suited up with a dickie bow, slicked black hair and a Clark Gable pencil moustache. 'Ask her?' he shouts at Frank! 'I was just getting down to business and she went nuts!'
'I went nuts because you called me a dirty fucking bitch. Who the hell do you think you are saying stuff like that to me?'

'You took my money for sex that's why. Call me stupid but I thought that was how it worked?'
'This is my job you little idiot! It's what I do. I've got bills to pay. What do you do in your day job that makes you so fucking superior?'
'I'm an actor actually and a damn good one!'
'Oh, right then, so you perform for other people for money am I right?'
'Well done genius. Yes I do.'
'So you're prostituting yourself like me then?'
'I beg your pardon you mad woman?'
'You're playing a game little man by putting on a performance. The same as me. How would you feel if somebody calls you a dirty fucking dwarf?'
'Right, that's enough!' shouts Charlie. 'Enough!' He jumps between them. Both stare at him like they are hallucinating.
'Fucking hell its Coco the clown!' exclaims the man.
'He's called Charlie actually,' replies Father Finn.
'Thank you Father. You two calm down. First we'll start with your names. You go first Missy?'
'My name is Mary Rose if it's any of your business.'
Charlie smiles. 'That's a lovely name Mary Rose and you are my good man?'
'My name is Trevor Large the second. I'm very pleased to make all your acquaintances.'
Mary starts laughing. 'Fucking really suits you that!' One look at Trevor's sad expression is enough to prevent the rest of us from collapsing into fits of laughter. 'Aw, come on now Mary that's not a very nice thing to say now,' says the Priest. A smiling Mary spots and I'm sure recognises me. Here we go!
'Fucking hell it's Georgie Best! Hello George. All the girls love you darling, but none more than me!'
'Hi Mary, thank you. These are my friends here, Frank, Father Finn and Charlie Canzone. Pleased to meet you, and you too Trevor.'
'Hello to you George, I'm also a huge fan!' says Trevor.

'So love your style George,' adds Mary. 'Tell me what are you doing down on the canal with Mr Al Capone here and these two in fancy dress? Didn't think it'd be your scene somehow handsome!'
'I just fancied a walk Mary and along the way I picked up some new pals. What's your story then?'
'Oh, I'm just a working girl George who was having an ordinary Saturday night until I bumped into Clark Gable's toy doll here!'
'Can we please leave it now Mary!' pleads Trevor. 'I was wrong to say what I said about you during our shall we say performance, and I profusely apologise.' Trevor holds out his hand for Mary to shake and she does so. 'I'm sorry also for what I said and let me say you may be small in size but not in stature!' Mary winks at a red faced Trevor.
'Well thank you,' he replies.
'Hail Mary I say!'
A smiling Father Finn crosses himself. 'Praise the Lord we now have peace in our time.'
'Where are you all heading?' asks Mary. 'There's not really a lot going on around here at this time of night except for people like me of course.' Frank lights up another cigarette and inhales slowly.
'We're all going for a late night drink love. You're both welcome to join us if you like?'
'I would be delighted, thank you,' replies Trevor.
'Thanks for the offer Mr Capone,' says Mary. 'But I best be off to see if there's any late night punters, stragglers still doing the rounds.'
Trevor looks aghast at what Mary's just said. 'No, no, no! I insist you come for a drink. I would consider it an honour to buy the queen of Sheba a drink.'
Mary smiles wide. 'How on earth can I turn down an offer like that from such a gentleman like you?' Trevor offers his arm for Mary to link and she reaches down to accept it. So, once more we head off with our numbers now swelled by another two. There's me, the clown, the Priest, the hitman, the hooker and the dwarf actor. It's now well past the witching hour and I've no idea who or what is waiting beyond the next bend. And I really don't care!

Father Finn sidles up to Trevor and Mary Rose. 'So you two new members of our happy flock. Please tell me something about yourselves? Would you like to go first Trevor?'
'Well yes but I'm not sure you lovely people would really want to hear Father. It's all a rather distressing tale I'm afraid?'
Charlie puts an arm around Trevor, 'Hey mate looking at me you may think I'm a laugh a fucking minute clown, well little do you know sunshine. Only a couple of hours ago I was ready to jump off Blackfriars bridge until George here talked me down. So, out with it!'
Trevor sighs, 'Very well.'

LOVING JUDY GARLAND

I'll begin by telling you about how my Mother and Father met. They first clasped eyes on each other at the Culver hotel in Hollywood, California, back in 1939. They were both working on a film you may have heard of? The one where Judy Garland's innocent Dorothy runs off to save her dog Toto?'
'The Wizard of Oz?' replies a smiling Mary
'The very one my queen of Sheba. As Dwarves or midgets as we were known back then, both won parts as Munchkins. The money was a joke because the dwarfs earned less than they were paying the damned dog Toto. It was no coincidence that on day one of filming a munchkin tread on the mutt and damaged its paw. However, moods never improved much amongst the dwarves when Toto was ruled out for two weeks and it's stand in was still on more money than them! Incited by such insults to make up for it they treated their time in Hollywood, as one long holiday partying every night during filming, like it was the end of the world! Oh, it was mind-blowing, the stories, my god! The unholy tales of drunken dwarf orgies. They'd be swinging from the lampshades! Rooms were ransacked and drunken dwarves were fucking in the corridors and lifts. Wherever took their fancy. They were the most motley assembled gang of sexual deviants, pimps, hookers and gamblers you could ever imagine. The Culver hotel just rocked and rocked! Things got so bad they stationed police officers with shotguns on every floor to keep order and prevent mayhem. It was always said to make a picture like The Wizard of Oz, everybody had to be a little drunk with imagination, but this lot took it to the extreme. None more than my Father. He even went on a date with Judy Garland. Father was one of the dandiest dwarves and no female was safe from his charms. My Mother being one of many who fell under his spell at the Culver. Being only seventeen, Judy took her

mum along and my Father on meeting them quipped...
'Fair enough, two broads for the price of one. That'll do for me!' He was simply insatiable! Needless to say it was a one-time thing and Judy kept her distance for the rest of the filming. You can actually see him winking at her during the movie. Because you see for the first time in his life my Father was truly in love. Sadly for him Judy had witnessed enough of the Munchkins carrying on around set to not want anything to do with him or indeed any of them. For every chance when the cameras stopped it was party time again and they'd get smashed! The Police forever on permanent stand-by used to scoop them up in butterfly nets. I was told a story about the film's make-up artist Jack Dawn. He found one German dwarf who called himself the Count. This being a typical example of why they had to be watched all the time. Once when the Count was due on set he went missing. The call went out...
'Somebody go and find the fucking Count!'
Then a whining noise was heard coming from the men's room. The Count had got himself that plastered during the lunch break he'd fallen down the toilet and couldn't get out! His legs hanging in the air! Bert Lahr who played the Cowardly Lion got friendly with some and claimed many made their proper living by pimping, extortion and whoring. These were real hard-nosed bastards who'd survived the great Depression by living on their wits and nothing else. Many carried knives and pistols. You crossed them once but never again. Others from around the world. Europe, Germany especially were fleeing the Nazis' doctrine of 'social hygiene' which demanded the elimination of 'handicapped' people. Against this you must realise that at the time Hollywood was viewed as a modern day Babylon, where everything and anything went. Power, sex, glamour, drugs and drink was the name of the game and the dwarves wanted a share. They demanded a piece of the action and set about making their own little notch. Naturally, soon as they had money in their pockets from the filming the behaviour got even worse and they fucked and partied away, until the Culver hotel simply bounced to the sky every night!

The dwarves had landed in Hollywood and for a short time we the little people rocked the world!
 As for My Father? Well his earlier lothario attitude shown towards female dwarves included my by now impregnated Mother changed overnight. He was in love. More so infatuated with Judy! He sent huge bouquets of red roses to her that were returned back with messages of: 'Stay the fuck away!'
 His every attempt to speak to Judy was blocked until finally word was sent that he was no longer welcome on set. My Father was duly fired.'
I'm stood along with the rest of us listening on open-mouthed to Trevor's story. It really was so extraordinary that you couldn't make it up. He appears upset. 'So was that it Trevor?' asks Mary. 'Did he get it together with your mum then?'
'Oh, no happy ending I'm afraid,' he replied. 'Sadly, my good lady the rejection off Judy was simply too much for my Father to take. One night he sneaked on set and hung himself from one of the forest trees. I have been told that the image of him swinging is visible on one scene as the camera cuts off the yellow brick road into the forest. But never having watched the film I can't say. Nine months later I was born just as the movie hit the theatres. We moved to England in 1946. My Mother got a job with a kind family in London where she served as a kitchen maid. Mother never mentioned him until one day when I was 12 years-old, she sat me down and we spoke about my Father for the very first time. She'd only known him for such a short while and even though they'd hardly spoke her eyes blazed with a lost love and passion. What a man he must've been but also what a complete and utter, stupid bastard to do what he did. She also told me that he was said to be the best dwarf actor of them all and so in my own way, I've tried to follow in his footsteps.'
'Big shoes though eh?' smiles Frank.
Frank it appears simply couldn't resist it! I try hard not laugh.
Looking around I'm not on my own and happily Frank's comments don't register with Trevor. 'Of course,' Trevor continues. 'I was

named after him. Trevor Large the second. And if I'm only half the man he was said to have been then that shall do me fine.'
Again, we try so hard not to chuckle. Frank looked set with another quip, but thank god he thought better of it! Mary glanced around at all of us, 'After listening to Trevor's story I suppose I best tell you my own tale now.'
Father Finn puts an arm on her shoulder, 'Only if you're comfortable with this Mary and you think it'll help you?'
Mary smiles. 'Aye, I think so Father. I think I'm ready to tell it for the first time.' Mary takes centre stage and motions across to Frank.
'Light me up a cigarette Mr Capone before I start. I think I'm going to need it. Frank hands one over and lights it for Mary. She inhales.
'Cheers for that,' she says.
'You're welcome sweetheart,' smiles Frank.

RAG DOLL

'Okay listen up everyone. I'm going to tell you all a true story about a young girl from Manchester who was nothing more than a rag doll. She was raised by her mum because her dad was killed during the war. As a child she loved to read. Books were devoured like other children eat ice cream and jelly. At 12 years-old, our rag doll was reading Shakespeare, Dickens and Tolstoy. From the Bible to the Torah to the Koran. Ancient history and modern. Comic books, Enid Blyton she loved and adored. Our rag doll dreamed of being an author. Of travelling the world and visiting all these wonderful countries and cities that she'd only ever read and dreamt about. At school, teachers watched in wonder as this slip of a girl, this rag doll with the huge blue eyes and heartrending smile who wanted nothing more than to read and absorb what books had to offer. Who would soak up every word, line, chapter and verse read. This rag doll so innocent, sweet and pure. This rag doll so trusting. This rag doll who when just 13 years-old was taken by a 'favourite Uncle' a friend of the Mother. Isn't that how they always work? To what she was told a children's party but waiting was a group of older men who took it in turns to rape her. There was one called the schoolteacher. He was the worst. A pig of a man. He slapped her face. The rag doll was made to undress and when they'd finished with her these older men, some well-known for the rag doll had read about them. The rag doll read everything see. She'd seen their faces in the newspaper. The 'favourite Uncle' grabbed her around the throat.

 'If you ever dare tell anybody we shall come to your house and kill both you and your fucking Mother!'
The rag doll simply nodded her head and wiped her eyes clear of tears. She got changed and the 'favourite Uncle' took her home. The next week he came back, the week after that, and the week after that.

The rag doll never said anything because she didn't want them to hurt her Mother. Her lips stayed sealed but she hurt so much, and so she read and read. Anything to stem the pain. Then one day she came home from school to find the local Priest and the 'favourite Uncle.' They told her that Mother had died and she was being taken away to live in an orphanage. After the funeral she was driven by the Priest in his car to her new home. The rag doll closed her eyes for she knew what was coming as he stopped off on the way, and raped her in a lay-by. Then he made her pray for forgiveness. And so the rag doll stayed at the orphanage where every week the uncle continued to call and take her to his important friends. Until one day when she was 16 years old the rag doll snapped and refused to go. She hit her favourite uncle with an iron bar and killed him. She smashed his fucking brains in. For this they locked the rag doll away until just two years ago. After leaving jail the rag doll worked the streets. She still reads. She reads and fucks for a living and drinks and drinks. The rag doll gentlemen, I'm sure you know is me.'

After listening to Mary's horrific story nobody moves. I look across to Frank. He's ashen-faced and catches my eye and I'm certain knows what I'm thinking. Frank glares at me and normally I wouldn't be brave enough to continue staring, but after listening to Mary I do. Indeed it's him who blinks. He smiles towards me before lighting up another cigarette. Hopefully, any notion of carrying out his job of work tomorrow morning has now gone forever?

Charlie steps towards a sobbing Mary. 'Come here you.' She all but collapses in his arms. A tearful Trevor too has an arm around her as the Priest watches on. Just for a moment I catch Frank staring across towards him. There's a strange look in his eye, something I can't quite understand. Then we were six. Our stories now told, well almost. The Priest has truly to reveal his inner-self and then there's little old me. Georgie fucking Best.

GEORGIE BOY

My new friends indeed the whole bloody world think they know the story. Well nobody knows nothing except me but I'm not going to stand before these lovely people tonight and bare my soul. I'm neither brave enough nor ready to do so. I've just listened to Mary and I think I've fucking suffered? I'd be embarrassed to have this lot listen to my woes. Because what problems do I really have? I have the whole world at my feet, I'm Georgie boy and every girl in this city wants to fuck me, but still I need to reach the bottom of the glass every fucking night? Now excuse me but what exactly is the problem here?
In the light of day the trumpets blow, the girls and the boys both scream my name. On the pitch I make grown men go weak at the knees. Off it grown women, married and not hand me their telephone numbers. They knock on my hotel door. I'm the boy who's got it all. So why do I only feel safe and sane at the bottle of a glass, and in the dead of night? Amidst the backslapping and cheering crowds the love and adulation. Why am I always in a crowd of one? I look up to the black skies, for me they're like a cloak. They make me invisible. I love the peace and the stillness of night. I can hide in shadows, I can walk the streets without people looking in my eyes and being in my fucking space screaming:
'You're Georgie fucking Best! I love you and I fucking hate you but I really want to be you!'
And, like Charlie the clown I give them a painted smile whilst thinking at the same time 'Fuck you!' No one should be me because I don't want to be me. I'm treated like a god and thought of as special because I can make magic on the football field. I don't need a fucking wand to pull rabbits out of a hat because I can make defenders appear drunk and staggering as I tear past them with the ball tied as if by an invisible string to my feet.

'Because of the wonderful things he does! La, la, la, la, la, la !'
Best by name, best by fucking nature. Well that isn't me. Let the trumpets blow for somebody else. Out of everybody here most who have real problems, I'm just a sad and sorry bastard who can't handle the fame. 'Sympathy for the devil' sing the Rolling Stones, but I'll be damned if I want my new friends that I've made here tonight have any for me. What follows is a continuing journey into Manchester's darkest heart. The cruel beat of this Northern outpost. Where money, power and sex are the true religion. A Mancunian Babylon by the Irwell awaits and as my adopted city gently sleeps, if you listen closely you can hear the sound of millions of people softly breathing. Eyes wide shut. While here down on the canal our story has hardly begun.

ACT THREE

THE SALFORD SIOUX

Cromwell Hospital. 2010.
 Don't worry, I'm not going anywhere just yet. Now before we go on I need to tell you a tall tale, one strange but true. One that will become relevant in a very short time as we move on.
 In 1887, the legendary American Army scout Buffalo Bill brought his Wild West show to Salford. Manchester's troublesome little brother across the waters of the River Irwell. It was a travelling company of 97 Native Americans, 180 bronco horses and 18 buffalo, that camped for five months with their tepees on the freezing banks of the Irwell. Foremost amongst them was the giant Sioux warrior and legendary horseman, the six-foot-seven, wonderfully named Surrounded by the Enemy. One can only imagine what they and especially he looked like to the people of Manchester and Salford in Victorian Britain. Exotic, exciting, ferocious and fearsome. Many of the Sioux were veterans of the Battle of Little Big Horn. General George Armstrong Custer's last stand where Custer and his troops were massacred down to the last man. These had good reason to be in Salford for they were still being hunted down by an unforgiving US government. The warriors were Lakota Indians from the Oglala tribe of the Sioux Nation, whom counted amongst their numbers two names all schoolboys know well.
 Sitting Bull and Crazy Horse.

The company performed nightly to ecstatic, packed crowds in what was the biggest outdoor arena ever constructed at the time in Western Europe. Sioux warriors and their cowboy counterparts recreating classic gunslinging scenes from the Wild West or performing daring acts of horsemanship. All took place in what is now Salford Quays, two years before the canals were even built! It proved so popular the show stayed for five whole months before finally the wagons rolled, and they pulled out of town back onto its European tour. But not all left. Having an unquenchable taste for whiskey (firewater), and the local women, the three warriors all close friends had been out the night before the circus left town and missed the train. They were Surrounded by the Enemy, an Ogala medicine man called Black Elk, and a hugely respected chief called Charging Thunder. With all three still on a US government wanted list none had little wish to return back to the United States, so they decided to stay and settle in Salford. In no time at all they found themselves accepted into the local community. They were proper men's men! Their love of a drink, a good laugh and almost superhuman appetite to sow their wild oats made me appear like a monk! Salford and the ladies in particular fell in love with them. However, tragedy struck when Surrounded by the Enemy caught a lung infection and died of chest complications at the criminally young age of only twenty-two. He passed away in a tepee on the Irwell banks. To the despair of his friends the authorities took Surrounded by the Enemy's body to Hope Hospital, where only a few hours later it mysteriously vanished. For that very same night Black Elk and Charging Thunder broke into the mortuary and stole the body away. They buried him with a true Sioux funeral ceremony by dancing, hollering and singing the holy words around the fire to ensure their beloved friend Surrounded by the Enemy entered the land of his ancestors. Salford legend has it that one small girl who was baptised at St Clément's church was indeed Surrounded by the Enemy's daughter, before all necessary information was 'Lost' by the Catholic church's record books. Only Black Elk returned to their prairie homelands. Charging Thunder married and raised a family and eventually moved to West Gorton, where he changed his head dress for a cloth cap to become George Edward Williams. He got himself a job working for many years at Belle Vue Circus looking after the elephants. Tending to their needs, talking to them and cleaning out the stables, it was a remarkable relationship. Both he and them far from home.

A couple of stories!

His favourite elephant was called Nelly and when Charging Thunder got drunk which was quite often, he'd head for the circus, climb in with the elephants and sleep off his hangover with Nelly standing guard over him. No one was allowed near until he awoke and heaven help any who tried!

Another time a huge circus snake got free and found its way into the elephant's stalls. On sighting Charging Thunder picked it up and immediately the snake wrapped itself around his neck. Carrying his trusty tomahawk, Charging Thunder lopped of the snake's head killing it instantly. The owner of the circus went spare at the Red Indian. 'Why didn't you just leave it alone?' he screamed!

Charging Thunder was in no mood for apologies. 'You can always get another snake but there's only one Charging Thunder!'

Around Gorton, Charging Thunder swiftly became a well-known and very respected figure in the area. Apart from his job at Belle Vue, he worked as a handyman for a local engineering firm and a doorman at the local cinema. Nobody chanced any trouble when Charging Thunder was around. However, there was so much more to this man. Locals would knock on his door and seek advice. Whoever had a problem their first port of call would be to go and see the Indian. The 'Wise man' who came from the Great American West. From the wild prairies where the buffalo roamed to live amongst them.

But Charging Thunder's health was never good. The constant Mancunian, drizzle, damp and smog finally took a terrible toll and he died from pneumonia in 1929, at the age of just fifty-two. Charging Thunder's passing mourned by all and not just in Gorton and Salford, but legend has it that on passing the wolves howled out his name on the giant Sioux plains of Charging Thunder's birth place. Today he lies buried in Gorton cemetery, but Charging Thunder's spirit left town many years ago. However, the bloodline of the Sioux remains throughout Salford, many unknowing that their great forefathers were the ferocious Red Indians who surrounded and slain General Custer, and later danced and drunk firewater on the bank of their own River Irwell. That same canal we traipsed down in 1970, and why am I telling you all this? You'll soon see. Now back to the story…

OZ

So, on what felt like a never-ending cobbled path with countless bends, we made our way.
'What's this pub like Frank?' asks Charlie. 'Are we getting close? My bloody floppy feet are killing me!'
'It's not a pub Charlie, it's a madhouse! It's for the midnight owls and people like us and it's not far off now.'
'By us I take it you mean spirits of the night Frank, lost souls searching for salvation?' says Father Finn.
'I mean people who need a fucking drink Father and have had better days. Nothing else.'
'Or some with maybe worse days to come maybe?'
'Let's hope not eh Father, for both our sakes.'
They again share a look. There's something going on between those two that I just can't nail down.
Trevor suddenly starts to point. 'What the fuck is that?'
In front has appeared a neon sign beaming down upon the water a hundred yards further on. It's illuminating the surface with two huge lime green letters spelling the word OZ.
'Oh my god!' exclaims Mary
'Bloody hell!' says Charlie
'Fuck me, I'm home,' adds Trev.
Frank puts an arm around me. 'George, do yourself a favour when we get there. Have a good drink but stay off the pills son. Believe me they're not for the likes of you.'
'What do you mean Frank?'
'If you take one pill then the chances are you won't be coming down until 1975. I don't think Mr Busby would be too happy with that. Do you get my fucking drift as they say these days?'
'Cheers Frank, I'll keep that in mind!'

Frank smiles. 'Good lad, this place has a very special clientele and I'm deadly serious George. They're not your people. Trust me take nothing you're offered or it will destroy you. Come on let's go.'

With Frank's warning foremost on my mind we walk ever closer with him leading. He turns back towards us. 'Just stay here for a minute.'

Frank steps forward ten yards until he's stood facing the neon sign. A light suddenly appears from the top of the warehouse opposite onto him. He shields his eyes and then across the water the doors to the warehouse slowly rumble open making a gigantic creaking noise. As we watch on open-mouthed, a draw bridge starts to drop from the far wall and fastens itself onto our side of the canal. Then once more all is silent. The doors to the warehouse reveal only an inside wall but also what appears an entrance. A smiling Frank turns back towards us. 'Well what are you lot all waiting for? Come on lets go and get a drink!'

Frank sets off across the drawbridge and we follow closely behind him. Once over we huddle up together outside the door. 'Do we knock on Frank?' asks Charlie.

'No need Charlie, they already know we're here. They'll open up in a minute.'

Charlie sighs. 'Oh, right, I thought there would be like a secret password or something. You know, knock three times like you see in the movies. I'm a little disappointed now to be honest with you.'

'You can always piss off back over to the other side of the canal Charlie. We'll bring you some crisp and a glass of lemonade out while we have a real drink. Your choice?'

Charlie appears suitably chastised. 'Sorry Frank mate.'

'Why all the bloody secrecy Frank?' asks Mary. 'All my time working the streets around here and I've never heard of this madhouse. You must be a very important man Mr Capone?'

'No, just damned lady,' smiles Frank.' You have to be for membership. When we go inside stay close to me and I'll sign you all in. No smart arse remarks because they're very touchy. Just behave, all of you. Especially you Charlie!'

'Don't worry about me Frank, I'll be good as gold!'
Father Finn can't let Franks comments of being damned go without saying something. 'Nobody is damned in god's eyes whilst still living Frank. Absolution of sin is the given right of all God's children. You can repent your sins now. I'll take your confession right here myself.'
Frank lights a cigarette but his eyes never leave the Priest.
 'I can't let you do that Father because if I did they'd know inside and wouldn't let us in would they? I'd no longer be damned. Their eyes are so keen beneath their horns you see and we all need that fucking drink right? Now be a good man and go and save somebody's soul who actually gives a fuck.'
'Oh, I believe you do give a fuck Frank, I really do. There's good in you, I can feel it and it's never too late to change your ways.'
Suddenly, the sound of the door unbolting can be heard. One bolt, two, three, four times. It slowly opens inwards. Then appears a huge figure. A Red Indian dressed in doorman's attire, truly handsome, six foot seven, dark skinned with long black hair and piercing, unforgettable, blue eyes. He walks out and stands with arms folded facing us. Nobody moves. Frank smiles and nods towards him.
 'It's good to see you again Surrounded by the Enemy.'
The two men shake hands.
'It's good to see you also Frank Collins.'
The Sioux Indian speaks with a broad Salford accent. 'Surrounded by the Enemy, please let me introduce you to my friends. Father Finn, Mary Rose, Charlie Canzone, Trevor Large the second. And last but not least. George Best.'
Surrounded by the Enemy smiles wide. 'A pleasure George, I'm a big red and a huge fan of yours.'
 Thank fuck for that I think!
'I'll vouch for everyone here,' says Frank. Surrounded by the Enemy goes along the line looking in all our eyes. 'There is only one rule here but it has to be obeyed at all times. What happens in Oz stays in Oz. Am I clear?' We all nod.
'Eh mate,' says Charlie. I fear the worst. Oh, no. Surrounded by the Enemy looks towards Charlie. 'Is Surrounded by the Enemy your real

name or just a stage act. A weekend name like?' He just can't help himself can our Charlie. The doorman glowers at him.
'It was my Grandfather's name. He was Salford Sioux. Originally of the Ogala tribe who wiped out Custer at the Battle of Little Big Horn. They came to this country in 1887 and never went home. He died on these banks many years ago, but my Grandfather's spirit lives on in me. Now have you got a problem with that Mr clown?'
'No, no, none whatsoever,' replies a clearly worried Charlie. 'I think it's a lovely name.'
Why is this place called Oz, Mr Surrounded by the Enemy?' asks Trevor.
The red Indian smiles wide. 'Because it's simply over the fucking rainbow little man. Now if you're all coming inside follow me.'
In we go as a single-file, the doorman first then Frank with us all behind. We enter into a long corridor with lime green walls that are adorned by scenes from The Wizard Of Oz. Trevor's eyes almost popping out of his head! At the far end is another door and outside it there's a desk where sits a woman dressed as the wicked witch of the West. 'This way please,' says Surrounded by the Enemy firmly. He points towards the witch and Frank reaches her first. She looks up and is truly fucking frightening! Frank smiles. 'Hello gorgeous!' The witch says nothing. Instead she hands Frank over a small penknife. He cuts a finger and lets the blood drip onto an open, large black book the witch has placed in front of him. We watch on in shock!
'Now sign your name and those of your friends Frank, and less of the sarcastic comments you cheeky twat!' The witch smiles back at Frank and he winks at her. She's truly horrifying and I'm finding it hard to figure out what's make up and what isn't.
'I wouldn't touch it with yours George!' whispers Charlie to me.
'And I'm not normally fussy.' Frank signs us in on the page where the blood still lies fresh. The witch licks a tissue showing her black teeth, and an even blacker tongue before passing it to him.
She smiles wide at Frank. 'Here you go lover boy, don't try and tell me you don't dream about me every night because I know you do!'

'Sadly, I don't dream anymore about anything darlin.' In fact I don't even fucking sleep.'
'The Scarecrow is in tonight Frank.'
On being told this by the witch we all notice Frank's eyes narrow into a murderous dark. 'Thanks doll.'
'He's in a foul mood as well Frank. Don't fuck around. Make your peace and explain what's gone on then go home safe.'
'Don't worry I've got it all in hand.'
'Make sure it is sweetness. You know the rules.'
The witch blows Frank a kiss. 'Now in you go, oh, and lover boy. I'll be in later to fuck your brains out!' The witch starts to laugh. A shriek that goes on and on! We walk past her, all eyes on this strange woman who is utterly hysterical. Mary offers her a glowering stare.
'Sort yourself out love eh. You look a fucking mess.'
The witch hears this and looks up to see Charlie is staring back.
'Are you really a witch?' he asks her? 'Witches are old and ugly,' she replies. 'What do you think clown boy?'
'Well appearance can be deceptive but in your case I don't fucking think so!' Charlie moves away quickly so she doesn't have time to answer. Frank stops at the door and turns to face us.
'Right listen up. One piece of advice. Nothing is ever as it seems in Oz so keep your wits about you at all times. That apart well fucking enjoy!' He opens the door and in we go.

WE'RE NOT IN KANSAS ANYMORE

Oh my fucking god!
 What greets us all as we walk in is a giant warehouse space, more like an aircraft hangar. The Zombies *Season of the Witch* is blaring out at a deafening tone.
It's the time, of the Season...
There are a thousand lights of every colour in the rainbow and more exploding in a kaleidoscope of multi-lit beams, cascading down from the ceiling. Around us dancing wildly, squatting in huddles, or sat quietly in dimly lit corners, must be at least five hundred people of all creed, shape, sexuality and in various life changing degrees of drunken and drug fuelled stupor! Nothing appears off bounds. There are many fucking openly in every position. Some even I haven't tried! A few I'm sure that are not even legal. Charlie is stood next to me gripping my arm.
 'Fuck me George, we're not in Kansas anymore!'
We head across to a long bar that stretches the entire length of the warehouse. Those serving are dressed in various outfits out of the Wizard of Oz movie. From munchkins to tin men and cowardly lions. Also, a worryingly number of Dorothy Gales both female and male. A few with beards trying too hard in small blue frocks and red shoes.
'My shout!' says Frank. 'What do you say to champagne all around for starters?' A cheer goes up from our group. I glance around, I thought I knew every late night drinking hole in Manchester, but this place is a total mystery to me.
A beautiful, blond-haired young girl with huge blue eyes dressed in nothing but high heels and a black bra set sidles up to me. She's smiling wide, obviously stoned and clutching a large glass of wine. Her faces inches away from mine.
'Hello George, would you like to play?' She goes to kiss me and I feel her tongue in my mouth slipping in what feels like a pill. I can't help but swallow. She pulls away and starts to laugh and swirl around on her heels! 'Come out, come out wherever you are and meet the young

lady who fell from the stars! You're all mine now Georgie boy!'
Again, she laughs wildly. Frank appears with a glass of champagne. 'Are you okay George?' I dare not mention to him I've dropped acid after what he warned me. 'Yeah I'm good thanks Frank. You were right this is some crazy joint.' I watch as the girl dances off still laughing like a lunatic.
Frank smiles. 'You don't know the half of it old son. Stay close and no drugs.'
The others gather around and Trevor raises his glass.
 'I would like to make a toast. To my new friends whom I have discovered on this strange but wonderful night! Our time together maybe short but I feel it will not be easily forgotten! To new friends!' Trevor raises his glass and we all join him in unison.
 'To new friends!'
'Right, I'm off to mingle,' says Charlie.
'And me,' adds a smiling Mary whilst grabbing Trevor's arm.
 'Come on you, I may need a chaperone.'

DONE THE DEED

I'm left with Frank and the Priest, who is still gazing around in shock at the surreal scenes all around him.

'Good heavens this fine lot would make some congregation. I think I'll take a walk amongst them. See if I can soothe some souls and maybe save a few.'

'You do that,' replies Frank. 'Pennies from heaven eh, you just can't leave it alone can you?'

'I don't think I'm with you Frank?'

'What I'm saying is you can't save everybody Father. What are you after a little pin off the Pope? Look around you, some people might not want to be saved and may enjoy dancing with the fucking devil in the pale Mancunian moonlight. Have you even considered that?'

'Tell me something Frank, why haven't you done the deed yet?'

I'm listening on in utter shock but the effects of the acid tab are slowly creeping up on me. I think best to stay quiet, the reality of this grim scenario lost in my fucked-up, state of mind. I wonder off in search of the blond girl. The conversation between Frank and the Priest goes on with me out of earshot.

'I've not yet made my mind up Father. When the sun comes up in a few hours I'll make a decision.'

'There's no decision to be made Frank, if you don't do your job then they'll come for you instead.'

'I need you to explain something to me that I'm really struggling to understand.'

'If I can, go on Frank.'

'The person who blew the lid in the confession box Father? Do you really think he deserves redemption with a couple of Hail Marys and Our Fathers for what he's done? The will to repent and confess surely

doesn't take away the sheer evil of the committed sin. Please tell me your fucking god doesn't work in such mysterious ways?'
'God is kind and forgiving Frank. Every one of his children deserves a chance for redemption.'
'Do you really understand the crimes this bunch of murderous perverts have committed? The amount of kid's lives abused and ruined? All because they have money and power and believe they exist above the law. Everybody else is deemed as fucking subservient to their sick needs. I'll tell you what happened. One of these fuckers suffered a sickening, sudden rash of conscience, and nipped in your church praying on the fact that you could never open your mouth to the Old Bill. He took the piss Father. He used you like he did those poor kids from the homes that are treated worse than cattle. You've been had and I fucking hate and pity you for it. I really do.'
'I don't think you understand Frank.'
'No, I don't think you do Father. You see being a good man, being a holy man doesn't give you power over these people. There are some in your own church involved with this. So high up they're probably on nodding terms with the fucking Pope himself. But you? You're just a small man with a dog collar out of his depth. You messed up the only thing that gave your life reason. You've forsaken all you hold dear and broken your vows. All to ease the miserable soul of a goddamn pervert.'
'No Frank, you don't see. It wasn't one of the guilty parties who came to see me in my church to confess their sins?'
'Who was it then?'
'It was one of the innocent. A young child who felt guilty for letting them do this to him.'
Frank appears shocked to the core. 'You're lying to me.'
'Why would I lie? The boy was ten years old. He'd lost his parents in a car crash two years ago and was put in a Catholic children's home. Yes Frank you're right, one of mine. A Catholic children's home. They put him in there and then they came. Every week, every Tuesday they came for him. And do you know something Frank, he thought it was all his own fault. They told him what was happening

equalled god's revenge for him letting his parents die in the crash. And you stand there Frank, you mock me? I may be just a small man with a dog collar but when I heard that boy's stories I realised losing my religion, my vocation is such a small price to pray. If you do have reason to kill me when the sun rises in a few hours well go ahead and do it. Indeed, I welcome it but please when you talk about a small man with a dog collar don't you dare ever say my actions were a waste of time. This small man in a fucking dog collar has caused an earthquake in your city tonight and the bad guys are running for cover. Not bad for a man of the cloth found after hours drunk in a pet shop doorway don't you think?'
For a moment Frank simply stands and stares at the Priest before…
'Let's go and get a drink Father. I think we need to talk.'

THE MANCHESTER MERMAID

Somehow,
 without knowing or remembering how, I've wondered back outside and found myself on a disused canal path. It's an offshoot that leads to what appears a deserted dock. The pill is kicking in. I'm sweating and my heart is beating like it's set to burst. I look up at the stars and feel like I can reach and touch them. A comet appears and is heading towards me. Closer and closer until it crashes into the once, still black waters that are now bubbling with colours of red, yellow and green!
I rub my eyes, walk on and then I hear somebody singing.
I recognise the voice and remember the words…
'Come out, come out wherever you are and meet the young lady who fell from the stars!'
 It's the blond girl who popped the pill into my mouth. I look in front and behind me but don't see anybody. 'George I'm over here!'
I turn around to the canal edge and I see the blond girl smiling and waving at me from the water. 'Are you coming in the water with me George, it's lovely in here?' The girl is naked from the waste up, but unfortunately I can't see beneath the dark canal surface!'
'Aren't you cold?'
She laughs. 'Kiss me George! Kiss me once more!'
My head is spinning! Why, oh, why did I swallow this fucking thing? But what the hell she's gorgeous. I lean down to kiss but then she bites my lips and pulls away. Her face suddenly contorted with rage.
'Fuck off George, I'm not like all your other girls!'
'I'm sorry,' I reply, my head all over the place.
'You're not sorry at all George.'
'But you asked me to kiss you?'
'If I asked you to jump off a cliff for me George would you do that too?'
'I don't know. I'm not sure'

She smiles. 'Oh, so you might do. You're not falling in love with me are you George. You can't do that because you can never have me. I will only break your heart Georgie boy.' I feel nothing but utter love for this strange girl. Even if she is making me sing for my dinner, but I know I'll get her in the end. I always do. I'm Georgie fucking Best!
'Climb out of the water, I want to talk to you.'
'Oh, no you don't George, because you want to fuck me. You see that's your problem, you think love and fuck are the same word but They're not, the only similarity is they each have four letters.'
'That's not fair.' I've no idea what the fuck she's going on about.
'Life isn't fair George, death isn't fair. What isn't fair is that you won't get in the water with me.'
'I can't do that, I don't want to, I'll drown in my state.'
'That makes me very sad George, because I have to go now. Will you give me a goodbye kiss?'
'No because you'll bite me again.'
She laughs loud. 'Oh, I promise not to lover boy, I promise not. Just a simple peck on the cheek.' She points to a spot and I lean down and gently kiss her face. 'That was so lovely George.' She blows me a kiss back in return. 'You still have time to turn it all around you know. Do as the man tells you and the yellow brick road can lead you down another path. I love you George, I love you!'
An almighty splash and this girl spins high out of the water to reveal her bottom half is a mermaid! That same moment the comet erupts back out of the water and into the night sky from where it originally came. Then all is quiet and still. I watch the comet until it vanishes from sight. What man could she be talking about? What path? The effects from the acid feels to be wearing off a little. I'm going fucking mad, I'm going insane! Never again, sorry Frank. Line me a drink up.

CHARGING THUNDER

'Fuck the champagne!
This calls for a pint of vodka and lemonade.'
'Come on George that's not the answer,' I hear. I turn around and facing me is a Red Indian with arms folded, wearing a traditional white head dress in full warrior regalia and carrying a huge tomahawk in his belt. The only difference being his is a broad Salford accent like the doorman, Surrounded by the Enemy.
'Are you real?' I ask.
He smiles. 'What do you think?'
'Well I've just been blown out by a Manchester mermaid so it's up in the air to be honest. No offence.'
'None taken George. Rough night?'
'Aye, it's been different, a strange one. Are you a friend of the doorman?'
'Surrounded by the Enemy is the grandson of an old friend of mine. We go way back a long way.'
'You're the man aren't you? You're the man who the mermaid was telling me about. 'Do as the man tells you and the yellow brick road can lead you down another path.' It's you. You're the wizard of Oz!
'Not exactly,' he smiles. 'My name is Charging Thunder, George. I left your world in 1929.'
'So, you're dead then?'
'No I've been on holiday! Have a day off George come on! There's no such thing as death, just a pass over, a change of worlds. Anyway, as a favour to a friend I've come back to have a word.'
'To have a word with me, why?'
No George, the wall. It appears you're getting one last chance.'
'One last chance at what Charging Thunder?'
'To turn your life around.'

'What makes you think I want to turn it around?'
'We the Sioux have a saying.
'We will be known forever by the tracks we leave.'
I start to laugh. 'Smokey Robinson said the same thing!'
'Don't make me use my tomahawk George!'
I immediately stop laughing only for Charging Thunder to then laugh out loud. 'Don't worry George, I'm not here to scalp you unless it's absolutely necessary. Just to remind you that many greats have fallen with a bottle in their hand. Our own history is littered with such men.'
'I can handle it Charging Thunder.'
'A brave man dies once George but a drunk many times. I've seen your future. The old tale of being blessed with a special talent coming with a curse is not true. For you are strong and wise enough to change, and I urge you to find the strength to do so.'
'You say you saw my future well that proves at least I have one.'
'Well then you must set your sights low.'
'In what way?'
'You'll hear these words many times. 'Where did it all go wrong George?' And you'll be either too drunk or arrogant to care. But one will know. You. For though you can and will speak in riddles and fork tongues. You will tell all your tall tales of women and wine. Of how you care little when nobody knows or cares more than you. A broken heart that lies to itself can cause a thousand silent deaths. Each one not telling you that you're dead. Oh, you'll exist but you will be lying to yourself and that's not living.'
'Why do I get this chance to turn things around Charging Thunder? There are so many people more deserving than me.'
Charging Thunder smiles. 'Because when a blind man hears your name George, he smiles.'
'I'm not a good man, I wish I was, but I'm not.'
'Yes you are, do you think I would be wasting my time here if I did not think this is true?'
'You say I'm strong enough, I'm not. When it comes to booze I fold and drop like a leaf in the fucking wind. All that's happened,

everything tonight I don't know what the fuck is going on? But then why do I feel it's all been leading to this?'
'Not exactly George, it may come as a shock to you but the world, both of them don't revolve around you. Amongst your friends there are a lot of things being sorted tonight.'
'Can you help me change Charging Thunder?'
'I can only tell you that it is the wise thing to do. There must be a natural way of things. Everything just happens. Nothing is ever written.'
I'm trying to hold back the tears. 'I just want to do what's right.'
'You have to do it for yourself George, for they will gather around and urge and scream at you not to do this. You must have courage and belief.'
'You know about courage Charging Thunder, you've seen some things. Stuff I could only ever dream about. Tell me about the Battle of the Little Big Horn?'
'Very well George. A story of real courage is Custer's last stand. In 1875, we the Sioux and Cheyenne Indians left the white man reservations because we were outraged over the continued intrusions of whites into our sacred Dakota Black Hills. We came together in Montana, with the great warrior Sitting Bull to fight for our lands. Never had there been such a gathering and to try and defeat and force us back to the reservations they sent their finest general. A vain, arrogant but courageous soldier who viewed us as nothing more than savages on horses. General George Armstrong Custer. Leading his Seventh Cavalry we led him forever onwards into our midst and a trap along the Rosebud river. Custer came across a group of around forty warriors. Ignoring orders to wait for reinforcements he instead decided to attack not knowing we lay in ambush and were three times his strength. We charged and together with the Cheyenne and Hunkpapa Sioux slammed into Custer and his soldier blues forcing them back to a long, high ridge. Meanwhile another force, we of the Oglala Sioux under Crazy Horse's command swiftly moved downstream and then doubled back surrounding Custer and his men, pouring in gunfire and arrows. As we closed in he ordered his men to

shoot their horses and stack the carcasses to form a wall, but they provided little protection against our bullets. In less than
an hour Custer and his men were wiped out. After the battle we stripped the bodies and mutilated all the uniformed soldiers believing that the soul of a cut up body would be forced to walk the earth for all eternity, and could not ascend to heaven. But not Custer, with his we stripped and cleaned the body. He had been the last to fall and was viewed as a worthy enemy. Even as a dozen braves closed in on him with a pile of dead soldiers at his feet, he stood clutching their flag before falling in a hail of arrows. That was real courage George Best.
'Did you see all this Charging Thunder?'
'I was the one who fired the last arrow that brought Custer to his knees. I saw the light go out in his eyes.'
'I promise to try and change Charging Thunder I really do.'
'I know you will George. Now go back inside, your friends will be worried about you.'
'There's just one thing I need to know before I do?'
'Go on?'
'Who asked you to have a word with me?'
'You will know soon enough now go.'
I walk off, only then wanting to take one last look at my Red Indian but when I turn he'd gone. I smiled at the thought of him.
'So long big guy.'

MEETING GOBBO HORNFACE

Frank comes towards me as I enter back into the warehouse. He's on his own. 'Where the fuck have you been George?'
'I just went for some air. Where is everybody?'
'Mingling would you believe!'
I spot Charlie sat next to another guy dressed as a clown. They've a bottle of whiskey in front of them. Trevor and Mary are dancing and appear to be getting on like a house on fire. As for the Priest? I look around but he's nowhere to be seen. Frank seems to read my mind.
'What's going on between you and the Priest, Frank?'
'None of your business George. Don't get involved.'
'It's him isn't it. He's the one you're going to kill?'
'Go and have a drink son this isn't a game, you're well out of your league on this.'
'I'm not drinking anymore Frank, I've given it up.'
He laughs. 'Oh, don't make me laugh you're George fucking Best!'
I look at him and decide best just to walk away, but I can feel Frank's eyes as I go. I head across to a smiling Charlie who stands up on seeing me. 'George mate, I'd like to introduce you to a new friend of mine, this is Gobbo Hornface. A fellow clown as you can see.'
Gobbo is dressed in full clown regalia. 'Nice to meet you Gobbo.'
We shake hands. 'You too George, a real pleasure, I'm a big fan.'
'What are you drinking George?' asks Charlie.
'I'm not mate. I've given it up.' A shocked Charlie scratches his curly wig, but then smiles wide again. 'Well good for you mate I'll just get you a glass of lemonade then.'
'Thanks Charlie.'
Charlie stands to go leaving just me and Gobbo sitting facing each other. 'Are you a full time clown Gobbo or is it just a hobby?'
Oh, between me and you George I'm not just a clown. I have many faces in my job.'

'Ah, I get it, you're a hack then, a private dick maybe?'
Gobbo laughs on hearing this. 'Not quite. Interesting news on you giving up the booze though?'
'I made a promise Gobbo and one I intend to keep.'
'Shame though don't you think George? All the fun of the fair. A lot more enjoyable with a drink in your hand?'
'I'm not so sure, all good things end Gobbo.' Gobbo raises his whiskey glass towards me. 'Well here's to you George, it takes some fucking bottle what you're doing.' Gobbo downs it in one then wipes his mouth on a sleeve. 'So who did you make the promise to then?'
'Well let's just say it's somebody you wouldn't like to upset.'
'Ha! He sounds just like the man I work for!'
'Hard work then is he your boss Gobbo?'
'Oh, you could say that George. He's a man who always gets what he wants and woe betides anyone who lets him down. Hell and fucking brimstone with him George.'
'Sounds a real hard-faced bastard.' Gobbo starts to laugh and pours another drink. 'He has his moments! There isn't anybody like him that's for sure.'
'What is it you do for this hard-faced sonofabitch Gobbo?'
'I collect mostly and sometimes I do a little acting.'
'Is he some kind of loan shark?'
Gobbo smiles. 'He most certainly is George. The best in his field. What that man gives he can easily take away.'
'Can't be easy for you sometimes?'
'What do you mean George?'
'Well threatening people to pay up what they owe?'
'I very rarely have to threaten. It's all done by trick and deception you see. I normally only show when there's no way back. When the party's over and they're resigned to the inevitable. I'm a fucking busy man. There's always somebody needs a good kick up the arse.'
'I'm not sure I understand you Gobbo?'
'It's quite simple really George. You see, I'm the Grim Reaper. I collect lost souls and my boss has a particular fondness for yours tonight.'

'You're just a fucking lunatic. Piss off!'
I'm in no state of mind to listen to this rubbish.
'Oh, wake up and smell the roses George. You know it's true.'
'Well I'm sorry to disappoint you Gobbo, but I've no intention of going anywhere with you. Whether it's to heaven, hell or some purgatory debtor's prison!'
'Do me a favour George! I only work for one and it isn't the man upstairs with the long beard and the white pearly gates who pretends all is well in his world. Took him only six days to make and a fucking eternity to break. Seems to enjoy letting his brethren suffer.'
'Not a fan then eh Gobbo?'
'So George you've had a friendly chat with the Red Indian? Always sticking his nose into my business him.'
'How'd you know about Charging Thunder?'
'Well I can't think of anybody else in my line of work who could've talked the great George Best off the booze.'
'He was very persuasive.'
'I must say I'm disappointed. I was looking forward to showing you off.'
'What do you mean showing me off?'
'You're a big prize George! A treasured soul. Bloody hell isn't it obvious? If you hadn't come off the booze tonight your pints of vodka and lemonade would've delivered you right into my lap. What do you think I'm doing in here? I don't enjoy dressing up as a fucking clown. I've got far better things to do.'
'Fucking hell Gobbo, excuse me for ruining your night! Tell me how exactly would it have happened and what makes you so certain I'm destined for hell?'
'It doesn't matter now but don't worry we'll meet again. Don't know where, don't when. But I know we'll meet again some sunny day! So, dress warm Georgie boy.'
Charlie returns from the bar. 'Here you go George mate, I've got you a glass of lemonade. Hey what's happened to Gobbo?'
I look back and he's vanished which I'm happy about.
'He had to shoot off fast to see a man about some horns.'

'Ah well, never mind George. He wasn't a proper clown anyway. I noticed he had his fucking wig on back to front!'
Trevor and Mary return to join us as does Father Finn, who has reappeared. Much to my relief.
'Everybody, I'm off the booze.'
'By god it's a miracle!' says the Priest. 'A darn fine one at that. I've been mixing but none here is interested in being saved tonight. But it seems you are George. Congratulations my son.'
'Well done George,' adds Trevor, as a smiling Mary leans across and kisses me on my cheek. 'Wonderful news! The boy from Belfast with the twinkle in his eye. Thank you for tonight.'
Mary and Trevor then kiss whilst holding hands.
'What's going on with you two?'
'Ships in the night George,' replies Trevor. 'Alone we were lost and together we found a port.'
'You were the lighthouse man George,' says Mary. 'You guided us home.'
'We've found love on your yellow brick road my friend,' adds Trevor. Charlie looks set to burst with delight on hearing. 'This is wonderful news! Congratulations both of you. By the way where's Frank? I think it would be nice to share a last drink together before morning comes and we all go our separate ways.'
I look over at the Priest and he smiles. 'Don't you worry George. Everything will be fine now.'
All fine? So Frank isn't going to kill him after all? At that moment it appeared like our time together, brief as it has been was set to end on a good note. But looking around there was still no sign of Frank. Something was going on. Time to switch and continue with his story for it was far from over. Frank had unfinished business...

OVER MY DEAD BODY

Frank is at the bar nursing a bottle of champagne when he feels a tug on his trousers. On looking Frank sees a dwarf dressed in a green Oz munchkin outfit. 'Hello Frank, the Scarecrow would like a word in your shell-like. Follow me.' The dwarf walks off a few yards only then to stop and turn around. 'Well come on then you best hurry up! He's not fucking happy with you.' Frank finishes the glass, picks a lighter up off the bar and follows the dwarf. He quickly catches up. 'Who is he here with?'
'The Monkey twins, Emerald Eddie and the schoolteacher. He's playing cards and losing big. After what's gone on as well I don't think I've ever seen him in such a bad, fucking mood. I hope you're ready to clip that Priest for your own sake.'
'Let me worry about that.'
The dwarf turns to stare at Frank. 'Big balls you Frank. Big fucking balls!' The dwarf scuttles on as they turn down a short corridor until arriving outside a door. He points towards it.
'In you go Frank, they're expecting you.'
Frank enters into a cigar and cigarette smoked-filled room. Sat playing poker at a small round-table is the top Manchester gang lord, Scarecrow. A small but robustly built middle-aged man with a balding head and slits for eyes that convey the evil in his soul. A true creature of the Mancunian underworld. Nobody knows his real name or background and none ever dare to ask. In this city his word is law amongst not just gangsters, but also those who pretend to uphold it. Scarecrow has the city's leading politicians, police and church figures in his pocket. For ten years he has ruled from the shadows. A dark empire financed mainly on the back of the sex trade. One that included the ghastly use of children to those sick and rich enough to pay for them. Once in Scarecrow's web influential people would be filmed and photographed, ensuring their loyalty remained guaranteed.

Some so famous their exposure to the newspapers could result in not just plunging Manchester into political, law and order and religious chaos, but indeed the entire country. Making certain Scarecrow's every order is adhered to are his inner sanctum. These men playing poker with him now. All murderous by nature and prepared to stoop to any levels to prove their loyalty to Scarecrow. The Monkey twins 31 year-old Michael and Martin Maguire. So nicknamed for their simian-like features due to birth defects. Though god help any whoever dared to mock them. Those who've made the mistake swiftly realising the Monkey twins have no sense of humour and enjoy torturing victims with hammers and nails. Then leaving their handiwork on view for an entire city to see so nobody dared try the same again.
 Then there is Emerald Eddie. The Scarecrow's Consigliore. If the Monkey twins are the chief muscle, Eddie is his main confidante. So named Emerald for his Mayo birthplace and fierce passion for his native Irish. The two rose together to stand tall, their former enemies now all dead, slaughtered without mercy. Their families also to ensure no future generations dared challenge them. Last at the table a slob of a 60 year-old with a fat belly, a dozen chins and red cheeked. The man is nicknamed the schoolteacher. Another who's true identity is unknown. He runs the Scarecrow's paedophile ring. The dark excesses for rape and torture especially children by his boss tolerated, only because of the huge amount of money this part of the business generates. Even for a man with a black soul such as Scarecrow, the perverted cruelty of the Schoolteacher leaves him cold. These are the men now stood facing the hitman.
 Frank Collins.
 'Pour yourself a drink Frank,' says Scarecrow, who speaks without even looking up from his card hand.
Emerald Eddie smiles on seeing Frank. 'How's trick's son?'
'All good thanks Eddie. I can't complain.'
Frank pours himself a glass of whiskey from a bottle on a nearby sideboard. 'Have you killed that fucking Priest yet?' asks the heavily wheezing Schoolteacher. Neither of the Monkey twins even bother to

acknowledge Frank's entrance. Both like their boss just concentrating on the playing cards. 'Let Frank have his drink before he answers Schoolteacher,' replies Scarecrow, who still doesn't make eye contact with Frank. 'Something tells me he's going to need it.'
Frank downs the whiskey and waits. After a full minute Scarecrow finally looks up. 'A little fucking munchkin has informed me that our problem is still breathing. Would you care to explain yourself Frank?' Suddenly, a loud knock at the door.
'Who is it!?' calls out Emerald Eddie
'It's Jimmy the DJ, I need a quick word.' A voice from outside the door. 'Let the ponce in,' says Scarecrow.
'Come on in Jimmy son!' shouts again Emerald Eddie.
In walks Jimmy the DJ. His long white hair and well known features off the television. 'What the fuck do you want Jimmy?' asks Scarecrow.
Jimmy has a manic smile. 'It's regarding our very famous politician friend in London. He wants to say thanks for the little present you delivered to him whilst he was staying here last week. He also said that when in the big house with the number ten on the front door he'd be sure to remember you.'
'Well you tell him from me we appreciate that,' replies Scarecrow. 'But also be sure to remind him that if he ever wishes to try and fuck me over, we have plenty of photos taken of his little adventure.'
'I will do Scarecrow.' Jimmy puts a cigar in his mouth and glares at Frank. 'Who are you fucking looking at!?'
'Calm down Frank!' says the Schoolteacher. 'Jimmy is a good friend of ours who does wonderful work with the community. He has his hand in many pies haven't you Jim boy. As well as other things.'
Jimmy starts to smile and Scarecrow looks up towards him.
 'Thanks for letting me know about our friend in London James, now fuck off.'
Jimmy the DJ turns to leave but on reaching the door turns to face Frank and smiles wide. 'I'm the real life Wizard of Oz Frank. I'm the smoke and mirrors. I'm the one they never see coming and never will.

It's a fucking dangerous thing around here these days to develop a conscience. Jimmy the DJ disappears.
Scarecrow turns his attention to Frank. 'Right then what the fuck are you playing at Frank?'
'I don't know what you mean?'
'Why is that grassing Priest sat out there with fucking George Best, a clown, a dwarf, a tart, and not being eaten by fucking worms in the Irwell?' All at the table are now staring towards Frank awaiting his answer. He takes out a cigarette and calmly lights it before inhaling. The atmosphere inside the small room suddenly turning a notch up from already tense to fearful.
'I've had a real good think about it Scarecrow and decided he didn't deserve to die.'
Frank goes into his pocket and throws a pile of notes on the table.
'Here's all your money back and just so you understand the Priest is under my protection now. Anybody tries to harm him they'll have to answer to me.' The Monkey twins look ready to leap on Frank but Scarecrow on noticing this puts a hand up. 'Calm down lads, there's obviously been a misunderstanding on our Frank's part here. He must have forgotten the rule that once you take on a job and the money has changed hands then there can be no going back. If you do so well the bible says you get fucking clipped. Had that slipped your mind Frank? Is it you're tired? I know how you work long hours. Maybe this can all still be sorted out. What do you say?'
'I'm not tired Scarecrow and my head is clear.'
Scarecrow picks the money up off the table and counts it. 'Well then we're going to have to agree to fucking disagree!' Scarecrow throws the wad of notes back in Frank's direction and it hits his chest. As the Monkey twins stand to rush him he pulls out a pistol fitted with a silencer and fires four times! The bullets taking out the twins, Schoolteacher and Emerald Eddie. Only the Scarecrow remains alive, the others slouched and lying dead around him. Frank points his pistol at Scarecrow, who sits in disbelief, his mind failing to register what's just occurred.
'Any last words Scarecrow?'

The Scarecrow wipes spattered blood off his face that belonged to the schoolteacher. 'You think killing me ends this Frank? You're fucking delusional. My people will ensure you don't live to see out the day.'
'Who says I want to? Besides look around, all your so called people are dead. It's over Scarecrow, anybody with links to you now will just cut and run.'
'I don't get this Frank. How many people have you killed for money? My money. Yet for this rat of a Priest who was going to burn our whole fucking world down you decide to be Gary Cooper in High Noon.'
'Kids, Scarecrow.'
'What?'
'Kids. They should be off limits, it's against all laws.'
'Oh, as if you didn't fucking know what was going on Frank?'
I didn't and if I had, I'd never have taken your money!'
'The Priest will still be killed Frank, there's simply too much at stake for him to be allowed to live.'
'Over my dead body.'
'Believe me it will be. By the way, Malcom Gore.'
'What is?'
'Malcom Gore, Frank. If you're going to put a bullet in my eye at least give me the courtesy to use my real name.'
Frank smiles. 'Whatever you're fucking called you die tonight. I'm going to end this sickness Malcom.'
'Where did all this suddenly come from Frank? What the fuck has happened to you?'
'The yellow brick road.'
'I don't understand?'
'Because of the wonderful things he does?'
'You're not making any fucking sense Frank?'
'I've met some people tonight Scarecrow, good people. I listened to their stories as one by one we became closer and they bared their souls. It made me realise that people like me and you, and these bastards lying dead at your feet. We have to go. They shouldn't have

to put up with us in their world. We're just like dog shit that they don't deserve to step in.'
'Frank, come on we can sort this?'
'It was a 10 year-old kid.'
'Who was?'
'Who broke his fucking heart crying to the Priest. A 10 year-old kid. You said before I was Gary Cooper, well fuck you Malcom Gore, that kid is going to burn your whole cesspit to the ground. He will be an avenging angel, with every breath I have left I'll make sure the likes of you get what's coming to help him.'
'Frank, please come on, I can give you names. We can go to the Police together, I'll blow the fuckin' lid on all of them. I promise, I know where the bodies are buried, the names involved that'll explode your fucking mind. This thing is huge!'
'Can't do I'm afraid. It's all too far over the rainbow now.'
'You kill me now and you die too Frank. People know your nature. They'll easily piece it all together. Those who have vested interest will hunt you down. Let's do a deal, you know it makes sense, let's me and you go and have a drink. A proper fucking drink!' Scarecrow motions towards the dead bodies around him. 'Just me and you Frank, we can run the show now.'
'Are you a religious man Malcom?'
'Why do you ask?'
'Do you believe in heaven and hell?'
'After what I've fucking seen and done Frank. Are you serious? Are you kidding me? What kind of god allows this stuff to happen to kids?'
Frank smiles. 'Maybe me and you could be sat next to each other on the rollercoaster downhill then?'
'Don't be too hasty Frank. Listen I've got two million quid that can be yours. It's in a house nearby buried in the back garden for emergencies. Why don't we get a taxi there just me and you? Now we've got rid of these fucking ponces we'll rule the roost. We can clean it all up. I never wanted it like this. That schoolteacher turned my stomach. Look at me a kid from Manchester. Do you really think

a scumbag like him could've turned me? It was all just about the money and the power. I know you're thinking of killing me…'
'Don't kid yourself Malcom. You know what's coming.'
A sweating Scarecrow tries to compose himself. Again, pointing to the dead bodies. 'See this lot around me, well fuck them! I never rated them. You were the one Frank, it was always you. All the jobs I handed out to you and you never asked questions. You nailed them. The bookie in Salford, the fucking loud mouth rat in Newton Heath. The bank robber in Moston. Tell me again where was the fucking conscience then Frank? You knew what we were into. You knew all the fucking time what was going on, you just lied to yourself and took the money. If I remember rightly you rode shotgun a few times for clients?'
'I thought I was taking them to working girls? Not kids.'
Scarecrow smiles. 'Pull the other one Frank, it's got bells on! Come on now wise the fuck up and put the gun away.'
'I know what I believed, now make your peace Malcom Gore.'
Make my peace with who Frank? Please don't do this. I don't want to die. This isn't how it's supposed to end for me.' Scarecrow is on his knees pleading.
'So long Scarecrow see you in hell!'
Scarecrow raises a hand. 'Frank no!' he screams as the bullet hit him between the eyes. Frank lowers the pistol.
 'Good fucking riddance.'

ALMOST SUNRISE

We're all sat chatting and Frank reappears. He looks at his watch.
'Almost sunrise. Why don't we go outside and watch it?'
Charlie laughs. 'Never took you for a romantic Frank.'
'There's a lot you don't know about me clown boy.'
We all stand to go out and I watch as Frank approaches the Priest.
'You need to disappear Father, leave the city today.'
'What have you done Frank?'
Frank takes a large wad of cash and puts it in Father Finn's pocket.
'Go and save souls elsewhere. Go home back to Ireland please.'
'I'll ask you again what have you done?'
'Only what I should have done a long time ago Father.'
Outside we go past the witch who smiles at us. Especially Frank.
'Ding dong the witch is dead!' she sings towards him.
Franks smiles and winks at her as he walks past. 'Run Frank! Run and don't ever stop!' she shouts.
We reach the door where Surrounded by the Enemy still stands with arms folded. 'I met a friend of your Grandfather's tonight.'
'I know George. Are you going to take his advice?'
'I'd be a fool not to. He's a wise man.'
'Then don't be a fool. He is the wisest George. He also has a huge tomahawk! Good luck.'
George laughs. 'Thanks but what's the score with you, are you of this world?'
'Not really,' he replies, while smiling wide.
'I'm from Salford!'
'There really is no answer to that!'
We head out just as the sun cast a morning shadow on the canal waters. Dancing speckles of light glimmer, sparkle and shine. The night is over and as a new day dawns we shelter our eyes.
So this it then,' says Charlie. 'I suppose from here we all go our separate ways now?'

'What are you going to do Charlie?' I ask.
'First thing George I'm going back to the circus for a shower, then get changed into something more comfortable! I realise now after an evening with you beautiful lot that I don't need no silly bloody wig and painted face to make people smile. I'm just going to be myself from now on. I've spent a lifetime hiding behind a mask, well not anymore. Charlie Canzone the clown is dead. Charlie Canzone the man is reborn!'
Me and Charlie shake hands. He does so also with The Priest, Trevor and Frank. 'So long Charlie you look after yourself.'
'Thanks Frank and cheers for calling me Charlie and not clown!'
'That's your name son. Be lucky'
Mary hugs Charlie tight and kisses him on both cheeks. 'I love you Charlie Canzone. You're a funny and lovely man.'
Charlie wipes a tear from his eye. 'A clown walks into a bar. Bet that hurt!' We all laugh even though it's a bloody, horrible joke! Charlie puts a hand up to say goodbye, turns and walks away. We watch as the clown with his big red floppy feet heads off.
Father Finn claps his hands together. 'Well you lovely people I too best be on my way. I have to be honest with you all last night I believed I'd lost my faith and the ground beneath my feet had fallen away. But you've all in your own way helped pick me up again. I can never thank you enough. May god bless you all my friends.'
Father Finn turns to Frank. 'Angels come in all shapes and sizes Frank. They even come wearing trilbies and carrying colt 45's!'
'It wasn't a colt 45 Father. You've watched too many Westerns!'
'You're a good man Frank Collins.'
'We're going to get off as well,' says Mary, her and Trevor holding hands. 'Good luck,' I say. 'I hope it works out for you both.'
Trevor shakes my hand and Mary hugs me tight. 'Oh Georgie, Georgie, I shall never forget this evening.'
'Mary Rose you're one beautiful lady.'
'You, George Best are a beautiful man!' Mary kisses me on the lips. 'We'll meet again George I promise you. One day we'll meet again and I'll be there when you need me with a rose in my hand.'

After saying goodbye to Frank they too are gone leaving just me and him. 'So George I suppose this is our goodbye. I'm not a great fan of them to be honest.'
'So long Frank.'
'Take care George. Best of luck with staying off the booze. I'll be rooting for you both on and off the pitch mate.'
'I'm determined to do it Frank. If I told you what happened last night, you'd think I was mad but for the first time in a long while, I can see straight again. I feel I've been given a great chance to sort myself out and I don't intend to blow it.'
'Good to hear son. You take care now.'
'What are you going to do Frank?'
'Well first I'm going to get some sleep then I'm going to save the world. Be lucky George.'
Frank walks away and I'm left alone. It now feels a lifetime ago that I first found Charlie threatening to jump off the Blackfriars Bridge. Then, the Priest, Frank, Trevor, Mary. The mermaid, the Red Indian. Nobody will ever believe me. Nobody. Was it the acid? Did that free up my mind to help me sort myself out? If so the question remains. Charging Thunder said a friend asked him to talk to me but who? I still don't know and I probably never will. I decide to head back to the Brown Bull and get cleaned up. Then instead of a Sunday session I'll go home. Already I feel better in myself. I'm going to miss my new friends but as the old saying goes…
'Today is the first day of the rest of my life!'
Or something like that!

I come off the canal onto the main road at the bottom end of Deansgate. As I head up the steps a car speeds past me and just for a second, I think I see Frank sat in the back of it between two other men. I rub my eyes, I'm so tired. It couldn't have been? I continue on the road still bereft of traffic, the pavement long and empty. Silent and still. This suits me but not in a sad, lonely way. I'm genuinely happy. No cloak of darkness needed and hopefully not ever again.
'So you've had a good night then George?'

I turn around and stood facing me is Charlie once more.
'Charlie, I thought you'd gone back to the circus?'
He smiles. 'I've a confession to make. I'm not really who I claimed to be.'
'Not the fucking News of the World please?'
Charlie laughs. 'No George I'm not the News of the World!'
'Well who then?'
'I'm your guardian angel George. The clown story impressive I must admit. I apologise for my little white lie but I needed to get you to meet Charging Thunder.'
'So you were the friend he spoke about?'
'Yes. I was out of ideas George. I was worried watching you drinking yourself into a stupor every night and knew I needed to do something drastic. My responsibility after all. You're a full-time job and more mate!'
'Well Charlie if that's your real name. Your plan worked. If this revelation hasn't made me want a drink then nothing will.'
'Charlie is my real name. We can't meet again now until, well let's not talk about that. I'll be seeing you George.'
'One last question Charlie.'
'Of course George, ask away?'
'Please tell me you don't really support Manchester City?'
Charlie smiles wide. 'Don't be ridiculous George. I'm a guardian angel not a clown!'
Then he was gone…
'Bye Charlie.'

A VODKA AND LEMONADE

I let myself in at the Brown Bull and go upstairs to my room. Feeling exhausted I collapse on the bed. I look at the ceiling and it starts to spin. I shut my eyes. I'll just have thirty minutes sleep then head home. My head on the pillow, my mind reeling, what a night! The madness of it, the sheer bloody madness!
It's the music from the juke box downstairs that wakes me up. Smokey Robinson's *Tears of a Clown*. This makes me smile. I look at my watch and it's ten minutes past two, meaning the pub is going to be full. I contemplate sneaking out the side entrance but then think no, I'll just have a lemonade before I go. If any of the boys are about I can let them see the new George Best! I head downstairs and come into view.
A cheer goes up from the entire room!
Many of this lot are only here because of me. They feed off my presence, I'm like a drug to them. They buy me a drink and then they think I'm one of them, well no more. At our table is the usual motley crew. Good mates but I know now deep down I can't risk their wonderful company if I'm to stay sober.
'Hello George, good night was it?' smiles Parky.
'Who was the lucky girl or girl's George?' asks a laughing George QC.
'Afternoon George mate,' says Waggy. 'What can I get you mate?'
I sit down. 'I'll just have a lemonade please Waggy.'
They all start laughing.
'Fucking hell George, your hilarious!' chides Parky.
'No I'm serious, just lemonade. I'm off the booze.'
'Well bugger me sideways George,' adds Waggy. 'A pint of lemonade coming up?' He stands and walks over to the bar.
'So what's brought this miracle about George?' asks George QC

'A promise to a friend George.' Waggy returns from the bar.
'I'm just off to the loo George. There's a guy at the bar insisting he knows you and wants to buy you the pint of lemonade. He's going to bring it over.' I glance across and the man does appear somewhat familiar but I can't think from where. Over he comes with my pint and his own. The man places the drink in front of me.
'Hello again George here you go mate.'
I look closer at his face. He's wearing a pin-stripe suit, combing his slicked-black hair and has the appearance of a lothario man about town type. If getting on a little. 'Thank you, you say we've met before. I'm sorry, I don't remember?'
'Oh, I've change a little since then George. A toast first if you don't mind?'
'No, not at all.'
'What the man gives he can easily take away! Cheers George.'
'Cheers.'
I drink and immediately can taste the vodka as it vanishes down my throat and my belly goes ice cold.
'I just asked for fucking lemonade?'
He smiles. 'So your friend said. But I believed you needed a stiff livener after all that went on last night? Thought it may make you see sense.' The penny drops. the painted smile and the wig. Then that fucking toast. 'What the man gives, he can easily take away.'
Gobbo. The Grim Reaper.
'Down the hatch George. All is fair in love, death and war.'
Gobbo walks back into the midst of a crowded pub. At first I think about going after him but then I look at my glass, my pint of vodka and lemonade. I take another swig, a large one and another.
And another…

LAST ORDERS (Part Two)

London. Chelsea. Cromwell Hospital. 2010. (Part Two)
I was tricked, manipulated, call it what you want, but it was forty years later before I found myself finally in this bed with no hope and resigned now to finally dying. I lived the life after that evening. I drank and I fucked with an almost desperation to blank out the horrible feeling of letting down my friends. Especially breaking the promise I made to Charging Thunder. That so hurt, it killed me inside because everything he said came true. 'Where did it all go wrong George?' Well in so many people's eyes it didn't. But it did. In my heart and soul I never left that fucking canal path. I was angry because I was duped. Then again I never had enough courage to just spit out the vodka and say fuck this! Oh no, not me, the temptation proved overwhelming and on I went. But hey it's gone and I find myself past the last bell. Time gentlemen please for the passing of the soul of this soon to be departed is underway. I'm not scared, just tired and ready because now I think it's time to go. I open my eyes and it's such a beautiful sight. My friends have come to see me cross over. There's Charlie in his clown attire. My guardian angel. He's seen enough since that night to write a book, maybe three books! The Priest, Frank, Trevor and Mary. All smiling. Mary walks across and hands me a rose. 'A rose from Mary Rose, Georgie boy. One night with you lasts a lifetime for anybody else.' Mary kisses me on the cheek. Then I see him. 'I'm sorry I let you down Charging Thunder.' 'As we say in Salford, no bother George. You're over the rainbow now.'

THE TALE OF FRANKIE ANGELS

"It was Christmas Eve in the city that can't sleep, and all wasn't quiet and still".

PROLOGUE
To the riverside (Part One)

Today. Christmas Eve.
Mancunia.
Somewhere in the North.
It's two hours to midnight and a ferocious snowstorm has covered the city that can't sleep. The assassin Frankie Angels is in the back of a black taxi cab staring through the window trying to figure out what's just happened on this Christmas Eve. Frankie's eyes appear transfixed by the relentless, blinding snowflakes falling. Time is short now, and the taxi driver in his red and white festive bobby hat busy desperately trying to get Frankie involved in a conversation is not helping anything.
'You going anywhere special tonight?' he asks, with a huge grin on his face. 'I'm sure you've got someone lined up for under the mistletoe eh? The lucky so and so.'

Frankie ignores him and just continues to stare out trying to equate the evening's mad events and make sense of them. A song is playing on the radio.

Frank Sinatra's *Have yourself a merry little Christmas.*
Frankie was named after 'Old Blue Eyes' but has no love for Christmas. There's no magic, no festive spirit and certainly no goodwill to all men and women. Too many bad memories, plus if these things truly existed Frankie Angels would be out of a job.

Merry Christmas one and all?
You must be fucking joking!
'So, you're the silent type,' continues the taxi driver, in his annoying irritating manner. Now he's blowing kisses at Frankie through the mirror. For one second Frankie contemplates. Besides, what does one more dead asshole matter after tonight…

ACT ONE

IN THE BEGINNING

Many years before.
To hit fast and kill has always been an absolute necessity for Frankie Angels. A talent one grim maybe, but a sight to behold that's been needed since a young teenager. Though only ever to those who had it coming. Because for Frankie, it's always been nothing more than just a journey of survival. At just 9 years-old Frankie was sent to an orphanage after both parents were killed in a police shootout. Memories are very vague being so young, but one thing that did resonate for Frankie, was the Frank Sinatra music both parents loved, and how they adored and doted on their only child.
'You're our whole world sweet Frankie, and we'll make sure your life is a far safer road to travel than ours whatever it takes.'
  Frankie remembers like it was yesterday that awful moment the Priest and the policeman first came to the school and being taken out of class. Then crying and sobbing after being told they had been killed till the tears had run dry. Screamed at and slapped across the face by a man wearing a dog collar.
  'You were the child of devil's now you're coming with me!'
The first of a million and more heinous words uttered by the Priest, Father Patrick Cassidy to Frankie. It was only years later that somebody let slip to Frankie the reason for such a cruel jibe made by a man of the blessed cloth. Frankie's parents it turned out were going around killing Priests known to them as being part of a paedophile ring. Both as children suffered at the hands of such scum and had vowed to seek revenge. One night all went horribly wrong and after a

failed attempt to kill Cassidy, they themselves were killed. Shot dead by three crooked policemen lying in wait.
'We got them Wendell! We've earned our money, now let's get the fuck out of here!'
In the city that can't sleep true power existed in the shadows, where none dared to venture, and the unholy abuse carried on unabated. There was no loving god just Father Patrick Cassidy. A devil with a crucifix and a free pass to do whatever the hell he liked.
Frankie was sent to a Catholic school home, that was more like a children's brothel for the city's supposed grand, good and fucking perverse. It was called *Our Lady of the Light*. Being such a beautiful child meant Frankie was in much demand, but survived such wretched horrors by drifting into another world and a time that existed with a Frank Sinatra soundtrack playing loud. Frankie's main tormenter was Cassidy, whose perverted habit was to make Frankie kneel and pray before the abuse began. Aged fifteen, enough was enough and a life of squalor on the run was preferable to the ritual beatings and rapes occurring in the home. Frankie ran away but never forgot those faces that came to visit in the night vowing revenge. There were four to deal with, plus the Priest. His would be a special kind of death. In time Frankie was planning on getting them all.
A rare chink of sunlight, albeit temporarily appeared for Frankie in the manner of a Northside club owner and gangster called 'Kind' Eddie Johnson. So named for his countless good deeds in giving money to children's charities and donations for churches. Eddie's name was praised across the city. Some even said prayers for him. On the surface a pillar of the community, beneath a snake. His true reasons for a supposedly kind heart hid a much darker truth.
"Kind" Eddie had a smile and a wink and a cheque for all occasions in the public eye. But the truth being "Kind" Eddie always hid his true nature until he simply could not help himself. Another creature of the night. Another paedophile and he had his eye on Frankie Angels. Working up from cleaning tables and washing glasses in the club and running errands, Frankie became a favourite of "Kind" Eddie. One of a trusted few allowed into his inner sanctum. The gangster was fond,

far too fond of this quiet but tough kid who possessed a touch of class, and always showed proper respect.

'I'm going to look after you Frankie,' he would say.

'Stick with me kid. Do what I tell you, keep your nose clean and mouth shut, and you'll go far in this business.'

'Thanks Eddie, you're a good man.'

After all what Frankie had gone through, "Kind" Eddie became some kind of father figure. That rarity in Frankie's life. A good man. A decent man. Then, the mask slipped. One night after a late drinking session a drunken "Kind" Eddie shown his true self and attempted to abuse Frankie.

'Come on Frankie Angels, you owe me.' Only to see the youngster put a carving knife through his eye. Killing him softly as the knife went deep. "Kind" Eddie has been murdered by a young ungrateful scumbag!' screamed out the do-gooders.

'An angel is on his way to heaven.' But Frankie knew the truth if nobody else did.

Justice was swift, brutal and refusing to even listen to Frankie's plea of self-defence, the gavel came down and a hard-nosed judge, handed out a ten-year sentence without flinching.

'I'm sending you away for a long time Frankie Angels, so you may learn the errors of your wicked ways. The city that never sleeps may even get some shut eye with young brutes like you off the streets of Mancunia.' Behind the city's Strangedays prison walls, lined with watch towers and guards armed to the teeth with shotguns and sniper rifles, it was like a school for rascals, and Frankie learnt lessons swiftly. But every day still remained a fight for survival. Though young and slight in size, it soon became apparent Frankie was not one to be messed with. Lightning quick with a blade and faster with both fists, Frankie was left alone and even took to looking after other prisoners much less capable. Once the word went out 'They're with Frankie' the bullying stopped. One such inmate was cell mate Jackie O'Malley, who Frankie helped out more than once. Jackie would never forget this and would in time put in a good word for Frankie with someone who all but ran the city that never sleeps.

'If you ever come across someone called Frankie Angels, Uncle Jimmy you could do a lot worse than bringing the kid on board. Frankie is fucking fearless.'

After serving the full ten years on release, a short spell in the Army followed for Frankie and this only served to brutalise even further. Never one for taking orders, Frankie was a walking timebomb and after spending more time in the stockade than actual uniform was finally thrown out. Frankie's commanding officer who knew the back story argued strongly with his superiors for one last chance, but they were adamant. This was a soldier simply out of control who had no respect for authority. 'No chance Frankie, you're out. I tried, but you want to fight the entire world Frankie Angels, and that's no good to the army. We just need you to fight the enemy. You don't see uniform you just see people.'

'Give me a gun Captain, I'll win your war.'

'I dare say you would Frankie, but then you'd start another one.'

Civilian life proved equally troubling and it wasn't long before crime became a constant partner. Frankie's talent were noted. A hired hand, a freelance assassin. First though there was the crimes of the past to be dealt with. The demons of childhood. Four well known past and present faces from the city, a senior policemen, a politician, a famous soap star and a well-known Mr fix-it DJ, with long, white scraggly hair, and customary cigar in his mouth were all found hanging, with a card around their necks declaring *SCUM*.

Only Father Patrick Cassidy still walked this earth. Rumours were he had fled the city and even moved abroad to escape Frankie's revenge. but Frankie would bide his time and hopefully one day.

Now the four had been dealt with Frankie could move on and start thinking about earning a decent living. It was always scumbags. Mostly it was out of town contracts to keep life simple, because the city that never sleeps was a complicated place to do business in. Secret alliances meant you never really knew who you were working for, and to kill the wrong person spelt trouble, and possible your own end. So Frankie's motto to stay alive became 'Never kill on your own doorstep.'

There was a bank job. Six grand, easy money for the Christmas festivities. No civilians hurt, the police were not interested, because they had far bigger problems to deal with. All appeared to have gone off perfectly. But then in one of the backstreet pubs on the Northside, where folk of similar minds gathered, Frankie was given word the city's most feared gangster's, Jimmy 'The Vicar' O'Malley, who ran the Northside, wanted a meeting with him straight away.
'You should've paid him his dues from the bank job Frankie. You're in a lot of trouble now. You've committed the worst crime possible in the Vicar's eyes.'
He was known as the Vicar because of O'Malley's time back in Ireland as a man of the cloth, but after realising the calling wasn't for him, the dreary confessions and monastic lifestyle, the Vicar found his true vocation across the water in the city that can't sleep. Murder, corruption and absolute mayhem. All were vices the Vicar excelled in and enjoyed. It wasn't long before he stalked out his own patch. Blessed be those who help themselves,
 for they shall inherit Mancunia.

THE VICAR

The Vicar lives in a luxurious gated residence known as the Riverside settlement. His personal apartment is at the top of the tallest skyscraper that overlooks the Vicar's Northern domain. All seeing and hearing from this vantage point. He misses nothing. It sits on the River Irwellian that slices through the city. Hidden beneath it's dark waters lay buried many dark secrets for the dead tell no lies or truths. They just rot. The city is split between four families who each run their own patch. The North, South, East and West. An uneasy peace exists between what is called The *Foundation*. If everyone stays within their given realms then business carries on in a calm peaceful manner. But woe betide an outsider, another gang ever dares to interrupt the status quo. They would be hit so hard and vanish in the blink of an eye. Cut up as instant treats for the Irwellian fishes who never went hungry, but just got bigger.

In the midst of a sweeping, fully-blown snowstorm, a pensive Frankie Angels arrives to meet the Vicar. Dressed immaculate as ever in a smart suit and trilby, Frankie walks across the swing bridge towards a huge electronic gate. Suddenly, they start to open and waiting behind are two black-suited guards clearly shivering. These are two of the Vicar's inner circle and most trusted bodyguards. The Irish Quinlan brothers, Kane and Abel. Suitably named from biblical characters by their alcoholic father, whose idea of fatherly love was to brutalise and sodomise both his boys until they killed him for it. Much admired around these parts, the brothers can easily be described as psychotic, merciless killers but only in matters of *Foundation* business. Mid-twenties, both are tall with dark murderous eyes, black hair and devilishly handsome in a satanic kind of way.

'Well, I'll be,' smiles Kane. 'Look whose coming our way.'

Frankie is greeted by both with a warm handshake and a bearhug.
'Hey Frankie, how you keeping?'
'I'm good Kane.'
'Looking sharp as ever Frankie Angels,' adds Abel. 'You keeping out of trouble?'
Frankie smiles. 'I'll let you fellas know in the next hour or so.'
'Ah, you'll be fine Frankie,' adds Kane. 'Relax, if the old man wanted you dead he wouldn't waste his time by having you come all the way over here.' Still the snow falls heavy and the bitter cold wind sweeps across the three. Abel puts an arm around Frankie. 'Come on, let's get you inside. I'm freezing my fucking balls off here.'
Escorted by the brothers Frankie is taken up to the apartment overlooking the city that can't sleep. Kane and Abel start to leave, but Kane then turns back towards Frankie. 'Don't worry you'll be fine, we've heard nothing bad and it would've been us he would ask to slot you. And that's not happened. So, you're good.'
'Thank you Kane.'
Frankie smiles. 'That's good to know!'
Waiting for Frankie on the balcony sits the Vicar. He has heard them entering the apartment. The Vicar is a huge man in a creased white shirt, black braces and a large stomach hanging over his pants, but this is a man who gives off an aura of real power. Some men just don't have to try too hard. Frankie is deeply worried about the bank job and now so regrets as is the tradition, and indeed number one rule on the Northside.
'Don't forget to feed the Vicar.'
Knowing Frankie has come inside, the Vicar looks over towards his bodyguard. 'I'll be fine Nathaniel, go inside and tell the kid I'm ready to see him.' Nathaniel Butesi is an ex-Paratrooper and ex-Britannia Heavyweight champion, and now the Vicar's shadow as his bodyguard. Butesi would give up his own life in a second for the boss. Once upon a time Butesi took a dive for the Vicar in the boxing ring that brought him shame, but also enough money to live comfortably

for the rest of his life. Unfortunately, Butesi was a degenerate gambler with an unhealthy, far too huge taste for powder and prostitutes. Everything went, not a penny left. In stepped the Vicar to hand him a job and more importantly, straighten out his addictions. Now Butesi has only one passion left in his life. To keep the Vicar safe, and god help anyone who ever tried to harm him.

He heads off the balcony to see Frankie waiting.
'You can go on but I'll be fucking watching you,' growls Butesi. Frankie nods, not even daring to reply and swiftly heads to see the Vicar. With a flick of his hand the Vicar motions for Frankie to sit down facing him. He says nothing for a few moment, just simply stares at his guest. 'It's good to finally meet you Frankie Angels.'
'You too Mr O'Malley sir.'
'You won't be aware of this but I've been watching you for a long time. I'm impressed.'
'Thank you.'

From inside the apartment Frank Sinatra is on the radio singing *White Christmas* and it resonates onto the balcony loud.
'I fucking love this time of year. Frank is the king for me. What about you Frankie, do you love your name sake?'
'Not so much Christmas but I love Sinatra. I got it off my parents.'
'The Vicar smiles, 'I thought as much, I can tell by your attire. So I hear you've been busy playing with banks?'
'I need to talk to you about that Mr O'Malley.'

The Vicar pours two glasses of whiskey from a bottle on the table between them and passes one over to Frankie. 'I can only guess my cut got lost in the post. Or maybe I need to cut the head off my fucking postman because he robbed me. What do you think?'
Frankie realises it's pointless to lie so just comes clean.
'I made a mistake. I can only promise to make it up to you.'
Unexpectedly, the Vicar breaks into a huge smile.
'You really think I give a fuck about your money?'
Frankie appears shocked. 'Well if it's not about the money, what am I doing here?'

The Vicar raises his glass. 'Share a toast with me. Let's drink to an old friend of both mine and yours. To that good soul "Kind" Eddie Johnson.' Alarm bells immediately go off in Frankie's head.
'Ah don't you worry your pretty head about it,' replies the Vicar. 'I'm just playing with you. I know he was a sick fuck and his thing for kids. Johnson had it coming Frankie. If not you some other poor wretch would've stuck a knife in. What you did, no one could ever blame you for and to get ten years for it. That was just fucking criminal. An outrage.' The Vicar smiles at his own joke then points out over the balcony.
  'Look out there Frankie.' The city that can't sleep is lit up by a million lights. 'Beneath those lights so many schemers, chancers and dreamers. They're the fucking worst, let me tell you. But they're all looking for that edge to get a little in front or make a move. There's an ocean of money out there to be claimed that I'm missing out on. Things need organising. You know what I see Frankie, I see a city crying out for change. One that's being dragged four ways.' The Vicar turns to face Frankie. 'I've had enough of it. I need to ask you a serious question, and I need an honest answer.'
'Ask away Mr O'Malley.'
'Can you help me do this? Can you help me clean up this fucking mess and bring it all under one flag? My flag. I don't want to share the cake anymore more Frankie, I want it all for myself.'
'If I can. What exactly is it you want off me?'
The Vicar re-pours both their glasses to the brim. 'I want you to come and work for me. I believe you're special. You've got something I need.' He hands Frankie the drink. 'I know how good you are at how you make a living kid. Those four bastards you got rid of. I want you to do the same for me. Take away any problems I have. Make them disappear. Do you understand me?' The look of sheer disbelief on Frankie's face surprises even the Vicar. How the hell does he know about the four?
  'What, you're telling me I'm wrong and you can't do this?'
'No,' says Frankie. 'I just don't understand how you know?'

'This is my city Frankie. I own it. Forget how I know. I know everything. The rats are my eyes and they get everywhere even under the fucking dirt.'

'Okay then, but why me, what have I done to earn such an honour? You must have a thousand guys working for you more suited. Take Kane and Abel for instance they would do anything for you.'

'No, no, it's not that simple. You're different to them.'

'In what way?'

'You come very highly recommended. I'm told you have character and are naturally loyal. That's a fucking rarity these days.'

'Dogs are loyal.'

The Vicar smiles at Frankie's remark. 'Look, everyone who works for me, family apart, does so out of money. My people are loyal, yes, but loyalty can be bought and so can betrayal. Also their faces are too well known throughout the city. You might also say I have trust issues with some of them.'

'And what makes you so sure you can trust me?'

'I can't fully, I'm going with my instincts. There's something else.'

'Go on.'

'When you was in prison. Do you remember a certain Jackie O'Malley?'

'Sure, I remember Jackie well. We were good friends inside. Is he a relation to you?' The Vicar crosses himself remembering how he himself put a bullet in Jackie's head.

'I need to be honest with you Frankie regarding Jackie. He was a fucking addict and selling drugs to kids on the Northside to feed his habit. I found out, for anyone else selling the powder to kids is an instant death sentence. But I gave him a chance to get clean because he was blood, but he was bad blood. He refused my offer and started selling to kids again. That was it. I felt if it had to be anyone, it must be me. There are lines that cannot be crossed and sadly Jackie crossed them twice. The Foundation knew of what he had done. This is our only rule. A tick in our box off Saint Peter at the gates of heaven against all the crosses. Good for the soul, good for public image. So, I had no choice. If you haven't got trust Frankie, you've got nothing.'

Frankie has listened closely. Jackie was his friend but he had no knowledge of this. 'You'd be right to trust me Mr O'Malley, but there's just one thing I need you to know.'
'Speak up,' replies the Vicar, 'Let me hear it.'
'I'll never kill anyone who doesn't have it coming to them. No civilians. Just bad people.' For a moment, the Vicar is angered by Frankie's insistence on this but swiftly realises it's just a passing thought. There will be plenty of time in the future to work on Frankie's soul when the immediate business has passed.
He smiles. 'I see no problems with that. Welcome to the family Frankie Angels.' The two shake hands. 'Okay then, there's no time like the present Frankie.' The vicar leans in closely. 'I already have one for you to break your cherry with for me. Let me tell you about the scumbag…'

ACT TWO

PULLING THE TRIGGER

It's the day before Christmas Eve in the city that can't sleep. Frankie Angels is sat at the bar in The *Strangler's Inn* nursing a large whiskey. Frank Sinatra's *My Funny Valentine* is playing on the jukebox. Every time the door opens Frankie's eyes glance over. Finally, the woman they call Rosie May enters. Small with long black scraggly hair, a pretty if dirt-caked face with huge dark almond eyes, and dressed almost in rags. She loves and lives to drink more than most, a temper fast and none dare take advantage for they risk a knife between the eyes. Rosie May is here to pass a message onto Frankie. An address of a Northside drug dealer selling powder to kids outside a school gate. She sidles up at the bar and passes over a small piece of paper. 'Hi Frankie. He's there alone now.'
Frankie reads it.
'Thank you Rosie.'
'My pleasure darlin' anything for you. So, how about a drink for Rosie May huh?'
Frankie motions to the bartender. 'Two more whiskeys please Joe.'
'Sure thing, coming up Frankie.'
'Just leave the bottle Joe!' calls out Rosie.
Joe looks across to Frankie who nods back as if to say it's okay.
'How have you been keeping Rosie May?'
'Not to good, I ache without you Frankie. Life is dull. Why don't you come around no more huh? We had a lot of fun together.'

Rosie puts a hand on Frankie's knee. 'Come on now Rosie, it was just the one time. By the way you look awful. What's going on, what the hell are you doing with yourself?'
'I'm drinking Frankie, I'm drinking far too much So I forget.'
'Forget what doll?'
Rosie May smiles but it's one tinged with sadness. 'I honestly don't know Frankie, but it must be working because I can't remember.'
Frankie takes out a bundle of notes and slides them into Rosie's hand. 'Here you go Rosie. You have to promise me you're going to eat proper?' Rosie slides the notes under her blouse.
'I promise you Frankie. I do, I do!'
'Good girl, I have to go. Thanks for the you know what.'
'Get the sonofabitch Frankie. He's poison.'
Frankie kisses Rosie May gently on the lips then head off. She watches Frankie head out the door. 'Hey Frankie!'
Frankie turns around to see Rosie smiling wide.
'Don't you go breaking my heart Frankie by getting yourself killed okay. I love you Frankie Angels!' Frankie winks at her and pulls the trilby down low. 'Eat Rosie May. Merry Christmas!'
Rosie May pours another glass as Frankie disappears out the door. She holds the glass up high. 'To Frankie Angels my one true love! Merry Christmas baby. Don't you ever fucking change.'
Slowly Rosie May fills the glass once more. 'Don't you ever change Frankie.'

'This is it. Stop here please driver.'
Frankie pulls up in a taxi directly opposite the drug dealer's 'Dead-leg' Dobson's apartment. Dobson is Frankie's trial hit for the Vicar and it has to go well. The idea of this man selling powder to kids abhors Frankie, meaning there will be no doubts whatsoever when it comes to pulling the trigger. Dobson is one of the bad people. After paying the driver it's just a short walk up a set of steps to Dobson's door. Inside, there's the loud noise of a dog barking. Frankie knocks on and doesn't have to wait long before the latch turns and Dobson stands facing with a growling bull mastiff on a lead alongside

him. Mid-twenties, white and bearded, his neck and arms covered in Swastika Nazi regalia tattoos. Dobson glares at Frankie with a look of utter disdain on his face. 'Yeah, what do you want?'
Frankie smiles. 'I'm here with a message for you.'
'A message, is that right?' sneers Dobson. 'Who the fuck is this message from? If it's that's asshole landlord, I'm not getting rid of the dog. Tell him to come round himself and I'll set Adolf on him.'
What a rotten name for a dog, thinks Frankie. No wonder it has a bad attitude to life, like its owner. 'No it's not off your landlord.'
'Well who the fuck is it then?'
Frankie reaches inside a jacket pocket and pulls out a letter with Dobson's name on. 'This is for You.'
'I can't read, you're going to have to read it for me.'
'I think we should go inside Mr Dobson. You may want to sit down after I've read it to you.'
'Just read the fucking thing for me man before I set my boy here on you!' shouts Dobson, into Frankie's face, as the dog starts to growl louder showing its teeth. Frankie can now see where it got the name 'Absolutely no problem,' replies Frankie, remaining cool. He rips opens the envelope. 'Here we go. 'It has come to our attention that you've been dealing drugs to schoolchildren at St Stephen's High and The *Foundation* have found you guilty.' On hearing this Dobson's face turns ashen-grey. 'As you know this is totally forbidden on the Northside and the penalty for doing so is execution.' Before Dobson can blink Frankie bursts into action firing two bullets. One at the dog and the other into Dobson's forehead killing both instantly. Standing over them Frankie calmly puts the letter back in a pocket and sighs. 'I didn't even get the chance to finish it. Merry Christmas scumbag.'
A quick glance around and Frankie walks back down the steps. There's no sense of guilt just simply the feeling of a job done well. Frankie starts to make a phone call to the Vicar.
'O'Malley speaking.'
'Our friend and his dog won't be at any school gates no more?'
'Well done Frankie, great work! Any problems?'
'None at all. Who's next boss?'

The Vicar laughs. 'Hey that's enough for one night, go and enjoy yourself, it's party time in Mancunia tonight at this time of year. Go have a drink and get yourself laid Frankie. We'll speak again tomorrow.' The line goes dead.
What now thinks Frankie? It's far too early to go home. Too much time to think about the past. Frankie just needs to keep heading forward in life and never look back. Suddenly, from deathly black skies, the snow starts to fall heavy again. Frankie puts out a hand to catch it and feel the icy cold touch. In the distance is the hum of a freight train rattling leaving the city that can't sleep. With going home out of the question Frankie decides to go and have a good drink and see where the night leads to. Vanish down the many back streets, the hidden drinking joints that exist for people like Frankie. Those who don't know what they're searching for, but like the city in which they live find no solace in sleep. Along the white coveted pavements Frankie traipses until finally a black cab appears on the scene. 'Where do you want to go friend?' asks the driver. Frankie takes off the trilby and smiles. 'One guess. Where do you think?'
'No problem. Live and let live I say. I know just the place,' he says smiling back. 'Leave it to me, we'll be there in fifteen.'

THE CHINAMAN

Christmas Eve morning.
Frankie awakes to the sound of Frank Sinatra on the radio singing *Killing me Softly*, and a bed with a beautiful, naked blond girl either side. Both are still fast asleep. Then for Frankie, the first death knell of a killer hangover hits hard. There's a swift, gentle shuffle off the bed being careful not to wake the girls. Finally, a fully dressed Frankie puts on the trilby and takes a last look at what's still lying in wonderful tranquillity on the bed. Now wrapped in each other's arms. Frankie smiles at the sight and last night's vague, but so sweet memories. 'So long girls.'
On leaving the building Frankie's phone buzzes and the Vicar's name shows up. 'Christ he's early.'
'Good morning Mr O'Malley.'
'Hey Frankie, how you doing. How was your night?'
'I had a really good time thanks.'
'That's great, listen, what have you got planned for today?'
'Nothing really, I was just going to head back to my apartment and probably watch some tv. I think the Wizard of Oz is on.'
'Ah, fuck the Wizard of Oz! That's not happening because nobody should be alone on Christmas Eve. Get your trilby ass over here now straight away Frankie.' Frankie winces at the thought of this.
 'Boss it's okay honest, I prefer…'
'I'm not taking no for an answer Frankie Angels. Get over here that's a fucking order. Okay?'
'Yes,' sighs Frankie, 'I'm heading over now.'
'Besides, there may be something that needs sorting later. I'll tell you all about it when you get here. Jump on a fucking sleigh if you have to!'
'Yes sir.'

'The Wizard of Oz. Fucking hell Frankie, isn't this city weird enough for you?' The line goes dead and Frankie takes off the trilby.
'Hey mister!' Frankie turns to face a young boy no more than seven or eight. 'Oh, I'm sorry.'
'It's okay,' smiles Frankie, 'It happens all the time, no harm done.' Frankie puts the trilby back on. 'What can I do for you little guy?' The boy smiles back and shrugs his shoulders, 'I just wanted to say Merry Christmas!' Frankie's eyes well up as he rustles the boy's hair. 'You too!' Frankie walks off fast trying desperately to stop the tears falling. 'Where the hell did they come from? Sort yourself out Frankie Angels, come on now.'

Deciding to walk in an effort to get rid of the hangover Frankie heads off. Suddenly, the thought occurs that to turn up empty handed at the Vicar's would not be just rude and bad mannered. 'It's Christmas for damn sake. 'I better get him a present.' Across the street, a chink of light amid the many shutters and closed signs shines bright.

Mr Chang's Magical Gift shop.
A window display of dancing wooden figures with smiling eyes on strings and never-ending waterfalls catch Frankie's eye. So much that the owner, a smiling Mr Chang notices and waves through the window. Now Frankie is feeling guilty and obliged to go across and buy something. On entering Mr Chang bows to Frankie in traditional Chinese manner. 'Good morning, I wish to you a very merry Christmas.' A smiling Frankie bows back in similar manner, this hardly helping the still raging hangover!
'Merry Christmas.'
Mr Chang stares long and hard at Frankie, his eyes showing real concern. Then he smiles once more. 'I have just the thing for you please just wait here a moment.' Mr Chang vanishes behind some blinds into a back room. Frankie looks around and notices a selection of charms. One above all catches the eye. Beautiful doesn't do it justice and Frankie stares utterly enchanted. Mr Chang returns holding a small teacup containing what appears steaming black mud.
'This will cure your hangover but all must be drunk in one go.'
'How did you know I had a hangover?'

Mr Chang simply rolls his eyes. 'Please just take and drink!'
Frankie does so and even though it tastes disgusting the results are incredible with the hangover easing before finishing the cup.
'Thank you that's amazing.'
'I know it taste awful but sometimes the horrible things in life are required to cure the horrible things!'
'What exactly is it?' asks Frankie.
'Best you don't know,' replies a smiling Mr Chang.
Frankie points towards the charms. 'They really are beautiful, especially that one.' Mr Chang picks it off the display and wraps it around his hand. 'A very wise choice. This comes from the ice mountains of the Ti Chi province in Eastern China. A hemp gathered from a lake said once to belong to a magical snow queen, who spent all her days and nights walking alongside the bank after her lover died in a war. The legend goes she placed a spell on all the flowers and plants nearby giving them the power of love. This one is for you, yes?'
'No,' smiles Frankie. 'A friend has invited me to their house and I want to take a gift but I'm not sure that's appropriate. I think a bottle of wine is more what I'm looking for.' Mr Chang nods but is still a little uncertain. 'The friend you are going to see, do you have special feelings for them? Because this charm will make them fall in love with you.'
Frankie laughs. 'It's my new boss actually, and that's not really a good idea in my business!'
A smiling Mr Chang hands it to Frankie. 'I give as gift to you. Please, may I ask you something?'
'Thank you for this. Of course.' Frankie's eyes are drawn to the charm. There really is something quite alluring about it.
'I see real sadness in your eyes, what is your name?'
'Frankie. Frankie Angels.'
'I sense a darkness in you. Please Frankie, you must change your direction in life and do it now, for where you are heading is not good.'
Frankie looks up and is shocked and hurt by these words but tries hard not to look offended. 'Thank you for your concern but I'll be fine.'

Mr Chang moves a little closer to Frankie, his eyes full of worry at what he sees. Shaking his head he appears distressed,
'Can I be honest with you Frankie Angels?'
'Can I stop you?'
'Frankie, I am blessed or more cursed the same as my mother in being able to see what has not yet happened.'
'You mean you can read the future Mr Chang?'
'In a way yes, although nothing is certain, I see enough to tell you the tidings are not good for you Frankie, and unless you take my advice this could well be your last Christmas.'
Frankie smiles. 'Like the song?'
'No, not like the song,' replies Mr Chang.
Frankie is starting to lose patience with this kind but strange old man. 'I think I should be going Mr Chang. Thank you for the charm and a Merry Christmas to you sir.' Mr Chang steps forward and goes to whisper into Frankie's ear. 'Please find another life for yourself. Before it's too late…'

COMEDIAN

With Mr Chang's doom laden words still resonating loud, Frankie heads off and jumps onto a packed tram heading into Mancunia's city centre. Although it's still early morning already people are out and about doing their Christmas shopping.
A brass band is playing *God bless Ye Merry Gentlemen.*
The Vicar's home on the River Irwellian is about another five miles away and straight from the tram Frankie hails a passing black cab to get there. The driver, a big man is dressed as Father Christmas. He glances at his new passenger through the front mirror and is clearly intrigued. 'Morning squire, where you going?'
'The Riverside settlement.'
The driver sets off but continues to eye up Frankie through the mirror.
'You off out partying for the day then?'
'Not exactly, I'm still working.'
The driver sighs. 'Me too.'
In blinding snow and treacherous driving condition the taxi makes it's slow, winding way through the Mancunia Christmas traffic. Horns are blaring, drivers gesticulating and swearing, giving out two fingered insults, there appears no Christmas spirit whatsoever! One man behind them is screaming abuse at Frankie's taxi driver.
'Screw you Santa! Get out of my way you fucking asshole!'
'And a merry fucking Christmas to you too, you grumpy bastard!' he hollers back. 'I hope your fucking Christmas tree burns down!'
Frankie is listening in and smiles at the sheer madness of it all.
'Where's his Christmas goddamn spirit?' The Taxi driver suddenly remembers his passenger. 'Hey, I'm really sorry about all this. Some people just have no patience or manners around here anymore.'
'A different world since Covid,' replies Frankie. 'Everybody is in a rush these days.'

'So true my young friend.' The taxi driver smiles wide. 'Well, you're looking smart and dressed to thrill. You look different.'
'In what way?'
Hey, don't get me wrong. It looks great on you. I mean no offence by the way.'
'None taken.'
'I can only imagine you're a model or a singer, am I right.'
Frankie smiles. 'No, I'm not a model or a singer but thank you. I'll take that as a compliment.'
'It was meant as one.' The driver isn't letting up and Frankie is starting to think this is going to be a long journey. 'But you're on the stage yes? You work in theatre?' Frankie listens on, whilst watching a snow-blasted young couple kissing passionately in front of a Pawn shop called *HARD TIMES*.
'No Mr driver, I'm not in the theatre or on the stage?'
'Okay, okay then I give the hell up! Go on tell me what you do for a living?'
'Well if you really want to know, I kill people for a living.'
The taxi driver bursts out laughing. 'Ah, I get it now, you're a comedian?'
Frankie sighs and stares out the window once more. 'Yes that's right, I'm a comedian. I don't kill people, I make them laugh.'
Seemingly content with this answer the taxi driver goes quiet and returns to his driving leaving Frankie at last in peace. Finally, they arrive at Riverside. Frankie pays the taxi driver and also hands him a huge tip. 'Much obliged the name is Billy by the way. Merry Christmas!'
'I'm Frankie. Merry Christmas Billy.'
Billy watches Frankie walk off into the ferocious, cascading snowstorm. There's something he simply can't put his finger on. It's troubling. 'Eh Frankie!' he shouts out.
Frankie turns around.
'Do you really kill people for a living?'
'Merry Christmas Billy,' smiles Frankie.

THE FOUNDATION

Inside the Riverside security tower, a CCTV operator and another man wearing a gun shoulder holster notice Frankie walking across the swing bridge towards them. He zooms in close and the operator smiles. 'It's okay, it's just Frankie Angels here to see the boss. Get the brothers down there and let the Vicar know who's coming for dinner.'
The gates open and stood waiting for Frankie once more are Kane and Abel. Both pleased to see who's stood in front of them.
'Season's greeting Frankie!' says Kane.
'Christ, Frankie,' laughs Abel, 'I think the boss wants to fucking adopt you!'
Frankie smiles. 'Looks that way boys.'
'Did you hear what happened to that scumbag Dawson?' asks Kane.
'No I didn't,' replies Frankie. 'I was busy last night what's happened?'
'He got fucking blown away on his own doorstop,' smiles Abel.
'Probably some junkie he ripped off. No loss to anyone.'
'Amen to that Frankie,' says Kane.
Kane puts an arm around Frankie's shoulder as they walk off.
'The lord may love a sinner but not on the Northside. The eleventh commandment isn't that right Frankie? You sell drugs to kids, you get clipped. It couldn't be anymore clearer. Everybody knows the rules.'
'It's good to have you on board Frankie,' adds Abel. 'We need people like you in The *Foundation*.'
They arrive at the Vicar's apartment and inside the sound of music, laughter and people chatting resonates loud. Abel opens the door and looks towards Frankie. 'In, you go, enjoy yourself!'
'Yeah enjoy Frankie Angels,' laughs Kane. 'Don't do anything we wouldn't do!' Frankie smiles at both of them then goes inside.

The door shuts behind. The party is in full swing with Sinatra's *Fly me to the Moon* playing loud. People are dancing in the centre of the room, while around them others sit and stand drinking. At the hub, conducting proceedings whilst clutching a large glass of champagne is the Vicar. Frankie spots some famous and infamous faces. None more than the heads of the other families that make up The *Foundation*.
The Southside. Jacob 'Careful' Cohen.
The Eastside. Luigi the 'Corpse' Scarone.
The Westside. Johnny the 'Pearl' Diamond.
  All three are sat laughing and chatting away like old friends at a school reunion. A show of unity and friendship for this the most wonderful time of the year, when in reality if the chance arose they would love nothing better than to rip each other's throat's out. The Vicar spots Frankie and heads across.
  'Frankie!' he announces loud, as if to let everyone know here is someone who has arrived at the party of real gravitas. Frankie is grabbed in a large bearhug by the Vicar. 'Thanks for coming. Come on let's go and get you a drink.'
  The Vicar takes two glasses of champagne off a passing waiter's tray. 'To our friendship Frankie Angels, may it last forever and a Mancunia day. And also to a first job well done! Congratulations on sending that slug to hell.' The two toast.
Frankie smiles. 'Cheers boss.'
The Vicar leans close and goes to whispers into Frankie's ear.
  'I heard off one of our detective guys that Dobson was seen off real good. 'Ultra professional' he told me. Just what I expected and want Frankie. Welcome aboard.' He moves away but gently, if firmly grabs Frankie's arm. 'Come with me there's some people I want you to meet.' The Vicar and Frankie head towards the table where all the bosses are sat enjoying themselves. 'Gentlemen, I'd like you all to meet a real good friend of mine. This here is Frankie Angels. The latest member of The *Foundation*.' Frankie leans down and shakes all their hands. Cohen is smoking a fat Cuban cigar. 'Nice hat kid,' he says. Scorone eyes Frankie from head to toe and appears impressed. 'You dress like a real star Frankie. I hope you're as good as you look.'

'Oh I can vouch for Frankie, he definitely is,' smiles the Vicar, acting like a father seeing his own child being praised to the heavens.
'Good to have you aboard Frankie,' says Diamond. 'You listen to the Vicar here and you'll go far.'
'I will, thank you.'
'Will you excuse me for a while Frankie? I need to speak business with these three rascals for a while. You go ahead and mix, make some new friends.' Not needing to be asked twice Frankie is only too grateful to get away. The Vicar sits down. He watches Frankie disappear amongst the partying crowd.
'Well gents what do you think?'
'Just a fucking kid Jimmy,' replies Cohen. 'Are you quite sure about this?'
'Believe me Jacob, later tonight our friend won't see Frankie coming.'
'Does Frankie know yet?' asks Scarone.
'No, not yet. I'm giving the kid some time to relax a little. Besides, it's fucking Christmas Eve after all.' They all laugh and Scarone lights himself a cigar. 'Was it Frankie who did the dealer from the school gates?'
The Vicar nods.
'Impressive,' says Scarone.
'It was Luigi and believe me there's been many more also. This wasn't Frankie's first hit by any means. The kid is already a veteran. A born killer.'
'And does our Frankie have a conscience?' asks Cohen. 'Because if so then we all know it's a waste of time. The wrong fucking choice.'
The Vicar's eyes are back on Frankie who's talking to a beautiful, young blond girl in a fetching, low cut red dress.
He smiles wide. 'Our Frankie has good taste and believe me gentlemen, if there is a conscience there, then it's just teething problems. I'll sort that out.'
'I hope you're right for all our sakes,' say Diamond. 'Because if that sonofabitch talks we all go down. The *Foundation* is finished.'
Cohen is another watching Frankie. 'To kill a Priest though, especially in Mancunia can see you lynched in the streets. This has to be

foolproof Jimmy. There can be no trails leading back to us. We have to be fucking invisible in all this. We have to be ghosts.'
Diamond's eyes are also transfixed on Frankie. 'This is a beautiful kid. Don't they say the devil has a face of an angel and a black heart? Maybe this is just what we need because if not we're truly fucked.'
'Look, just fucking relax all of you!' snaps the Vicar. 'We're in good hands. Come twelve o'clock tonight our shared problem will be no more. I know what makes Frankie Angels tick. Beneath the cool and calm persona there's a truly fucked up kid, and I can make that work for us all. Frankie will turn out to be our gift from the heavens. Trust me, we got lucky here gentlemen.'
Totally unaware of all the attention Frankie is busy talking to the blond girl. 'So, do you ever take your hat off?' she asks him, whilst smiling wide.
'Only in the shower!' laughs Frankie.
'What's your name anyway, and how come I haven't seen you around the Riverside before?'
'You don't want to know my name. I'm a nobody. I'm just here to fix the drains.'
'Well you're certainly dressed for it!'
Frankie smiles. 'Since when is it a crime to take pride in your appearance?'
'Oh you're good!' she laughs. 'Tell me drain person do you carry a gun?'
'Of course I do there's some big rats down there. You have to take precautions.'
'There are some big rats up here as well. I should know I work for one.' Frankie senses looking into this girl's eye that behind the mask there exists great sadness. 'What is your name?'
The girl smiles clearly enjoying flirting with Frankie.
'I asked first remember. You tell me yours and I'll tell you mine?'
'Frankie Angels.'
'Heather Mancini. Pleased to meet you Frankie Angels.'
'Likewise, Heather Mancini!' The two share a lingering hand shake.

Suddenly, any idea of Frankie getting to know Heather better is interrupted by a smiling Vicar who has appeared alongside them.
 'So lovely to see you two getting along well. Would you mind Heather sweetheart if I had a quick chat with our Frankie here? Whilst I do go and mix with the bosses. Tell them a few dirty jokes and refill their glasses. Make them smile huh?' Heather appears a different person now and Frankie recognises the fear in her eyes. 'Yes Mr O'Malley,' she replies. Heather casts a last glance at Frankie before heading off and the Vicar watches her go. 'She's a good girl Frankie, but she's not for you. Do I make myself clear? Heather belongs to me. She's my property. You can look but never fucking touch.'
'We were just talking boss.'
The Vicar smiles. 'I know. Come on I need to talk to you. Let's go somewhere a little more quiet.' The Vicar puts an arm around Frankie and they head out onto the balcony. Snow is still falling but they're sheltered. Away in the distance the city that never sleeps has turned white. The Vicar pours two large whiskeys from a bottle on a nearby table and hands one over to Frankie. 'You did a really good number on Dobson. Let's drink to his soul going to hell.' They toast and the Vicar immediately refills their glasses. 'I have another job for you Frankie and it can't wait. I know, I know it's Christmas Eve and it can't sit well with you, but we have no choice. This one must happen tonight.' The Vicar looks out across the river. 'Look over there Frankie. Until it all belongs to me this *Foundation* of ours only works if everyone plays by the same rules. Ours. There's nothing fucking mysterious about them. The North, South, East and West survives and prospers by employing none, fucking negotiable terms.' Frankie remains quiet. 'We have a fucking rat in our midst Frankie, and it needs to be exterminated. Can you do this for me?'
'Who is it?'
 'It's a Priest by the name of Father Brendan Nolan.' The Vicar watches Frankie's face carefully searching for a reaction. Looking for the merest sign of weakness but there's nothing to be seen. He's a happy man. 'Frankie, this fucking piece of work passed over

something he heard in the confessional box to the police. He broke the seal of confession, a solemn vow that all Priests swear to abide by. Can you believe this piece of shit. How dishonest is that? He even went against his own god? And now to make matters even worse he has well and truly fucked us all over. The *Foundation*. That's me and you now Frankie. The family.' The Vicar takes a sip of whisky. Again, he turns away from Frankie and gazes out over his Northern fiefdom. 'Nolan works at *Our Lady of the Light* children's home. I take it you remember that place?' Frankie's throat goes dry as memories of a tortured childhood comes flooding back. *Our Lady of the Light*. The rapes and the beatings. 'Are you okay Frankie?'
'Yeah I'm okay. Tell me, is Cassidy still alive, I've searched everywhere for him.'
'No the old pervert died of cancer years ago. I'm sure you'll be glad to know.' Frankie closes his eyes and prays the worms had a glorious day when he was lowered. 'There have been rumours about Nolan though. More than rumours from what I'm led to believe Frankie. Trust me on this, why would I lie to you? Him and Cassidy were a pair together. We are the same kid, we want these bastards choking to death beneath the mud or the rats chewing their fucking eyes out.'
'What has he said to the police?'
'Let's just say a certain politician has suddenly decided to cleanse his soul over certain dealings he's had with The *Foundation*. Seems to believe a few Hail Mary's and Our Father's would solve his problem. But luckily we've got friends on the other side Frankie. People who care about this city. One of our people in the police department got wind, so here we are having this conversation and been given the opportunity to solve the problem before events get out of hand. We need to clip this Priest though Frankie, a.s.a.p. He needs to fucking go and go tonight.'
'It's almost unheard of for a Priest to break the seal of confession,' replies Frankie. 'Something must've really spooked him to do that?'
'Yeah well don't you go worrying about that. You do this for me tonight and all your troubles are over. You'll never have to want for anything again. I might even throw in Heather.'

Frankie appears not to be listening, staring also now across the river through the falling snow. 'Hey Frankie, where the fuck have you gone? Come back we're fucking talking here!'
Frankie turns to face the Vicar. 'Remember when we first met I told you I wouldn't kill anybody who didn't have it coming to them?'
'Yeah I remember what of it? Where are we going here?'
'I need to know why I'm doing this?'
For a moment, the Vicar glares murderously at Frankie, only for a huge smile to then appear on his face. 'Frankie, my Frankie!'
The Vicar sits down and pours yet another whisky. This time just for himself. 'Okay then, just this once I'll tell you. Maybe because it's Christmas you caught me in a very good mood. Sit down Frankie Angels.' Frankie does so. 'Listen this goes no further Frankie. I'm sure you've heard of our esteemed Lord Mayor Fergal O'Bannion?'
'Fergal "Clean" hands?'
The very same. Remember O'Bannion's speech when he got elected. 'I'm going to clean up this city. I'm going to get the filth off our streets. I'm going to protect our children. The bad guys I'm coming for you!'
'Yeah I remember it well. All talk and he's as crooked as the rest of them from what I've heard.'
'You're damn right. The first thing O'Bannion did was to send out feelers to all four families explaining what he wanted to keep him off our backs. You know Frankie, it's not wise to hit a government elected official, because the heat from above would simply wipe you out, so we had little choice but to agree to his every, dirty, fucking whim.'
'And what was that?'
'He's a fucking degenerate and he's also took us for millions. O'Bannion has a bank balance the size of a small nation. He likes whores Frankie and the younger the better. Boys and girls.'
Frankie's eyes glaze over and the Vicar notices and smiles.
'That's right Frankie he's a fucking pervert, he fucks kids and here's where our friend the Priest comes in. O'Bannion went too far with one kid and cut up rough. So rough the poor kid died. Oh, of course

we covered it up. We had no choice. This kid had no family, no background. All was sweet and then what does O'Bannion do in a moment of madness. He has a fucking epiphany and goes to confess all to Nolan. Not only that he tells him who helped clean the mess up. He mentions names, mine included. Also, Cohen, Scarone and Diamond. If this goes any further he's fucked us Frankie. Fucked us! The Priest has to go.'
'What about O'Bannion, what happens to him?'
'We'll deal with O'Bannion. You just make sure that Priest doesn't see Christmas day. Are we clear here?'
'The Priest is a bad person, Mr O'Malley, yes?'
'You have my word on that Frankie. He and Cassidy shared kids. This is information from people I know and trust.'
'If that's how it's all gone down, then yes, I'll kill the Priest tonight.'
Inside though Frankie is far from sure. Something about the Vicar's story doesn't ring true. A huge smile appears on the Vicar's face as he stares at Frankie. 'You're going to go far kid. Me and you are going to do great things in this city. I have big plans as you already know and you'll be a huge part of them. I promise you.'
Suddenly, Frankie remembers the charm from Mr Chang's and not really thinking straight passes it over to the Vicar. He's clearly impressed with it and slide the charm onto his arm.
'They say it brings you luck boss.'
'I don't know what to say kid, it's...'
'At least that's what Mr Chang told me. Merry Christmas.'
The Vicar embraces and kisses Frankie on both cheeks.
'May all the saints in heaven bless you Frankie Angels. You stick with me and your enemies become my enemies. You're my family now.'
The Vicar goes into his pocket and produces a small photograph of the Priest and hands it over to Frankie. 'This is the sonofabitch. I've already told you where he'll be. Do this for me Frankie. Make our world a better place.' The two head back inside. Frankie heads for the door, only for a smiling Heather to appear and block it.
'Are you really going to go without saying goodbye?'

Frankie looks behind and notices the Vicar in deep conversation with the other bosses. 'I don't think it's wise for you to be seen talking to me Heather.'
'What did he say to you Frankie?'
'Not so much what he said, more how he said it.'
Heather glares across towards the Vicar. 'He's a monster Frankie. Don't let him kid you otherwise. Are you scared of him?'
'No, but I'm scared of what he might do to you though?'
'There's nothing the Vicar can do to me what he hasn't already done. He took me in when I was 13 years-old. He tells everyone I'm his family. He's a sick fuck and I want out. Can you help me? I need to get out of this city Frankie.'
'Look, I have to go. We'll speak later.' Heather appears close to tears. 'Okay.' Frankie gently touches her face and then is gone through the door. Never noticing the Vicar has witnessed this. He walks across to Heather. 'You're mine,' he says to her while smiling, so as not to attract attention. 'You go near Frankie again, I'll slash your fucking face. Is that clear?'
'Yes,' replies Heather, clearly terrified. The Vicar smiles wide and strokes her hair. 'Good girl.'

Stood on the swing bridge shivering and having a cigarette are Kane and Abel. They see Frankie heading back towards them.
'Hey Frankie!' shouts Kane. 'What the fuck, why are you going so early?'
'He didn't like my Christmas card,' smiles Frankie.
Both Kane and Abel laugh. 'You doing anything later Frankie?' asks Abel. 'If not me and Kane and the rest of the clan are heading over to *Mulligan's bar* to see in the midnight hour. You're more than welcome.'
'Thanks guys, I've a few things to tidy up but hopefully will see you there.'
'Oh, that's grand Frankie,' says Kane. 'Stay lucky huh. It isn't good to get yourself killed on Christmas Eve!'

Frankie smiles and watched by the two brothers heads once more into the snowstorm and back over the swing bridge. Kane is watching him.

'I won't be happy whacking Frankie brother.'

'Me neither,' replies Abel. 'But we follow orders?'

Kane nods. 'Orders are fucking orders. They're all going tonight'

ACT THREE

THE WAY YOU LOOK TONIGHT

Frankie is on a packed tram with people in packed like sardines. There's a busker stood nearby and he catches Frankie's eye. Suddenly, the busker starts to strum his guitar to the tune of Sinatra's *The way you look tonight,* and begins singing. All the time not taking his eyes off Frankie.
 'Someday, when I'm awfully low. When the world is cold. I will feel a glow just thinking of you. And the way you look tonight.'
 He goes on to finally finish and loud applause off all the passengers! Frankie claps also and goes into a pocket to hand the busker some notes. 'No this one was on the house,' smiles the busker to Frankie. He holds out a hand for Frankie to shake.
'You have a great voice,' says Frankie. 'Merry Christmas.'
'Merry Christmas beautiful stranger,' replies the busker.
The bell sounds to depart the tram and Frankie walks over to the busker and kisses him on the cheek before edging past to step off.
'Hey!' shouts the smiling busker.
Frankie turns around. 'From now on every time I play that song I'll think of you.' Frankie pulls the trilby down low to shelter from the snow and smiles wide. The doors shut and the tram sets off with the busker's face up against the glass watching Frankie vanish into the snowstorm.

FLYNN'S CAFÉ

  Flynn's café sits in a nondescript backstreet alley of the city that can't sleep. Above its door hangs a broken-down neon sign that occasionally fizzles back into life then out of it again.
  There are few customers but those that do make the effort always to return, for ex-pugilist Mickey Flynn is a genial host and a good listener. Also for a few extra coins the coffee can be sweetened by decent malt whiskey, and if Mickey thinks you need it and that you're a good egg, then it's on the house. They're a good friendly crowd at Mickey's place and Frankie Angels loves it in there.
  Needing some time to think and shelter a while from the still, blistering snowstorm, Frankie heads down the alley to Flynn's, passing on the way nothing but graffiti strewn walls, burst black rubbish bags and overfilled garbage wheelie bins. With feet disappearing deep into the snow and finding it hard to walk, Frankie spots an old man sat huddled beneath a blanket in a doorway pulling it tight around him. He's also trying desperately to light a roll up with a wet match. Frankie goes across and hands him a lighter. The old man lights up and stares at this kind stranger.
  'Thank you.' He hands Frankie the lighter back.
  'Now get inside somewhere, there's no use the two of us freezing our assess off out here.' Again, the old man pulls the blanket around even tighter but Frankie puts out a hand and lifts him to his feet. 'Come on old man let's go and get something to eat.'
  'I'm afraid nobody will let someone like me through their door, but thanks anyway stranger. You best kindly be on your way.'
  'Come on,' smiles Frankie. 'I know such a place.'
  Frankie points to Flynn's café. With the old man alongside he enters the café. It's all but empty except a bearded man in a dress and high heels sat in a corner reading a newspaper and drinking coffee, and a

policeman chatting to the owner at the counter. A small, fat, balding red-haired figure with a boxers' pug-nosed face and surprisingly, friendly green eyes. 51 year-old Mickey Flynn. Never a high ranking contender in the boxing game but a tough character in and out of the ring, Mickey made his living as a journeyman fighter and was never short of bouts. He fought on only until he had earned enough to buy the café. To most nothing but a broken-down old hole but to Mickey Flynn, a lifetime's dream. This was his place. Mickey's place. Flynn's café. 'Hey Frankie Angels!' exclaims Mickey. The two embrace. Mickey is one of the few people in this city who knows Frankie's past tale. They're good friends and have always had each other's backs. 'Good to see you as always Frankie, who the hell is this?' He points at the old man. 'Has he been bothering you for money? I've seen him before in the doorways and going through the bins.'
'No Mickey, he's an old friend of mine who's just hit a bad time.'
'The name is Wendell S Fairchurch,' says the old man.
'Looks like he could do with a good wash Mickey!' calls out the policeman. His face full of disgust. 'You don't want to start letting his type in. Bad for business.' Frankie stares daggers at him and Wendell starts to head back out the door. 'Hey where do you think you're going old man?' shouts Mickey. 'Any friend of Frankie's is a friend of mine. Get back in here and sit yourself down.' A smiling Frankie leads Wendell to a small table with two chairs by the window before heading back over to the counter. 'I really appreciate this Mickey.' The policeman is sat behind Frankie on a high stool glaring angrily towards him. 'No bother Frankie, it's Christmas! How's life with you, are you out partying tonight?'
'Maybe later but I've some business to take care of beforehand.'
The policeman taps Frankie on the shoulder who turns around to face him. 'Don't I know you from somewhere?'
'No, I'm sorry, I don't think so,' replies Frankie. The policeman starts to laugh. 'Now I remember. It was the Menswear window on the high street. You were a fucking mannequin!'

This comment clearly angers Mickey. 'Hey Bobby cut it out. You're not funny, Frankie is a good friend of mine.'
'Well, I have to say you've got some strange friends Mickey. It's enough to make me worry about you.'
'Meaning what?' replies Mickey.
The policeman continues sipping his coffee whilst still smirking.
'Drink your coffee and get out Bobby. Next time you want to insult me and my friends, whether in uniform or not, I'll knock your head flat off your fucking shoulders. Is that understood?' Frankie watches the policeman close waiting for any sudden movement, whilst Wendell and the bearded man in a dress can't take their eyes off the officer's gun holster. Then a huge smile suddenly appears on his face.
'Don't you worry yourself Mickey. I'm going. I know when I'm not wanted. I'll be sure to tell the other boys at the station to avoid this shithole too.' He points a finger close to Frankie's face. 'I'll be keeping a special eye open for you mannequin.' The policeman then walks towards the door only to turn around facing everybody. He's still smiling, albeit now in a menacing, mocking fashion. 'Merry Christmas freaks, one and all!' That said the policeman puts on his cap and trudges off into the snow. All in the café watch him go. When almost out of sight the bearded man in a dress stands up to leave and heads to the counter. 'What a fucking arsehole! What do I owe you Mickey?'
'No, it's Christmas, it's on the house. Merry Christmas George.'
The bearded man blows him a kiss. 'Merry Christmas Mickey Flynn. You're a good man.' A swift nod to Frankie and George makes his way out of the café.
'Seems like a nice guy,' smiles Frankie.
Mickey nods in agreement, 'The best Frankie. He's a cop. A fucking good one too who works the streets looking out for underage kids and bringing them in. Or catches the bastards trying to abuse them.'
 Mickey slaps Frankie on the back. 'Right Frankie Angels my treat! For you and old Wendell here. How about my homemade stew, some chocolate cake and steaming hot coffee?'

Frankie smiles wide. 'That sounds great Mick.'
'Go and park your ass down with Father Time over there. I'll bring it over.' Frankie goes to sit opposite Wendell who's staring as if hypnotized at the falling snow through the large café window.
'In all my years on the streets I've never seen snow like this. It's never ending and is going to bury this city tonight.'
'How long have you been out there Wendell?'
'Too long, I'm sorry, I still don't know your name?'
'Frankie.'
'I'm much obliged Frankie. You had no need to do this. Are you a cop?'
'No, I'm not a cop,' smiles Frankie. 'Anything but.'
The old man starts to laugh. 'Well then if you're not a cop you must work for the church. Do you want to save my soul and help me find god? Because I'll tell you now you're wasting your time. That heartless bastard left this city years ago for me.'
Again Frankie smiles. 'No Wendell, you can relax. I'm not trying to save your soul.'
'Well that's okay then.'
Mickey appears at the table with the food and coffee. He lays it down.
'Here you go gents my specialty. Enjoy!'
'Much obliged Mickey.'
'Thank you sir,' says Wendell. 'You're a gentleman. Just like your young friend here.' Mickey heads back to the counter and they start to eat. 'So, come on then Frankie. I'm at a loss. If you don't want to arrest or save me just what the hell is it you do?'
'Jesus, Wendell, just eat your stew.'
'I thought you said you wasn't religious?!'
The two laugh. 'Let's just say Wendell that I'm in pest control.'
'In that outfit?'
Frankie smiles. 'I've already had this conversation today.'
'Frankie, my new young friend, you're as much in pest control as I'm a male model.'
'You don't want to know what I do for a living Wendell. Just enjoy your stew. Don't ruin a good meal for yourself.'

'I'm not judgmental Frankie believe me. I'm the last person in the world in a position to judge anyone. I'm just curious that's all. Face it, when we walk back out that door our paths are most likely never to cross again. So what have you got to lose by telling me?'
Frankie stops eating, puts down his spoon and stares across at Wendell. 'Okay then old man you win. I'm a problem solver.'
'Oh yeah, what kind of problems?'
'Bad guy problems.'
'Are you some kind of superhero then? That would explain the costume.'
'I kill for money those who have it coming.'
'An assassin?'
'Like I said, a problem solver.'
'Is that right, and how exactly do you know they have it coming Frankie?'
Frankie has no answer and thinks the old man has a valid point. Wendell laughs out loud. 'Oh, come on Frankie, what do you take me for. You're no killer? You're a good person with a good heart. I can tell, I know about these things.'
'How exactly would you know Wendell?'
'Because I was also a fucking assassin Frankie. I know the type and you are definitely not the type.'
'How can you be so sure?'
'Because there's no smell of death about you. You smell clean.'
'I don't know about that Wendell. Maybe it just doesn't stick on me?'
Wendell pushes his stew bowl aside and starts on the chocolate cake. 'No, no, it sticks on us all. It's a fucking curse but you're a good kid, I can tell. Maybe you've done a few bad things but there's no mark of Cain in your eyes. You're a decent person.'
'Maybe I just hide it well?' He thinks of Mr Chang.
' Frankie pushes over all the chocolate cake in front of Wendell.
'Are you not having any cake, it's really good?'
'No I'm full, you enjoy it.'
'Thank you. Very much obliged.'
'So who did you work for Wendell?'

'Various people, I freelanced mostly and made a great living from it. If you don't have a soul then the killing business can be extremely lucrative. I was raking it in. The plan was make so much dough then retire abroad and get away from this fucking, poisoned city.'
Wendell pushes his plate away and tastes a mouthful of coffee.
'What you have to understand is that everything is corrupt Frankie, it's not just the way of this city but the fucking world. For men like me back then who had no morals, I was laughing all the way to the bank. I had everything a man in my position could desire.'
'Forgive me then Wendell but what went wrong then? How did you get from there to here living in a doorway and scavenging through garbage?'
'A Priest, Frankie. A fucking supposed man of god ruined everything for me.' Wendell takes another sip of the coffee and stares once more through the window at the driving snow. He appears close to tears.
'I know that world,' replies Frankie.
Wendell smiles. 'His name was Father Patrick Cassidy. May god pour burning oil on his rotting soul.'
Frankie goes cold. Did the old man really just mention Cassidy?
'What happened to the Priest Wendell?'
'It began as a hit I was involved in. A husband and wife who had been hunting down a Priest paedophile ring led by Cassidy. One night they went after him and we were waiting. There was me and two other guys. We dressed as cops and killed them. Job done or so we thought back then.' The thought of stabbing this old man in the eye is going through Frankie's mind but somehow the need to know what happened next is overwhelming him.
'How did this prove to be your undoing Wendell? Just before you said that you didn't have a soul?'
'I didn't think I had Frankie, I honest to god thought I was immune to any kind of suffering, but when I found out what Cassidy was up to. Jesus fucking Christ, kids? The hit on those two people gave him carte blanche to do whatever he wished in the care homes and god knows how many lives were ruined. There was rumours they also had a kid who Cassidy used as his own. Like some kind of trophy prize

offered out to friends when seeking favours. It all came to a head when I finally came face to face with the sonofabitch and he offered to give me an hour alone with the poor little wretch. Well, I'm not proud of this but I'd had a few drinks, and he'd made out this was a beautiful kid? They took me to a room and there on the bed tied up naked with rope and gagged was the …' Wendell has tears falling down his cheeks. 'I had no idea, I swear to god I had no idea the kid would be that young. I just turned and walked away and kept walking. Past the fucking Priest, out of the door, out of that life. I never looked back.' By now an ashen faced Frankie has a gun aimed at Wendell under the table as the old man wipes his eyes clear of tears.

'Like I said Frankie, I ran from there. the image of that kid broke my heart. Every penny I had, I gave over to charity. I drank and I drank and ended up where I am today. What the fuck was I thinking, Just what the fuck? I wasn't naïve, I just kidded myself from the reality of it all.' Wendell closes his eyes, opens them back up and smiles.

'So you see Frankie, if that experience taught me anything it's that I now recognise good from evil. I know the smell.'

Frankie fires!

The look of shock on Wendell's face lasts only for a moment as the bullet catches him low in the stomach and his head drops to the table. Mickey comes racing over. 'Frankie, what the fuck?'

Frankie looks up. 'He was one of them Mickey.'

'Okay, look, you have to go and make yourself scarce. Let me get rid of this scumbag. It's no problem at all.'

Frankie appears in shock. 'I'm sorry this happened here, I really am.'

Mickey smiles. Merry Christmas Frankie Angels you're burying ghosts. Now get the fuck out of here my friend.' The two embrace before Frankie leaves. After walking twenty yards the urge to turn around is all-consuming, and the sight through the window is of Mickey dragging Wendell's lifeless body from the table. Frankie can also hear music blaring out from the café Jukebox. Frank Sinatra's *That's Life*. 'Some Christmas,' says Frankie, starting to whistle the tune as the snow continues to fall and swallow up the city that never sleeps, in ever, increasing white mountain peaks.

OUR LADY OF THE LIGHT

It's 5-30.pm,
and the city that can't sleep is alive with last minute Christmas shoppers. The streets are jammed packed. Buskers, jugglers and religious cranks all competing for attention. A Salvation Army Christmas choir roaring out *'Joy to the World!'*
A Father Christmas is ringing a bell loud at all who pass.
'Merry Christmas one and all!'
Frankie is lost amid the festive madness and still in a sense of disbelief as to what has just occurred. Suddenly, Frankie's phone rings. It's the Vicar.
'Hey Frankie, I just had a call. Our friend will be at the orphanage in an hour handing out presents. Can you believe it? A fucking gift. You still okay with this?'
'All good boss, I'm on my way there now.'
'Don't let me down Frankie. Soon as it's done you head right back here and we celebrate. Is that clear?'
'It's clear.'
'I'll see you later kid, good luck.'
The line goes dead and Frankie puts the phone away and takes out the photo of Father Nolan. 'I'll be seeing you very soon Priest.'
It's only a twenty-minute walk from the city centre to *Our Lady of the Light*. For a hundred years now a home for children. A local institution. The pride of the North's Catholic church. Covered head to foot in snow Frankie brushes some off the suit on arriving at an electric gate. The building itself is monstrously Victorian. Deathly black, quiet and still like Dracula's castle. Lights that shine from every window signalling a broken heart. The distant verses of *Silent Night* drifts outwards. Frankie rings a buzzer and a woman's voice starts crackling through with an Irish accent.

'Hello, who is it, do you have business here?'
'Good evening, yes I have a meeting with Father Nolan. I have some late Christmas donations and I wanted to give them to him personally tonight. I thought it would make a nice surprise.'
The gate slowly opens and Frankie walks through. Memories of this place though locked away for years come flooding back.
'Hold it together Frankie, just hold it together for a little longer.'
On reaching the main door Frankie is greeted by a grim-faced, 62 year-old nun with arms folded. This is Sister Teresa. A fearsome lady originally from Cork who runs the home with an iron hand in a velvet glove. Inside, the sound of children's voices playing echoes loud. 'So you say you're here to see Father Nolan?'
'I am yes.'
'As it's to do with god's work I'll make an exception to this late calling and let you through.'
'It most certainly is god's work and thank you Sister.'
'Well you best get yourself in here out of the snow then.'
Sister Teresa leads Frankie into a small sparse room with just a desk, a cabinet and a huge crucifix hung on the wall.
'Father Nolan is due back shortly you can wait in here for him. Try not to break or touch anything.'
'Thank you.'
'Do you know the Father personally by the way? I'm sorry your name is?'
'Angels, Frankie Angels. No, I don't know him personally Sister. We've never met, we've just spoken over the telephone.'
'He's a wonderful man Mr Angels. This home has not always been the happy place it is today. Terrible things have happened in the past before I arrived, but thanks to Father Nolan, the children can now sleep safely at night.' Frankie is intrigued because this sure doesn't sound like the man described to him by the Vicar. Rumours, he said. Rumours. Again, something doesn't ring true.
'I spent a long time here as a kid Sister, I know exactly what went on. If Father Nolan has put an end to all that, then he is indeed as you say, a truly wonderful man.'

'I'm so very sorry young man.'
Frankie smiles. 'It was a long time ago.'
'Father Nolan cleaned out the cesspit. Those Priests who disgraced themselves were handed over to the authorities. We both vowed so long as he and I are around no one will ever hurt the children of *Our Lady of the Light* again. We will defend them with our lives.'
Frankie feels sick. Suddenly, the office door opens and a man dressed as Father Christmas carrying a sack appears. It's 56 year-old Father Brendan Nolan. Born in Dublin, a tall, burly man with a big smiles and kind, warm eyes. 'Ho ho! Well then who do we have here Sister Teresa?'
It's me Father remember, Frankie Angels. We had that talk on the phone?' Father Nolan notices Frankie's gun pointing towards him but out of sight from the Sister. He lowers his false white beard.
 'Ah yes, I remember now. Sister, can we have the office for a few moments please?'
'Of course Father. I'll leave you two gentlemen in peace. Merry Christmas Mr Angels.'
'Merry Christmas Sister Teresa,' replies Frankie.
Sister Teresa leaves shutting the door behind her. Father Nolan goes and sits behind the desk staring at Frankie. 'So, you're here to kill me then?' Father Nolan smiles. 'Bad form to kill Santa on Christmas Eve. Even in this god forsaken city.'
Frankie doesn't reply.
'A man of few words eh. Is it okay if I smoke? Normally if I did so inside the Sister would kill me, but in these circumstances, I don't think she'd mind as much.'
'Go ahead.'
'Thank you. You're a decent bringer of death my son.'
Father Nolan lights a cigarette, his hands clearly shaking.
'All I ask is when you do this don't hurt anyone else. Nobody knows what I did. Especially Sister Teresa. Without her these children are lost.'
'I'm not here to kill you for what you said in confession. I'm here because of what you've done to the kids.'

'I've never laid a hand on these children. Whoever told you that is lying.'
'How do I know you're not lying?'
'You don't, but do you really think a woman like Sister Teresa would let me near her children after all that has gone on here in the past?'
'She told me you blew the lid on this place?'
Father Nolan nods. 'Aye, I blew my chance of being Pope in one mad moment of deciding to do the right thing.'
'What happened to the Priests?'
The authorities took them into custody and then very quietly they were released back into church care. The power of the lord! My god, I feel ashamed.' Father Nolan inhales on the cigarette. 'It makes me sick what happened. The Priests were scattered across the globe. Africa, Asia. Out of sight and mind except for the poor kids they had all abused for years on end.'
 Frankie has watched carefully Nolan's eyes. This is no liar, this is no child abuser. It's become clear now the Vicar is lying. Frankie puts the gun back in his jacket. 'I'm sorry for all this Father. There has been a huge mistake.'
Father Nolan smiles. 'You don't say!' He puts out his cigarette in an ashtray. 'Bad for my health, Sister Teresa keeps telling me. She is a good woman. The best.'
' Please Father, take my advice now and go. Get out of the city tonight and don't come back. There's no other choice. Someone in the Police department has broken your cover with O'Bannion's confession. You can't give yourself up because there's no one you can trust. The *Foundation* can't and won't let you live so you have to make yourself vanish.'
He smiles. 'What, leave dressed like this? No I can't leave, and if I did vanish what happens to the children and Sister Teresa?'
'I'll protect the kids and the nun.'
'No, I'm going nowhere. You tell whoever sent you here that I don't regret breaking the confessional seal for one moment. I would do it again and again. You tell your ghouls I'll be right here and ready to

fight them. They can go to hell and in the words of our *Lady of the Light,* can fuck right off!'

Frankie knows it's a losing battle to change the Priest's mind, but also to not kill this man will mean a death penalty for himself. There's only one option left open to him.

He smiles. 'Did she really say that Father?'

'No my son! My mouth tends to get carried away sometimes!'

'Well then, I best go. I wish you a Merry Christmas Father.'

'What exactly are you going to do now Frankie Angels?'

'I'm going to do what's right. I'm going to end all this.'

Frankie leaves the office and steps back out of the children's home. The sound of them still playing and laughing resonates loud. On reaching the electronic gates they automatically start to open. Frankie turns one last time and sees Father Nolan and Sister Teresa stood watching him go. They both raise a hand to wave goodbye. Frankie returns the gesture and then heads off back to the Riverside for some unfinished business.

To the Riverside (Part Two)
THE LAST HIT

'Now be honest with me,' laughs the taxi driver.
'Do you believe in Father Christmas!? The driver bringing Frankie back from the orphanage has not shut up since they set off. Frankie gazes out the window taking in the view. Dimly lit street lamps illuminating the falling snow. The roads and pavements thick and white. Amazing how clean the city looks when the dirt is buried beneath and out of sight. There are few people around now because most are in bars, pubs or at home waiting for the magical hour. The stragglers, drunks, loners, sporadic and broken-hearted wonder the streets alone.
'I've always loved this time of year,' continues the taxi driver. 'They say it's just for kids but it's nice to see people smiling and laughing don't you think?' Frankie stares through the front mirror seeing the smile on the taxi driver's face. Nodding though still remaining quiet, preferring to just gaze out the window.
'So have you been working tonight or just enjoying a few drinks?'
'I've been working.'
'You must love your job to be working on Christmas Eve. What is it you do?' Outside the air is thick with so much snow now it's becoming hard to view. This irritates Frankie who wants to see as much of the city as possible after what's occurred. Time maybe short.
'What do I do, more what did I do? I resigned tonight. I quit.'
'Oh, I'm sorry to hear that.'
'Don't be, it's a good day.' Frankie smiles. 'It's a good day after so many bad.' Finally, they arrive at the Riverside and the taxi pulls up at the swing bridge. Frankie goes to pay the driver and steps out. On the other side the gates are already starting to open and stood waiting are Kane and Abel. Kane comes to greet Frankie. 'I got some news.

The bosses got nervous and wanted him out the way. We hit O'Bannion at nine o'clock tonight. They're having a party upstairs. If you're done for the night now Frankie, do you fancy that beer at Mulligans?'
'I'm done for good Kane.'
Kane laughs. 'Come on what are you talking about? How's the Priest?'
'I reckon he's probably handing out presents to the kids by now.'
'What do you mean handing out presents?' asks Abel.
'He's supposed to be fucking dead Frankie? You were supposed to clean it all up. The bosses are up there celebrating now thinking all their problems are over.' Kane appears almost apoplectic with rage. 'Are you fucking telling me he's still alive?'
Frankie just shrugs his shoulders. 'He was when I left him.'
Abel stiffens up. 'Hey Frankie, you had orders man. This isn't good.'
'Let me pass now boys. I've got unfinished business inside.'
Frankie spots Kane going for his gun but before he has a chance, fires twice in quick succession and both him and Abel hit the floor dead. Frankie notices the light in the CCTV tower is switched off meaning that Kane and Abel are the only security on the gate. The Vicar won't have any idea what's coming his way. A reckoning.
The Riverside is quiet with the only noise coming from the Vicar's top apartment. Music and loud laughter. Frankie reaches the half-opened door and goes inside. Frank Sinatra's *My Way* is playing and four men clearly drunk are singing along to it on the balcony, clutching their wine glasses. The Vicar, Cohen, Scarone and Diamond. Frankie enters and the Vicar is first to spot him. He appears delighted. 'Frankie, what the fuck?' The others stop singing and Cohen points to the gun in Frankie's hand. The Vicar's features suddenly turn from laughter to stone cold, as he hadn't at first noticed. 'Why the gun Frankie?' asks Cohen.
The next moment Cohen, Scarone and Diamond are lying dead in a hail of bullets. The Vicar stands frozen as the song finishes.
'Frankie, have you gone mad? What the fuck are you doing?'
'I'm ending this. Think of it as a Christmas hit.'

'Frankie, come on now whatever has happened we can sort it out. Suddenly, Butesi appears on the balcony and makes a rush for Frankie, and he too is gunned down. The Vicar appears horrified. There are four dead bodies at his feet. He needs to think fast.

Hey kid, what you've just done here has done me a huge favour.' The Vicar points out across the city. 'Look out there, it all belongs to us now. It's our world now Frankie.'

'You lied to me about the Priest. He's a good man and you're filth.' The Vicar smiles. 'I supposed he told you that?'

'For once just tell me the truth?'

The Vicar starts to panic. 'Frankie, please god don't do this, we're family for fuck's sake, I don't want to die!' He has both hands together in prayer pleading for his life. 'Frankie, no!' shouts the Vicar. He falls as two bullet tears into him, only it's not from Frankie, but Heather stood behind. The Vicar's disbelieving eyes as he dies remain wide open. Frankie turns to see Heather, who drops the gun and falls into Frankie's arms.

'Come on, we have to go.' Frankie picks up the charm, grabs Heather's hand and they race from the apartment past Kane and Abel's bodies, and over the swing bridge. The two finally stop running and Frankie takes off the jacket and puts it around Heather's shoulders. 'So, what now Frankie?' she asks.

'Whatever we want, it's all over. I'm retired.'

'Frankie, please tell me something?'

'What do you want to know?'

'Be honest with me, I'm going to ask you again. Why don't you ever take off that damn hat?'

Frankie smiles. 'Because it keeps my head warm, what else?'

Heather takes the trilby off and Frankie's long, blond hair swirls down. She kisses Frankie on the lips. In the distance a clock strikes twelve and crowds cheer loud. Fireworks explode and the skies above the city that can't sleep erupt in a plethora of cascading colours! Frankie hands Heather the charm. Heather smiles. 'Thank you. Merry Christmas my girl. Frankie Angels!'

Post Note.

Frankie and Heather lived Happily ever after!

STARMAN

"I looked, and I looked, but I did not see no God". Yuri Gagarin

Today there are more than 500,000 man-made objects in space, ranging from satellites to junk, to an International Space Station. On Wednesday 12th April 1961, there was just one.

ACT ONE

THE FIRST MEN ON THE MOON

NASA COUNTDOWN.
'5.4.3.2.1. Zero–all engines running, and we have lift off on *Apollo 11!*'
So, the Starman begins. Launched by a *Saturn* V rocket from Kennedy Space Centre, in Merritt Island, Florida, on Wednesday 16th July 1969, *Apollo* 11, roars forever upwards into the heavens and beyond. Rather strangely, this truly historic event occurs in the same area as from where *Columbiad*, the giant cannon shell-spacecraft, in Jules Verne's 1865 classic novel, *From the Earth to the Moon*, took to the stars. The astronauts, Neil Armstrong, Buzz Aldrin and Michael Collins travel for three days and nights, until they enter into the Moon's orbit. Mission commander Armstrong and Pilot Aldrin put the lunar module *Eagle* down on Sunday 20th July 1969, at 20:18 UTC. (Universal Time Coordinated).

Neil Armstrong quotes those immortal words.
"Houston: Tranquillity base here. Be advised. The Eagle has landed!..."
Huge applause breaks out from Mission Control, the dream realised but the mission far from over. Whilst still on the ladder, Armstrong uncovers a plaque mounted on the landing Module bearing two drawings of Earth (of the Western and Eastern Hemispheres) and an inscription reading…
Here men from the planet Earth first set foot upon the Moon, July 1969 A.D. We came in peace for all mankind.

Armstrong becomes the first to walk on the lunar surface and describes the event for the world to hear.

"One small step for man, one giant leap for mankind..."

Six hours later, on 21st July at 02:56: UTC; Buzz Aldrin joins Armstrong. Together, they spend about two and a quarter hours outside the spacecraft. Watching from above Michael Collins pilots the command module-*Columbia* alone in lunar orbit, whilst his fellow astronauts stride where no one has ever gone previous. They plant a specially designed U.S. flag on the lunar surface, in clear view of the TV camera.

Sometime later, President Richard Nixon speaks to them through a telephone-radio transmission from the White House.

"Hello, Neil and Buzz. I'm talking to you by telephone from the Oval Room at the White House. And this certainly has to be the most historic telephone call ever made. I just can't tell you how proud we all are of what you have done. For every American, this has to be the proudest day of our lives. And for people all over the world, I am sure they too join with Americans in recognising what an immense feat this is. Because of what you have done, the heavens have become a part of man's world. And as you talk to us from The Sea of Tranquility, it inspires us to redouble our efforts to bring peace and tranquillity to Earth. For one priceless moment in the whole history of man, all the people on this Earth are truly one: one in their pride in what you have done, and one in our prayers that you will return safely to Earth."

"Thank you Mr President," replies Armstrong...

"It is a great honour and privilege for us to be here, representing not only the United States, but men of peace of all nations, and with interest and curiosity, and men with a vision for the future..."

Armstrong and Aldrin spend just under a day on the lunar surface, before returning back to Columbia and the lonesome, but smiling Collins. 'What happened to you two? It's been a little quiet around here!' The astronauts jettison *Eagle*, before performing the manoeuvre that blasts them out of lunar orbit on a trajectory course back to Earth. They return and land in the Pacific Ocean on Monday 24th July 1969. Broadcasted on live TV to an ecstatic world-wide audience. These men are to be forever immortalised for their glorious deeds. But what very few people know is that before he left the Moon surface, Commander Neil Armstrong performed one last mission before heading home. This being done on the behalf of a young boy on a far-away planet and distant English shores. To place a memorial to a fellow pioneer of the stars. A man who led the way, as Mankind made its first foray into the heavenly unknown, that exists beyond the clouds. Armstrong bent down, gently brushing away the Moon dust, and placed the letter and a Russian Rouble coin in the ground, before standing back and saluting. ''God bless you Yuri, and you too young Charlie Baker. You do him proud with your life and make sure our Starman lives forever in your heart.''

THE CHOSEN ONE

Moscow. The Kremlin.
Nine years previous. December 1960.
27 year-old Soviet Air Pilot Lieutenant Yuri Gagarin, has been summoned to the Kremlin for an audience with Russian Premier Nikita Khrushchev. A nervous Yuri had come a long way from the small village of Klushino. His father a carpenter, his mother, a milkmaid. Like countless millions of people in the Soviet Union, the Gagarin family suffered dreadfully during the brutal, Nazi occupation in World War Two. Klushino was occupied in November 1941, during the German advance on Moscow. An officer took over the Gagarin residence. Unlike so many other peasant families who were simply slaughtered out of hand, the Gagarin's were allowed to build a mud hut on the land behind their house.
"You can stay in there," said the officer. "But if I have one scrap of trouble, I will shoot you all myself."
The Gagarin's spent eighteen months in the mud hut until the end of the occupation. Even during that frightening period, Yuri was always of academic learnings, a bright boy who loved to read and had an eye for technical details that were well beyond his years. Five years following the war, at the age of sixteen, in 1950, he entered into an apprenticeship as a Foundry man at the Lyubertsy Steel Plant, near Moscow, and also enrolled at a local Young Workers' school. After graduating from there in 1951, with top grades, whilst also earning honours in Foundry-work, Yuri was selected for further training at the Saratov Industrial Technical School. There, he studied tractors, but it was whilst in Saratov, Yuri volunteered for weekend training as a Soviet air cadet at a local flying club. Here he learnt how to fly. At first just in a biplane, suddenly, Yuri had found his vocation in life. The journey to the stars was underway.

After graduating from the technical school in 1955, the Soviet Army drafted him and he was sent to the Air Force Pilot's School in Orenburg, and taught to fly MiG-15's.
In 1957,
Yuri met the love of his life Valentina Ivanovna Goryacheva. A medical technician graduate of the Orenburg Medical School. They were married on Thursday 7th November 1957, and following graduation, Yuri was assigned to the Luostari airbase in Murmansk Oblast, close to the Norwegian border. There, he rose swiftly through the ranks to Senior Lieutenant. Little did Yuri know he
was being assessed constantly for an extraordinary mission. The Soviet Union was in a space race with the United States, and amidst great secrecy taken huge strides to leap in front of the Americans.
In 1960,
after an exhaustive selection process, Yuri, along with nineteen other Pilots was chosen for the Soviet space program. He then found himself selected again for an elite training group, known as the *Sochi Six*, the best of the best, from which the first Cosmonauts would be chosen for the *Vostok* project. Yuri and other prospective candidates were subjected to experiments designed to test physical and psychological endurance to the maximum. Out of the twenty selected, the eventual choices for the first launch were Yuri and fellow Pilot Gherman Titov. In the end the decision was made.
Now, as Senior Lieutenant Yuri Gagarin is escorted into the Premier's office, and the door shuts behind him. He waits to hear the news that this son of a carpenter and a milkmaid, is set to become the first man in space.

Sat behind his huge desk, the small bull-like, bald headed figure of 67 year-old Khrushchev is busy writing. He looks up on hearing Yuri enter, who is stood to attention.
'At ease Lieutenant.'
Khrushchev sits back and studies the diminutive five-foot-two uniformed figure before him. Extremely handsome and soon to become the most famous man in all history. Yuri takes off his cap and

places it under an arm. His eyes staring straight forward, inwardly unable to believe he's stood facing the great Nikita Khrushchev.

'So, Gagarin, it appears you are the chosen one. I'm sure you will be pleased to know that you are loved by your peers also. When the twenty candidates for *Vostok 1* were asked to anonymously vote for which other candidate they would like to see as the first to fly, all but three voted for you. How do you feel about this?'

'I am truly honoured sir, I vow to not let the Motherland down.'

'Oh, I know you won't, but I asked you how you're feeling Lieutenant. Not to kiss my ass. Relax son.'

The Premier points towards a chair facing him.

'Come, sit with me for a while.'

Yuri steps forward and sits opposite Khrushchev, who pours two large glasses of vodka from a bottle on the desk, handing one over. He raises his glass high for a toast.

'Nostrovia!'

Yuri joins him and the two men drink the vodka in one hit.

'Now, answer my question Gagarin?'

'Well, I am honestly not afraid, just wary of what may lie in wait for me beyond the stars.'

'Such as?'

'The unknown, the loneliness. If anything goes wrong, I don't want my family to see me as a floating coffin in the night sky for the rest of their lives. I hope you don't think of me as a coward because of this?'

Khruschev smiles. 'You are only human Gagarin. It is only natural. This mission will require a different kind of courage. Not the type needed to fight the Nazi hordes, or in our stand-offs with the imperialist Americans today. No, when you take off in four month time from our world to beyond the stars, yours will have to be a bravery no man has ever before needed. For Gagarin, in your time in that tiny *Vostok* cockpit looking back upon this world, you shall be the loneliest man in the history of the planet. Such feelings could send lesser mortals insane. Are you ready for this kind of life changing experience?'

'I cannot honestly say until I'm in that situation. But what I can promise is that when the moment arrives I shall with all my heart think only of the Motherland. That alone should give me the strength I need.'

Khrushchev laughs out loud and refills their glasses. 'A head for politics I see. You are very guarded for one so young. I think you will make a great Politburo man.' Khruschev raises his glass once more. 'What shall we toast to now Lieutenant?'

'Whatever you wish sir?'

'How about God? Let us drink to God. I hear you believe in such nonsense. I have it on good authority from the KGB, that you and your family celebrate Christmas and Easter, and keep religious icons in your house. Am I correct on this? Is the KGB doing their job well?'

A clearly flustered Yuri is struggling. What the hell does he say to this? 'Sir, I…'

'Just be honest with me Yuri Gagarin. Do not worry, do you really think we would have invested all this time and effort in your training and preparations, without having your background fully checked out? Come on now. No, you are the Starman. You have been handpicked to perfection for the space mission. The chosen one. I just need you to understand one thing, and for you to be totally honest with me?'

Yuri finishes off the vodka in yet another single hit and puts down the glass on Khruschev's desk. 'What exactly is it you wish to know sir?'

Khruschev stares at Yuri for a moment. As if looking for some secret hidden deep behind his eyes. 'Are you really expecting to find your God out there in the heavens Gagarin? Is this the loneliness you talk about, that you fear there will be nothing, no heaven, just total silence and an eternal black sky?'

Yuri smiles. So this is what the old bastard has been after. As if he hasn't got enough worries on his mind to deal with. 'In all honesty sir, I believe I shall be concentrating so much on the controls of the spaceship, this God who you speak about could fly past me on a cloud and wave, and I still wouldn't notice!'

For a moment Khrushchev says nothing but stare once more at Yuri. Then begins to laugh out loud before downing his vodka. 'Oh, we have chosen very well, but I will tell you this just one time, and you will do good to remember Comrade Yuri Alekseyevich Gagarin. From this moment on, no more false idols boy. God is not good, he can put you before a firing squad. No singing angels. just the party. That is your mother and your God. Do I make myself clear?'

Yuri looks his Premier back in the eye, knowing well if he had answered incorrect a possible bullet in the head could have been his prize, no matter what Khruschev said about him being the chosen one. He smiles. 'Yes sir, and I swear to you that if I do see anything up there. Whether it be angels, a large, bearded man on a white cloud, or even Father Christmas himself, I will never drink again!'

Khrushchev again stares for a moment at Yuri, looking for signs of false bravado. He then smiles himself. 'Very well then, I shall trust you Gagarin. You have convinced me. But always remember this one thing.'

'What is that sir?'

'I am not a man to disappoint. Don't cross me Yuri. Do not ever try to cross me.'

THE CONSTELLATIONS

England. Manchester.
 9 year-old Charlie Baker is always being told by mum, dad, grandparents, teachers and friends that his head is in the stars. Charlie is a dreamer, a young boy happiest gazing at the night sky from his bedroom window, wondering what's up there. For his birthday Charlie's mum Eileen and dad Les bought him a telescope and through its lens, magic and wonder explodes before this young boy's eyes. The constellations, the shooting stars. The strange, but also, somehow friendly image of a man's face chalked out and looking back from the Moon. Some evenings, Charlie tries to stare him out and is convinced the man is smiling back, and that one day they'll meet. Mad as that may sound this young boy knows. He just knows, and nobody will ever tell him otherwise.
 Also Charlie loves the space comics, his hero Dan Dare. Pilot of the future. Fighting the alien villains across the vast Universe. *Marooned on Mercury. Operation Saturn.* So many adventures as Dare attempts to ultimately defeat the evil Meekon. A super-intelligent, interplanetary criminal-mastermind, who escapes and avoids capture at the end of every episode, only to return again and again, with even more dastardly schemes. Charlie laps these stories up.
 ''A head full of broken biscuits is what you have Charlie Baker!'' This what his mum tells him almost every day! ''You live in the stars, you do son!''
 Charlie is used to hearing such comments and takes no notice, for there's another problem brewing. In the school playground he's hearing strong rumours that Father Christmas isn't real. Charlie laughs like the other boys when Teddy Thompson tells all who'll listen…

"Santa isn't real, I know this for a fact, and anyone who still believes in him is a big girl's blouse!"

Charlie still believes for now, although he's not saying anything to Teddy Thompson or anybody else. Charlie Baker will make his own mind up on Christmas Eve.

Walking home from school, alongside his best mate Harry Doyle, Charlie decides to approach the subject very gingerly.

'What did you think of Teddy saying all that stuff about Father Christmas today, Harry?'

'Well he does have a big mouth Charlie, but I have to admit, I agree with him.'

Inside, Charlie's heart sinks. He was hoping, like himself, Harry was still a believer. 'Me too Harry. Me too.'

Harry pulls out a bag of sweets and offers Charlie one.

'Here you go old chum, I suppose you're star watching again tonight?

'Of course Harry,' smiles Charlie. 'I have to say hello to the man in the Moon. He'll wonder where I am if I don't!'

A laughing Charlie and Harry sit down on a wall. Harry looks up at the miserable grey, murky heavens.

'I'm surprised you can see anything through that dirty sky?'

'Oh, I can see everything Harry.'

Harry smiles, because he knows what's coming next. His friend is going to talk all about the magical stars, and nothing can stop him!

'They're called constellations Harry. Humans have been looking up at them since we lived in caves. We think there are about eighty-eight named. So, it says so in my book anyway. And sometimes, sometimes they feel so close and are so beautiful, you just want to reach up and touch them.

Like paintings in the sky.

There's Andromeda, who is known as the chained maiden. She appears during November and December and is named after a mythical Greek princess. Andromeda was first noted by the Greek astronomer Ptolemy in the second century. The second century Harry! Can you believe that?' Harry shakes his head in mock wonder, and puts another sweet in his mouth!

'Then, there's The Big Dipper Harry. This is part of the constellation Ursa Major. The Great Bear.' Charlie stands and postures like a grizzly bear, pretending to attack a laughing Harry!
'There's Canis Major. The Great Dog. Now, every hunter needs hunting dogs as companions Harry, and Canis Major and Canis Minor are the hunting dogs for Orion. The Great Hunter of the sky. Most importantly, Canes Major is home to Sirius, the brightest star in the night sky. The brightest of them all!' Harry offers Charlie another sweet. He accepts it gladly. 'Cheer Harry. Cygnus the Swan. This great bird soars high in the night sky during the early mornings in late Summer, and in the evening, during Autumn. Then, Gemini. Known as The Twins. These are companions of Orion. Gemini is visible in the early, morning skies during Autumn and early winter.
A smiling Charlie looks over at his friend. 'Am I going too fast for you?' Harry shakes his head, lying, whilst sucking furiously on his sweet and totally lost!
'Then we have Leo the Lion. Leo is just one of a group of constellations around Orion. A lion in the sky Harry. A lion! How brilliant is that? Orion is The Great Hunter and the largest constellation in the sky. This giant figure, a warrior dominates all of them. Scorpius. The Scorpion. You don't see this often Harry, only in Southern skies during the months of July, August and September, but it's A beauty. Taurus. The Bull. Another close friend of Orion, Taurus is directly above the Hunter in the sky. Then there's the giant red star Aldebaran…'
 Suddenly, a laughing Harry stands up, puts his hands over both ears. 'Please stop! You've lost me. I give up, I really, really give up Charlie Baker!' Harry hands a smiling Charlie yet another sweet, and he looks back up to the sky. 'I could go on all day.'
'I know,' replies Harry. 'That's what was worrying me!'
The two boys laugh and carry on walking home.
'Can I tell you something Harry, but you must promise not to laugh.'
'Of course I won't laugh silly, I'm your best friend.'

They stop walking and Charlie turns to face Harry. He takes a deep breath. 'Well the thing is Harry, I'm still not convinced Father Christmas doesn't exist. When I look through my telescope and see such wonderful things, I still want to believe, and I don't care what bloody Teddy Thompson says. How can you trust someone who picks his nose and eat the crows?'

Harry is laughing out loud at this. So much he sets Charlie off! Finally, they both stop to catch breath.
'I'll tell you another secret Charlie.'
'What's that then?'
'I still believe as well.'
Charlie smiles wide at his friend. 'Thanks Harry.'
There's still some hope, thinks Charlie.

MAN ON THE MOON

Manchester. Christmas Eve.1960.
 Charlie is in bed,
 but so far from sleeping. It's close to midnight and he's listening out for any movement on the stairs outside the bedroom. Foremost amongst his thoughts, mum and dad taking the presents downstairs, and then the much, more important task, listening out for sleigh bells.
'Come on Santa,' he whispers. 'Your last chance tonight.'
Charlie closes his eyes and hopes beyond all Christmas hopes, but sadly can clearly hear the creaking of stairs and the sound of mum's voice shushing dad. 'Quiet Les love, he'll hear you and don't drop anything!' Charlie concentrates harder listening for noises outside, but nothing. He leaps out of bed and sneaks onto the top hallway, just in time to see his parents disappear into the living room, downstairs, clutching a host of wrapped presents.
'You go back up and get the rest Les. I'll set these up under the tree, and don't wake him.' Hearing this, Charlie races back into his room, jumps into bed and puts the covers over him. The light on the landing beams bright, as his smiling dad pops his head in.
 'Merry Christmas little man,' he whispers.
 Charlie has tears forming in his eyes. This annoys him and he wipes them clear. Once dad has gone, Charlie goes to his window and stares out at the night skies. Snow is falling heavy, he tries to focus hard through it, desperate now in search of a childhood dream, but failing. No reindeers pulling a magical flying sleigh being driven by Santa Claus, with a sprinkling of silver dust in its midst. Nothing, Charlie sighs heavy, only then to notice once more the face again. The man in the Moon is smiling back at him!
 'One day we'll meet. One day I'll shake your hand Mr Man in the Moon. You just wait and see.'

COMING HOME

Moscow. Christmas Eve.1960.
Yuri Gagarin is sat in his apartment on the sofa, with arms around heavily pregnant wife Valentina. In front of them a table with a half, empty wine bottle upon it and a large, warm, red-lit log fire glowing bright. Valentina is becoming increasingly worried about her husband. Although totally in the dark as to Yuri's mission, due to the secrecy involved, she knows one look and this is a man with an awful lot on his mind. Yuri is staring into the log fire, his thoughts a million miles away. 'Yuri, what is wrong my love?'
He smiles. 'Nothing is wrong.'
'No, there is something. I know you better than you know yourself Yuri Gagarin. Talk to me husband.'
Yuri finishes his glass of wine, then reaches for the bottle and refills it. He kisses Valentina softly on the lips and touches her belly.
 'Is he or she behaving well?'
Valentina laughs. 'Ah, whoever it is boy, girl, they are kicking their mama like a wild horse. But don't you try and change the subject Yuri. What is wrong?'
'If there is something bothering me, you know Valentina, that I can never speak of it with you. It is far too dangerous.'
Valentina jokingly looks behind the sofa and under the table.
'I see nobody else here, what, is it something so terrible and dark you cannot share it with your wife. The mother of your child and soon to be another child?'
'Yes. That is exactly the reason Valentina.'
'I don't understand Yuri, at least let me in just a little.'
He smiles. 'When you look at the night sky what do you see? How does it make you feel?'
'Yuri I…'

'Valentina, please, just answer my question. It is important.'
Valentina stands, goes to the window and stares up at the moonlit evening. 'Well, I see stars, thousands of them twinkling like little diamonds, I see a full Moon, sometimes, especially, when I was a child, I would see a man's face in there smiling back at me. I would also see comets and shooting stars. I loved to watch them hurtle through the skies.'
Valentina turns to face Yuri. 'But why do you ask this?'
'Because that's always what I what you to see. Our children also. And our grandchildren.'
'Is there going to be a war with the Americans Yuri? Is this what you are trying to tell me? Are we all going to die soon?'
'No, my darling wife,' smiles Yuri. 'There is not going to be a war. Yuri hugs a tearful Valentina tight. 'Ignore me husband, it is just the wine and the time of year. Are you upset because we can no longer celebrate Christmas and Easter, Yuri? Is this why you are not your normal self?'
A smiling Yuri nods and kisses his wife on the forehead.
'Yes Valentina, that is the reason. You can read my mind girl. I can have no secrets with you.' Yuri's mind is already high above earth looking down from his *Vostok* rocket ship. He has been told by his superiors the success rate for the mission is rated at just fifty-per cent. Frightful odds, but one's not necessarily enough to make him break out in a cold sweat. As a child in post-war Russia's decimated landscape, Yuri and his brother would often wonder in the woods and find countless amounts of abandoned, military hardware. Yuri's favourite game was taking the pin out of a grenade with a ten second delay, holding tight until counting to six then throwing it. He and his brother diving for cover as the grenade exploded! Now he faces similar odds and Yuri is going to ensure the rocket will not become an eternal tomb encircling the Earth skies forever more, and breaking the hearts of his family, every time they looked into the night sky. Yuri Gagarin is determined that he will be coming home.

LIFT OFF

Wednesday April 12th 1961.
Shortly after 0700. BST.
  Major Yuri Alexeyevich Gagarin, is led onto the boarding path for *Vostok 1*. He takes a deep breath before entering the spacecraft at the Baikonur Cosmodrome launch pad in Kazakhstan, Soviet, central Asia. Once all last minute checks are completed, *Vostok 1* is launched, and the Starman is on his way.
A crackle of noise and the historic radio communication between the control room and Yuri at the moment of rocket launch.
"Control. Preliminary stage…intermediate...main... lift off! We wish you a good flight. Everything is all right."
  Yuri checks all his controls. Takes a deep breath. He is ready.
"Let's go!"
This a phrase that will swiftly enter the annals of Russian folklore.
'Come on Yuri,' he says quietly to himself. 'Deep breaths, you're only going to the stars, it's not that far!'
  For the next two hours the rocket simmers and smokes silently on the launch pad, awaiting its cue to launch into history. Finally, the word is given and amidst a blazing sea of flames, *Vostok 1* ascends, slowly at first, but gathering speed with each passing second, until soon it is arcing through the atmosphere at a terrifying velocity. Yuri endures ten minutes of gruelling acceleration, before the rocket's final stage shuts down. Ten seconds later, the spacecraft separates and for the next hour and a half, *Vostok 1* will orbit the Earth.
  Travelling at more than 17,000 miles per hour, (27,000 kilometres per hour.) *Vostok 1* is guided entirely by an automatic control system. There is only one message Yuri officially relays back to Earth during his one hour and forty-eight minutes in space.
"Flight is proceeding normally. I am well..."
Alone amongst the stars, Yuri has little time to think, never mind take in the mind-blowing views from the porthole window of the Earth,

and deep space. All the time at the back of his mind is Valentina and their children. He has no intention of making them orphans at such a young age, and being forced to see their father's coffin in the night sky forever more, so, Yuri concentrates every thought on the control panel, ensuring all is functioning properly. Only once is his attention distracted, as a flash of light on the porthole blinds him, albeit momentarily. As Yuri opens them once more, what he witnesses outside the spacecraft just a short distance away leaves him utterly staggered. He rubs his eyes, looks again, it's gone. A smiling Yuri remembers his promise to Premier Khrushchev.
'Nobody will ever believe me anyway.'

The mission is complete and the time has come for Yuri Gagarin to return. Once through the Earth's atmosphere, he prepares for the final phase of his journey, a last descent into Southern Kazakhstan, the Saratov region of central Russia. Huge applause and bear hugs await him, as the Cosmonaut lands safely back on Earth. A hero of the Motherland, a legend is born!

Yuri is also famously welcomed back to our planet with a hospitable offer of bread and milk by locals Anna Takhtarova and her 4 year-old granddaughter Margarita. Anna smiles wide.
'Welcome home Comrade Gagarin.'
'Thank you for the bread and milk, Yuri replies, also smiling. 'It is good to feel my feet back on solid ground!'
'I watched you in the sky,' says Margarita, pointing upwards.
'You are the Starman.'
Yuri leans down to talk to Margarita. 'I am a Starman who is eager to enjoy your lovely bread and milk.'
Margarita hugs Yuri and the many cameras flash.

On hearing the news, the Soviet premier Nikita Khrushchev, sends word from his holiday home on the Black sea, congratulating Yuri Gagarin on his monumental achievement. A message of truly, historic, undertaking.

"The flight made by you opens up a new page in the history of mankind in its conquest of space. You are now our Russian Christopher Columbus!"
Khruschev also sends word that Yuri be flown to him, soon as possible. Khrushchev needs to see and look into his eyes. Only then can he truly relax. "I need to see you boy. I need to know."
To an astonished, awestruck world, the Soviet news agency *Tass* make the first official announcement of Yuri's flight, at just before 0800. BST. Radio Moscow then interrupts its schedule to give full details to a jubilant nation. A world listens in shock and awe.
A new age has dawned.

Four days after Yuri Gagarin returns from his flight,
 the Soviet Government holds a press conference during which he addresses his country and the world. Yuri is introduced by famed rocket scientist A.N. Nesmeyanov.
'Everything is symbolic in this achievement. The fact that the first Cosmonaut is a Soviet citizen, the fact that the first cosmic spaceship carrying Yuri Gagarin was named *Vostok,* meaning East or Dawn, and also the fact that the flight was completed in the morning, these are all symbolic. For the morning is the dawn of a new era. From now on the day of Wednesday 12th April 1961, will be connected with the achievement which was accomplished by Yuri Alekseyevitch Gagarin. The entire flight around the Earth was completed in just 108 minutes, every one of these precious seconds have shaken the world. Comrades, it is with great honour that I present to you, the Starman!'
  As the huge applause starts to wane,
 Yuri stands waiting to answer questions.
'Comrade Gagarin, many people are interested in your family biography. Can you tell us of your background?'
Yuri smiles on hearing this thinking, here we go. Brace yourself in Gagarin. 'I have read in the newspapers that some irresponsible persons in the United States of America, who are distant relatives of the Gagarin's consider that I am one of their offspring's. Well, I am sorry to say they cannot be more wrong, for I am a simple Soviet

man. I was born to the family of a peasant. A proud man, my father was a fine carpenter. My mother a milkmaid. The place of my birth was in the Smolensk region. There were no princes or nobility in my family tree. Before the revolution, my parents were poor peasants. The older generation of my family, my Grandfather and Grandmother also. There never has been any blue blood in our family. Or indeed red, white and blue!
Therefore, I will be forced to disillusion my self-appointed relatives in America. I can assure you we will not be meeting anytime soon!'
 There is great laughter around the room on hearing this, before finally dying down.
'How did your journey to the stars begin Comrade Gagarin?'
The questions fly for hours until, finally, the last two.
'Comrade Gagarin, can you explain to us just what you witnessed whilst in orbit?' Yuri's wry smile luckily not giving ruse to his true feelings. If only they knew, the Cold War would end tomorrow?
 'Well, the Earth's surface looks approximately the same as seen from a high-flying plane. Clearly distinctive are large mountain ranges, huge rivers, forest areas, shorelines and islands. The clouds which cover our Earths' surface are very visible, their shadow on the Earth can be seen distinctly. The colour of the sky is completely black, meaning the stars against this backdrop are so much brighter and clearer. The Earth itself is surrounded by a blue halo. This particularly visible at the horizon. From a light-blue colouring, the sky blends into a beautiful deep blue, then a darker to violet and finally complete black. Darkness comes over instantly and nothing can be seen. During this period, the spaceship passed over the ocean, sadly not cities. Otherwise, I would have probably been able to see their shining lights and waved! Finally, when the mission was complete, we activated my return to earth. This passed smoothly and without incident, but it was still with great relief, when I once more felt the Motherland's soil beneath my feet. As you all know, it is always good to be home Comrades!'

Once more a standing ovation for the Starman, before a final question. 'Comrade Gagarin, what lies ahead for yourself and the Soviet space program?'

'I am immensely glad that my beloved Motherland was the first in history to penetrate the cosmos. The first airplane, the first satellite, the first cosmic spaceship, the first manned flight into orbit. These are the opening stages on the great road of our journey towards discovering the mysteries of outer space. We shall go on and conquer the stars, but it shall be done in the true spirit of peace and not militarism. Personally, my biggest wish left now is to fly towards the Moon, then onto Mars. That is the dream and with our magnificent crews of Cosmonauts and scientists, it shall hopefully be achieved. Thank you all.'

Cue, yet another standing ovation, but there remained one thing Yuri never mentioned...

'I just couldn't,' he says quietly to himself.

A DAMNED MOVIE STAR

The United States are left reeling in shock at this sudden and totally unexpected Space coup by the Russians. A deadly blow to the Americans who had hoped to be the first to launch a man beyond Earth's atmosphere. They had scheduled their first space flight for the following month of May, but now with Yuri's successful mission, this feat would elude the U.S. space program, until February 1962, when astronaut John Glenn makes three orbits on *Friendship 7*.
However, back in 1961, The *Cold War* is suddenly igniting as another bear, a ferocious, unfriendly one now sits alongside the Ursa Major constellation-the Russian version taking its place amongst the stars. Despite the gravity of their defeat, President John F Kennedy realises it is wise to soothe panic amongst his military hawks, who amongst these are an influential, formidable few who believed almost with holy decree that the only way to defeat the Soviet Union is to 'Hit them before they hit us' attitude. A lunatic plan of action that can result in only one outcome. Armageddon. Wise and savvy enough to realise it is best to reach out with an olive branch, and not DEF CON 3, Kennedy immediately phones Premier Khrushchev to congratulate him on his country's magnificent achievement. Rumours that a Russian launch attempt was imminent had been circling for days, but few in Washington believed their great adversaries had advanced so far in such a short time. The previous era was one of fierce competition between the US and the USSR, with the link between space exploration technology and military technology all too apparent. A clear example, the *Vostok* rocket that took Yuri on his pioneering journey, was adopted from a Soviet Intercontinental Ballistic Missile, the *R-7 Semyorka*.
  This triumph of the Soviet space program in putting the first man into space has hurt not just the United States with its propaganda

value, but also bruised badly their ego and pride. As Kennedy meets with his brother Bobby and close confidante Kenneth O'Donnell, in the Oval office to discuss this crisis. It's clear calm heads need to prevail, and that now the race to put a man on the Moon is one they simply can't afford to lose.

The President has his back to the desk looking through the huge windows onto the White House lawn, when Bobby and O'Donnell, a former World War Two bomber Pilot enter.

'Bobby, Ken, what the hell happened?'

O'Donnell looks at Bobby as if expecting him to answer. The President now facing them with arms crossed, looking stern-faced.

'They won Jack,' says Bobby. 'Those sonofabitch, Commie bastards caught us with our pants down, you have to hand it to them.'

'It isn't good enough just to say that Bobby, what were the CIA doing, walking about with their goddamn eyes shut? I want to speak to Allan Dulles, someone's head is going to roll for this. He's always so damn quick to point the finger in our direction.'

'We got caught off guard,' replies O'Donnell. 'All our eyes have been on preparing for the Bay of Pigs invasion. I would advise against going after Dulles and his mob for the moment. God knows things are tense enough between us as it is.'

'Who is the goddamn hotshot they sent up there?'

O'Donnell rustles through a file he's holding.

'27 year-old senior Lieutenant Yuri Gagarin. One of their very best. A Pilot from Soviet Air Force group One. Born Klushino, 1934. A prodigy. That's about all we know.'

O'Donnell passes the file over to the President, who stares at a photo of Yuri in uniform. JFK smiles. 'Well, Comrade Gagarin, you appeared to have let the wolf loose in the chicken coop, young man.

He shows the photo to Bobby and O'Donnell. 'Have you seen this guy, he looks like a damned movie star? They are going to milk this for every Rouble its worth, and Yuri here appears to be the perfect leading man?'

'I have to admit Jack,' replies Bobby. 'There is a part of me admires what this fellow did. It must have taken real guts.'

'All well and good Bobby, but we can't let this stand. The United States has to be seen to be winning from this day on, from this moment, the race to the Moon begins. Get my speech writer Teddy Sorensen to start work on something that will put the hell and brimstone under our guys and fire us towards the damn stars. Am I clear?' Bobby and O'Donnell both nod. A smiling JFK stares again at Yuri's photo. 'All kudos to you Starman, but this is not the end, it is merely the beginning.'

ACT TWO

A REAL LIFE STARMAN

Manchester. Wednesday 12th April 1961.
 Now resigned to the fact that there is definitely no Santa Claus, Charlie Baker is sat in his bedroom reading a book he received at Christmas about the planets. Ever since learning the truth Charlie has said nothing to nobody, not even to Harry, but inside he's deeply upset. As Charlie looks at the pages, so many different worlds, he finds it impossible to think that there can be nobody else out there in the universe. Strange, but since Christmas Eve, even the man in the Moon's face has vanished. He doesn't even bother looking through his telescope anymore.
Charlie feels so alone…
Suddenly, his door opens and there stands Les, all red-faced and out of breath. 'Charlie lad, come downstairs now, you have got to hear this! It's amazing son. We've done it, our Comrades have only gone and bloody done it! Les turns and races downstairs with a flummoxed Charlie close behind. They head into the living room, where his mum is sat listening to the radio. She smiles wide towards him.
 'Listen Charlie! Listen to this it's wonderful!'
 Les is jumping about like a jack in a box! 'Listen Charlie son! You're not going to…'
'Quiet Les! Let the boy hear!'
With his dad's arm around his shoulders Charlie's heart soars.
'The BBC can now confirm that the Soviet Union have successfully launched a man into space. 27 year-old Cosmonaut Yuri Gagarin

orbited the planet and has returned safely. We will bring you more news as we receive it.'

An incredulous Charlie smiles wide for the first time since Christmas Eve, so there is magic in the sky after all. A Starman, a real life Starman! Suddenly, the thought that Santa didn't exist isn't so painful anymore.

'A socialist did this Charlie!' said Les. 'One of us! A bloody Comrade in arms!' Les is a trade union official who works for the Amalgamated Union of Foundry Workers based on Chorlton Road, in Manchester, Moss Side. An amused Eileen watches Les with a look of mock derision on her face. 'Les, calm down love, you're making this sound like one of your Foundry workers flew the spacecraft around the Earth himself!'

An ecstatic Les kisses Eileen on the cheek. 'That's just it Eileen, he has. Don't you see, it was a collective effort by the workers. It's one in the eye for the big bosses. This is our victory. Mr Gagarin has done us proud!' There's tears in Les's eyes as Eileen hugs him tight.

Suddenly, it dawns on Charlie just how much this means to his dad. A thought occurs, he runs back upstairs and sets up the telescope on his window ledge.

Charlie focuses in on the Moon, there he is again smiling wide. The man in the Moon is back!

'Yes!' shouts out Charlie. 'Welcome back Comrade Moon!'

A smiling Charlie punches the air! 'I can't wait to see Harry at School tomorrow!'

I SAW NO GOD

Moscow.

In scenes not witnessed since the monumental victory parades at the end of World War Two, Cosmonaut Yuri Gagarin is paraded and lauded through the capital's streets in an open top car. Hundreds of thousands line the routes, all desperate just to catch a mere glimpse of the unassuming young man with the huge smile who they are calling the Starman. Dressed splendid in a bright green uniform adorned with medals, Yuri waves to the adoring masses. He is being showered with flowers and confetti, a true hero of the Motherland. When finished Yuri has an appointment at the Kremlin, once more with Premier Nikita Khrushchev. Sat in the front is 38 year-old KGB intelligence officer Sergei Belikov. He watches on in disbelief at the astonishing scenes unfolding around them, as it appears all of Moscow has turned out to welcome Yuri. As one of the KGB's best men, Belikov is honoured to be given the role of his handler. He is expected to act as both spy and bodyguard on Yuri. To never leave his side, and report anyone or anything that might deflect or hinder the Soviet Union's plans for him. For to the Party now, the extremely, handsome and affable Cosmonaut, Yuri Gagarin, has suddenly become their most potent weapon in the ongoing *Cold War* against the United States and its allies. Yuri is priceless, it has been decided in the highest Soviet echelons of power that new battle plans must be drawn up so that the Starman can go forth to capture hearts and minds. Finally, amidst the fervid, surging throngs of people in Red Square, all creating a sea of waving flags and desperate just to be near their hero, Yuri's entourage arrives at the Kremlin. He and Belikov are swiftly escorted into the inner sanctum by a stern-faced military attaché. On arriving outside Khrushchev's office, the attaché points to Belikov.

'You must wait out here.'

Belikov and Yuri have become close in just the short time they have shared together. 'It appears you are on your own Starman. Behave yourself in there.'

Yuri smiles. 'Sergei, I spend more time with you than I do my wife. A little break should do us both good.'

Both men laugh and Belikov goes to sit on a nearby chair.

'When you come out I'll be waiting for you right here!'

'Don't be so sure Comrade, I might just jump out of the window and head back to the rocket. It is the only place I can get peace and quiet!'

Belikov laughs. 'I wish you luck with that. But the days of peace and quiet are over now Comrade. I'm afraid you and me belong to the Motherland.'

Premier Khrushchev is stood waiting when there's a knock at his door. Yuri enters. Khrushchev goes across to greet him with a huge bearhug and kisses on both cheeks. He's smiling wide whilst clutching Yuri's shoulders with his arms.

'We of the Soviet Union are in your debt Yuri Alekseyevich Gagarin. You have brought so much pride and joy into our hearts and earned for yourself a glorious place in the Motherland's history.'

The Premier takes from a small box containing a Hero of the Soviet Union medal, and places it on Yuri's lapel.

Khruschev smiles. 'You are now my son Yuri Gagarin, I feel the love of a proud father for you.'

He points to his desk. 'Come, come let us toast your magnificent achievement.' The Premier pours two large vodkas. He hands one to Yuri, whilst raising his high. 'To the Starman for bringing everlasting glory to the Soviet Union!'

The two men toast and down their drinks in one hit. Immediately, Khrushchev refills the glasses. 'Such a historic occasion as this demands we drink long into the night, but we shall have to postpone to a later date, for the Motherland has great plans for you.'

Again, they toast and drink the vodka in one hit. Finally, Khrushchev sits down and motions Yuri to do similar.

'Your life is now no longer your own, I am sure you understand this?'

'I am aware of my responsibilities. I will do my duty sir.'

'I have no doubts you will Comrade Gagarin. Your weapons now are your smile and your personality. You will be meeting Kings and Queens, Presidents, Prime Ministers and Politicians across the world. You must treat them all with this magic you have boy. You will charm them. You will be our flag Yuri. You will open factories, you will give speeches and kiss babies. No longer are you a man of war. There will be no more flying for you my son.'

A horrified Yuri cannot believe what he's being told. 'Sir, please, I am a Pilot, I…'

Khrushchev puts his hand up to silence Yuri. 'I know this is difficult for you Gagarin, but we simply cannot allow you take the helm of another MIG15 or space rocket. You are too important now to the Motherland. What, did you honestly believe we would let you take that risk?'

'What do you mean, my wings to be taken away? I always believed this publicity tour was merely temporary, then I would be allowed to return to my normal duties. But to ground me permanently? Sir, I am a Pilot, you may as well cut off my arms and legs.'

'Believe me, I am sorry boy, but this is how it has to be. The reality is you are simply far more important to us alive than dead. There are others, many ready to take your place in the cockpit, but there is only one Starman. There is only one Yuri Gagarin. A man who has looked down upon the Earth and not up. That is you, Yuri.' A smiling Khrushchev pours them both another vodka. 'Ah, I think we can allow ourselves one more of these whilst we speak of this.'

Khruschev passes Yuri his drink over the desk.

'Thank you sir.' Yuri is clearly still reeling from the notion of being told he's not allowed to fly anymore.

'Do you remember our previous conversation Gagarin?'

'I do.'

'So then,' smiles Khruschev. 'Did you find your God out there beyond the stars? Did he wink and give you a nudge, as to whether

he exists?' Yuri ponders this question whilst keeping eye contact with his Premier. What he saw up there, Yuri is certain must remain a secret. Although there remains no doubt whatsoever in his mind, that it was real. 'I saw absolutely nothing sir, my time was spent mostly pressing buttons in the spacecraft keeping myself alive.'
Khrushchev starts to write a line on a piece of paper. He passes it over to Yuri. 'We shall arrange an interview where you shall be asked a question, this shall be your reply.'
 Looking at the paper Yuri reads it. 'I looked and I looked, but I did not see no God.' Yuri stares back up at Khrushchev. 'I have already told you sir. The answer is I saw nothing. Why do we have to go through all this again?'
'For the good of the people Lieutenant Gagarin! It is part of your new role. Khruschev appears close to a meltdown! 'To hear these words coming from your lips that this absurd notion of a higher being, this Holy Trinity, this Father, his Son and the Holy Spirit. Where people drink his blood in churches and their sins are forgiven. What witchcraft is this? No, there is only one who should be obeyed, that is Mother Russia. Only to her should we answer. Is that understood?'
'Yes sir.'
 Yuri stares at the red-faced Khrushchev, whose rant has clearly left an ailing effect on him. What he saw in space at that moment was undoubtedly his Premier's worst nightmare. For a second, Yuri contemplates telling Khrushchev, because it would probably give him a heart attack, but it's only a passing idea. Thoughts of Valentina and their two baby girls, Yelena and Galina swiftly overwhelm any urge to come clean. For what good could possibly come from it? A firing squad? His family killed also or shipped off to a gulag. No, he thought, best live with it. That way nobody gets hurt.
 'When I am asked, I will say as ordered. I saw no God.' Khruschev smiles. 'Good, so we clearly understand each other?'
'Yes sir. Absolutely.' Khruschev eyes Yuri Gagarin with caution. He knows this young man who has already captivated the world and looked down upon it with secret eyes is hiding something. Call it a

sixth sense, but it disturbs Khrushchev, much worse, scares him rigid. Just what did this Starman see out there in the darkness of space?

As Yuri reappears from the office, a smiling Belikov stands up and points to the Cosmonaut's lapel. 'Don't tell me, another medal off the Motherland? Congratulations. How many is that a hundred, two hundred, a thousand?'
 Yuri tries to smile at his friend's joke but doesn't really have the heart for it. 'A great honour yes, though as I am sure you already know, they are not letting me fly anymore. Too dangerous, claims Khrushchev.' Yuri and Belikov walk side by side down a long winding corridor, with magnificently, framed photographs of former leaders and great Soviet deeds hung upon its walls.
'No, I did not know Yuri. I am truly sorry.'
'It appears now until my end of days, I am nothing more than, to quote our great leader, a flag.'
'Well Comrade, on the bright side, I get to see some weird and wonderful places, and drink fine wine, and meet beautiful women, whilst you have to deal with the boring side of things, like shaking hands with all those imperialists bastards!'
'Whatever happened to watching my every step and listening in on my every word?'
Belikov smiles. 'My Father was a fisherman from the Crimea Yuri. He had a saying, 'Never try and teach a fish to swim.' In other words, no one plays the game better than you Comrade Gagarin. I would not dare embarrass or risk harming our friendship by spying on you.'
'Just what kind of KGB officer are you Sergei Belikov?'
'I am loyal to the Party, but also to you Yuri, and would give my life for both. Personally, I see no distinction. You are one and the same.'
 'Ah, but Comrade Belikov,' smiles Yuri. 'What if I was to admit I am a huge John Wayne fan?'
 Belikov shakes his head in a mocking grave manner. 'Well that changes everything Comrade Gagarin, for then I would be forced to shoot you!'

Both men start to laugh, the sound echoes far down these famed, gold braided-red carpeted corridors. Through the years so much blood-stained history, all spilt in a savage revolution, and a war fought against Hitler, almost to the Nazi's last man. Now, the same conquerors had their eyes on the stars.

ONE OF US

England. Manchester.
 Les Baker is in his office at the Foundry Union building in Moss Side. He's pondering an idea, one so fantastic he can't figure out whether it is lunacy or sheer genius. Les writes down a name and smiles. 'For Charlie. I wonder, I just wonder?'
 He picks up the piece of paper and steps out. Les walks fast and brisk to the office next to his. There, the Union boss, 61 year-old Frank Evans, is sat with his feet up on the desk, reading a newspaper and drinking a large mug of tea. Les knocks on his open door and Evans glances up, appearing rather perturbed on being disturbed from his relative slumber. Though he is smiling. 'Yes, brother Baker.'
Evans reluctantly puts his newspaper down on the desk.
'What can I do for you?'
Les steps in, shutting the door behind him. His face a little pensive. He scratches his head.
 'What's eating you lad? Your face isn't suited to keeping secrets. Speak up.'
 Les hands the piece of papers over to Evans.
'Yuri Gagarin?'
'He's the Russian Cosmonaut who orbited the planet three months ago Frank.'
'You don't say Les. There's me thinking he was Manchester United's new centre forward. What are you up to?'
'I've been reading up on Gagarin, Frank. Well, you're not going to believe this, but before he became a Pilot, Gagarin worked in a Foundry. He's one of us!'
'Les, are you feeling okay? Maybe you should go home and have a lie down? Get Eileen to make you a large whisky toddy.'

A clearly excited Les sits down opposite Evans. 'I think we should write a letter to the Kremlin and invite Brother Gagarin to come and visit us. We, this building, right here in Manchester. Solidarity with his fellow Foundry workers, and one in the eye for the bosses. What do you think?'

'I think you've gone stark raving bonkers Les. This is the most famous man on the planet. Of all time even and you think we can get him here to Manchester. To Moss Side?'

'Well, we do try to keep the red flag flying Frank. Brothers in arms and all that. Can't do any harm to ask?'

Frank leans back in his chair, he sighs heavy. 'Okay Les, write your bloody letter, but don't get your hopes up. Trust me, if anyone even bothers to open and read it over there, chances are it will go straight in the bin.'

Les smiles wide. 'Cheers Frank, I'll get cracking on it straight away!' Les leaves the office, and a smiling Frank sits watching him utterly dumbstruck. He shakes his head. 'The Starman in Manchester? You're mad Baker. You've most definitely lost the plot Comrade!'

SUPER-BEING

Moscow. The Kremlin.

Premier Khrushchev is at his desk, when a knock on the door and the uniformed, Soviet propaganda Minister Colonel Alexei Petrov enters. A thin man, with slicked, black hair and hawk-life eyes. He carries a long, jagged scar on his cheek to the forehead, a permanent reminder of a German grenade at Stalingrad. Petrov has in his hand a letter. He stands before Khrushchev. 'Sir, I believe there is something you should be made aware of that we have received.'

Petrov passes the letter over to Kruschev.

'We have translated it for you.'

Khrushchev takes a minute or two to read the said letter. He appears engrossed, before finally looking up towards Petrov.

'Is this the Manchester of Frederick Engel, Alexei?'

'Yes sir,' smiles Petrov. 'The very same. A city in the North of England with huge Socialist leanings. The letter you have just read, this invitation for Yuri Gagarin to visit the headquarters of the Amalgamated Union of Foundry Workers. This is a wonderful propaganda coup. Think about it, a Soviet spaceman being cheered to the rafters by one of the largest unions in Europe. The workers of the world united by our very own Yuri Gagarin.'

Khrushchev continues to read...

'This Comrade Les Baker states that the Foundry Union wish to honour Gagarin with a medal and grant him honourable membership of their Manchester branch. Make this happen Colonel, give it top priority. Where is Gagarin at the moment?'

'We are still drawing up his schedule for the world tour, but are keeping him busy across the Motherland unveiling statues of himself, and attending invites to witness streets being named in his honour. I have word from his handler that our hero is hopelessly bored, but smiling like the legend he truly is. Belikov says our people are in total awe of him. It is like they are coming face to face with an out of the world, super-being. Apparently, Gagarin finds it all quite overwhelming, but he continues to kiss a thousand babies a day and shake ten thousand pair of hands! No doubt sir, Comrade Gagarin is performing his duty.'

The words 'super-being' have clearly irked Khrushchev. Something about Gagarin's demeanour when quizzed on the existence of God, and the look in his eyes on asked whether he'd experienced anything out in space, has left him cold, almost frozen in fear. He knows the Cosmonaut is hiding a secret, but it is something Khrushchev simply doesn't know how to confront. So, he thinks best do nothing for the moment. 'Bored you say? Well, maybe a trip to England and meeting Comrade Baker and his English brothers may just be what Gagarin needs to shake him up and realise the importance of his role. Make all preparations Petrov, I want him to travel to England, soon as possible. Contact Manchester. Tell them the Starman is coming.'

Petrov smiles wide. 'Yes sir. This is a letter I am very much looking forward to writing.'

GUESS WHO'S COMING TO DINNER

England. Manchester.
 Tuesday 23rd May 1961.
Charlie Baker and best friend Harry Doyle, are walking home from school. As ever Charlie is in raptures over Yuri Gagarin. Since the Cosmonaut's spaceflight, every inch of his bedroom wallpaper is covered with pictures of the Spaceman and his rocket ship *Vostok 1*. A shrine to Gagarin's historic mission. Charlie has read every newspaper, comic and magazine article on it since, and is arguably Manchester's finest expert now at just 9 years-old! At least that's what Harry thinks anyway. He walks along sucking on his sweets, now and again offering one to Charlie, so he goes quiet for a moment, and letting him breathe. Only then to begin once more explaining to Harry, in the minutest of details, how it was possible for Yuri to enter space legend, and now adorn his bedroom walls.
'Next stop is the Moon Harry! Nothing can stop us now. It's all systems go. The boffins will be working as we speak on some kind of super propulsion system that will be able to take spacemen to not just the Moon, but even further. Maybe even Mars!'
 Harry is listening on with one ear. He doesn't possess his mate's adoration of all things Yuri Gagarin, but does tend to enjoy Charlie's sheer excitement, and the stuff about the Moon and Mars makes even both his ears pick up.
 'Really Charlie, really? We're going to travel through space. Put spaceman on Mars like Dan Dare?'
'Just a matter of time old pal. The genie is out of the lamp Harry!'
The boys reach Charlie's house. I'll see you in school tomorrow Harry.'
 A smiling Harry offers Charlie a last sweet which he accepts.
'Bye for now Charlie, say hello to Yuri on your wall for me!'

The boys laugh, only to suddenly see Les appear at the front door.
'Lads!' he shouts over. 'Come in here now, both of you!'
Charlie and Harry exchange quizzical looks, then run up the garden pathway and into the house. Once in the hallway…
'In the living round boys, hurry up!'
Charlie and Harry enter in to see a smiling Les and Eileen both stood facing them. Les is holding up a letter.
'Do you know what this is?'
The boys both shake their heads.
'No dad, but my guess is a letter?'
'Absolutely no idea Mr Baker,' adds Harry.
'Well then, let me give you both a clue.' Eileen playfully punches Les' arm. 'Stop teasing the boys Les, tell them.'
Charlies appears mystified, whilst Harry is starting to think the entire Baker clan are all quite mad!
'Okay then,' continues Les. 'This here is a letter I've received at work today from the Kremlin.'
'Is that the Kremlin in Moscow Mr Baker?' asks Harry.
'The very same Harry. I take it Geography is your strongpoint at School?'
'Dad, you're not a spy are you?'
Les starts to laugh. 'No Charlie, no son, I'm not a spy! we're going to have a visitor. Guess who's coming to dinner?'
'Dad, I don't understand, who is it? What are you going on about?'
'It's the Starman, Charlie lad, the man on your wall upstairs. Yuri Gagarin is coming to Manchester!'
Such is the joy these words mean to him, Charlie feels tears welling, then he yells and jumps into his dad's arms! 'Yes, yes, yes!'
Meanwhile, a smiling Eileen puts an arm around a shocked Harry's shoulders. He is standing there with his mouth open, unable to speak.
'Come on poor Harry, you can help me in the kitchen, we'll leave these two spacemen to it. I'll ring your mum, tell her you're having tea here with us.' They both leave the room as Les and Charlie continue to cheer and generally go mad!

WELCOME TO MANCHESTER

England. Manchester.
Wednesday 12th July 1961.
 Exactly three months on from his journey into space, Yuri Gagarin, finds himself on a specially chartered Vickers Viscount 800 airliner, aptly named Sir Isaac Newton, heading for England, Manchester.
 He's sat staring out the porthole, his eyes lost high up amongst the clouds. Alongside him as ever is Sergei Belikov, who is watching him closely. Yuri has hardly spoken since they left their last stop of Finland. His first official call on this world public relations tour.
 'A rouble or two for your thoughts Comrade? You look lost in space.' Without turning to look Yuri smiles, but it's one tinged with sadness. He continues to stare through the porthole.
'I belong out there Sergei. High in the heavens. These days I just feel trapped on the ground. Like a bird with no wings.'
A smiling Belikov suddenly has an idea. He grabs Yuri's arm. 'Come with me.' A quizzical Yuri stands and follows Belikov, as they head up towards the cockpit and enter. Flying the plane are Captain James Firth and his younger Co-Pilot, Hugh Stannard. Both ex RAF.
 Belikov smiles towards them. 'Excuse me Captain, my friend here is a Soviet Air Pilot, but has not flown for a while. He has a heavy heart. Would it be possible for him to take over the controls and with your assistance spend some time at the helm?'
 Both Pilots stare and are clearly in awe of Yuri's presence. He's stood facings them in his bright-green Air Force uniform.
 'I don't think we would have a problem with that,' says a smiling Captain Firth. 'What says you Hugh?'
 'None whatsoever sir. It would be an honour.'
Stannard stands and removes his headset and hands it across to Yuri.
'Please, Lieutenant, be my guest.'

'Thank you,' replies Yuri. 'I promise to look after it!'
Yuri takes the vacant seat next to Captain Firth.
'Would you like to take over for a while Lieutenant Gagarin?'
'I would love to, thank you Captain!'
Back at the helm for the first time since the space mission, and feeling once more like his old self, Yuri Gagarin takes over whilst crossing the North sea. He checks all is good on the control panel. Belikov watches on, this is the first time he has seen Yuri genuinely happy and smiling. The true face of the Starman. Belikov pulls Stannard over to one side of the cockpit. 'Please, never breathe a word of this. I will be shot!'
Stannards laughs. 'Only to my grandchildren many years from now sir!'

In typical Mancunian fashion, even on an early July afternoon as the Spaceman touches down on the tarmac at Ringway airport, the rain is falling in torrents. Now sat back in a passenger seat, Yuri unfastens his seat belt and stares through the rain-strewn porthole. What he sees is a murky, miserable grey scene. In many ways reminiscent of home. As the airplane turns and makes it way towards the terminal, through the mist for one moment, Yuri thinks he sees huge crowds of people, but puts it down to being weary and the fog making his eyes play tricks on him. He rubs them hard. Belikov has said to expect a small delegation, but nothing more. Finally, the airplane comes to a halt, and as Yuri and Belikov are gathering their belongings, a beaming Captain Firth heads towards them.

'Firstly, I would just like to say to you Lieutenant Gagarin, that it has been an absolute honour to fly alongside you today.'
'The honour is all mine Captain Firth.'
Yuri and Captain Firth shake hands.
'Also, gentlemen, I must inform that waiting for you on the runway, and back in the terminal building are quite literally thousands of people. You may have been born in Russia, Lieutenant Gagarin, but to the people of Manchester, you have come from the stars!'
As the airplane doors are swung open and a smiling Yuri appears into sight, utter pandemonium breaks out amongst the waiting crowds.

Hundreds are on the tarmac behind a thin line of Policemen, whilst back in the terminal building, thousands await to catch a glimpse of the Soviet Cosmonaut, who has soared beyond the heavens. Shouts of his name go up from screaming young girls. Manchester has never seen anything like this. The man from the stars has come to the rainy city. There's no *Cold War* in this Northern outpost today, just an outpouring of love, respect and mystique for the boy from Klushino, who has tripped the light beyond the clouds. Whilst waving to acknowledge this fantastic reception, Yuri tries to speak into Belikov's ear but can hardly be heard! 'What the hell is going on Comrade?' A laughing Belikov waves also to the soaking, ecstatic, Mancunian masses. 'I have no idea! Just keep smiling Yuri, remember this place is called Manchester and how happy you are to be here. Do not worry Comrade, I will be by your side throughout.'

A laughing Yuri turns towards Belikov. 'Sergei, you worry far too much, You KGB types. You must learn to relax my friend, otherwise you will have a heart attack!'

Yuri makes his way down the airplane steps, only to see the crowd surge forward past the haplessly, outnumbered Policemen, and carry him joyfully away on their shoulders. Belikov watches on in utter disbelief! 'Hey, bring him back now!' he shouts. 'He is ours!'

A horrified Belikov watches on as this hero of the Motherland is swept further from the airplane, and the KGB man's grasp. Yuri catches his eye and with a huge grin gives him the thumbs up!

'They are going to shoot me,' says Belikov quietly. 'Then they are going to wake me up and shoot me again!'

As the Police try desperately to snatch their VIP guest back and into the arms of a desperately, worried official welcoming committee, including the Lord Mayor of Manchester, the honourable Harry Lyons, Yuri is the very model of good natured, patience and composure. The Cosmonaut is waving, smiling and shaking hands, before finally managing to persuade the adoring Mancunians to put him down onto the floor, so he can proceed with his day!

'Please, my friends. I do not bounce well, please put me down!'

This, the locals do with a loving care and respect, as if Yuri was one of their own. All officialdom has vanished as Ringway airport resembles a madhouse, with thousands upon thousands now encircling Yuri, welcoming him to their city. A line of harassed Police officers, some with helmets still in place, most not, force a path for Yuri to swiftly meet the jostled and clearly, embarrassed city representatives. An official holds an umbrella over both the heads of Yuri and the Lord Mayor. 'We are so sorry for all this pandemonium Mr Gagarin,' says Harry Lyons.
'Please do not apologise. This reception is beyond my wildest expectations.'
'We do have a car waiting,' continues Lyons. 'But the crowds beyond the airport are huge also. It could be a while before you reach any of your set destinations.'
 Finally, Belikov turns up, utterly staggered by the scenes around him, and so relieved Yuri Gagarin hasn't been kidnapped!
'Thank God they never dropped you Gagarin!'
'Agreed!' smiles Yuri. 'We best get started don't you think?'
The Lord Mayor turns to an airport official. The open Bentley is at the far of the hangar. Can you arrange to bring it here? We are never going to make it through this lot on foot.'
 The official nods and walks swiftly away. All this time the crowds continue to chant Yuri's name. 'Yuri! Yuri! Yuri!'
Belikov pulls him to one side. 'I don't want you standing up in the car. It makes you too easy a target.'
Yuri stares back at Belikov like he's gone mad, and starts to laugh.
'A target for what, all this?' Yuri points around at the thousands of people cheering his name in the Mancunian downpour.
'Have I ever listened to a word you said Sergei?'
Belikov has a wry, but amused looked on his face. 'For what it's worth, I do outrank you Lieutenant Gagarin. I could officially have you shot for disobeying orders!'
 A smiling Belikov takes Yuri's arm. 'Please, just promise me you will stay in eyesight? For me.'
'A deal!' replies a grinning Yuri.

The open Bentley pulls up alongside them. 'Hey you!' The Lord Mayor calls out to the driver. 'Put the hood back up, we can't have Lieutenant Gagarin getting drenched all the way from here to the Union headquarters in Moss side.'

Yuri is listening in. 'Please no, if all your people have been good enough to come out to say hello, then I must insist the hood stays down. Besides, what is a little rain?'

On hearing this a smiling Belikov shakes his head. He can already see tomorrow's newspaper headlines across the world.

'Starman dies from common cold in Manchester!'

'As you wish Mr Gagarin,' says Lyons. Hardly willing to argue with a living legend, and thinking of the better photographic opportunities for his good self to be seen alongside Yuri Gagarin.

The twelve mile journey from the airport to Moss side, sees the pavements packed five to six deep with rain-lashed, but joyful Mancunians. The weather is unrelenting, but even under dark and gloomy thunderous skies, nothing can dampen Manchester's enthusiasm to take this young Russian Pilot to their heart. Yuri is showered with flowers, red roses and carnations whilst stood up, and seemingly intent on waving to every single person. Soaked to the skin, he's offered an umbrella by the Lord Mayor, but politely declines. 'No thank you sir, if all these people have turned out to welcome me and can stand in the rain, then so can I. It is the least I can do.'

Amongst the cheering crowds are legions of schoolchildren, some taken to see the visiting spacemen by enlightened teachers, others arriving via more enterprising routes, such as bunking off school for the day! Finally, Yuri arrives in Moss Side, outside the Foundry Union's headquarters, and once more an adoring mob of well-wishers who have waited hours in the teeming rain are on hand to greet him. Belikov simply shakes his head in astonishment. 'You don't even get this kind of reception in the Motherland. It is like you are the Russian Elvis Presley! What have you got on these people Gagarin?'

'So long as I don't sing, then I think we shall be okay,' smiles Yuri! Belikov bursts out laughing. Yuri never ceases to amaze him.

'How do you stay so calm with all this going on my friend?'
'When you have witnessed what I did Sergei, you realise, all this, the world, everything in it. We are simply a raindrop in a storm.'
Belikov follows behind as two Policemen stand either side of Yuri escorting him into the Union building. He thinks back to what Yuri just said. What did he mean, ''a raindrop in a storm?'' Suddenly, from the crowds, a young girl no more than 5 years-old breaks clear, and runs to hand him a small bunch of flowers. A smiling Yuri bends down to accept them. 'Thank you young lady, you are very kind.' Yuri accepts the flowers and kisses her on the cheek, before taking the girl back to her parents. The father offers his hand.
 'Welcome to Manchester Yuri lad. It's so good to see you mate!'
Yuri shakes the man's hand before heading back over and taken inside.

WHEN CHARLIE MET YURI

Waiting for Yuri in the lobby is Union Foundry leader Frank Evans and alongside, smiling wide in his best suit, shaking like a leaf is Les Baker. Les has a special favour to ask Yuri Gagarin, one he knows risks losing him his job, but a promise is a promise. Especially, when it is to your son.

Earlier that morning as Charlie was getting ready for school and properly miserable because he risked missing out on seeing Yuri Gagarin, his dad walked into the bedroom. 'You okay son?'
'Not really dad, I would have loved to meet Yuri, but if a chance pops up could you try and get his autograph for me?'
'I think I can do better than that Charlie lad. School won't miss you for one day. Get changed you're coming to work with me!'

Now, staying quiet with the light off in his dad's Union office, sits Charlie, who is obeying orders off Les. 'Stay out of the bloody way!' Charlie is hoping and praying that the next people to walk through the door are his dad And the Starman.
Meanwhile, elsewhere in the building, Yuri and Belikov are introduced to Frank Evans and then to Les.
'I'm so very pleased to meet you Comrade Gagarin. It is truly an honour.'
'I recognise your name Mr Baker. You are the person who wrote the letter, am I correct?'
'Yes sir.'
Belikov smiles wide. 'Thank you. You have done a great deed.'
'It was my pleasure,' replies a blushing Les.
'What gave you the idea Comrade?' asks Yuri. 'Never in my wildest dreams did I believe I would receive such a wonderful reception from your people.'
'It was my son Charlie. He's your biggest fan Mr Gagarin. A real dreamer, but a good lad. I believed that with you being a fellow

Foundry worker and Charlie's love for the stars, well, I thought nothing ventured, nothing gained. And as you proved yourself just three months ago, anything is possible sir.'

'I would have loved to say hello to your boy Mr Baker.'

'Les inches closer to Yuri and whispers into his ear. 'I've actually got him hiding in my office, if you possibly get a minute?'

Les steps away leaving Yuri smiling and nodding towards him. 'No problem Mr Baker.'

Harry Evans coughs loud. 'Comrades, if we can all move into the main hallway, we have a special presentation for you Mr Gagarin. Now, shall we?' Evans points to the hall, whilst glaring at Les, who doesn't meet his boss's eyes. He daren't!

At a formal ceremony before a large audience of Union workers, Yuri is presented with a specially designed gold medal, which he immediately pins to his uniform along with the many others. The medal has on it a design that is also to be the new logo for the Foundry Union showing the hands of two people cradling a globe with the words...

Together Moulding a Better World

Yuri is also appointed the first ever "honorary" member of the Amalgamated Union of Foundry Workers. Grand speeches are made. All this time the huge crowds outside continue to shout his name. Yuri insists on breaking away from the festivities to go to the window, where he remains for some time, smiling and waving to the adoring Mancunians. Then, Yuri remembers his favour to Mr Baker.

He catches his eye across the room, nods, and Les motions for him to follow.

Charlie is sat patiently in the dark office. He can hear clearly all the cheering outside, the festivities going on elsewhere in the building. But orders are orders off dad, Charlie Baker isn't moving. Suddenly, the sound of footsteps approaching makes him slide down under the desk. The door opens, he can see from below two men enter. One pair of legs appear familiar, the other?

Les switches the light on. 'Come on Charlie son, get up! I've got somebody with me who would like to say hello.'

Slowly, Charlie rises and can't believe his eyes.

Yuri smiles on seeing him. 'Hello Charlie Baker, I'm very pleased to meet you.' Yuri steps forward and an open-mouthed Charlie moves from behind the desk. They shake hands.

'Hello Mr Gagarin sir!'

For once in his young life Charlie is speechless, much to his dad's amusement! 'Thank you for taking the time to come and see me.'

Yuri sits on the desk with arms folded. So, young man, we don't have much time. Do you want to ask me some questions about my spaceflight?'

Charlie joins him on the desk, his legs dangling, his eyes never off Yuri. Les steps back enjoying the scene. His boy and the Starman.

'I have three questions if you don't mind Mr Gagarin?'

'Fire away Charlie,' smiles Yuri. 'But please keep them short.'

'Will do sir.'

'My handler will find us soon, he is like my mother!'

'Okay, here goes. Number one. What will you remember most about being high amongst the stars?'

'I saw two dawns in one day Charlie, that was truly special, and is something I will tell my two young daughters about until they tire of it.' Charlie nods in agreement. He would never tire of being told this.

'Mr Gagarin, do you think if you and the Americans joined together to conquer the stars and go further to the Moon, maybe Mars even, then it might make us realise we are all really just the same, and there's no need to blow ourselves up. There's no such thing as Russians, Americans or English, we're all just Human Beings, don't you think?'

'Wow! Charlie, you are a smart lad!'

Yuri stares across to a very proud, looking Les. 'I so hope too Charlie, this world belongs to all of us. To you and your children also. Nobody wants a war, there are many good men on both sides who think as we do. Trust me, I will do my best to ensure there is more cooperation,

and who knows, in just a few years we may have a joint mission to the Moon?' Yuri looks at his watch and just as he does so a smiling Belikov enters. 'So, this is where you are hiding. There are many important people looking for you Starman?'
'Hello Sergei, let me introduce you to my new friend Charlie Baker. Charlie, this is who I was telling you about. My second mother!'
'Please to meet you Charlie Baker, Yuri, please. We have to go?'
'I know, very shortly, but Charlie has one more question to ask, go on boy.'
'Thank you, Just a short one Mr Gagarin, when are you going back to the stars?'
For a moment Yuri's smile disappears. He looks across to Belikov, who can't meet his eyes. Yuri puts an arm around Charlie.
'Not for some time my friend. But can I tell you a secret?'
Charlie nods vigorously, whilst Belikov looks set to self-ignite!
'The truth is Charlie, there is not a day goes by when I don't dream that I'm still up there, because in my heart I never left. Do you ever look up to the skies at night, and see the man in the Moon?'
'Yes sir, he's my second best friend after Harry Doyle.'
'Well, that is me up there. Every night you must look up and say hello. You promise me this, yes?'
'I promise you Yuri, er, sorry, Mr Gagarin!'
Yuri smiles. 'Call me Yuri, Charlie Baker, we are friend now. Right?'
'Yes Yuri!'
Yuri jumps up. He straightens down his uniform and points towards Belikov. 'I must go now before my mother over there gets really mad and throws something at me!'
Charlie stands facing him. They shake hands again, and Yuri slips a Russian rouble coin into his hand. 'It has been a privilege meeting you Charlie Baker.' Yuri nods towards a smiling, tearful Les.
'Hey, Yuri!' calls out Charlie.
The Starman turns around to face Charlie.
'At Christmas, I found out there was no Santa Claus, it was my dad over there putting the presents under the tree. I didn't believe in magic

anymore, that was until you flew to the stars. Then you became my new Santa Claus. My Starman.'

Yuri smiles wide before leaving with Belikov. Charlie appears in shock as he watches them head out the door.

'Dad, did that really just happen?'

'Yes son. Don't forget to tell your mum when you get home!'

PRIME MINISTER IN A WEEK

After saying a last farewell to all at the Foundry Union headquarters, next up for the visiting Russians is a tour of the vast, Metropolitan Vickers Works at Trafford Park. Again, thousands of workers mob Yuri. Police are forced to stop the traffic, and move back the crowds to allow Yuri's Bentley through the gates. His welcome is tumultuous, but does not alter the Cosmonaut's, smiling, composure. On his mind though is Charlie's last question.
 The hurt never leaves.
Once inside, the vast crowds are clapping and cheering as they follow Yuri on a factory tour. Again, Police Officers need to force a path through the sea of people lying in wait, all struggling to catch just a mere glimpse of him. Hundreds are giving Yuri congratulatory slaps on the back, and as he stops to sign a few autographs, pure mayhem erupts! Factory security men and Police detectives encircle Yuri to prevent him being pushed over by the ecstatic, overly enthusiastic crowd. Belikov grabs hold of Yuri. 'This is getting too crazy Comrade!'
'Do not worry Sergei. Nobody ever got killed by kindness my friend!' As the commotion continues something attracts Yuri's attention.
 'That is not right.'
Yuri heads across to a photographer, who is standing on a casting to capture a better shot. 'Hey, please come down. This casting is unfinished and can be spoiled by someone standing on it.'
 Sheepishly, the photographer steps off.
'I'm very sorry Mr Gagarin.'
'It is okay,' smiles Yuri. 'I was once a Foundry worker and although I do a different job now, I am still the same old Foundry worker at heart!' These comments cause another explosion of applause and cheering. Again, Belikov shakes his head. 'If the rest of England is like Manchester, Yuri will be Prime Minister in a week!'

After the factory tour, the Police link arms to make a pathway through for Yuri to reach the car park. There, a lorry has been set up as a temporary platform for him to address a crowd of over five thousand people, made up mostly of workers from Vickers, but swelled by hundreds more from surrounding factories that have given up their lunch hour to come and see the Starman. Still, the Police are grappling with the crowds to keep some sense of order, as many try to climb onto the lorry, only to be pulled back down by the Manchester Constabulary.

Yuri's speech is brief.

'I carried no armaments or photographic equipment on my flight. All the devices on board were for scientific and technical purposes.'

Thinking again of Charlie, he stops for a moment.

'There is plenty of room for all in outer space. Plenty of room for the Americans, the Russians and the British. I look forward to the day when Soviet space ships will be flying to the Moon and working with American and British scientists who will be there too!'

Cue, unadulterated scenes of joy as the crowd explode on hearing these stirring words. Finally, in what resembles more a getaway, than any sense of civic formality, the Bentley speeds out of Vickers and heads to Manchester Town Hall for the official reception.

There, the crowds around the building number over six thousand Now half an hour late they are again handed a large Police escort to get through. Nothing has been spared to salute the visiting space hero. The Russian national anthem is played and the red flag has been raised over the Town Hall. As Yuri salutes on the building steps, a small boy breaks through the Police cordon, takes a quick photo and then stands staring at him in complete shock. All as if he can't believe who is stood before him. A smiling Yuri ruffles his hair. 'I hope your photo is a good one!' The boy appears hypnotised as the Police lead him back to the crowd.

ANGELS

Later at the luncheon, the head of Jodrell Bank, Sir Bernard Lovell is introduced to Yuri. 'Mr Gagarin, there are so many things I would like to ask, but I'm sure you will not be allowed to answer any of them?'
Lovell smiles, as he notices Belikov who is nodding to agree.'
'I would like to thank you Sir Bernard for the assistance Jodrell Bank has given our space programme in tracking the early launches.'
'Anything we could do to help. I was hoping you may find time in your schedule to come and visit us at Jodrell Bank?'
Yuri looks across to Belikov, who shakes his head.
'I am sorry, we have to be in London later tonight, but I hope to return one day. Please, then you ask me again?'
'Excellent, would it be okay if I called you Yuri?'
'Of course,' smiles Yuri.
'Yuri, this current obsession with destroying our world that exists today. You have given us hope that we can rise above it and look to the stars for a shared dream. One that hopefully sees us enter a period of enlightenment and away from this nuclear madness that currently engulfs us. For that I sincerely thank you sir.'
 Lowell offers Yuri his hand and the two men shake.
'Believe me Sir Bernard, do not despair, I can promise you when I looked down upon our planet, I saw only one world, one shared not by different countries or religion and ideologies, but by the human race. I am just a Pilot, much wiser men than myself will prevail on both sides to ensure a better future for our children.'
 'Ah, but you forget Yuri, I don't know if you are a religious man, but you have been closer to God than anyone ever in the history of civilisation. Out there in space, a Starman, alone.'
 Belikov is watching Yuri closely, he appears edgy with this conversation, and is readying to step in.
'I can promise you Sir Bernard, I saw no God up there. Just the black of space.' Belikov breathes a sigh of relief.

'Of course you didn't Yuri. Besides, if you did see anything, you would never tell me, would you?'
'If you want confirmation of a higher being, I advise you to just pray harder Mr Lovell.'
'Quite,' smiles Lovell.
Belikov goes to whisper into Yuri's ear. 'Time to go Comrade.'
'Please excuse me Mr Lovell it appears I have to, as you say, mingle.'
'Are we really alone then Yuri Gagarin?'
A smiling Belikov shakes his head on hearing this, only then to have his attention grabbed by a Town Hall official desperate to have Yuri be photographed with another publicity seeking politician.
'Mr Lovell,' says Yuri quietly. 'Whilst my mother is not listening, trust me, tell your people with their fingers on the atomic trigger. We are not alone. Take care now.'

Later that evening,
the Russians return to Ringway airport for the flight to London, unbelievably, there are still thousands of people lying in wait to wish their hero a fond farewell. As Yuri reaches the top of the airplane steps, he turns, grins wide and blows a kiss before entering, the doors shutting behind him. The Starman has come from afar and just for a short while, his wonderful smile has lit up this rain-soaked, Northern city. One thing is certain, Yuri Gagarin may only have been in Manchester for a day, but he will be a Mancunian for a lifetime.
The Manchester Evening News wrote the next day about Yuri's visit. "His was a human achievement, a victory for man's spirit and courage. That is why any sort of hesitation in the hospitality would have jarred so much. But any suggestion of that has been swept away in the tumult and the shouting, for the ordinary people's cheers have blown away the cobwebs of protocol. It is the human warmth of the welcome that counts."
The Soviet press were equally extolling the virtues of the visit. Pravda. "Manchester's toiling masses accorded Major Gagarin a reception unsurpassed in its cordiality. Never over the past many tens of years has Manchester met anybody with such an embrace. They

were greeting the Cosmonaut as a glorious son of the Soviet toiling masses, who had demonstrated to the whole world what the people of triumphant Socialism could do.''

Once airborne, Yuri puts his head back against the chair and closes his eyes. Sat next to him, a smiling Belikov watches this with an amused look on his face. 'I do not believe it Gagarin, you are human after all!' Yuri smiles, but doesn't reply. Belikov is worried, his Starman and friend is troubled. 'Before you drift off Starman, tell me, what was the nonsense talk with Lovell all about.'

Yuri's eyes remain closed. 'If, I am not wrong he wanted to talk to me about angels.'

'Really? I thought he was a serious man?'

A smile comes across Yuri's face. 'Even serious men need some magic in their life Sergei.'

'But Angels? Are you playing with me Gagarin?'

'Maybe Sergei. Maybe not! Maybe our feet should always remain on solid ground, for that is where we belong?'

Before Belikov can question Yuri more, he turns around to see him fast asleep. He smiles on seeing his friend grab some much needed rest. 'Sleep well my friend, but please not of angels up there. Unless they are on our side.'

That same evening Charlie is at his bedroom window, staring up at the sky, waiting for the moon to appear from behind the black, misty-swaying clouds. Suddenly, it shows and Charlie smiles wide.

He clutches tight on the Rouble coin.

'Good evening Yuri!'

ACT THREE

THE MAN WHO FELL FROM THE STARS

Following the world tour,
 the sudden rise to fame and grim realisation he will never be allowed to fly again takes a heavy toll on Yuri. Whilst long-time friends and acquaintances say he's always been a "sensible drinker" the touring schedule places him in countless, social situations where to drink was always expected. The Starman would smile, raise his glass, a toast, then another and so Yuri drank many times to the extreme. Blocking out the misery of never again being higher than the heavens. Yet still the honours keep on coming. This hero of the Soviet Union constantly wheeled out in view of an adoring audience to pin yet another service medal onto his chest.
 In 1962,
 Yuri is posted to Star City, the Cosmonaut facility. There he spends several years helping to work on designs for a state of the art, re-usable spacecraft. However, even being back amongst fellow Cosmonauts is small comfort, the pain inside at not flying remains, it cuts deep, but every time he asks to be recommissioned, it is treated with short shrift by commanding officers…
 "Stop complaining, you know the situation. You are far too important Gagarin, your duties now lie elsewhere."
 Yuri is fed this same line endless times. He feels each medal is like throwing him a fish to stay happy about having his wings clipped.

Even more honours are passed Yuri's way. Promotions follow, he becomes a Lieutenant Colonel of the Soviet Air Force. As if in an ongoing erstwhile rush to keep Yuri content, he's soon promoted again. This time to the rank of a Colonel. The honours, tributes and even more medals are stacking up, but they mean little, for nothing even comes near, or could ever replace the flying.
he Starman, it appears has fell to earth.

Paris International Air show.1965.
  US astronaut Neil Armstrong has recently completed his first space mission off *Gemini 8* and his encounter with Soviet Cosmonaut and legend Yuri Gagarin comes about completely by chance. Both men are in Paris representing their respective space programs at the Air show. Yuri has already been photographed shaking hands in a public relations exercise with two of the NASA Astronauts off the recent *Gemini 4* mission, Edward H. White II and James A. McDivitt. Away from the cameras, Yuri manages to have a good chat with White and swiftly comes to the conclusion, the only difference between them is a flag. It ends in handshakes, bearhugs and with promises that they must meet again in more peaceful times. Yuri wishes White all the best for future space missions, and that night is sat alone, seemingly unnoticed, drinking vodka in a hotel bar in the centre of Paris. A small anonymous figure dressed in a dark business suit and simply staring at his glass, dreaming as ever of the stars.
Or at least Yuri thinks he hasn't been noticed.
  A tall man dressed casually in an open shirt and smart suit approaches his table.
  He's smiling. 'Would you mind if I buy you a drink?'
The man speaks with an American accent. Yuri looks up and recognises the face immediately.

BLESSED

Neil Alden Armstrong was born on Tuesday 5th August 1930, in Wapakoneta, Ohio, the eldest of three children. Though both of his parents are extremely devout Christians, Armstrong is no great believer. His first experience of aircraft comes at the Cleveland Air Race, when he is taken at the age of two. Four years later, Armstrong is in flight after his father pays for the two of them to be taken up in a Ford Bi-Plane. Thereafter, flying gradually becomes an obsession, expressed first through model aircrafts, followed by in his early teens, flying lessons. Armstrong is presented with a licence on his sixteenth birthday, even before he has learned to drive a car!
After leaving High School, Armstrong studies Aeronautical Engineering as a naval air cadet at Purdue University. After two years at College, in 1949, he is called up for active duty, undergoing flight training in Florida, before being sent to Korea, where Armstrong flies seventy-eight combat mission over the next three years. After the war he returns to Purdue, teaching Mathematics, while completing his qualifications. Armstrong graduates in 1955, and successfully applies to be a Test Pilot with the National Advisory Committee for Aeronautics (NACE), soon to be renamed the National Aeronautics and Space Administration. NASA.
Based at Edwards Air Force in California, he's quickly deployed on space-related programmes, and for seven years he test flies many of America's future, supersonic fighters. His seven flights in the top secret X-15 aircraft take him at speeds of up to 4,000mph, to the edge of space. By then, John Glenn has become the first American to make an orbital flight of Earth, and an initial group of seven astronauts are halfway through Project Mercury, the first of the three programs leading to the Moon landings. Then, in September 1962, Armstrong and eight others are accepted to form a second cohort of astronauts billed as the *'The New Nine'*.

They are all superb candidates, America's finest. The prestigious Newspaper, The Washington Evening Star is already busy forecasting that Neil Armstrong will be the man to take control of America's first attempt to land on the Moon. He makes his first space flight as Command Pilot of *Gemini 8*, becoming NASA's first civilian astronaut to fly in space. Armstrong performs the first docking of two spacecraft with fellow Pilot David Scott. This mission is aborted after he's forced to use some of his re-entry control fuel to prevent a dangerous spin, caused by a stuck thruster. If it wasn't for Armstrong's swift thinking, disaster could well have occurred. Back at NASA control, Neil Armstrong's card is marked.
He's Moon bound.

Yuri smiles wide. 'Only if I can buy you one back Mr Armstrong.'
He stands and shakes Armstrong's hand. He looks around the empty bar and feels safe. 'Let us go and drink at the bar. It is much more fun.' Yuri and Armstrong head over to the bar, and settle on a couple of stools. A smiling young barman in smart attire comes across.
'Yes gentleman. What can I get you?'
'A beer for myself, and you Yuri? Your magic potion sir?'
Yuri laughs. 'In the spirit of space international relations and co-operation, I will happily share a beer with you!'
'A true gent Mr Gagarin.'
'Please, call me Yuri.'
The waiter returns with the beers placing them on the bar. A smiling Armstrong passes one to Yuri. 'Please, call me Neil.'
Armstrong raises his drink high.
'To the stars and a better future for our kids.'
The barman smiles and starts to wash glasses nearby.
'I know you lost a very, young daughter three years ago. From the bottom of my heart Neil, I pray she rests in peace. As for our toast? To the stars, our kids and Nostrovia Comrade!'
'Nostrovia Yuri!'
The two men drink.

'Thank you for your kind words about my daughter. Her name was Karen.' For a moment they say nothing, but stare, both smiling. Yuri decides he's going to break the silence. 'So, you are the enemy yes?'
'It appears so Yuri!'
'I read about you saving your people on *Gemini 8* Neil. What you did was remarkable.'
'Thank you, but I just remembered my training. There's no time to be scared up there Yuri, nobody knows that more than you.'
'Still, I salute you.' Yuri raises his glass and Armstrong joins him. They drink once more. 'Your beer is really good Neil,' smiles Yuri. 'You Americans have surprisingly good taste!'
'That maybe so Yuri, but myself, I'm also partial when not working that is, to a glass of your Mother Russia's finest!'
'These days it is my space fuel Neil, I am sad to admit. I have kissed so many babies, shook so many hands since the mission. Ha! It is the only thing that keeps me sane.'
'You're not going back up anytime soon then?'
'That is highly confidential. Don't forget my friend, we are officially enemies, sworn to bring each other's ideologies down, even if it means destroying the world in doing so.'
'What say we take off our uniforms and speak man to man, Yuri Alexeyevich Gagarin. Spaceman to Spaceman?'
A smiling Yuri nods in acknowledgement. 'Sounds fine by me Neil.'
Yuri and Armstrong chink glasses once more and drink.
'So, let me guess. The boys in charge over there, they figure you are too much of a Flash Gordon sonofabitch to risk putting you back in the chair?'
'In a manner of speaking, yes. They have turned me into a living statue, and will not let me near a plane, never mind a rocket ship.'
'That's because you are priceless to them Yuri. You beat us into space, you done it fair and square. But I'll be damned if you are going to beat us to the Moon!'
Both men laugh.

'I hope you are chosen Neil. It will be a wonderful thing to experience. To see the earth from the Moon? Our life's dreams complete.'

'As the good Lord made us. I take it you are not a God fearing man Yuri?'

'I have my faith Comrade. As you can imagine it is something I must keep in my heart.'

'Did they know of this when you flew?'

Yuri nods and takes a drink. 'I was just the best man for the job.'

'I always read Khrushchev was a real hardliner on religion, you surprise me. They must have rated you very highly Yuri.'

'When I first met Khruschev, I was convinced I was going to be pulled off the mission. Especially when he informed me that they knew I was a practising Orthodox Christian. I got a warning and also told to stay quiet if…'

'If what?'

A smiling Yuri laughs, but it's a nervous one.

'Khrushchev was somehow convinced that once out in space, I would see God and tell the world of it over the transmitter.'

'That's just crazy Yuri!'

Something of a worried glint in Yuri's eyes, makes Armstrong believe he is trying to reach out and tell him something.

'Did you see actually see anything up there?'

Yuri stares back at Armstrong as if he's desperate to talk but can't.

'Well, did you?' asks Yuri.

Armstrong laughs. 'I asked first!'

Yuri looks around the bar. It remains empty, accept for the seemingly bored, disinterested barman rearranging a drinks display.

'I saw something Neil, that to the day I die, I will never be able to explain.' Armstrong looks across to the barman.

'Two large vodkas please!'

The drinks arrive, Yuri picks his up. 'If I told you what I saw, you will think I am a madman.'

'Let's be honest with ourselves Yuri. Nobody has any idea about space. It is an open book up there. Hell, we have hardly scratched the

surface, and possess absolutely no idea what lies in wait for us deep in the Cosmos.'
'What I saw Neil exists only in myths and folklore.'
'Tell me Yuri, what exactly did you see?'
'Back in 1961, after the mission, when I was touring England, I met a young boy in Manchester called Charlie Baker. Charlie told me that the Christmas just gone, he had finally discovered that the one you call Santa Claus did not exist. Charlie was devastated, but then when I orbited the earth, he started to believe in magic again. I had become his Santa Claus. This kid asked me three questions about the flight. One of them was what I would remember most about the flight? I lied and told him seeing two dawns in a single day, when I should have told him the truth. For some reason this has haunted me since. I also told him that every time he looked to the stars I would be smiling down. I would be his man in the Moon.'
' But surely that's a good thing Yuri.'
'No, you do not understand Neil, it just proves that I'm not Charlie's Santa Claus. Or his man in the Moon. There cannot be two of…'
An incredulous Armstrong stares at Yuri. 'Are you seriously saying what I think you're…?'
Yuri downs his vodka, and motions to the barman for another two, before turning back to face Armstrong. He's smiling wide. 'I will tell you, but I think you should have another drink first my American friend!'

The next morning Neil Armstrong is sat in the hotel lobby drinking black coffee, nursing a slight hangover. Two men in casual clothes, shirts and slacks approach him. They are CIA.
'Mr Armstrong,' the first one says. 'May we have a word sir?'
Armstrong motions for them to sit down facing him.
'Thank you sir,' says the second man.
'What can I do for you two gentlemen?'
It's regarding your conversation with Mr Gagarin last night,' replies the first man. Armstrong smiles. 'CIA? The barman, I presume.'

The second man shakes his head. 'French Intelligence actually. They just passed you on. We are just doing our job sir.'

'Is this about my conversation with Mr Gagarin?'

'We feel it may have been somewhat inappropriate regarding the present climate,' answers the first man. 'Gagarin is after all the enemy.'

'I don't see Yuri as my enemy. He is a fellow Astronaut. Or Cosmonaut as his people call them.'

'He is a serving officer in the Soviet Air Force sir,' replies the second man.

'They've clipped him. Gagarin no longer flies.'

'Be that as it may we still have to ask you?' says the first man.

Armstrong takes a sip of coffee whilst staring at both men.

'What exactly do you both need to ask me?'

The first CIA man smiles wide. 'I believe you know well sir. It's regarding Gagarin's extraordinary, bizarre claims about what he witnessed in space.'

The second man places a small taping device on the table and starts to play Yuri's voice. …'I will tell you, but I think you should have another drink first my American friend!…'

The same man turns it off. Armstrong shakes his head and places the coffee down onto the table. He sits back in the chair with arms folded.

'You want to know if I believe him?'

'No sir,' replied the first man. 'We want to know if you think Gagarin is mad?'

Armstrong smiles. 'No I don't. Indeed, quite the opposite. I believe Yuri is the sanest man on earth. And what he witnessed or thinks he did makes him the most blessed also. Now, next question gentlemen?'

GOOD FRIENDS

The Space race grows even more intense as the charge for the Moon is now truly on. Yuri's Gagarin's constant pleas to be included are at last heeded. Yuri is called to Moscow for a meeting with Air Force General Nikolai Lubanov. He's sat before Lubanov in his Kremlin office.

'It is with great reluctance we do this Gagarin, but someone of your vast experience can no longer be ignored.'

'I will not let you or the Motherland down sir.'

Lubanov smiles on hearing this. 'Just do not crash and burn on me Comrade Colonel, or they will have my balls.'

'I promise not to sir.'

'You are to be the back-up Pilot to Cosmonaut Vladimir Komarov, for the *Soyuz 1* flight. I believe you two know each other?'

'Yes, we are good friends.'

'As you know it is set to launch 23rd April 1967. Our first manned spaceflight in over two years to be given the green light. The Moon is calling Yuri Gagarin.'

'I am sure you are aware of the numerous, technical issues regarding *Soyuz* 1 sir.'

'Of course Colonel, but my hands are tied. Our people, the engineers, the technicians have discovered over two hundred faults and counting. These have been reported to Party leaders, but we are simply told to fix them.'

'Surely that is unacceptable sir. Have you asked for a delay?'

'Yes but, I am simply overruled. They insist everything must go as planned. We need you more than ever Yuri.'

'Sir, it is unforgiveable to ask any Soviet Pilot to undertake such a risk. It will be a death trap. There are no parachutes from space.'

'I agree, but these are political pressures. A successful show of Soviet superiority is desired to mark the anniversary of Lenin's birthday.

Also, this obsession of keeping up with the Americans is all consuming. We must be the first in the race to the Moon. Return to Space city Yuri. Go over every inch of *Soyuz 1*. There is nobody more qualified than you to fix this.'

'I will head back straight away After what happened recently with the Americans, they will be reeling. That was a tragic incident, we must ensure that does not happen to our boys. I was introduced to one of the astronauts killed whilst in Paris. Lieutenant-Colonel White.'

'It does provide us with some vital breathing space, despite the horrific circumstances of their deaths, they are still the enemy Gagarin.'

'There are no enemies in space sir, except space itself.'

On Friday 27th January 1967, tragedy struck the Apollo program, when a flash fire occurred in a command module, during the launch pad test. Three Astronauts, Lt. Col. Virgil I. Grissom, Lt. Col. Edward H. White and Roger B. Chaffee, an Astronaut preparing for his first space flight, were burned alive. What happened to the Americans horrified Yuri. Gagarin. The dangers of their profession now fully realised. The *Apollo 1* tragedy makes Yuri even more determined. After working with his technicians and engineers, he becomes aware the design problems on *Soyuz 1* are indeed impossible to overcome within the time frame allowed. The pressures from the Politburo to proceed with the flight are unrelenting. They will instead have to be worked around. A desperate Yuri has an idea and meets again with General Lubanov to discuss it.

'General, you have to pull Komarov from the flight. He is a good Pilot, but not experienced enough to deal with *Soyuz 1*, and the ongoing, technical difficulties. You require someone with far more experience.'

'Such as who Gagarin?'

'Me, Comrade General. I can do this.'

'No, never! This conversation is over Gagarin, before it even begins.'

'I can handle this flight sir. I can take her up and bring her back in one piece. Is that not the best present Comrade Lenin could have had on his anniversary?'

'If I was to take this idea upstairs Yuri, they would shoot me. The leadership will never risk a national hero on a flight as dangerous as this. Surely, you understand your importance to the Motherland?'

'I am not a flag General. I am a Pilot. I want to serve the Motherland the best way I can.'

'Very well, I will pass on your request, but do not expect them to adhere to it.'

'Please explain that to send Komarov up is a death sentence. I implore you General. Make them understand.'

'I will do my best. Now, get out of here Gagarin before I change my mind.'

Yuri stands and salute. 'Yes sir.'

Once back at Space city, Yuri seeks out Cosmonaut Vladimir Komarov. He finds him coming out of a test capsule in full Cosmonaut regalia. As ever a smiling Komarov is glad to see his old friend.

'Starman!'

Yuri and Komarov shake hands.

'It is good to see you Vladimir.'

'Where have you been, I was asking about you. The place is too quiet without you complaining about some piece of equipment or other on the ship.'

'I've been to Moscow.'

'Do not moan at the wrong people Comrade. You may be a living legend, but those big shots have ego's bigger than their bellies.'

'I have big worries Vladimir. This is an extremely dangerous mission.'

'Hey, don't worry. You are worrying far too much these days Yuri. I will bring this baby back in one piece, and me to!'

'I have to be honest with you. I asked Lubanov to take you off the flight. I do not think you are ready.'

'You did what?'
'Lubanov is taking it to the Politburo. If they agree, I shall go in your place.'
'Yuri, you cannot do this, we are supposed to be friends? This is a betrayal.'
'You are my friend, that is exactly why I am doing it. *Soyuz 1* is a junkheap. It needs to be taken apart panel by panel, bolt by bolt and rebuilt.'
'If I am removed I shall protest. I deserve to go, I have done my time in the programme. I am ready!'
'You may be ready but the ship is not. I will not let you take that risk.'
'What makes you think you can handle it Yuri Gagarin?'
'You said it yourself Comrade. I am the Starman. I am our best chance.'
'If you do this you are a son of a bitch Yuri Gagarin!'
'Maybe so, please don't hate me Vladimir. You have to believe I am doing this for all the right reasons.'
'This has been my dream since I was a small boy Yuri. Now, you want to take it away from me?'
'There will be other space flights for you my friend. Far safer, I will make sure.'
A seemingly distraught, Komarov walks off and Yuri watches him go. He stops and turns to face him. 'If this mission is as doomed as they say, well I hope you get turned down Yuri Gagarin. If it is to be anyone then I would rather it was me.'

Yuri is in his office when the telephone rings. He picks it up.
'Colonel Gagarin speaking.'
'Yuri, it is Lubanov. Your request has been turned down flat. I advise you stop your complaints about *Soyuz 1*. They have not gone unnoticed. Take this as a friendly warning Colonel.'
The line goes dead, and a furious Yuri throws the phone on the floor. He has his head in his hands.
'Idiots!'

NO HEROES IN SPACE

The date of the *Soyuz* 1 launch.
 Sunday 23rd April 1967, Yuri meets with Vladimir Komarov, only hours before lift-off.
 'If there is the slightest murmur or odd noise of malfunction coming from the control panel, you call it before the countdown, do you understand me Vladimir Komarov?'
 'Yes dad,' smiles Komarov.
 'I am serious. Promise me, there are no heroes in space, just dead idiots. So, you promise me now Comrade.'
 'I promise Yuri.'
 A clearly nervous Yuri pats Komarov on the shoulder. 'Good boy.'
 'I have an apology to make Yuri. I am sorry for calling you a son of a bitch. I was angry, I did not…'
 'Listen to me Vladimir. This mission is being rushed. There is no dishonour if you feel uneasy once on board to transmit a no go. Believe me, you will know within minutes if something is not right.'
 'Yuri please. No more. I am ready to do this. Just wish me luck and have a bottle ready for us to share on my return. Maybe two!'
 Yuri and Komarov embrace.
 'I will be here waiting with two full glasses.'
 A smiling Komarov nods at this. 'I shall see you very soon Starman.'

 Finally, *Soyuz 1* is launched from Baikonur Cosmodrome. Problems begin shortly after take-off, when one solar panel fails to unfold, leading to a shortage of power for the spacecraft's systems. Further trouble rapidly follows, it soon becomes obvious something is going terribly wrong. A decision to abort the mission is ordered from the ground. *Soyuz 1* fires its retrorockets and re-enters the Earth's atmosphere. Despite all hell breaking out around him, Komarov at this point remains confident and transmits.
 … "I have this control…Do not lose faith in Vladimir Komarov…"

To slow the descent, Komarov deploys the bonus parachute, followed by the main one. However, due to a defect it doesn't unfold. He then activates the manually deployed reserve chute, but that fails also. Everything is failing. Disaster now looms as the *Soyuz* re-entry module begins to fall like a blinding, speeding, downed rocket. It crashes to Earth.

A rescue helicopter spots the descent module lying on its side with the failed parachutes spread across the ground. It is in flames with black smoke filling the air and streams of molten metal dripping from its exterior. The entire base of the capsule burned through. Another group of rescuers in an aircraft arrive and attempt to put out the fire in the blazing spacecraft with portable extinguishers, but these prove insufficient, and they instead are forced into using shovels to throw dirt onto it. Ultimately, the rescuers are able to dig through the rubble to find Komarov's smoking, incinerated skeletal remains still strapped into his seat.

All this time, a grim-faced Yuri had been listening to the terrifying, heart-breaking events unfolding over a transmitter, back at the Cosmodrone, along with many others, tear-stricken. He hears unspeakable things that will haunt him forever, for as Komarov finally falls to earth knowing his death is certain, he starts to rant and rave. Komarov curses the engineers, the flight staff, the Politburo members, Generals, and tells his wife how much he loves her, then, the screams as Komarov is exhumed by fire and burnt alive.

Fuming at his friend's savage, brutal death, Yuri Gagarin demands a meeting with General Lubanov back in Moscow at the Kremlin. A furious Yuri cuts a fraught, angry figure. Lubanov sits back in his desk on him entering.

'We killed him.'

'Comrade Komarov died a hero of the Soviet Union Colonel. He will be remembered forever more by the Motherland.'

'Who was the bastard who turned down my request General?'

'Step back Gagarin.'

'You heard the General, Colonel. Enough!'

Stepping out of the office corner, previously unseen, is 45 year-old KGB Colonel Ivan Akulov. A ferocious bear of a man with scarred features and a hook for one hand. All souvenirs of the Battle of Kursk. 'You go too far. Your status as some kind of living legend stretches only so far Gagarin. Men have been shot for far less than what you have got away with recently.'

'All I claimed would happen came true, and my friend is dead. *Soyuz 1* was a death trap. This is not some game, when you play politics with the space programme people die. Vladimir Komarov died, burnt alive!'

'Every word you mutter Gagarin takes you closer to the grave, and not the stars. Do not fool yourself, your importance is over rated to people like me.'

'What are you saying?'

'It is over for you. You are grounded once more. And be grateful we don't put a bullet in the back of your head, and send your family to Siberia.'

'You threaten me with my family?'

'Opinion is split on you Gagarin. Oh, you do have friends in high places, but you also have enemies. More increasingly so. Take some advice from an old soldier. Go back to kissing babies, opening tower blocks in your name and getting drunk. You will live longer Comrade, as will your family. I can guarantee you that.'

On the mention of his family, a shocked Yuri knows he's beaten, and heads for the door. 'Colonel Gagarin!' shouts Akulov. Yuri turns around to face him. 'This will be the best way for you to serve the Motherland. Forget about the Moon. You are yesterday's Starman. We will be going there without you.'

THERE'S NO RULES ANYMORE

A year passes. 1968 arrives.
  In a vain hope, Yuri applies to re-qualify as a Jet Fighter Pilot. Astonishingly, surprising none more than himself, he's granted permission. This Yuri passes with flying colours, and again to his sheer joy, the Starman is allowed once more to take flight. The situation being that the space race is now so critical for the Soviets, they badly need Yuri back in the fold like never before.
  But there is a hidden agenda, for sadly other forces are at work also to ensure Yuri Gagarin never walks on the Moon.

Russia. The Crimea.
  Yuri's one-time KGB handler Sergei Belikov is in the back seat of a Cadillac with blacked out windows. Next to him is a bald-headed, six-foot-six brute of a man in a dark suit. Two similar are sat in the front. Belikov has been summoned for a meeting with former Soviet Premier Nikita Khrushchev, at his holiday home in the Crimea, on the Black sea in Sevastopol. Since being ousted from power by a Kremlin plot led by a whole host of fellow Politburo leaders, who despaired at what they considered Khrushchev's backing down to Kennedy in the Cuban Missiles crisis, he has spent his time drinking heavily, seething, plotting revenge and forever haunted by what Yuri Gagarin seemingly witnessed out in space.
  Word has reached him through some still, loyal KGB contacts that Yuri has been granted permission to fly again and is being groomed to lead the charge in the Soviet's, imminent assault to beat the Americans to the Moon. The thought of him broadcasting to an entire word as he takes man's first step on another planet horrifies Khrushchev. His fear that the Cosmonaut experienced some kind of

spiritual encounter during the *Vostok 1* flight, but never spoke up, means the opportunity must never be allowed to arise again. However, the waters have been dirtied by the fact Khrushchev has almost a father's love for Yuri. Before he puts certain plans into motion, Khrushchev needs his fears confirmed. Thus, Sergei Belikov has been summoned back from Cuba, where he has been serving as the Soviet attaché to Fidel Castro. Assigned, after the near, calamitous, war with the Americans over the stationing of Russian missiles in Cuba, Belikov was taken from Yuri's side to keep a wary eye on the volatile Castro. One dance with Armageddon was enough, and word came down from the Kremlin to Belikov...
"Rein in the Beard."
This he has done successfully, forming a close relationship with Castro in doing so, but Belikov misses his friend Yuri Gagarin. On pulling up outside Khrushchev's, holiday home, the driver leans his head around to face Belikov. 'Speak honestly to Khrushchev, Comrade Belikov. He will know if you are lying, the stakes are such, the price for dishonesty these days is simply not worth the price you will pay. These are different times, there's no rules anymore.'
'What does he want with me?'
'Like I say, no bull Comrade Belikov. The old man has a sixth sense for it. Tell him what he wants to know.'
Belikov is led inside through three luxury-suited rooms, and onto an outside balcony. There, sat in dark glasses is a hugely, overweight Khrushchev, wearing loose fitting clothes, his face reddened and clutching a large glass of vodka. The bodyguards leave Belikov alone.
Khrushchev points to a chair facing him.
'Come, sit with me Belikov.'
The view from the balcony is stunning, the vast expanses of the Black sea shimmering in the late, afternoon sun. Khrushchev pours his vodka in a long glass then drops ice onto it. 'I feel it is respectable to take ice in my drink during daylight hours. The sun here in Sevastopol tends to give me a thirst, so a small sacrifice don't you think to enjoy a good drink into the evening?'

Khrushchev hands Belikov a drink and raises his own high. 'Nostrovia!' Khrushchev drinks his in one, whilst Belikov, just a mouthful. 'So, Belikov, tell me how is Fidel? Has he forgiven me yet for not igniting World War Three for the sake of his oversized ego?'
'No, he never mentions your name sir.'
Khruschev smiles. 'Very smart Belikov, just like your friend Gagarin, your defences are forever up.'
'I do not understand why I am here sir?'
'I need you to help me sleep again Comrade Belikov. When handling Yuri Gagarin, did he ever mention his religious beliefs to you, and remember Belikov, you are sworn to tell the truth. Do not lie to me son, for I will know.'
'So I have already been warned. I have no reason to lie to you.'
'Well then?'
'No, Gagarin never mentioned any such thing to me.'
Khruschev stares long and hard at Belikov, who tries not to blink.
'You are lying to me.'
'Comrade Khrushchev, forgive me, but why are you doing this? Yuri Gagarin is a hero of the Motherland. Never in our time together did he utter one word against the state. I fail to see the reason behind your question.' Khrushchev has already poured himself another large drink. 'Just answer the question, you are out of your league here boy.' Belikov can feel the anger building up inside him. 'On whose authority was I brought here? I insist you tell me before I answer any more of your questions?'
'What am I listening to here? You will not insist and you will reply Belikov. This is official matters of state. What, has all that Cuban sun gone to your head? Do not ever think this nonsense of revolution you are hearing about from your new Cuban friends applies here. You obey orders, your heart and soul, your conscience belongs to the state.'
'With the greatest respect sir, just who are you speaking for? This is not the Kremlin.'
'So, you think you can go running tales to the kremlin? To Brezhnev and his band of treacherous leeches. What are you going to say to

them? That their former Premier had worries about where Gagarin's true loyalties lay, and you refused to co-operate?'
'Yuri Gagarin is no traitor.'
'Do not dare to underestimate me Comrade Belikov. I will ask you one more time. Did you ever hear Gagarin talk about his religious beliefs?' Knowing well now that Khruschev can smell lies, like a dog hunting down rats, Belikov feels there's little choice but to tell what he knows, or at least thinks. Belikov so yearns to just go back to Cuba. 'There was something, just the once.'
Khrushchev leans towards him. 'Tell me?'
'Though he never spoke of it directly, I believe Yuri witnessed something on the space flight that he simply could not explain. It moved and disturbed, even tortured him.'
'Did Gagarin ever hint to what it was?'
'Angels.'
'Do you believe Gagarin saw his God Belikov?'
Belikov stares at Khruschev, but says nothing. However, in the silence his answers lies, for it is clear from the look on Khrushchev's face that Yuri Gagarin is now a dead man. A light switches on in Belikov's head. He has been brought here to act as judge and jury on the life of a man he cares deeply about, and it sickens him to the stomach.
'Now, leave me Belikov.'

PARADISE DOWN HERE ON EARTH

On an icy cold day with mountains of snow in the air,
 Yuri Gagarin is walking around the huge lake in Moscow's, beautiful Gorky Park, with wife Valentina and young daughters Yelena and Galina. The children aged seven and ten are playing a chasing game in front of their parents. A concerned Yuri worries as they stand close to the water. 'Girls move away from there!' he shouts.
 The girls look up, smile, wave, and do as their father says.
 'Oh, how they love and obey their Starman!' smiles Valentina. Valentina is linking Yuri. 'His word is their command.'
 Yuri is laughing! 'You are joking yes? I live in a house with three women. I have to take more orders at home than when I'm working!'
 Valentina punches him gently on the arm. 'Ah, you love it Yuri Gagarin.'
 'What man could ask for more?' he replies.
 Yuri stops and kisses Valentina. 'I have a wonderful wife who is my best friend also, and two beautiful daughters who look like their mother. I am blessed.'
 'So, why Yuri, why are you in such a rush once more to go back to the stars when you have paradise down here on earth? Why risk everything?' A smiling Yuri links his wife once more, and they walk on. 'Because it is who I am Valentina, surely you understand that?'
 'Of course I do, but look at them.'
 Valentina points toward the two girls. 'They are you Yuri. Yelena and Galina should be the only stars you think about.'
 'I cannot explain it my love, but this is something I must do.'
 'I don't understand Yuri. First you had to fly, then you had to go to the stars, now you must go to the Moon. Why? Why not just be happy here on Earth with what you have? A wife and two beautiful young daughters, who love and adore you.'

Yuri can't look his wife in the eye, everything she says is right, but ultimately he is the Starman, and has no choice but to go forever further. This is a man born to soar beyond the heavens. There's no personal choice, just what is meant to be.

'Then go!' cries a tearful Valentina.

THE LAST FLIGHT

34 year-old Yuri wakes early.
It is Wednesday 27th March 1968,
 a foggy, snowy, ice cold-windswept morning. He's stationed at Chklovsky Military airport, about twenty miles Northwest of Moscow. Yuri has thrown himself into retraining on Fighter Jets, and remains confident that if the opportunity arises to be considered for a Soviet Moon landing, he will be ready. No longer drinking, the years of being used as nothing more than a propaganda tool have taken a heavy toll. Yuri is world-weary and concentrates now only for one last gigantic effort to reach past the heavens, and beyond. To keep going until finally he is able to look at the earth from the surface of the Moon.
 Yuri is scheduled to fly three times today, two solo, one alongside his good friend and experienced Co-Pilot, Vladimir Seryogin. This is to be the first flight. He boards a bus with Seryogin, taking them to the airport, only to realise his identification is missing. Terribly superstitious, Yuri appears a little anxious, but a smiling Seryogin places a calming arm around his shoulders.
 'Hey, Starman, we are hardly going over the clouds, for you my friend, this is like going up a ladder!'
 Both men laugh, but still inside Yuri is a little uneasy.
A little after 10.am, they take off in the two-seater Jet towards the flight zone in weather conditions that appear to be deteriorating. Thirty minutes go by before Yuri comes over the radio…
"We have completed the exercise and are heading back to base."
Then, nothing. Radio silence. After a further ten minutes of no sightings or communications with the aircraft, panic sets in.
The base commander moves into action. "Dispatch rescue teams. Find out where the hell they are!"

Consternation has taken hold with the realisation kicking in that Yuri and Seryogin maybe down. Around 3.00.pm, crews discover the still, burning, smoking charred plane, lying silent amongst the snowclad trees of the Russian countryside. Seryogin's body is immediately identified, but there's no sign of Yuri Gagarin? Hopes are that Yuri has managed to eject before impact, if so, where is he? A deep sense of foreboding and unease settles over Chklovsky airport as every search and rescue vehicle, both airborne and on the ground is mobilised to find him. A cloak of secrecy falls, the KGB arrive on the scene. The Kremlin wants answers as to what happened, but most of all they need to discover whether Yuri is dead or alive?

The search continues throughout the evening, all night, by torch and under floodlight, until finally, early the next morning, shortly after 10.am, they find him.

The Starman is no more.

Yuri's remains are bagged up and the call is made.

When news breaks, the world goes into mourning, Soviet authorities hastily assemble a commission to determine the cause of the crash. Once done, the Communist party head Leonid Brezhnev closes the investigation and deems it top secret. Something isn't right. Those involved are told to stay silent, for their conclusions could unsettle the nation. "Keep your mouths shut," they are warned. "Nothing is worth a bullet in the back of the head."

A national hero dies under supremely, mysterious circumstances, nobody is talking, the perfect recipe for conspiracy theories. Some that will persist for decades.

Yuri was drunk?

Another proposed that he and Seryogin were joy-riding and taking pot-shots at deer below.

One whispered constantly, a persistent rumour that Yuri's plane was sabotaged by unknown forces for reasons relating to a supposed UFO encounter, whilst on his space mission.

Other theories, Yuri was poisoned by the CIA, or that even he was a secret CIA agent himself?

Another claims Yuri actually survived the crash, only to live out his days in a Soviet psychiatric ward until his real death in 1990.
There are even people who believe Yuri is still alive today, his identity protected for all these decades by intensive plastic surgery. All far-fetched, steeped in myth, legend, the stuff of wild conspiracy theory. Nobody really knows.
Except a chosen few.

At a state funeral, with hundreds of thousands lining the streets of Moscow to pay last respects, the bodies of Yuri and Seryogin are cremated, their ashes buried in the walls of the Kremlin on Red Square. Dressed all in black and veiled, Yuri's ashen-faced wife Valentina and crying daughters Yelina and Galina watch on. Alongside them, a long line of Soviet Generals saluting, all red braid and medals adorned. Finally, it appears Yuri Gagarin has got his wish, and been returned to the stars.
But the story of the Starman is not yet over.

In 2010, Russian researchers discovered that a faulty air vent led to a quick descent and a crash. According to their findings, the Pilots discovered it in the cockpit mid-flight. This ultimately caused both men to black out and the plane to crash. Yuri and Seryogin realised the cockpit was not hermetically sealed, took emergency action to descend to a safer altitude, only to drop too fast and crash. As a post-note it was also discovered that before take-off, this same air vent was left partially open.
But by who?

THERE IS A SANTA CLAUS

England. Manchester.
Thursday 28th March 1968.
 16 year-old Charlie Baker is sitting watching the television with his mum and dad, Les and Eileen, as the BBC news report on the tragic crash involving Yuri. A tearful Charlie is clutching tight on the rouble coin given to him by the Starman. Les is ashen-faced, whilst Eileen is sniffling into a handkerchief.
 'This is so, so very sad.'
Les puts an arm around her. 'I can't believe it love.' He looks across to Charlie, and can't bear to see his son so upset. 'Are you okay Charlie lad?' Charlie can't talk, for his heart is breaking. He so hoped his friend would one day walk on the Moon, and that when older they could even meet up once more. Charlie looks at the coin and suddenly has an idea. If Yuri can no longer go to the Moon, then Charlie Baker will ensure at least in spirit, a piece of him will one day make it there. So, he goes to write his letter.

"Dear Mr Armstrong.
 My name is Charlie Baker.
Please find enclosed the Russian Rouble given to me by the Russian Cosmonaut Yuri Gagarin back in 1961, when he visited my home town of Manchester, England. I was 9 years-old then, and my father arranged for me to meet and ask him three questions. He was a true gentleman. Yuri was, and always will be a hero for me. He said that every night when I look up to the stars towards the Moon, it will be his face smiling back at me. Funny, back then I had just discovered Santa Claus wasn't real, but then Yuri became my Santa, he still is. If you ever go to the Moon, please will you place this letter and the coin

upon it. Then, we can truly say that Yuri Gagarin, the first man in Space is where he belongs, and that the Starman is resting in peace. Yours sincerely, Charlie Baker."

Sunday 20th July 1969.
  All at NASA space control, in Houston, whoop and holler as *Apollo 11*, begins a return journey to Earth. It has been a monumental success, for the *Eagle* had landed and is now soaring home. All aspects of the mission have been met, astronauts Neil Armstrong, Buzz Aldrin and Michael Collins are set to be heeded for all time as true pioneers of the space age.
  The first Men on the Moon.
A crackle of transmission fills the control room, but it is badly muffled. All ears listen in.
"Be advised *Apollo* 11. Please repeat your last message?"
"I repeat, Mission control be advised...
There is a Santa Claus..."

"Orbiting Earth in the spaceship, I saw how beautiful our planet is. People, let us preserve and increase this beauty, not destroy it!"
  Yuri Gagarin

SMALL FACES

ACT ONE

It is the winter of 1927.
 40 year-old Laurence Stephen Lowry is sat on a wall overlooking Bolton Wanderer's Football ground, Burnden Park.
 He's watching as thousands of people make their way from all directions into the ground. Slowly, Lowry starts to sketch what he sees before him. Unbeknown to Lowry, a young boy is staring up toward him. 11 year-old Charlie Riley.
'What are you doing up there mister?'
Lowry looks down.
'I'm sketching for my next painting young man.'
'Can I have a look then?'
'Can I have a look please?' replies a smiling Lowry.
Charlies sighs and rolls his eyes. 'Can-I-have-a-look-please?'
'Good lad! Of course, you can. Come on, hop up here.'
 Charlie climbs up and sits beside Lowry. He appears fascinated by the sketching. 'Your people are so tiny, they need a good stew. They're like little match stalk people.'
Lowry can't help but smile at this young visitor who has entered his normally lonesome existence while painting.
'What's your name young man?'
'Charlie, Charlie Riley. At your service sir!'
Charlie puts out his hand for Lowry to shake.

'And you are, may I ask Mr Painter?'
My name is Laurence Stephen Lowry. Also, at your service Charlie Riley!'
'I'm very pleased to meet you Mr Lowry.'
The two shake hands.
'It's lovely to meet you too Charlie. You asked about my figures?'
'Yes, they're just like little match stalks. I'd be scared they'd snap.'
'Oh, they won't snap, they are tough as teak! Imagine a jigsaw, the match stalk people are just strokes of a brush of a much bigger canvas Charlie.'
Charlie coughs and points towards Lowry's sketch.
'I could draw that.'
Lowry nods and smiles. Not taking offence. 'I'm sure you could.'
'I'm sorry, I didn't mean to be rude Mr Lowry.'
Of course, I know that. Let me explain. These figures, or match stalk people as you say. In my mind, as I draw them, they're all so very different people. They're alive in my head Charlie.
Mr Jones from the post office.
Mr Brown the butcher.
Mr Collins who works in a bank.
Lowry taps on his head. 'They're all up here. When I start the actual painting on a brand, new blank canvas, they'll come back to life. As you shall see young man, when it's finally finished.'
Still Charlie doesn't appear convinced as he studies the figures carefully. 'How can you tell who is who Mr Lowry, there are so many of them?'
'Oh, no, no, they're all so different Charlie, just Like real people. They all have names, they laugh and cry, joke, they get mad. Each one is a friend of mine.'
Charlie smiles. 'Invisible friends? Mr Lowry, I'm the kid. I think I'm the one who's supposed to have invisible friends.
Lowry bursts out laughing. 'Ah, I see, a very good point. It's like this Charlie. As my brush sweeps over the canvas, they'll slowly come to life. I shall see them appear and wave, and they'll wave back. Maybe nobody else will see it but I will.'

Charlie is rubbing his chin. 'I see. You're a kind of a magic man then, a magician?'

'No Charlie. I'm not a magic man. I'm just a painter. And a poor one at that.'

'You don't sell many of your paintings then?'

'Sadly, I hardly sell any at all Charlie.'

'I'd buy one Mr Lowry. I honestly wouldn't see you starve.'

Lowry smiles wide. 'Why, thank you that's very kind. You're a good lad.'

Charlie empties out both his empty pockets and shows Lowry.

'If I had any money that is.'

'Of course Charlie. But it's always the thought that counts.'

'And I have to be honest with you Mr Lowry, I'm not sure it would be this one I'd buy.' Charlie points at the sketch.

'Oh really?'

'But I would definitely buy another one…I think.'

'The fact you like them is enough for me Charlie. Thank you.'

'If you don't make any money from your paintings, how do you live Mr Lowry?'

'You do ask an awful lot of questions Charlie?'

'I love to know things about interesting people Mr Lowry, besides, we might never meet again?'

'Oh, I think we will. Well, can I trust you Charlie to keep a secret?'

'You certainly can, I always keep secrets and I always keep my promises.'

'Well, that's wonderful. I'll tell you then. During the day I work as a rent collector for the Pall Mall Property Company. But I do tend not to tell people this. People have a somewhat, dislike for this type of profession.'

'Why's that Mr Lowry? I don't understand, somebody has to do it, besides, it's nothing to be ashamed of.'

'Yes, I know Charlie, but it isn't nice to have to knock on people's door and ask them for money.'

'They did borrow it in the first place, but don't beat yourself up Mr Lowry. I'm sure they'd rather hand it back over to you than some nasty bugger.'

'Quite, thank you! A lot of these folk just desperately need the money to feed their families though Charlie. We're living in very tough times.'

'I suppose so, it's not your fault though.'

'It is just a job though Charlie, for I need the money to live, and look after my mother. Although I would hate to be known as just a Sunday painter.'

'Oh, Mr Lowry, you're anything but. Besides, if, if anyone does call you a Sunday painter, you tell them maybe, but what I paint on a Sunday, others could not paint in a month of Sundays!'

Lowry smiles at this. 'Thank you young man. I shall remember that.'

'My pleasure Mr Lowry, anytime. It costs nothing to be nice.'

'The thing is as well Charlie, with looking after my bed-ridden mother, the only time I really have time to properly paint is when she's asleep. I then go upstairs to my little heaven on earth, my studio in the loft. I prepare my canvas, and bring alive our match stalk people!'

'Wow! You're a good fellow Mr Lowry. I so wish I could paint.'

'You don't need talent to be a painter Charlie. Just a real passion to do it. You know what you are really trying to paint, to express. If nobody else can see it, well, that's their problem. Passion, and also time my new young chum. Time.'

'Time. Charlie sighs. 'I bet, they'll never be enough time for me though.'

'Don't be silly. You're a small boy, young man, you have all the time in the world!'

Charlie nods and smiles. 'Of course, Mr Lowry.'

'Yes, well, I really must be getting on. And you best run along, your father will be looking all over for you.'

'I'm not here with my dad Mr Lowry, I've come with my older brother, Harry. He's over there, one of your match stalk people. You can see him now waving!'

'I'm not sure he's waving Charlie, it appears he's raising a fist to me! You better move fast lad.'
'Harry's only joking. He tries to be like a dad, but he's dead soft really. He just keeps a really good eye out for me, because you might find it hard to believe, but I can be a bit of a nuisance. So, everyone says anyway. I seem to get on most people's nerves.'
'Well, let me tell you, you don't get on my nerves Charlie. Now, go on, get going. It's been very nice chatting to you.'
'Will you be here for the next home next match Mr Lowry?'
'Yes, I will. Myself and my sketch pad.'
'Will you be sat on this wall?'
Lowry smiles. 'Yes, I'll be sat right here on this very wall!'
Charlie sports a huge grin. 'Great! Well, I'll be seeing you then. Goodbye Mr Lowry, and farewell to all your invisible friends until we meet again that is!' Charlies races off to his brother Harry.
 Lowry watches him go. 'Goodbye Charlie, hopefully, I'll see you again!'
He continues to sketch as still the crowds pile into the ground. Lowry smiles at the character already sketched.
 'Oh, hello Doctor Brady. I never knew you was a Bolton Wanderers fan. I think I shall give you a little briefcase. Would you care for that, any particular colour?' Lowry sketches a tiny briefcase onto the hands of a new match stalk figure.
Meanwhile, Charlie has reached Harry. He starts to cough.
'Are you alright little man? Here you go take this.' Harry hands him over a handkerchief and Charlie wipes his mouth.
 'Come on chum, get your breath back, you know you're not supposed to run you daft'n.'
'Thanks Harry.' Charlie smiles. 'I feel a lot better now. You're not going to believe this, I've just been talking to a real-life painter. Mr Lowry he's called.'
'Well, good for you and not for him! I hope you didn't bend the poor man's ears. Come on, let's get inside, its nearly kick off.'
'But Harry...I'
Harry puts an arm around Charlie.

'Wrap it titch, now come on. Let's go and watch the match.'
Harry and Charlie join the queue to enter the ground.
Charlie is still on cloud nine after talking to Lowry. 'We're all match stalk men Harry! And we're never going to die! Isn't that great news?' Harry appears upset, but hides it from Charlie.
He smiles and ruffles Charlie's hair. 'That's great news little man, really great news…'
That same evening Lowry enters the loft that he uses as a studio with the sketch from the day's work under his arms. It is a dimly lit room by gaslight. He walks over to a small window and looks out from his home on 117 Station Road in Pendlebury. It is mostly black, only the glare of the streetlamps light the darkness.
 Lowry smiles. 'I love the night, the silence. The peace it brings. Just me and the canvas and my match stalk people. Time to say hello.'
 Lowry sits down in front of the blank canvas with his selection of paints, and goes to work.
'I wouldn't see you starve! Cheeky little sod!'

ACT TWO

Two weeks later.
 Lowry is back ensconced on his wall sketching away when he hears a familiar voice below him.
'Hello again Mr Lowry! How's your luck?'
Lowry smiles. 'Oh, hello Charlie, its fine thank you! How's yours'?'
'Its good thanks.'
Charlies climbs back on the wall. He stares at Lowry's sketch of the crowds flooding once more into Burnden Park, and the backdrop of Bolton's chimneys and buildings.
 'Definitely coming on this sketch Mr Lowry.'
'Good of you to say so Charlie. How have you been?'
'Oh, up and down. The usual, but I've been looking forward to seeing you though. Meeting my magic man and his match stalk people once again!'
'Are you here again with your brother?'
'Yes, always, he's my shadow. I told him all about you Mr Lowry. He's really looking forward to meeting you.'
'That would be nice, where is he?'
'The Pub! He'll be out in a bit.' Charlie smiles. Only way he can watch the Wanderers these days he says!'
Lowry laughs. 'I see. Are your mother and father at home then?
'Yes. Mum's at home with my little sister Eileen.'
'And your Dad?'
'He's not here anymore. Dad was killed in the war. I was only very small, so I don't really remember him. Just shadows sometimes when I'm asleep. I have his photograph in a little frame in my room though, and I always say goodnight dad before I go to sleep.'
'I'm very sorry Charlie.'

'Where are we up to in the sketching then Mr Lowry?' Wanting so much to change the subject.
'Still working hard on the match stalk people. I've many more of them to do yet.'
'Where do they all come from then?'
'They all come from Bolton of course!'
'Come on Mr Lowry! I'm just a kid, but even I can figure that out. Where else are they from?'
'I'm sorry Charlie.' Lowry smiles. 'Where do they come from you ask? Well, our match stalk people come from many places. One thing all of them have in common though is that they are very lonely. So, I take this pencil here, I bring alive one, two, three, and no longer are they on their own. This painting will bring thousands of lost souls together, and they'll never be lonely again.'
'Wow! What about you, do you ever get lonely Mr Lowry?'
'Oh, I think we all do sometimes Charlie. Don't you?'
'Not really. There's always someone tugging at my collar.'
'That's because your family loves you Charlie.'
'I suppose so.'
Charlie coughs, then, with a handkerchief wipes his mouth.
'Sorry about that Mr Lowry. I've a silly cough that just won't go away.'
'You certainly do young man. Zip your coat right up to the top. There's a bitter wind today.'
A smiling Charlie does as Lowry says. 'You sound just like my Harry!'
'That's because we care about you little man. This weather is horrible, you'll catch your death.'
Charlie points at the sketch. 'I like your chimneys pointing through the skies Mr Lowry. Such a horrible colour those skies though. Ugh!'
'True Charlie, but if you look hard enough, you'll always find some beauty, even amidst the darkest, drab of scenes. Try and look beyond them, those skies, tell me what you think could be up there?'
Heaven, at least I hope so?'
Charlie stares upwards, Lowry also.

'Maybe so, but there's also the moon and the sun, and a billion stars and constellations. It's like our match stalk people. Just because people can't see them wave and smile, it doesn't mean they're not doing so.'
Charlie nods in agreement. 'With this fog so thick in the mornings, I can't see in front of my face going to school. I always imagine there are giant and goblins, and white knights in shining armour fighting each other in the mist, and only I can see them.'
'Invisible friends,' eh, says a smiling Lowry.
Charlie laughs. Touché! Yes, Mr Lowry. Invisible friends!'
Lowry continues to sketch.
'Any idea what you would like to be when you grow up Charlie?'
'One of your match stalk people Mr Lowry, then I'll live forever!'
'I shall save you a spot on the canvas young man.'
'Thank you, Mr Lowry, you're a very kind gentleman.'
Suddenly, Harry appears walking towards them.
'Harry!' shouts Charlie. He jumps down off the wall, runs over to Harry, and grabs his arm. 'Come on Harry, hurry up, I want you to meet my Mr Lowry!'
Lowry clamours off the wall, and with the sketch under his arm goes to greet Harry. The two shake hands.
'Very pleased to meet you Mr Lowry. I've heard so much about you off this little rascal here.'
Harry ruffles a smiling Charlie's head. One of his favourite habits!
'Likewise, Harry.'
'Show Harry your sketch Mr Lowry!' insists Charlie.
Lowry starts to unravel his sketch.
'Oi you!' says Harry. 'Manners! What happened to please?'
'Peas out of a pod you two. Please-can-you-show-Harry-the-sketch-please-Mr-Lowry.'
Harry looks at it 'Very impressive Mr Lowry. Very impressive indeed.'
A proud Charlie watches on. 'Will be a thing of beauty when Mr Lowry has finished it Harry.'

'Thank you, Charlie, soon as it is finished, you shall be the first to see view it.'
'Sorry if young bugger lugs here has been a bit of a pest Mr Lowry.'
'Not at all Harry, he's been no bother whatsoever. Your Charlie is a good lad.'
'Well, we best be on our way into the ground, and let you get on with your fine work Mr Lowry. It's been a real pleasure meeting you.'
Harry and Lowry again shake hands.
'You too Harry. Goodbye Charlie, see you in a couple of weeks then.'
'You certainly will Mr Lowry, nothing like going to the match, and seeing you again of course!'
Harry and Charlie walk off. Then, Charlie starts to cough badly. He wipes his mouth with a handkerchief once more. Harry looks worryingly towards him. He puts a hand on Charlie's forehead.
'You're a little hot. Maybe we should give the match a miss little man, and get you home?'
'No, no, I'm okay Harry. Honest.'
'I'm not sure, I think we...'
'Oh, please Harry, I don't want to miss the game.'
'Okay then, but I have my eye on you. Come on.'
From afar Lowry watches on before Harry and Charlie disappear from his sight. He then continues to sketch, making the skies even more brutal. Dark, black...Foreboding.
That same evening, Lowry takes to his canvas with an almost feverish passion in order to complete the painting. All the time he's thinking what to name it? The gentle and fierce swish of the brush, the dabbing of paint with his figures to bring alive yet another match stalk person. Then, suddenly, Lowry steps back. It's all but complete.

There remains just one last tiny thing to do. He takes a final dab of paint and adds it to the canvas.

Lowry smiles wide. 'There we go. My invisible friend.'

ACT THREE

Another two weeks later.
 Lowry is again sat on the wall overlooking Burnden Park, although this time he's waiting for Charlie to show. His plan is for after the match to take Charlie and Harry to see the painting. As kick-off draws ever closer, there's still no sign. Then, he spots Harry walking towards him, but no Charlie? Lowry steps down off the wall. He notices Harry is wiping away a tear.
'Hello again Harry, what in heaven's name is up?'
'I thought it was only right to come and see you Mr Lowry.'
'Regarding what?'
'I'm afraid I've the most terrible news.'
'Oh, my poor chap, what is it, what's happened?'
'Our Charlie died last week. He had a fever. The poison got on his chest and took him from us.'
For a second it appears as if Lowry can't breathe.
'The coughing, was that?'
'Charlie was never fully well Mr Lowry. From being born he had a weak chest. We were told by the doctor's that if he reached his teens that itself would be a small miracle.'
'Did Charlie know of this?'
'He was a brave little boy. Yes, I think so.'
'I really don't know what to say Harry. Except to offer my deepest condolences, He was a wonderfully, inquisitive and bright little boy.'
'Charlie thought a lot of you Mr Lowry. So much that just before he closed his eyes for the last time, he asked me to pass a message on to you.'
'Oh, my. What was it Harry?'
'Charlie said he will always be your invisible friend.'

Lowry sheds a tear on hearing this. 'Please, after the match Harry. I've something I need to show you. Would you mind meeting me back here?'
Harry smiles between tears. 'I'm in no mind to go in without our Charlie, Mr Lowry. We could go now if you like?'
'Yes, of course...Of course. Come on.' Lowry puts an arm around Harry and the two walk off. Behind them the roar of the Burnden Park crowd grows ever louder as the teams appear to play the game.

Lowry and Harry enter his studio. There's a canvas on a stand, but it's covered by a white sheet.
'Please excuse the mess Harry.'
'That's quite alright Mr Lowry.'
Harry glances around at the many paintings scattered on the floor, and on the walls around the room. 'You're a very talented painter sir.'
Lowry takes off the white sheet to unveil the painting.
'Harry, please come closer.'
Harry steps forward alongside Lowry. The scene is Burnden Park, with hundreds of people heading towards it from every direction.
'It's beautiful Mr Lowry.'
Lowry points to a single match stalk figure that appears to be waving towards them.
'Do you recognise him Harry?'
Harry looks closer. 'Can't say I do sir.'
Lowry smiles. 'Well, that's your Charlie. He's going to live forever now in this painting.' Harry is trying so hard to smile through more tears. 'Oh, I can see him now! That's just lovely Mr Lowry. What are you going to call this?'
'I was thinking of Going to the Match?'
'Going to the Match. I think that's perfect. Our Charlie would have loved that.'
'Well, Going to the Match it is then.'
Lowry and Harry continue to stare at the painting for a long time. Both are convinced they can see Charlie smiling and waving towards them. They would be right.

MADONNA AND MR WILSON (A MANCHESTER LOVE STORY)

PROLOGUE

Anthony H Wilson was once famously quoted as saying, when forced to pick between truth and legend, print the legend. What is true is way back in the midst of time, Madonna performed, albeit miming, two songs at the Hacienda. The rest of this story, well?

Print the legend!

We're going to take you on a mystery tour of late-night early eighties Manchester with Tony Wilson as your guide, and a starstruck Madonna listening on to his every hyperbole. For one night only Anthony H is back! A love story about a city.

Manchester. Enjoy!

"I'm a minor player in my own life story."
Anthony H Wilson

ACT ONE

OPENING NIGHT (Bernard)

Friday 21st May 1982.
 British troops are landing at San Carlos Water on East Falkland. Three thousand troops with a view to establishing a beachhead for attacks on Goose Green and Stanley. Only two warships survive unscathed. HMS Ardent is sunk with the loss of twenty crew. HMS Argonaut and Antrim also hit by bombs which fail to explode. Argentinian losses include thirteen MiG Aircraft fighters reportedly shot down. The Falklands War seven thousand miles away is ablaze.
 Meanwhile,
it's opening night of the Hacienda night club on 11-13 Whitworth Street, on the edge of the murky depths of the Rochdale Canal. What was once a yacht builders yard (obviously much needed in eighties sea-faring Manchester), and a warehouse was set to be transformed not just into Tony Wilson's dreamscape, designed to put Manchester's music and bands on the world map. That was the idea. But also, maybe more important for Tony, somewhere for the weirdo's to hang out and listen to the music nobody else gave a fuck about.
 Early doors.
 Chaos rules inside the Hacienda as the sound of Mancunian traffic echoes through its huge Victorian walls, pouring past outside. Everything is going wrong. There has been a huge rush to ensure all is ready on time, but behind the scenes mayhem reigns. Plasterers and scaffolders are still at work trying, but failing gloriously to keep a low profile.

'Watch that fucking ladder!'
'Who left that fuckin' nail on the seat? You've just rammed a barmaid!'
'I should so lucky!' he smiled
The smell of freshly-licked paint hangs heavily in the air, alongside more exotic, illegal substances. A hopeful feeling of it'll be alright on the night appears to be the motto they are going to live or most likely fail miserably by.
Finally,
 Onto the stage he appears from his "World Famous" Embassy club, sat just a few miles away in Harpurhey, on Rochdale Road. There's little applause and more than a few boos from a sparse, uninterested audience. This isn't by any means your archetypal Bernard Manning crowd. Indeed, most hate Bernard's, rather large guts! He represents to the vast majority of students present what the milk snatching Margaret Thatcher is to the broken North. Her Tories have declared war and cities like Manchester and Liverpool are in the firing line, swiftly being eviscerated into rotting, industrial wastelands.
 Manning is dipped head to toe in out of date marmite.
 He cuts a sight amidst the seemingly, hip-dressed, (in their mostly drug induced minds), much younger audience. Greased, unruly black hair, sweating, a loud, (playing trumpets!) Hawaiian shirt over his loose-fitting trousers. Fat, crude and vulgar, the undoubted king of the Northern cabaret set, Manning shoots from the hip taking no prisoners.
 Especially, fucking students.
Bernard gazes around the Hacienda, shakes his head and sighs loud.
'Fuckin' ell, I've played some shitholes in my time, but this dump is up there with the best in Liverpool!'
 From the side of the stage, the owner smiles. He's booked Bernard and knows unlike most present what's coming next. The comedian looks out across the crowd and is clearly not impressed. 'I got paid for coming here tonight, what's your lot's fuckin' excuse?
 Jesus, Did you all get dressed in the fuckin' dark?'

A male voice from the crowd mutters something back, but its inaudible. Bernard puts a hand to his ear. 'What was that lad, I didn't fuckin' hear you?'
'I said you're not fuckin' funny!' This time around he's shouted loud.
'I've not even started yet! Maybe so,' replies Manning. 'But you're fuckin' ugly lad. Jesus Christ, they should've shot your mother when you were born, never mind just fuckin' slapped her!'
 Right, here we go,
'Quasimodo was running down the street chased by a group of kids.
'For the last time, I haven't got your football!'
 Silence…
'A Scouser went to a prostitute.' Bernard fires on!
'Do you want a blow job?' she asks him.
'Will it affect my dole money?'
Again, nothing, not a murmur or a cough.
'Man says to his wife…
'Pack your bags, I've won the pools.'
'What should I pack? Something light, something warm? Where are we going?'
'We're going nowhere. Just pack your bags and fuck off!'
 'I wish you'd fuck off!' finally shouts a voice!
 Bernard shakes his head and continues on for twenty minutes to a small sea of completely uninterested, hate-filled faces, until finally, running out of heart and patience, he cuts it short.
'I'd like to say you've been a lovely audience, but my wonderful mum has taught me never to tell lies, so I think you're a bunch of twats. Goodnight!'
 Bernard heads off the stage to the waiting owner who's smiling, but shaking his head. The comedian takes out the £500 fee from his pocket and hands it back to him. 'Here you go Tony mate, you're going to fuckin' need this a lot more than me!'
 So it was, Tony Wilson got a result!
 There would not be many more on 11-13 Whitworth Street.

TODAY (Part One)

It's night-time outside the Hacienda,
 way past midnight, and a full Mancunian moon is shining over Manchester. The clubs are shut, the many black cabs are parked up in the vain hope of a late fare of somebody desperate to reach their bed. Or somebody else's. The Hacienda, a place that once throbbed and rocked with so much life, love and energy is now live-in flats. All is so very still. The gentle rattle of a late-night train leaving Piccadilly station, and the quiet hum of a Metrolink tram nearby ushering past G MEX, the only sounds.
 Suddenly, from above, a beam of light illuminates and a very familiar face appears outside on the Hacienda doorsteps.
He coughs, steps forward and smiles wide.
 'So, it goes again.
Hello, my beautiful Mancunians, have you missed me?
I am the resurrection, to quote Mr Ian Brown. And this, Manchester, this here is the place, and the Hacienda, was the place.
 Good evening,
 in case you've forgotten already and shame on you if so, then my name is Anthony Howard Wilson, and for one night only, the man with the long white beard upstairs who calls himself God, has just said, how fucking pretentious I know!
''Tony son, fuck off for the evening, and let me try and run the place on my own. I've been here a while, I do know what the fuck I'm doing?''
'Not big enough for both of us, he claims…Well…he'll have to go. Anyway, the reason I'm back here amongst my fellow, wonderful, beautiful Mancunians is to recall a special night thirty-seven years ago. As for did it all really happen as we are about to read?
Well, truth, fiction and legend all merged into one at 11-13 Whitworth Street. You'll have to decide for yourself. Though the madness of

those times rests only now in Mancunian memories, our music, despite Buddy Holly's insistence, he still goes on about it now, has never died. So, shall we, as they say,

Get "Into the groove?"

The words of that New York Cleopatra, Madonna. Whom we shall meet very soon. Back now to a time when we were all far younger, and frankly off our fucking heads. Did we know how to run a nightclub? Did we fuck.

Did we care? Not really. Nobody got rich, that's for sure. I don't suppose Hooky is out there tonight or any of the others? Forgive me New Order, we did not know what we were doing! And, if any of the Mondays are reading this, watch your fucking pockets!

Lovely Northern ladies and gentlemen, it is with more than some trepidation, I now will tell you of Madonna and Mr Wilson.

I can promise it will be emotional. As for will it ever make any money? Behave please. This is the Hacienda we're talking about.

What do you lot fucking think?'

CLEOPATRA OF NEW YORK CITY

Friday 27th January 1984.

Doctor Who is on BBC One. The Pure Hell of St. Trinian's, BBC Two. The A Team, ITV. Meanwhile, at 5.30pm, arriving at full blast on Channel Four, following the Munsters, the Tube roars onto our television screen coming live from the Hacienda in Manchester! It features The Factory All Stars, Marcel King, The Jazz Defektors Breaking Glass, and some young buck from New York city, calling herself Madonna. Of who it was said could dance and sing a bit, but not necessarily at the same time. She'd been down to perform two live (miming) songs, *Burning Up*, and was in the dying remnants of *Holiday*. As the music fades off, and the television cameras cut away to an advertisement break, Madonna slowly winds down. Dressed as the streetwise girl from New York city, who didn't give a fuck, all black, cropped vest, sawn-off leggings, ra-ra skirt, and big crucifix earrings, she finally stops dancing.

'Someone get me a fucking towel, will you!' she yells, much to her dancer's chagrin. Madonna turns around on heading off the dance floor to face the small, seemingly, unimpressed backing dancers.

'Thank you everybody, you saw something very special today, my name is Madonna. Now don't you all fucking forget it!'

There are many stares of disdain and murmurings amongst them.

'Who the fuck does she think she is?'

'Cheeky cow!'

'She was fucking miming and still sounded terrible!'

'She dances like Cliff fuckin' Richard!'

Seemingly oblivious to the cutting remarks, some clearly made loud enough for her to hear, Madonna keeps walking off before reaching a smiling Tony Wilson, who hands her over a towel.

'Darling, that was fabulous, truly wonderful. The word from the people at The Tube is that they loved you. Jools Holland is here somewhere, he adored you. You're truly a star. Tonight Manchester, tomorrow, the world!'

'Who the fuck is Jools Holland?' asks Madonna

'That's a good question,' replies a laughing Tony. 'I'll remember to ask him next time we speak.' Madonna wipes herself down with the towel, whilst secretly enjoying listening to the mad Brit's warblings.

She smiles. 'You sound surprised about how good I was? You shouldn't be, in fact you should be in awe.'

'Did I sound surprised? I didn't mean to be. Please forgive me young lady, I truly was in awe.'

That's good then,' nods Madonna, checking Tony out from top to bottom. 'Hey, what did you expect man? I'm Madonna. I'm going to conquer the fucking world. You hear me?'

'In stereo my darling, and I'm truly on your side.'

Madonna stares at Tony with faked incredulity, trying hard not to smile. She likes him. ' You'd never heard of me before tonight had you?'

'May I call you Madge?'

'No you fucking can't! My name is Madonna, I'm a star. Besides, what the fuck is a Madge?'

A smiling Tony stares at her, she's definitely got something, but whether its actual talent, he's not so sure.

'It doesn't matter. Well, yes, yes of course, your star has already travelled over the ocean. I've heard many tales of your sweetness and your talent has wings.'

Madonna isn't sure what to make of him. 'Tell me, not that I give a shit, but are you gay?'

A laughing Tony shakes his head. 'Only on a Sunday!'

'You're a goddamn strange guy that's for sure. Where can I shower before I get out of this fucking joint?'

'Joint? Ah, yes, an Americanism.'

'A what?'

'Well, Madonna, I actually was hoping you'd do Manchester the honour of performing one more song. Spoil us so to speak. The people are demanding more.'

'I don't think so my weird Brit friend, besides, the cameras are wrapping up, my dancers are showering, so, why would I, honestly… Oh, I'm sorry, but just who the hell are you?'

Tony appears all mock aghast! Clearly enjoy himself.

'What, who am I? Who am I? What a strange question. My name is Tony Wilson to the peasants. Anthony H Wilson to the beautiful people like yourself, and I actually own this dazzling hovel. In fact, I'm the one fucking paying you!'

A smiling Madonna is impressed. 'Ah, Anthony H indeed. What does the H stand for?'

'Honourable,' he replies. 'Though many say horrible.'

'Fuck off!' she laughs! 'So you're paying me huh, How much for one more song then? I think I'll call you Tony, suits you more.'

'How about fifty quid?'

'Squid? You want to pay me in fish Wilson, get the f…'

Tony sighs. 'No, Madonna, quid, quid! An English colloquialism.'

'A col what?'

'It's another word for pound, therefore, fifty quid. We might not be making much money with this place, but I haven't resorted paying people in fish yet?'

Peter Hook is walking past and hears this.

'You could talk a goldfish out of a bowl you Wilson,' smiles Hook. 'Make it dance and still not make any fuckin' money out of it.'

'Thanks for that Peter, this here is Madonna, she's going to be a star.'

Hook acknowledges her. 'Alright kid, whatever you do, don't lend this fucker any money.'

Madonna laughs. 'I sure won't, thanks for the tip!' That said Hook continues on. 'Who was that Tony?'

He sighs. 'My number one fan Madonna. My number one fan!'

'So,' she replies. 'No fish?'

'No, my darling! Fifty quid?'

'Fuck off Mr Honourable Wilson!'

A smiling Tony knows he has his hands full. 'Quite.'
'I don't come that cheap Tony, I'm Madonna. One day you'll have my name tattooed on your arse man. Every punk, lawyer, politician, policeman, pimp and priest will.'
'I can quite imagine sweetheart. The Cleopatra of New York City. Your delicate beauty matched only by your voice, dear girl.'
'A hundred Tony?'
'Fuck off!' he replies with a huge grin.
'You know something,' laughs Madonna. 'You really are full of shit Tony.'
'So, it's been made known to me. Many times.'
Tony points towards a Ladies bathroom. 'You can grab a shower in there young madam. Make sure you lock the door, and put a chair behind it just in case. They're fucking quick in here. The hot water should be working. When you're done, why don't you come and join us for a drink in our VIP suite? It would truly be an honour.'
Madonna smiles. 'Fancy scrubbing my back?'
An embarrassed Tony looks around making sure nobody heard her. 'Well I wouldn't say…'
'Fuck off! I'm kidding with you,' laughs Madonna.
'Of course you are!' replies a red-faced Tony.
'I like you Anthony H, you're interesting. A challenge. Sure, why not, I'll have a drink with you. Although I have to admit you do seem like an asshole, but, cute with it. In a Brit type of way that is.'
'Cute isn't something I hear often,' sighs Tony. 'Pretentious tosser more so in these parts. Or just wanker.'
A smiling Madonna is fascinated by this strange Northern Englishman, 'I can't imagine why, where's this VIP lounge of yours then?'
Tony point across to a door. 'See that STAFF ONLY sign on the door over there?'
'Yeah, what about it?'
'You go through there my dear. Make sure you switch the light on though before you go down the stairs, or you'll break your fucking neck. Oh, I almost forgot, watch out for the bucket and mop when you

reach the bottom. Once in, you may think it resembles a barber's shop, that's because it is. We call it *Swing*, but it's also the quintessential, Mancunian, welcoming watering hole, and one fit for you. My redoubtable queen of New York City.'

'Fuck me Tony, you have the best lines!' laughs Madonna.

'You taken?'

'Only by your beauty princess!'

'You trying to talk me into bed Tony?'

'No,' he smiles. 'Just into our barbers!'

'A shame, Jesus, are they all like you around here?'

'Sadly, no Madonna! I am an unprotected species.'

She smiles. 'I'll protect you Anthony H. Let's see where the night leads…'

Tony watches as Madonna vanishes into the ladies' bathroom, but not before turning and giving him a wave before she does so. He shakes his head, 'Fucking hell, she could've been born in Moston that one.'

The Channel Four presenter of the Tube, Jools Holland spots Tony, and heads across. He's smiling wide. 'Tony, where's the sassy cow, quite something isn't she?'

'She certainly is Jools, a little off her fucking rocker, but she's definitely in the right place for that.'

Holland laughs. 'Have you asked her to do another song?'

'She told me to fuck off. Asked for £100, then I told her to fuck off. Unless you lot at Channel Four want to pay?'

'You must be joking! She's not exactly Chaka fucking Khan. I think we'll pass on that Tony.'

'Not yet she isn't. I don't know what it is she's got, but that girl isn't going away. Give her time Jools!'

'Time for what? She can't sing and I've seen better dancers on Top of the Pops behind that fucking Jimmy Savile.'

'We'll see,' smiles Tony. 'And don't mention that cunt Savile in here. He's barred.'

'What, has he tried to get in?'

'No, he's just fucking barred.'

SWING

Tony heads downstairs to the barbers and on entering spots a miserable, looking Steven Patrick Morrissey, sat in a corner, strumming away on a guitar. Morrissey and the Smiths are riding high with a number two album in the music charts. Also present is young local girl Tracey Donnelly, who's busy with a sweeping brush.
 Tracey has been by Tony's side since the early days of the club. There's no set job description for her, Tracey basically just does everything that needs to be done around the place. Keeping things ticking over and duly ensuring many people out of trouble!
 The type of person invaluable in a madhouse like this,
and her boss knows it.
 'Hi Tracey love, Moz, tell me something?'
Tony sighs. 'Do you ever fucking go home? You're famous now, you have a best-selling album at number two in the charts. Why not go out and enjoy life? At least go upstairs. Have a dance and a drink? Maybe even get a blowjob? There'll be plenty of willing takers.'
 Appearing deep in thought Morrissey continues to strum his guitar. 'I'm celibate Tony, you know that. My body and mind is a temple to creativity and making art. Besides, I'd rather suck my own cock.'
Tony and Tracey stare momentarily at Morrissey, then each other, both not really sure they can believe what he's just said.
 'Anyway, how'd it go with little Miss precious knickers Tony? We watched her perform on the portable didn't we Moz?'
 'And what was your considered opinion of Miss Precious knickers Moz, as Tracey calls her?'
 Morrissey stops strumming, he looks to the roof as if in sheer angst, then towards Tony. 'It's complicated Tony.'
 'Enlighten me Moz. I need your wisdom.'
Tracey laughs. 'Go on Moz, do what Tony just said! Enlighten him.'
He puts down his guitar. 'Well then, here goes, my considered opinion is that apart from the two songs being utter shite, and the fact

she can't sing or dance. The girl would have the cats running down the alleys in Salford and jumping in the fucking Irwell.'
'Not really a fan then?' replies Tony.
'She's going to be a star Tony!'
A smiling Tony for once appears lost for words. 'Moz, how on earth? How did you come to that conclusion, dare I ask?'
Morrissey picks his guitar back up and again starts to strum, albeit slowly. 'She may sound like a screeching banshee, but there's an attitude about her. An aura, she doesn't give a fuck about anything, but being a star. It's so obvious. Young girls and the gays will love her. She's a white disco queen from New York with bigger balls than any man. The girl is going to be huge.'
'Moz, please,' pleads Tracey. 'Will you stop talking about balls!'
'Sorry Tracey love, force of habit.' Tony points towards Morrissey's guitar. 'And, by the way, what on earth are you doing with that thing?'
'What this?' smiles Morrissey, strumming a little faster.
'Yes, yes, the fucking guitar!'
'Oh, Johnny Marr is teaching me! Another string to my miserable bow.'
'What's Johnny thinking, he must be off his head. You already think you're Oscar Wilde, please god Moz, don't morph into Bob fucking Dylan.'
'No Tony, you have to listen, he's good,' interrupts Tracey. 'Play Tony what you played for me before Moz, it's really catchy. I loved it, what's it called again?'
'I haven't got a proper name for it yet, but I'm contemplating Manchester virgin.'
'Autobiographical I presume?' asks Tony.
'My choice Tony, like I said, my body is my temple.'
'Christ preserve us' sighs Tony. 'Come on then, get it over with. let's hear this masterpiece dedicated to yourself.'
'I'm not sure it's ready yet for your scathing criticism Tony.'
'Go on Moz!' smiles Tracey. 'For me. Please, Tony will go easy, won't you Tony?'

'Anything for you Tracey love,' sighs Tony. Trying hard not to die of boredom. 'Moz, just play the fucking thing will you.'
'Go on then Miss Wiz'n draw!' smiles Morrissey. 'Please be nice now Tony!'
'Miss what?'
'Miss Wiz'n draw,' laughs Tracey. 'Wythenshawe, draw? Come on Tony!'
'Tracey dear, please excuse me for me not being down with the South Manchester council kids latest slang. I'm rather busy on the telly and running this fucking place. Talking of which, make sure there's nothing hanging around with these Channel Four types knocking about from the Tube.'
'Why, will they report us to the police?'
'No, my dear girl, they'll fucking rob it.'

Morrissey starts to strum the opening chords of what will later be Madonna's *Like a Virgin*.

Suddenly, she enters and smiles wide on hearing it!
'Nice! It's got a groove!'
All eyes in the room turn towards Madonna, 'That tune, it's so damn awesome. Hey Mr James Dean type over there. Love the quiff man. Do you have any lyrics for that?' A dubious looking Morrissey stares at Madonna. Despite only tiny, there's an enormous presence about her. She scares him! 'Erm, yes, I have a few lines.'
Madonna stares back like a leopard steadying to pounce and rip apart a deer, 'Love to hear them. Your name is?'
Tony is listening in, 'Don't you watch Top of the Pops Madonna? This man here is the last of the famous international playboys!'
'Thank you Tony' smiles Morrissey, scribbling down what he's just herd for future use.
'Top of the fucking what?' asks a confused looking Madonna.
'My name is Morrissey and my band are the Smiths.'
Madonna shakes her head still thinking about Top of the Pops.
'Sorry, never heard of you, but I love your tune. Can I hear some of your words?'

'Yeah go on Moz,' says Tracey, another warily eyeing up Madonna. 'They're brilliant. Sing it like you did before.'
Looking around Madonna shakes her head. 'Not exactly the fucking Carlton this is it?'
'Well, you're not exactly Diana Ross darlin!' snaps back an annoyed Tracey, on hearing her little palace described as such by this visiting gobby Yank. 'Are you the hired help hun?' remarks Madonna, clearly trying to agitate Tracey. 'Make yourself useful huh, get me a drink.'
'I'll give you fuckin' hired help in a minute!' she fires back.
A furious Tracey puts her sweeping brush against the wall, getting ready to deal with Madonna, only for Tony to step in. 'Wo, wo ladies! Calm your tits down. This is a place of peace, not all-out fucking war. Pipe down Donnelly!'
Suddenly, all their warring attention is attracted to Morrissey, as he starts to not just strum his guitar once more, but sing also…
''I made it through the Manchester wilderness.
Somehow, I made it through.
Didn't know how lost I was,
Until I found you, down on the Irwell.''
Morrissey finishes and stares up at his small, but open-mouthed audience, waiting for a reaction. 'Well, what do you think?'
'What the fuck was that?' asks an utterly perplexed Tony. 'Honestly, Moz, you really need to think again and dump the guitar. That was positively upbeat, it'll fucking ruin you!'
'Oh, I don't know Tony,' adds a smiling Madonna. 'It does have a certain something. Hey, Donnelly, or whatever the fuck you're called. Where's my drink?'
'I won't tell you again you fu…!'
A laughing Tony again moves fast to referee! 'Madonna sweetheart, you've got it all wrong. Tracey isn't my hired help. She's my Factory girl.'
Tracey remains glaring angrily at Madonna. 'Yeah, I'm Tony's Factory girl. You listenin' yank?'

'This young lady here,' continues Tony pointing to Tracey. 'This Mancunian star from the deep south of our beautiful city, where angels and devils mix like a bag of jelly babies.'
'Calm down Tony,' says Morrissey. He smiles. 'They bite the head off jelly babies in Wythenshawe and dump the fuckin' rest!'
'Oi you!' screeches Tracey towards him! Tony puts a protective arm around her making Tracey smile wide. 'Tracey has seen stuff no one her age should ever have to witness. Isn't that right love?'
'Too right Tony,' she replies. 'A child of the streets me, you listenin' to this New York girl?'
'Keep chatting gangster lady,' sighs Madonna, whilst popping some bubble gum into her mouth.
'Well, you're not really a child of the streets are you Tracey?' asks Tony.
'No, not really,' smiles Tracey. 'I have my own room and that at home, but I'm just getting my point across to madame fuckin' Buttersky here.'
'I think you'll find it's butterfly hun,' laughs Madonna. Clearly enjoying herself!
'Whatever!' snaps Tracey, with a truly, impressive, dismissive tut.
'Quite,' says Tony, now seemingly losing the will to live. 'But as Tracey will tell you herself. She's a Donnelly from Wythenshawe, and proud of it. She is sheer quality!'
'Erm, no comment Tony!'
'Compared to what she's experienced growing up in that concrete heaven of Wiz'n Draw, we here are merely kids fucking around in a playground. Aren't we dear?'
'Wiz n draw?' asks Madonna. What the fuck is 'Wiz n draw?'
Tony sighs. 'Oh, it's not important.'
'Okay then, but what exactly does a girl have to do to get a drink around here?'
'You can try being nice for a start,' says Tracey.
Madonna paints on a plastic smile. 'Can I have a drink, please?'

'Of course, you can!' replies Tracey, herself smiling, but through gritted teeth. Tony rolls his eyes as Tracey grabs four glasses, a bottle of red wine and starts to pour.

'What year is it?' asks Madonna. 'It better be vintage, I don't drink any old shit!'

'No, but you talk it,' grumbles Tracey, so quietly that no one hears her. 'It's vintage Wythenshawe market Madonna. Like the stuff posh people drink.'

Don't forget the vodka in mine Tracey love,' shouts across Morrissey. 'And don't be tight with it.'

'Hearing you Moz,' laughs Tracey. 'Vodka going in, plenty of it!'

'Where did that Vodka come from?' asks Tony.

'The Midland Hotel bar,' replies Tracey.

'First I've heard, I don't remember that happening?'

'Neither do they Tony, to be honest.'

Tony puts a hand up. 'Tracey love. I don't want to hear anymore!'

Tracey hands out the glasses, and ends up standing next to Madonna. 'So, tell me how a gal from Wiz n' Draw ends up in a cool dive like this?'

'The 105?'

'The what?'

'It's a bus Madonna,' helps out Tony. 'I'm sure you have them in New York?'

She smiles. 'Me? I'm more used to Cadillacs baby!'

Again, Morrissey starts to strum. This time a different tune.

'Oh, no, not another one,' sighs Tony.

'So,' asks Madonna, thinking of declaring a truce now she has a drink. 'What exactly do you do around here then Factory girl?'

'I started down here last year Madonna. My job title was a receptionist. Receptionist? I ask you. That really covered many things because with the hairdressers being off their heads most of the time, I'd be left to entertain the waiting customers.'

Madonna rolls her eyes...

'No, bloody hell not that!' shrieks a shocked Tracey!

Tony can't help but smile at Tracey's embarrassment.

'Many times, I'd walk in here and see a line of grumpy faces waiting for Laurel and Hardy, Andy and Nick, to get out of their fucking pits over in Hulme, and Tracey would be tap dancing, singing or telling jokes. Anything, to keep the waiting customers calm and happy.'

'But not that Tony…' adds a horrified looking Tracey.

'No, Tracey dear. Definitely not that!' laughs Tony.

'And did it work?' asks Madonna. 'The other stuff?'

'Yes, mostly' smiles Tracey, now calm again. 'Apart from the singing, that just pissed them off even more. The tap dancing always went down well though! Think I missed my way sometimes!'

Madonna laughs. 'You're sweet.'

'Oh, thank you,' replies a shocked Tracey. 'You're not such a stuck-up bitch after all!' she says quietly whilst drinking her wine.

'Sorry, what was that?'

'I was just saying Madonna, you're really rather lovely yourself!'

Meanwhile, Morrissey has continued to strum his guitar throughout, but is also now mumbling lyrics.

Tony appears fearful to ask, but does so anyway. 'What's this fucking epic you're working on Moz, a sequel to Bright Eyes?'

'It's called Mother don't Preach Tony.'

'Nice title,' smiles Madonna, again looking like she can't believe her luck!

''Mother, I know you're going to be upset.
Cause, I was always your little boy.
But you should know by now.
I'm not a baby.''

Tracey is dancing along with glass in hand to Morrissey's singing!

'Hell, today is like Christmas morning for me baby!' calls out Madonna. 'Keep them coming!'

'Oh, come on now Moz,' adds an exasperated Tony. 'That isn't even pretentious. What's wrong with you? That guitar is your crutch, you need to get rid before somebody hits you over the head with the fucker!'

A seemingly deflated Morrissey puts down the guitar and takes a drink. He then sighs heavily. 'You could have a point Tony, it is cheering me up a bit. Worrying that.'

'It's fucking career-ending Moz, trust me,' replies Tony. 'Dump it.'

'So' asks Madonna, silently now fully enjoying the company of Tony, Morrissey and Tracey. 'Tell me who else is coming to our little get together here. Any big hitters? Bono, Boy George, Cliff Richard?'

'Cliff fucking Richard?!' exclaims Tony, whilst looking around the barbers room. 'You have the cream already here my love. We may have the New Order boys coming in to scream abuse at me later, but everyone else in the place will be either working, dealing or dancing.'

'Pat Phoenix is in,' says Tracey. 'She might come down Tony?'

'Who the fuck is Pat Phoenix?' asks Madonna.

'Who the fuck is Pat Phoenix?' replies a high pitched Tracey.

'She's only queen of the street Madonna!'

'I thought she lived in London in a palace. Not a goddamn street?'

'For fuck's sake!' sighs Tony, very quietly. 'Americans?'

'Coronation Street, Madonna,' says Morrissey. 'It's a television show. Pat is an actress. She's beautiful and strong, and I truly adore her.'

'Oh, right,' smiles Madonna. 'Well if you like her quiff boy, that's good enough for me. She turns her attention to Tony. 'Hey Tony baby, I've been meaning to ask you. What the fuck is a Hacienda?'

'I thought you'd never ask!' He points to the roof where you can hear the music humming from the above dance floor. 'This place, my sweet-smelling rose from across the ocean is Manchester's heart and soul. Though, I do have to admit, nobody really seems to appreciate that yet.'

'Apart from me and you Tony, we do,' smiles Tracey. 'We get it.'

'Of course, that goes without saying my factory girl, apart from me and you.'

'But what does Hacienda mean, what is it?' asks Madonna again. 'Did you make it up Wilson?'

'Not exactly!' laughs Tony. 'It means whatever you wish it to be my magnificent mistress of Manhattan.'

Madonna is smiling. Anthony H is really starting to grow on her.

'Cut the crap, I'm from Queens actually, and the truth is you don't know do you Tony?'
'Some would say we are making it up as we go along Madonna, but this, this place…This place is definitely real.'
'Go on then Tony boy. I'm all ears, as well as tits!'
'Damn straight you are our kid!' laughs Tracey. 'Damn straight Madonna!'
'Shut up Tracey,' sighs Tony.
'Let me try and explain Madonna. Hacienda is a Spanish word; it means an estate. These were in the form of plantations, mines, even factories. The Haciendas aimed for self-sufficiency, to look after themselves. They didn't care about luxuries, though many were indeed beautiful buildings, but it was all about the illusion you see. In the eye of the beholder. That my dear.

That is our Hacienda.'

Madonna stares at Tony for a moment trying to figure out just what the hell he was going on about. 'So, let me get this straight. This here Hacienda is your beautiful home, you try and do things your own way to survive, but you have hardly any fucking money, no plan, and are dreaming of better days, and weeks, and happy Mondays to come. Am I right?'
Tony smiles wide. 'Yes! Something like that.'
For a moment there's silence…

'Bloody hell Tony,' a smiling, but shocked Morrissey finally speaking up. 'A miracle on Whitworth Street West! She's left you speechless! We need to get the date, time.'
'And the year!' laughs Tracey.
Tony raises his glass. 'A toast!'
'Can I have butter on mine please!' smiles Tracey.
'Behave Donnelly. A toast!'
Madonna, Tracey and Morrissey raise their glasses also.
'To our adopted Mancunian for the evening. The most beautiful and wonderful Madonna. What's your second name by the way?'
'I only need the one Tony!'
'To Madonna!'

'To Madonna!' repeat Tracey and Morrissey!
'May she long continue to shine, to fuck off and to conquer the world.'
'Amen. You hitting on me Tony?'
'No Madonna,' smiles Tony. 'I'm just in awe.'
'Fuckin ell…' says Morrissey quietly taking another drink. Suddenly realising something was going on between Tony and Madonna.
'The vowel and the Pussycat. Who'd have believed it!'
'Where are you staying Madonna?' asks Tracey.
'At a friend's, but I've no plans on going home just yet, I'm too wired for sleep. I was hoping that your prince of the city here, Lord Tony might show me the sights?'
'Sights?' shudders Morrissey. 'Good luck with that!'
'What a great idea,' adds Tracey. 'Go on Tony, be the gentleman we know you are, and not the pretentious tosser people think. Give our Madonna here a personal guided tour.'
'Erm, thank you for that, I think, Tracey darling.'
Tracey looks at her watch. 'There's still loads of time before throwing out. Manchester on a Friday night Tony. Give the girl a treat!'
A smiling Madonna flutters her eyebrows towards Tony. 'What do you say then, you going to take me Tony baby?'
'How can I possibly say no after that? Well, drink up; you do know it's raining, don't you, and this isn't normal rain my princess, it's Manchester rain.'
'It rains in New York as well Tony.'
'Not all the fucking time it doesn't.'
'I think you're overdoing the misery Tony.'
'We're a hum drum town Madonna. We excel under dark and gloomy miserable clouds. Fucking hell, look at him!' Tony points across at Morrissey.
'Ah, cut the crap Wilson!' she replies laughing. 'I was happy here in my drunken haze, and I'll be fucked if you're going to make me miserable now.'

On hearing Madonna, Morrissey looks across, picks up a writing pad and starts to write down what she's just said! 'Two giveth, one taken away,' he says smiling to himself.
Madonna finishes her drink then goes across to hug Tracey.
 'So long factory girl, any advice on how to handle our Tony here?'
'Oh, yes!'
'What's that then?'
Tracey starts to laugh. 'Just let him talk!'
'That figures,' smiles Madonna. 'Nice meeting you too gorgeous quiff boy. She waves across to Morrissey. 'If you're ever in New York, you make sure to come and look me up.'
'I'd like that,' he replies. 'What's your address?'
'Ah, you won't need it,' she laughs. 'Hey, I'm Madonna, I live my life in the lights. Just look on the Time Square billboards, you'll find me!'

ACT TWO

CAROUSEL RUNNING RINGS AROUND THE MOON

It's just turned nine o'clock in the Northern city of Manchester.
 On a bench overlooking the canal, with a wine bottle in hand,
  Tony is sat in his famous white raincoat. Next to him is Madonna. She's also adorning the same. 'I really appreciate the coat Tony, but I feel like fucking Colombo!'
 The rain has momentarily ceased, and on the bridge above them, crowds are making their way to pubs and clubs along the busy Oxford Road pathways. A head pops over the bridge and spots Tony. 'Wilson, you fuckin' tosser!' he screams down, causing Tony and Madonna to look up. The same then hands Tony a V sign, laughs and vanishes. A fuming Madonna can't believe what's just happened. 'Screw you, you piece of shit!' she shouts loud.
 Madonna looks back towards a smiling Tony. 'Are you going to let him talk to you like that Tony?' She starts to head up the stairway leading to the bridge. 'I'm going to find that asshole!'
 Tony is touched at her reaction, it also amuses him. 'It's quite okay Madonna. I get as many compliments as insults. I actually prefer the latter mostly. They're far more interesting. Please, come back here and sit down.'
 She's still livid, 'I want to go and find him and kick his fucking ass Tony. You're far too nice.' He points to the space next to him and smiles towards her. 'Your throne awaits you once more my queen!'

Madonna stares at Tony in quiet disbelief, and shakes her head before doing as he asks. 'You're a lot more polite person than I am Tony.' Again, Madonna turns to the direction of the stairway. 'Scumbag!' she roars at the top of her voice.
A smiling Tony puts an arm around her. 'Think of all this as a Swan Lake of the streets. A Mancunian opera. A tidal wave of human joy, despondency and despair. All off to get pissed out of their brains.'
'Pass the wine lover boy,' smiles Madonna. 'You just keep talking!'
'That lot up there in their pringle jumpers and adidas trainers. Their Lacoste shirts, some hooky, most probably. Those lucky enough to have jobs are simply blowing off steam, whilst those who haven't, and managed to scrounge a few quid to get down here tonight are simply a deafening, unwanted mass choir this country, and fucking government have given up on. Oh, they'll be fighting later, but those not lucky, or simply too bare-faced ugly to grab a fuck. They'll be crying, their tears and blood falling into the gutters mixing with the rain. Manchester rain.
Incessant, fucking, miserable Manchester rain.'
 'Not that rain again,' sighs Madonna.
Oh, but those lucky few,' continues Tony.
 'Those so lucky handsome few will be down some back-alley fucking, or riding over the rainbow getting a blow job in the back of a black cab. Others, dreamers who like to simply watch the stars, or poets, looking for that jaw-fucking dropping sonnet. Our midnight drinkers, some of the greatest minds scraping through bins, desperate for a mere sip to keep the madness away. All will be around somewhere. We'll see them later, harming nobody, penning their fucking angst or drinking it. Not everyone my dear Madonna in this city has a voice like me. Many, many have the talent, but not the gift to be a twat. Nor the arrogance. For Manchester is a fucking, wonderful place, but it can also be a cruel place. A dark city. A troubled town. Our sense of humour so sharp we could cut your fucking head off with a throwaway comment.'
 Madonna has listened transfixed. 'You could be talking about New York Tony. You really could.'

'Oh, no,' replies a smiling Tony. 'There's no city in the world like Manchester. Nowhere. Look at her down there?' He points towards A pretty, blond ballerina, 18 year-old Rachael Collins from Hulme, appearing into sight, dancing-pirouetting alongside the canal path. Tony appears close to tears. 'Look at her, Rachael Fucking Collins.' A smiling Rachael looks up and spots Tony. 'Hi Tony!' she shouts. He waves back. 'That there Madonna, is my darling Rachael, a princess of the fucking checkout. She'll be up for work in a few hours wishing miserable bastards a nice day and hating it. But dreaming all the time down those aisles of better days. A life free of strangling boredom to live her dreams.

To fucking dance!'

A spellbound Madonna watches as Rachael dances in the silhouette of a full moon shining bright down upon her. Full of grace, tiptoeing on the water's edge before pirouetting under the bridge, and out of sight. 'Bye Tony!' Rachael's voice echoing beneath.

'Love youuu!'

'Did that all really just fucking happen?' asks Madonna.

'Oh, yes,' replies Tony. 'Next time you're performing, you remember that girl, you remember my Rachael Collins, and you blow the fucking crowd away with your heart and soul. Do you promise me?'

'I promise Tony. I'm going to be a star, I'm going to conquer the world, it has no idea what's coming. Oh, I'm not fucking blinkered, I know I don't have a great voice, or the best dancer, but I have decent tits, a huge, sexy, fuck me smile, and the ambition to haul the moon down from the fucking skies. No one dare not underestimate me Tony. It won't be a case of them not seeing me coming, trust me they'll see me, but they won't be able to stop me.
Nobody will.'

'I can quite believe!' smiles Tony.

Madonna passes the wine back to Tony, and for a moment the two sit quietly, taking in the evening's sights and sounds. Then, the silence is broken by the sound of a grizzly voice humming a familiar tune. An old tramp, Lord Charles, appears, and walks slowly towards their bench. All the time clutching tight onto a half-filled whisky bottle finished off in the last hour.

He stops, and the moonlight now illuminates his well lived-in, haggard features. Lord Charles coughs. He spots Tony, recognises him and smiles. 'I have something for you young Wilson. They are more than words. They are the story of all our lives.
Listen hard young man…
''Round, like a circle in a spiral, like a wheel within a wheel.
Never ending or beginning, on an ever-spinning reel.
Like a snowball down a mountain, or a carnival balloon.
Like a carousel that's turning running rings around the moon…''
Finally,

Lord Charles comes to an end of his drunken, nasal, heartfelt rendition of *Windmills of your Mind*. On finishing, he turns to Tony and Madonna. 'How's life treating you son?'

'Interesting as always, but good Lord Charles. And yourself, you keeping well?'

He takes a huge swig from the whisky bottle, then wipes his mouth, 'I can't really complain Tony. I have my firewater here, a decent doorway put aside for later, and up there,' Lord Charles points towards the black starlit skies. 'A decent plethora of stars.
Ah,' he spots Madonna. 'I see you have a lady friend with you young Wilson?'

'This vision alongside me here is Madonna from the great New York city, Lord Charles. Tony is smiling wide. 'Isn't she beautiful?'

'She is indeed,' nods Lord Charles. 'A fine figure of a woman. New York you say?'
Madonna nods.

'An amazing city. So good they named it twice, sang my good friend Frank.' Lord Charles takes Madonna's hand and kisses it.
'Charmed I'm sure Lady Madonna! So, very lovely to make your acquaintance.'

'The pleasure is all mine Lord Charles,' she replies smiling.
'I adored your song, such beautiful words.'

'If you love that song it means to me two things. You always chose love over hate, and you possess a musical soul my dear girl.'
'It made me feel happy. We all love to be happy Lord Charles.'
'We certainly do Madonna. Well, I shall leave you young people to carry on with whatever young people do these days. Goodbye Tony, you too young lady, give my love to the Big Apple. I had a skyscraper there once, until I saw the light. A most wonderful view of the Hudson River, and all the scandal, and all of the vice.
I loved it for a while. Until, well…
So long my gentle children.'
Lord Charles turns and walks away, disappearing down the steps leading onto the canal path, and away beneath the bridge.
'Tony.'
'Yes, Madonna.'
'Who the hell was that?'
He smiles. 'I've already told you. That was Lord Charles?'
'Tony baby, what the fu..?'
'Okay, okay!' he laughs. 'You have just met the very loud and proud, the mad Lord Charles Nelson the second.'
'A Lord? What the fuck has happened to him. Doesn't a Lord have a mansion, servants and a horse and carriage? I don't believe they sleep in doorways and smell like shit!'
'I heard that Madonna!' booms Lord Charles' voice from beneath the bridge! 'Oh crap,' Madonna appears sheepish on being caught, whilst Tony bursts out laughing.
'Okay then, what's Lord Charles' story Tony?'
'Well, in the beginning he was the grand Lord of Lancaster, rumoured after the royals to be the richest man in England. But something happened, what? Nobody knows for sure, but because of it, he gave away every pound and every penny.'
'What happened Tony, I have to know?'
'I heard a rumour, but it doesn't really make sense in the world we know today.'
'Tell me. Please.'

'Well, it turned out Lord Charles discovered something far more important than money and material goods. Something he prayed would help make the world go around just a little better with his millions.'
'Yeah, and what was that?'
'Love.'
'You're fucking kidding me.'
'No Madonna, I'm serious.'
'And did it?'
Tony smiles. In the distance he can hear Lord Charles giving another rendition of his party piece. 'We can only hope so my dear.'
He takes a large swig of the wine and looks down upon the black, still silent waters of the canal.
'Well, I have to tell you. I think he was an asshole Tony baby.'
'What?' He laughs. 'I'd keep your voice down, if I was you!'
'Lord Charles was an goddamn asshole!' she shouts! 'We're living in a material world, and I'm a material girl. To get things done in this world, you need to push and push, and watch where shit goes. Not walk away, ah, the man is a fucking asshole. You can quote me on that.'
'He's a saint!' replies Tony
'He's an asshole...End of.'
'You New Yorkers are so fucking cynical Madonna.'
She takes the bottle back off Tony. 'Yeah, and you're the Queen fucking mum! Come on Tony, admit it, you agree with me. From what I've discovered the only difference between this place and my city, is we have two fucking towers over the Hudson River that'll stand forever. And, let me tell you, they're far bigger than anything you've got in this town.'
'Size isn't everything darling!'
'That's a fucking myth!' laughs Madonna. 'Who told you that Tony?'
'I get told all the time I'm a small knob, but people love me!' smiles Tony. 'I'm not surprised' she replies. 'You're a very loveable person Mr Wilson.'

The two go quiet appearing content in each other's company. Above them, suddenly, a shooting star hurtles across the night skies. Madonna notices it first and points up. 'Look, Tony!'

He does so, 'That thing better not fly to fucking low over here, it'll get shot down!'

'I love shooting stars Tony,' smiles Madonna. 'They remind me of myself!'

'Well, you certainly have made an impression tonight young lady!'

'I want to know about this city Tony. Your city. I want to know what makes it tick, makes it laugh and cry. What's it's heartbeat. Where the holy fuck do you Mancs come from?' Tony stands up and takes Madonna's hand. He's smiling wide. 'Come on, me and you are going for a walk.'

'Yeah, where are we going?'

'To the top of the world our kid!' laughs Tony.

'Isn't that a James Cagney's line?' asks Madonna.

'No, Matt Busby my love.'

'Busby? Never heard of him. What films was he in Tony?'

'The greatest story ever told!'

'Oh, I know that one, who did he play?'

'God' smiles Tony. 'Come on lady, time to go…'

ACT THREE

CITY LIGHTS

Together, hand in hand, Tony and Madonna head off the canal and onto Oxford Road, where Tony hails down a black cab. It stops. Both crouch into the back seats. The driver recognises Tony through his rear mirror. 'Hello Tony mate, I really enjoyed the show tonight. Where are you off then?'
'The CIS building please.'
 The taxi drives off with the driver still checking out Tony through the mirror. 'Have to admit though Tony, I thought the all-stars were brilliant, but where did you find that yank girl singer? She was fucking hopeless! Embarrassing even.'
Tony feels Madonna slouch low. He grips her hand tighter and waits for the eruption, but it never comes. Instead, Tony notices a tear in Madonna's eye before she turns away looking through the window.
 Not wanting him to see her upset.
 Finally, they pull up outside the CIS and step out. Tony goes to pay the driver, whilst Madonna walks a few yards on.
'How much?' he asks.
 '£4 please Tony. Enjoy your night with your nice lady over there,' he smiles. Madonna turns around on hearing this, and the driver suddenly realises it's the girl he's just been slagging off.
'I'm sorry love. No offence, I was just having a laugh like.'
'None taken,' replies Madonna. 'I know I'm going to be a star and you'll still be riding round in your stupid fucking taxi here. You fucking arsehole!' She appears ready to rip the driver's head off.
'Here we go,' says a smiling Tony quietly. He hands him a fiver.
'Keep the change and fuck off before she kills you!'

Will do' replies the driver. 'She's fuckin' mad her!' he says, before screeching off!

Madonna laughs as the taxi disappears back into town. She looks up at the huge CIS building. 'Are we going up there?'

Tony links her arm. ' We certainly are, there's something I want to show you.'

She smiles. 'Oh, Tony, You going to give a girl a nice time?'

He laughs. 'Just pray the fucking lift is working!'

Tony and Madonna are on top of the CIS building overlooking the entire city. A thousand lights, police sirens can be heard, the rattle of trains heading off, through and into Victoria and Piccadilly station. All beneath a still, starlit sky.

A smiling Tony points out across Manchester. 'So, it goes, look out there. Tell me what you see Madonna?'

'I see a city sleeping. It's fucking late Tony. What exactly am I looking for?'

'Close your eyes, imagine a smog-filled sky, endless chimneys, klaxon horns blaring. Once upon a time Manchester was the centre of the entire industrial word. We were home to the Industrial Revolution. Us, Manchester. We were a giant living and breathing machination of humanisation. Worker ants with attitude and not prepared to be fucked around. If not exactly for a fair day's pay, at least show us due respect, and the ability to feed our families. Our voices were loud against the gentry, the aristocracy, our fucking supposed, learned better. We rose up, Peterloo, listen Madonna, listen quietly you'll hear the ghosts of the fallen scream as the Yeomanry cut and slashed them down near our Central Library. Hidden history, blood and guts, men, women and children, innocent souls slaughtered on the Manchester streets. Our kids don't even learn about it in schools, because do you know why my precious lady of the Queens, those fuckers on high are scared to fucking death it may happen again.'

A smiling Madonna opens her eyes.

'I see it Tony. I see your city.'

He continues to point. 'Look beyond those twinkling lights, everyone out there, a beating heart. Bursting with dreams and desires to make

their lives better. To love, to create beautiful music, music that moves you to the fucking gut, that takes your breath away. Poets scribbling like mad dervishes writing down the words before the night takes both them and their masterpieces into a place of restless dreams. Others, sleepless, lost in mathematical equations to change or save the world. Alan Turing, he won the Second World War, an adopted Mancunian. One of us.'
'Who the fuck is Alan Turing Tony?'
Tony appears to choke up a little. 'Who the fuck is Alan Turing? He's lost in the history books Madonna, not even a crease, an afterthought, not a line on a page. A queer they called him. A poof, a criminal. A Fucking criminal? Those bastards who made him commit suicide would've been talking German, and their children and grandchildren screaming "Heil Hitler!" If, if it wasn't for our Alan. That's if the Nazi's hadn't murdered them all.'
'You okay Tony?'
He's smiling again. 'Look at that sight, look at my city. Welcoming to all. Jews, Gentiles, Irish Polish, Jamaican, Pakistani, Indian, Ukrainian and Chinese. The Manchester I know doesn't recognise creed or colour. Come one, come all, we ask little in return. Just like gravy on your fucking chips, and respect your neighbour.
'What's gravy Tony?'
'Heaven my dear!'
'You talk about Manchester as if it's an oasis, is that what you're talking about Tony? A refuge for those just wanting to live their lives in peace, and look after their families. Sounds like America man. Once upon a time.'
'Look over there Madonna, do you see that building with the tall clock tower?'
'Yeah.'
'Guess what it's called?'
Madonna smiles. 'Shock me Tony!'
'The Refuge Building.'
She laughs. 'Why does that not surprise me Mr Anthony Wilson?'

'You're a New York city girl Madonna, this, for you is a village, but for me and those like me. Yes there are a few! Manchester is the fucking epicentre of life itself.'

'Wasn't the Beatles from around these parts?'

Tony starts to smile. 'Sadly, for them no. Nearby, up the road in a place called Liverpool.'

'All you need is love huh Tony?'

'Love can, if we let it, tear us apart my dear, sang a good friend of mine once. May he rest in peace. It can be an all-consuming passion, but it's one we embrace here. Here, in this city where we invented the first railway stations, where we invented computers. Out there, us, we did! Then we put on the fucking kettle for a while, had a brew, and really got down to work. 'Have you heard of the Suffragettes Madonna?'

'Not sure I have Tony. Did they have any hits?'

A laughing Tony sit down and motions Madonna to do similar. She does so. 'There was a Manchester girl called Emmeline Pankhurst, from the Moss Side backstreets who caused the wizened, old, rich gentlemen of society hell on fucking earth with her Suffragette ladies. They fought them on the streets and racecourses for simple equal rights. And they won! Women's rights, the right to vote, that was our Emily.

Then there's the Unions.

The Co-op.

The fucking Mancs going crazy on the dance floor. Lost in the vibe, our musical souls, Northern Soul. When business was done, we danced. And danced, and danced.

And we're still fucking dancing!'

'You really adore this place don't you Tony?'

'It's my home Madonna, it's Manchester. We tend to do things a little differently here.'

She laughs. 'You don't say! Manchester getting into a groove!'

'Sorry?'

'Nothing Tony, just thinking out loud. You got anymore plans for tonight?'

He looks at his watch. 'It's gone three in the morning, not really.'
Madonna grabs his hand. 'What say we stay up here till the sun comes up, watch it together over your city?'
Tony smiles. 'Why not my beautiful lady? And whilst we are up here, let me tell you about the greatest football team in the world!'
'You mean that soccer thing?'
'I mean football!'
Madonna starts to laugh. This is one night she won't forget in a hurry, 'I'm all ears Tony baby!'

TODAY (Part Two)

Tony steps down from the Hacienda doorsteps,
 and prepares to say a last goodbye before returning upstairs.
 He smiles,
 'And, so it went,
for those of you with filthy minds I know well what you're thinking! Well, sorry to disappoint you, but nothing happened between myself and Madonna on that long, gone night. We simply sat and talked until the sun came up over the Irwell, well, mostly I did about the greatest city in the world. She, bless her, just listened on, I thought back then in silent awe. Sadly, I couldn't have been more fucking wrong! You see, a few years later, our paths crossed once more, only this time in New York. By this time Madonna was indisputably, as she claimed she would be, the biggest and brightest star on the planet. I introduced myself, and that dear, dear lady claimed not to remember me.
Me? I ask you.
Anthony Howard Wilson.
 Like so many things, since then, myself and the Hacienda are no more. Oh, and incidentally, those two towers on the Hudson River, Madonna talked about. Turned out they didn't last forever after all. I vacated this mortal coil at just 57 years-old, and was surprised to see how many people truly missed me. Not bad for a pretentious tosser, may I say. I heard there was talk of a statue. Fuck that, the pigeons and New Order would have a field day. I ask only of my fellow glorious Mancunians, as I wrap up now, two things, please, don't ever change, and don't ever forget me.
I'm Tony Wilson.'

THE SEA ALWAYS WINS

PROLOGUE
THE YEAR OF OUR LORD

Cork harbour.
　The young Irish sailor stares in utter disbelief for she's simply the most beautiful sight he's ever seen. Laden down with a large kitbag and a tatty suitcase the sailor salutes and shows the officer on deck his credentials, before being allowed on board. A last minute replacement for an unfortunate crew member, Jacob Mendy, taken seriously ill has resulted in good fortune for this boy from Drunamere on Ireland's West coast, who hopes to begin the first chapter of a wonderful adventure. A new life. Looking around at the majesty and sheer size of this seafaring wonder of the world the sailor takes a deep breath. He smiles wide can this really be happening to him, William (Billy) Rogan? A boy who has dreamed of going to sea for as far back as he can remember?
'Come on, move yourself now son!' shouts a Naval officer to William.
'There's no time for slouches or daydreamers on this ship.'
'Yes sir,' replies Billy, before swiftly heading onboard. He takes one last look at the Cork harbour brimming with people and cargo before heading inside. Billy smiles wide, his dreams coming true. The date is the year of our lord, April 11, 1912. The ship is RMS Titanic.

ACT ONE

KEEPER OF SECRETS

April 11, 1961.
 9 year-old Tom Rogan is sat on the end of Drunamere pier with his Grandfather, William "Billy" Rogan. Both are staring out across the wide expanses of the Atlantic Ocean. William is smoking a pipe. This is a man of the sea and a keeper of secrets few could ever even comprehend.
'Look out there our Tom across the wide ocean. Tell me what you see?'
 The boy shrugs his shoulders. 'Just the waves Grandfather and the seagulls.' William smiles and shakes his head. 'No you have to looker harder. Concentrate.' Tom doesn't really understand what he's supposed to be looking for but loves his Grandfather so stares anyway. 'Beneath those waves is a world we can only dream of. It's a magical wonderful place and just because we can't see what is there doesn't mean it isn't there.' William puts an arm around Tom's shoulders and the memories come flooding back. 'Now promise me that you'll never hurt the sea lad?' Tom turns to look quizzically at his Grandfather.
'I promise.'
'Good boy Tom.' William looks back ruefully towards the sea, his eyes drifting not just to the horizon but towards another time.
'One thing you must always remember is that the sea looks after its own and god help anybody that dares to hurt it's children. No matter how large you build your walls in the end the sea always wins.' A tear comes to the old man's eye. 'Believe me, I know.'

William ruffles Tom's hair. He looks at the young boy who clearly has no idea what his Grandfather is blabbering on about!

Later that same evening, a full moon illuminates the Atlantic ocean and the stillness of the black water is suddenly interrupted by the splashing of what appears to be some kind of a tail. It's a mermaid's tail. She surfaces and her golden hair shimmers. The mermaid's eyes staring towards the faraway shore of the flickering lights of the small Irish fishing village of Drunamere, sitting quietly between two mountains peaks. The sound of music and laughter can be heard resonating from Drunamere's only pub. The *Shark's Finn*. The mermaid smiles and listens for a moment and is then captured in a moonbeam. A heavenly glow. Then swiftly as she appeared the mermaid vanishes back under the water gone from sight. All once more is deathly still. Not a ripple on the ocean surface remains and the night goes on. And the music goes on.

And our story goes on…

TEARS OF A MERMAID

September 23, 1973.
In the terrifying midst of the most ferocious storm ever recorded off the Irish West coast, the fishing boat *Madame Marie* from Drunamere, rocks, sways and shudders on a tormented ocean. Lightning bolts flash and strike the raging waters illuminating the sea! On board being thrown around like rag dolls are five local fishermen. The Rogan brothers, Brendan and Tom, Sean Clancy, Patrick Kelly and Donal Malone. As the monstrous, tossing waves threaten to overwhelm the boat the men make the decision to cut the night's work short and bring in their catch. Despite the horrific conditions it's been a decent catch. A wave splattered and lashed Brendan and Tom pull in the bulging haul. This night something else has been caught in the *Madame Marie* nets. Brendan nudges Tom and points up.
'What the hell is that?'
Tom looks but hasn't a clue. 'Let's lower it!'
As the net drops nearer and it becomes clearer what they've caught Brendan and Tom stand open-mouthed. 'Holy mother of god,' whispers Brendan to his brother. Finally, the net hits the floor and amid the mass of wriggling sea life struggling in the last moments of their existence lies trapped a mermaid. An ashen-faced Tom leans down. 'That can't be what I think it is, can it?'
Brendan kneels beside him. 'All the angels and saints in heaven brother what have we here?' The mermaid cuts a terrified sight. Half a human and fish caught in the webbing unable to move. Her long, blond hair caked with blood, her eyes tormented, her tear-stained face etched in sheer terror. She stares at Tom but on trying to speak no words come from her lips. Tom is shaken back to life by an excited Patrick Kelly who slaps him hard on the shoulder.
'Tom, look at that thing, it's almost human!' he yells. All the fishermen crowd around the net as Brendan pulls out a knife and goes

to rip the nets open. The mermaid trembles and shakes. Her eyes filling with tears. A bemused Donal Malone begins to laugh.

'Would you look at that thing it's crying!' Tom sidles up to Brendan with both their eyes hypnotized by the agonised mermaid.
'She's dying, we've got to throw her back in the sea Brendan!'
'No Tom that's not going to happen, we're going to keep it.'
Tom shakes his head. 'This is so wrong. We got told the tales as kids Brendan. We thought they were fairytales but they're real and we have to put her back in the sea, we have to!'
'Ah, away with ya! Don't you give me that rubbish brother!' snaps Brendan. He turns his attention towards the others who are stood around the net. 'Lads, what do you think? Are you with me or Tom?' Brendan gestures towards the mermaid who is desperately gasping for air. 'Do we take it back on shore or return it from where it came? I vote we keep. Hands up if you're with me lads come on now, you know it makes sense?' With no hesitation Clancy, Malone and Kelly throw their hands immediately in the air.

Tom watches in disgust. 'What's wrong with you all? Look at her she's dying, I don't want anything to do with this.'

Brendan clearly isn't impressed with his younger brother insistence not to go along. He walks up to Tom. 'You've always been the same. Why do you always have to play the saint little brother? For once in our miserable lives we've been given a break and you in your infinite wisdom, you want to throw it back over the side? Not this time, with or without you we're doing this and me and the boys here are going to be rich! You can do whatever you want!'

As they talk Kelly and Malone have bent down and are within inches of the mermaid's face. A smiling Malone is whispering into her ear. 'Don't you dare die girl. Don't you dare, you're our fortune, me and the boy's from Drunamere here.'

Suddenly, the mermaid's eye's close and her dying breath drifts in a puff of air that floats high past a startled Kelly and Malone before vanishing in the dark rain lashed sky. 'Jesus Christ, Malone!' exclaims Kelly. 'Did you just see that?'

Brendan stares down at the mermaid's lifeless body. He puts a hand on her face and wipes away a tear that had formed under an eye but not melted away. 'No matter this makes no difference, dead or alive this is still a fine catch and will fetch us a fortune. One of you go and get a sack. Soon as we are back ashore we'll go and wake up Finn and get him to contact his famous brother in Dublin.'
Tom watches on from afar as Kelly and Malone struggle to put the mermaid's body into a sack dropping her in the process, before finally succeeding and tying it tight with a rope. He feels sick and leans over the side to throw up.

A huge crack of thunder makes him look towards a starless sky. All is deathly black as if the heavens themselves had suddenly gone into mourning. Tom crosses himself and swears he can hear crying from high above.

MOONDANCE

December 21, 1983.
It was as if the devil himself had turned up from the sea and cast an evil spell upon the eerily, deserted Drunamere. It's once quaint lines of small street houses and shops boarded up. The only sounds and signs of any life are bands of screeching seagulls picking for meagre scraps, whilst a washed up lone fishing boat sits rotting on the beach. The *Madam Marie*. All this whilst the incessant banging of an unlocked door caught in the wind resonates eternally in the air. Like a death knell. Drunamere has been left to die. It has paid a truly awful price.

Across the Irish sea in Manchester, England, hidden away from the city's busy Deansgate shopping area sits Mulligans pub. It's crammed to the rafters and Van Morrison's *Moondance* is blasting out on the juke box.

...It's a marvellous night for a Moondance. And the stars...

Sat in a corner reading his newspaper and enjoying a quiet pint of Guinness is Tom Rogan. Tom left Ireland many years ago and Manchester is now home, Mulligans his local. However, today is not a good day, for the pub is packed with lunchtime office workers all stood huddled close around him and making far too much noise for Tom's taste. One steps back knocking his table and almost sending the Guinness flying.

'Watch what yer doing fella!' snaps Tom, whilst grabbing his pint.
'Oh, sorry mate,' comes the apologetic answer.

Through Mulligan's side door walks the acclaimed author Paul Archer and his researcher Liam Conwell, who appear like two plain clothes policemen on the search for a criminal. The bespectacled Conwell points across to where Rogan is sitting and the two make their way through the loud, beery crowd.

'Are you Thomas Rogan?' asks Conwell.

'Depends whose asking?'

Conwell produces a small photo of Tom from his pocket and shows it to Archer. The two compare it to a startled Tom and both nod before sitting down beside him, much to his growing unease. Archer places the photo on the table and Tom picks it up. An old passport snapshot. 'Who the hell are you two, CID? Don't you lot ever get tired of harassing innocent Irishmen in pubs in this country?'
'No we are not CID far from it,' smiles Archer. 'Please excuse the interruption. Let me introduce myself, my name is Paul Archer. Amongst other things I teach English literature at Manchester university. This man here is my assistant, Liam Conwell.'
Conwell smiles but already Tom has taken an instant dislike to him. 'Would you mind if we put some questions to you Tom?' asks Archer. A perturbed Tom puts down his newspaper. 'What kind of questions?' He's annoyed but also more than a little intrigued as to what these two lunatics want with him.
'Oh, it's nothing untoward, they are just to confirm we have the right man. All this is nothing to worry about, I promise you.' Convinced now they are weird but harmless Tom relents. 'Go on then. Make it quick.' He puts down his newspaper.
'Thanks Tom, here we go. Number one. Do you believe in mermaids?'

A smile forms on Tom's face although his stomach is churning. He should have guessed, it was only a matter of time before the cranks arrived. 'Of course I do gentlemen. Doesn't everybody? Not just mermaids, I also believe in Father Christmas, leprechauns, fake moon landings, aliens and the tooth fairy. Now if this is going where I think it is, I would advise you both to leave now. There's no truth in it whatsoever.' Conwell has been to the bar and returned with three pints of Guinness. 'Thanks Liam,' says Archer. 'You see Tom, here's my problem, I know something happened that night. I have the story and I intend to write a book about it. I've also spoken to somebody else who was present and they've confirmed my suspicions of what occurred back on the night of September 23, 1973. On board the fishing boat *Madame Marie* when you along with four other local

men from Drunamere, trapped a mermaid in your nets. Good for you, that you wanted to put her back into the sea but the others, oh no, even though she died they voted to keep her and to tell the world about their astonishing discovery. And let's be honest here, make some money in doing so. Am I right so far Tom? I think so. Should I go on?'
Tom shrugs his shoulders. 'Very well,' smiles Archer. 'The mermaid died within minutes of being caught and that you and a priest, a Father Conlon buried her in an unmarked grave somewhere in Drunamere cemetery. I could go on and on. I know it all?' Tom stares at Archer for a moment, inside his heart is racing, how the hell did he find all this out? 'Mr Archer I have to congratulate you on a fantastic imagination. Whatever it is you're smoking at that university of yours I would definitely like some please. But you see I'm sorry to disappoint and burst yours' and your friend's fantasy bubble here but nothing actually happened that night. It's all just a crazy tale that people desperately want to be true but the real truth is it's all utter nonsense. Not a grain of truth. A mermaid? Come on now Mr Archer. The entire thing is nothing more than pub drunks looking for a free drink off American tourists. You know I have to tell you something. If you can't convince those plastic Paddies to believe in Leprechauns then mermaids are honestly the next best thing. For we are indeed a beautiful land of dreamers and story tellers Mr Archer, we love and do tell grand tales. And people like you just so want them to be true. Now please, take it from me I'm doing you a real favour here, someone is taking you for a fool. I was indeed there and all that was in those nets was a large seal. We were in the midst of one of the worst storms the West coast had ever seen. Lightning bolts exploding like bombs around us on the water. Torrential rain and waves that reached towards the heavens. Let me tell you fear does strange things to a man's mind and eyes in such circumstances. We were lucky to survive that night with our lives. There was no mermaid Mr Archer, and sadly for you then no story. Now if you and Mr Conwell here don't mind, I thank you for the pint and bid you both a good day.'

Tom picks his newspaper back up and starts to read it again whilst inside praying hard they'd both believed him. 'Tell me about the tears Tom?' asks Archer. Determined not to give up. 'Tell me about the tears of the mermaid?'

Tom puts down his newspaper once more. It's clear whoever Archer has spoken to knew exactly what happened back then. He needs to buy himself time to think.

'I'm going to get some air.'

Tom edges his way through the pub crowd and steps outside. He lights up a cigarette. Following behind appears Archer. Tom inhales whilst staring at him.

'How the hell did you find me Mr Archer? Don't tell me, the Wizard of Oz got in touch and told you I was drinking in Mulligans?'

Archer laughs. 'No not exactly it was your brother Brendan.'

'My Brendan?'

'He wants to make things right Tom. Brendan feels terrible about what went on. As for finding you? His son works at the tax office and traced you through your national insurance number. A very clever young man.'

Tom smiles wide. 'Just like his bloody father. A crafty one at that.'

'Brendan was absolutely adamant in telling me that out of everybody present that night you was the only one who acted with any kind of dignity and kindness. He also says he's sorry and that not a day goes by when he doesn't wish they had just listened to you and thrown her back into the sea.'

Archer hands over Brendan's telephone number. 'He begs you to ring him.'

Tom looks at the number. 'You truly believe you have the full story Mr Archer?'

Archer nods. 'Do you mean the disappearance of your younger sister at the same time as the mermaid dying and her body tragically never found? I'm so sorry about that Tom. The official police inquiry stating that she likely drowned, her soul lost at sea? Also about how the priest blessed the water time and again but it had become poisoned, the fish and all sea life vanishing around Drunamere.

Forcing the locals into having to move away leaving the village now deserted. Some say cursed even? Oceanographers, sea scientists couldn't explain what actually happened to the water but we both know it was a mermaid's curse. Your mermaid Tom.'

Tom finishes his cigarette and stamps it out on the pavement. So much for a quiet afternoon, a couple of pints and a read of his newspaper. Archer has it all it appears. He looks over towards him. 'Mr Archer, no offence but if by some wild chance this book of yours that you're writing gets published no one will ever believe it. Your reputation will suffer and they'll call you a crank. True or false, I'll leave that in your heart to make that decision. Believe me I know. Please, just trust me you would be an awful lot better just forgetting about all this.'

A smiling Archer takes out a packet of his own cigarettes and offers one to Tom but he shakes his head. 'They'll believe me if I write that last chapter Tom. When you tell me where you and the Priest buried the mermaid.' Tom stares for a moment at the passing Manchester traffic then back to Archer. 'I'm not sure. This is the stuff of fairy tales Mr Archer and the trouble with fairy tales is that they need a happy ending. You haven't got one. Never forget we lost a sister in all this madness. This means that I'm sorry because you seem a decent man, but I can't help you. I just can't.'

Archer appears wounded. 'Can't or won't Tom?'

'Can't. You see, a long time ago an old man warned me that the sea always wins. He was right. You don't mess with it for the consequences Mr Archer, can be truly horrific. As my family discovered.'

'Please, just speak to Brendan.' Archer hands Tom over his business card. Time to close the book Tom. I never wanted or expected a happy ending, I just want an ending.'

DON'T PAY THE FERRYMAN

Later that same evening,
   Tom is sat at home staring at Brendan's phone number. Finally, he plucks up the courage to ring him.
'Hello.'
'Brendan it's Tom.'
'Jesus Christ Tom! How are ya?'
'I'm fine, you and the family, is everyone okay?'
'Aye we're all grand. Ma is good. She's been living with us since well, you know. And Michael is getting married this year. Tom, I'm going to be a Grandad and you an uncle! But we're not telling Ma just yet if you understand. Hell and brimstone and all that bloody shite.'
Tom is close to tears. 'Brendan, I,…'
'No words Tom everything in the past between us is water under the bridge. Listen, I'm coming over to Manchester. I take it by this call you've spoken to Archer?'
'I did, he seems like a decent type.'
'He is. Archer came to see me in Dublin with that horrible little bastard assistant of his.' Tom laughs at this. 'We live here in the city now. I trust him Tom. He's the one to tell the story I'm convinced of it. Oh, it's so good to hear your voice after all these years! I'll ring you on this number when I get to Manchester. I love you brother.'
Brendan puts down the phone.
   'I love you too,' replies Tom to a dead line. He picks up Archer's business card and starts to ring him also.
   'Hello, Paul Archer speaking?'
'I'm in Mr Archer. For family reasons only. You want the full story sir I'll give it to you. I'll tell you everything but I need you to know we're going to a very dark place. This is no fantasy tale, it isn't Hans Christian Anderson. It isn't Disney this is reality. They were real tears

that night and we've paid a shocking price that still haunts my family today and will forever more. But I'm in.'

Tom puts down the phone and stares long at a photograph of his young sister Colette who went missing all those years ago. Bitter memories Tom tries so hard to keep at bay suddenly return.

'What happened to you baby girl?'

The next evening at Piccadilly railway station, Brendan Rogan stands beneath the arrival and departure screen waiting for his brother, when he feels a hand on his shoulder. He turns to see Tom smiling back at him. The two embrace with Brendan close to tears.

'Tom, you look grand, and you don't look a day older! Look at ya with all your hair! Always was the bloody lucky one!' For a moment, the two just hug once more. The emotion in both clear to see.

'Welcome to Manchester,' smiles Tom. 'Come on I've arranged for us to meet Archer.' Tom picks up Brendan's luggage but is momentarily startled when Brendan puts a hand on his arm.

'I just want to...'

'Brendan, no it's okay honestly.'

'No, no it isn't okay. I have to say this. It's something that has kept me awake for years. What happened that night on the boat you didn't deserve any of it. None of what happened is on you. We should have listened Tom. If so maybe Colette would still be with us.'

Tom shakes his head. 'No Colette drowned Brendan. You can't connect the two. It was a tragic accident what happened had nothing to do that. Now come on let's get a shift on! I think we could both do with a Guinness or two.'

Tom and Brendan enter a legendary old fashioned Mancunian watering hole, The *Peveril and Peak*. Small in size the *Peveril* is jammed tight. On the juke box blasting out is…

Don't Pay the Ferryman by Chris De Burgh. 'I love this damned song Tom!' smiles Brendan who sings along loudly! Sat waiting in a corner with seats saved are Paul Archer and Liam Conwell. Archer motions the brothers over and Tom and Brendan acknowledge them.

'Let them wait whilst we get the drinks Tom, the pair of shites!' Tom tries hard not to laugh, it feels great to have his older brother back. Finally, they go across and sit facing. There's a momentarily stand-off. 'Thank you so much for agreeing to this,' says Archer finally.
 'I know it must be very difficult for you both. I can only promise that this book will do justice to your sister's memory.'
'We both think that you're doing this for the right reasons Mr Archer,' replies Brendan. Otherwise we wouldn't be here would we Tom?'
 Tom nods in agreement. 'We believe you're the correct person to tell this story. We do trust you Mr Archer.'
Archer raises his glass. 'I'd like to make a toast. To a successful venture.'
'To Colette,' says Brendan.
'To Colette!' they all repeat.
'May she rest in peace,' Tom adds.
'I've arranged for us all to travel over to Dublin tomorrow then onto Drunamere. That's if it's okay with you both?'
'Sounds fine Mr Archer,' replies Tom, as Brendan nods in agreement.
'First Tom, I've so many questions to ask you but I've really no idea where to start.'
Tom smiles. 'Why don't we start at the beginning eh Mr Archer like every great story does.
 Brendan nudges Tom. 'You definitely okay with this brother?'
'For Colette, Brendan, like we agreed?'
'For Colette.' Brendan wipes a tear from his eye.
 Tom inhales hard on his cigarette and begins…

A GRAND CATCH

'We returned home to shore around 6.00.am. By that time the storm had vanished, it was strange because in an eyeblink the waters were calm, dead even. Once back to settle nerves and tempers, mine especially, it was agreed we would knock up the landlord of The *Shark's Finn*, Fergal Finn and share with him our dirty secret.'

Dawn. The sun is set to break and the battered, almost broken fishing boat, the *Madame Marie* docks once more on Drunamere's short pier. The five crew members disembark. They appear a shattered mob. Clancy and Kelly carry off the large sack containing the mermaid's lifeless corpse. They move slowly. 'Mind how you go lads be careful with it now,' says Brendan. Last jumping off the boat is Tom still blazing with anger and finding it hard to believe his brother could do such a thing. He grabs Brendan hard by the arm.

'For god's sake, this isn't right Brendan! She needs to go back in the sea and I believe deep down you know this. What the hell is going through your head? What we're doing here isn't worth all the money in the world!'

Brendan pulls Tom's arm away. 'We took a vote Tom, four to one and you lost, end of. Now come on let's just get this over with. If you can't stomach it fair enough but think of Ma and Colette. This is for them too. To give both the life they deserve. Your own blood or your conscience? That's the choice we have going on here.'

'No you're wrong, the choice is between what's right and wrong.'
'Ah Tom away with ya! All your missing is a crucifix and a crown of thorns. Give it up now.' Brendan walks off and Tom watches him go. He looks back at the boat then rushes to catch up and join the others heading down the pier. Brendan puts an arm around him. 'Trust me brother it'll all be fine. We'll be laughing about it in a few days when we're all rich!'

Across the road from the pier stood The *Shark's Finn* pub. Brendan bangs on the door and the top window opens. The furious landlord Fergal Finn appears looking down. 'Lads, bloody hell! Away with ya now! Do you know what time it is? Go home I'm shut.'

'Fergal please!' shouts back Brendan. 'Ya need to open up here because this is an emergency!'

Finn sighs and bangs down the window.

Brendan turns to the others. 'Let me do the talking okay boys, I can twist Fergal round my little finger when needed.' Tom stares at the sack carried by Clancy and Kelly and shakes his head. 'Be my guest' he says. 'I want nothing to do with this.' As Brendan glares daggers at him the pub door unlocks and Finn's face appears. He looks on in derision at the motley crew before him.

'Jesus, Mary and Joseph, you look like you've just had a close encounter with Moby Dick! Come on in.' He opens the door wide. 'What's in the sack?' he asks Clancy, who smiles and winks back at him. 'It's a mermaid Finn!'

'My god,' he sighs. 'They're already drunk!'

Finn and the fishermen take the stools off a table and sit down. Brendan has an arm around Finn. 'Go fetch us one of your better bottles Fergal, you're going to need a glass or two when you hear this.' Finn stands grumbling under his breath about them paying for it, but does as asked and returns with a bottle of whisky and six glasses. He sits himself back down and pours the drinks. Finn glances up at the five faces whom are all watching him back intently.

'Right then which one of you lunatics is going to tell me why you've got me out of bed at this ungodly hour and are drinking my whisky for free?' Brendan finishes the drink in one slamming his glass back on the table. He looks Finn right in the eyes. 'Last night we caught a mermaid in our nets.'

A red-faced Finn looks set to explode! 'Are you trying to make fun of me because, I'll tell ya now lads, I'm in no bloody mood, now get the...'

'Go look in the sack Fergal,' says Patrick Kelly, interrupting Finn in mid rant. He points over towards it. A reluctant Finn stares at Kelly then stands and goes across with every eye in the room upon him. He unties the rope on the sack and looks inside taking a sharp intake of breath on doing so. 'Oh my god! Oh boys this is a first even for you lot.' A shaken Finn ties it back up and returns to the table. He avoids all eye contact with the others whilst trying to regain his composure. Finn takes a drink and then another one. Brendan leans over towards him. 'We'll cut you in Finn. That thing in the sack is going to make us all rich.'

These words appear to be the final straw for Tom who stands pushing his stool away. 'That thing? I can't do this Brendan, I'm sorry.'
'Oh come on Tom,' says Clancy. 'Have a drink let's talk this over.'
'Sean is right,' adds Malone. 'Go on have a drink. You're being selfish here. What happened to all for one and one for all?'
'Aye,' joins in Kelly. 'Sit back down Tom and stop being so goddamn dramatic.'
Tom shakes his head. 'Can't do lads.' He storms out the pub door and heads across to the pier where the sea appears unnaturally quiet and still. Not a stir or a ripple. Gazing out to the horizon Tom swears he can still hear the crying from last night.

Back inside there are worried faces all staring towards Brendan who knows exactly what they're all thinking. 'Don't you all go worrying about my Tom, he'll be fine. I'll talk to him, my brother is a sensitive soul but he'll come round. Now, Fergal, we need you to ring your famous brother who walks for RTE. Tell him to get a television crew here for tomorrow morning. Hint we have a story that's going to rock the world.' Finn nods in agreement.

Brendan raises his glass. 'Good, gentlemen please join me in a toast. To a grand catch!' They all do but none quite so enthusiastic as Brendan and this clearly agitates him. 'Ah, what's wrong with you all now? This time tomorrow we're all going to be famous. The boys from Drunamere who've netted themselves a real life mermaid. We're going to be on the front page of every newspaper in the world! Imagine being on the front page of The National Geographic? Imagine being interviewed on Wogan on The telly? Hell, they'll even make a film about us. Us, the boys from Drunamere who risked all to bring to shore one of the great wonders of the world!'

Still Brendan doesn't get the looks on faces he's hoping for, instead settling just for refilling his glass and downing it in one.

'Sod the lot of ya,' he mumbles. 'I'll go on Wogan on my lonesome.'

CONFESSION (Part One)

That same afternoon in the village a weary and worried Tom Rogan makes his way up the steep path to the church of Saint Malachy, that sits halfway up one of its twin peaks. In the well-kept gardens outside, the white-haired, 68 year-old Father Michael Conlon is busy with a sweeping brush mopping up the leaves. Father Conlon is Drunamere born. After hearing the calling as a teenager his postings ranged from England, Africa, the Vatican until finally back home. Saint Malachy's and its congregation are Father Conlon's world and flock. His heaven on earth. The church itself, an ancient five hundred year old stone structure overlooking the village with breathtaking views of the ocean. On noticing Tom, Father Conlon smiles wide. He's always liked him much more than Brendan, who tended to spend rather too much time in the confessional for his liking.
'Tom lad, how went the night's work, I hope you caught more than a cold out there my son?'
'It's been rather eventful Father. I've a rather a big favour to ask of you if you don't mind?'
'Okay Tom but I hope it's not that red head from Tralee. If so then you'll have to make a decent woman of her. You know the rules around here. Fire and brimstone otherwise you'll be chased onto the next ocean liner to New York!' Tom smiles ruefully, he sighs, appearing truly despondent. 'If only it was that simple.'
'Tom what is it, what's wrong with you?'
'Will you take my confession Father?'
'Of course I will my son, come on, let's go inside.'
The two head off into the church. Father Conlon leads Tom into the confessional box and he kneels down to face the Priest through the veiled curtain connecting the two. 'Take your time Tom, take a deep breath. God is ready to listen to your sins and absolve them.'

In for a penny thinks Tom. He knows the priest is going to think the next few words from his mouth are those of a madman.
'Bless me Father for I have sinned. It's been well too long since my last confession.' There's a long silence and one that worries Father Conlon. 'Speak up Tom, come on now whatever it is god won't turn his back on you.'
'I'm not so sure about that Father.'
'Try us Tom, you're here now. We're good listeners. Clear your heart of all that's troubling you.'
'I've been involved in something so terrible Father. A sin against nature. For this, for me there can be no redemption. Not from heaven above, from you, nobody.'
'Let god be the judge of that, now out with it Thomas.'
'There's no easy way to say this except last night we killed a mermaid out on the ocean.'
'Tom Rogan this isn't funny! A confessional box is no place for practical jokes and childish humour. You'd be wise to apologise now, otherwise, god help me, I'll come in there and give you a good hiding myself! You should know better than this!'
'Father, you've known me since the day I was born. When I was a kid I was scared to death of you. I still am! I'd never lie to you. Never! I swear on my life and on the life of my younger sister Colette. If I'm lying may god strike me down this day. It all happened last night whilst we were out on the *Madame Marie*. The creature, she or whatever got caught in the nets. I said throw her back but the others wanted to keep her. "Boy's we're gonna be rich!" Brendan told them and they all agreed. It was out of my hands. As this went on the mermaid she got scared and cried. Tears fell down her face and then. Then she died. They have her in a sack tied up in The *Shark's Finn*. Tomorrow my brother has arranged for the television boys to come over from Dublin to film it. I can't let this happen, I just can't. If I fetch the body here will you stand over the body and say a prayer for her? We can bury the mermaid unmarked right here in the graveyard.

Please Father, please, I'm begging you?'
A shocked Father Conlon is convinced that no matter how mad or strange this may sound to others, Tom is telling the truth.

'God has heard your sins and he forgives you. Your penance can wait for the moment because we have to talk about this face to face Tom. Go and wait for me outside these walls. What I have to say to you can't be heard in such a sacred place.'

Father Conlon's hears Tom's footsteps leaving and follows him out. He stops at the church doors turns and bows towards the alter before crossing himself. 'May god forgive me for what I'm about to tell the poor lad.'

The two men are gazing out across the dark ocean. Father Conlon lights up a cigarette to steady his nerves, 'I hear strange and terrible things in the confessional box. Some of it keeps me awake for weeks on end. This is a strange island we live in Tom. One, seemingly cursed to suffer. One filled with ancient tales and legends. Of tortured spirits that stalk the countryside and ghost ships and mystical creatures that inherit our waters. But this?' He turns to face a distraught Tom. 'Nevertheless I do believe you. Do you want to know why?'

'I'm all ears Father, I really am.'

'Because my son. Many years ago I heard a similar tales about this same creature off a man you know only too well.' He points towards the ocean, Out there are a sea of secrets and just because we can't see them means nothing? Now what happened last night was terrible and has to be made right but at least you tried to do the proper thing. The important matter now is we give her a Christian burial as a child of god deserves and pray it's enough.' Tom recognises some of the words said by the priest as belonging to someone he indeed does know. He remembers a time long ago staring at the sea with a kind and a gentle old man at the end of Drunamere pier's end.

'You're talking about my Grandfather aren't you?'

Father Conlon smiles. 'William told me an extraordinary tale outside the confessional box over a whisky or two. I'm telling you this not as a betrayal of trust, but because I think you deserve to know the truth and even more importantly after last night, your Grandfather would wish me to tell you.'

'Please go on Father,' replies Tom, now desperate to hear what the priest has to say.

CAPTAIN AHAB

'On April 13, 1912, the RMS Titanic was sailing off the West coast of Ireland on her maiden voyage to New York. Tragically unknown to all on board, except one, that same night a mermaid got caught in her giant underwater propellers and was slashed apart. The only witness to this appalling incident was a 17 year-old sailor recently assigned to the Titanic after coming aboard at Cork by the name of William Rogan. You might have heard of him? It was your Grandfather Tom. A teenage seaman from Drunamere. William had to watch on in sheer disbelief and horror unable to help the creature. Even though they would think him mad William decided he had to speak up on what he had just witnessed. So, after saying a quiet prayer for the mermaid's soul, one that wasn't only heard that night by his god, William Rogan headed off to find a ship officer.

.... The afternoon of 14th April, 1912, and the Titanic Captain 62 year-old Edward J Smith is sat in his cabin when there's a knock at the door. 'Come!' he calls out. Smith is your archetypal, seafaring figure with his distinguished white hair and beard. A hugely respected figure amongst the White Star line company, thus him being their first choice to take the Titanic on its first voyage to North America. Entering is First officer Lieutenant William Murdoch and alongside him, able seaman William Rogan. Smith looks up from reading his book *Moby Dick* by Herman Melville. First published back in 1851, and just a year after Smith was born.
'My apologies for the disturbance sir,' says Murdoch. 'But I think there's something you need to hear.'
'Go on Lieutenant,' replies Smith, putting down his book.
'I think it's best coming from Able Seaman Rogan.'
'Out with it then Rogan what's going on here?' William cuts a nervous figure. Only the previous evening he'd watched on in horror

as the mermaid was sliced to pieces by the ships propellers. William has pondered on whether he should come clean about what he witnessed or stay quiet in case of ridicule.

'Tell the Captain, Rogan, go on now.'

Captain Smith can tell by William's demeanour that he's clearly petrified. 'What's your first name lad?'

'William sir.'

'Tell me what's troubling you William.'

'Something happened last night Captain, when I was on deck. Something terrible.' Smith looks across to Lieutenant Murdoch. 'Do you know what's going on here First Officer?'

'No Captain, just that I was approached by Able Seaman Rogan, who told me it was vital that he spoke to you because the safety of the ship could be at stake.' Captain Smith's features swiftly change from Grandfather-like to matters of ship safety. 'Out with it then Rogan! What's going on here? Talk to me.'

William knows if he opens up Captain Smith will think him unfit for service and have him locked up until they reach New York. But the other side of the coin is not telling him and they may not even reach there if he doesn't come clean, so William decides to tell the truth.

'It was around 11.50 last night Captain. I was looking over the side when I saw what I can only describe as a mermaid. She was swimming alongside when suddenly it disappeared and the next thing I saw and heard was our propellers ripping the poor creature to pieces.' Captain Smith has listened incredulously to William, his face a strange concoction of bewilderment and anger. He's tried to keep quiet until it's eventually proved impossible.

'Enough!' he shouts, loud enough to make both William and Lieutenant Murdoch jump!

'Let me explain something to you Rogan, what you witnessed last night was no mermaid it was simply a dolphin. Do you understand me?'

'But Captain I seen her face, she was smiling before…'

'Silence!' shouts Smith. Immediately, William knows he's gone much too far and should have kept his mouth shut.

'Do you drink Rogan?'
'No sir.'
'Do you like to be the centre of attention Rogan, a storyteller at parties back in Ireland to impress the ladies?'
'No sir, that isn't me.'
'Then why darken my door with this preposterous notion of what you claimed to see last evening?' William is struggling to think of an answer that wouldn't see even more ridicule being hurled at him, but also knows he has to tell Captain Smith what he heard following the terrible accident.

'Because I heard voices Captain. Terrible voices crying out from beneath the sea and the far horizon.'
'And what were these voices saying Rogan?'
'They spoke about revenge Captain.'
'Against who?'
'Against us sir.'
Captain Smith stares long and hard at William for a few moments, his eyes never leaving the young sailor's from Drunamere. He's convinced the boy is obviously traumatised. His first time at sea and seeing spirits and hearing ghosts from the oceans depths, when it's simply nothing but a natural phenomenon. The boy is mistaken, his eye and ears have played tricks under the Northern stars on the black sea. Smith decides to give William the benefit of the doubt. He picks up his book. 'Do you see this lad?'
'Yes sir.'
'There's a line in here when Captain Ahab who has been driven to madness in his desperation to kill the whale Moby Dick declares…
'This ship! The hearse! A second hearse!' Well William, the Titanic is no hearse it is unsinkable. Captain Smith holds up the *Moby Dick* book. This is just a tale lad. Let me tell you I have covered every inch of these waters as man and boy. I've heard the strangest stories from old seadogs but it was always just for another jug of beer or to impress a lass. Every ship had a storyteller who claimed similar as you do. I like to think I am a practical man and I like to believe a fair

man, so I'm not going to mock or punish. There are no such creatures as mermaids, we will leave it at that. Go and get some sleep son. Rest up and when back on duty remember our talk and we'll have no more of this.'

'Yes sir' replies William, knowing it's pointless to go on.

'Dismissed,' says Captain Smith. William turns and leaves the cabin. 'Keep your eye on that young lad Lieutenant Wallace.'

'I will do sir, he seemed so convinced with what he saw didn't he?' Captain Smith smiles. ' The sea is full of wonders and dangers William but I think I can guarantee there are no mermaids out there. Now if you don't mind.' Captain Smith holds up his book once more. 'I would like to continue my adventure with Captain Ahab.' Lieutenant Wallace smiles and salutes. 'I shall leave you in peace Captain.' When the Lieutenant had gone Smith settled down to lose himself in *Moby Dick* for a little longer, before returning back to the bridge. For a second once there Smith thought he could hear voices in the far off distance. Tormented, wailing and crying, but the Captain put it down to the huge machinations of the ship. What else could it possibly have been?

CONFESSION (Part Two)

'The next night the so called unsinkable RMS Titanic hit an iceberg and sank to the bottom of the ocean at the cost of 1514 human souls. Amongst the lucky survivors was your Grandfather, Tom, who whilst being one of the last off the ship after helping countless escape, finally jumped overboard. Exhausted and falling unconscious, William began to slip beneath the great murky depths that had already entombed so many. Only, this is where I need you to take a leap of faith my son, for a mermaid to appear and carry him towards a nearby lifeboat, where he was dragged aboard. But just before leaving the mermaid held your Grandfather tight and they both watched as the Titanic disappeared beneath the waves.
"The sea always wins," the mermaid whispered into William's ear.
"This was for the death of my sister."
Then she vanished.'
'Father, are you seriously trying to tell me that the Titanic sank because the sea was avenging the death of a mermaid?'
'Why would your Grandfather tell me such a crazy lie Tom? It just wasn't in his nature to do such a thing. The sea struck back in anger. One of her children had been cruelly taken away and you must believe me because history will repeat itself. This power that truly does exist will wreak revenge if last night's wrongs are not put to right. A Christian burial may help but it by no means guarantees that forgiveness will be forthcoming. Because what occurred on the *Madame Marie* was an act of violence against nature. Against the sea? I believe she will seek revenge. One way or another, I don't know when or how but we are all going to pay a heavy price for last night. They should have thrown her back Tom, they really should.'
'I'd always known my Grandfather served on the Titanic, that he saved people's lives, but this? It's just incredible. I don't really know what to say. Thinking back there was this one time. I was about

9 years-old and we were sat on the end of the pier here in Drunamere. He was talking all weird about life beneath the waves. What you said before they were his words back then. He must have been trying to tell me what had happened but thought best of it. The sea always wins. Throughout the years, that line has always struck a chord.'
'There's more Tom, much more though I think this is enough for you to try and take on board for one day. We'll talk again but now let's get to it. I'll prepare a grave for the mermaid and you go and fetch her. Just one thing you must never speak of this. Are we clear on that?'
'Father, who would ever believe me?'

AMEN

It's early evening in The *Shark's Finn* and Tom is stood outside listening in. He has a plan and now just needs to pluck up enough courage to carry it out. Music resonates off the jukebox, Creedence Clearwater Revival's *Bad Moon Rising*.

There's raucous laughter and loud voices. Tom takes a deep breath and goes inside. The fishermen are still sat celebrating their good fortune. On seeing Tom enter, Clancy nudges Brendan who's singing along with the jukebox.

'Your brother is back Brendan.' They all stare across towards him and he walks warily to the table.

'Look, lads this morning, I'm sorry, I was tired, stupid and want to apologise…' Before Tom can continue Brendan stands and goes to shake his hand. 'Little brother it never happened. Now come on let's all have a drink together.' Patrick Kelly brings over a chair whilst Sean Clancy pours Tom a whisky and hands it him. Donal Malone clinks his glass. 'Slainte Tom! Don't you go worrying yourself anymore about that thing on the boat. It was just a freak and not worth getting all twisted inside about. Just think about the money instead we're all going to make. Brendan here reckons we could be overnight millionaires and even get on Wogan!'

The night goes on.

Tom is sat next to a blind drunk Sean Clancy, who is struggling to stay awake amidst the merriment. He's been biding his time.

'Where is she Sean?' asks Tom.

'Where's who Tom?' replies a slurring Clancy.

'The mermaid, I want to take a last look.'

'Brendan told me to put the sack in Finn's yard around the back for safe keeping.' Clancy has hardly finished talking before he nods off. Tom pulls his chair back and stands up only for Brendan to notice him. 'You going somewhere Tom?'

'The toilet Brendan, the toilet. What are you my keeper?'

He smiles. 'Sorry brother old habits. I can't help but worry about you, it's my job!'

Tom acknowledges by grinning wide before heading past the bar and through a side door that leads to the toilet, then the outside yard. He instantly spots the sack and goes to look for something else to put the mermaid's body in. A large canvas bag catches his eye and Tom empties the sack and places her with as much care as possible into it. 'Please forgive me,' he whispers. Tom gathers up clothes from a washing basket and other items to refill the sack to a similar weight, before tying it back up. Finally satisfied it's sufficient to fool the others at least till morning, he places the mermaid over his shoulder, and heads through the back gate into the blackness of the Drunamere night to hide the bag behind a wall. His heart racing, Tom then returns inside. 'Brendan, lads I'm going home, I'm exhausted. God bless, I'll see you all in the morning.' A drunken Brendan staggers up and embraces his brother. Brendan goes to whisper into Tom's ear. 'Everything will be alright.'

He nods and ever so gently shrugs him off. 'I know Brendan, I'll see you tomorrow.' Tom leaves the pub and Brendan sits back down. He raises his glass. 'To the best brother in the world, Thomas Patrick Rogan!' Both Kelly and Malone join in the toast whilst Clancy still lies flat out in a drunken slumber. Knowing he's got time Tom rushes back to pick up the mermaid's body and sets off up towards the graveyard. Across the way the dark ocean. Its mysteries hidden deep and unseen, but they are all watching him. In the distance Tom spots a shining torchlight held by Father Conlon who stands waiting by the prepared grave. He goes to help Tom and the two carefully lay down the mermaid into it. Father Conlon picks up a shovel and begins filling the dirt back in. He points to another and one look is enough for Tom to pick it up and start digging himself. Just as the two men have nearly finished, from the ocean comes a distant crackle of thunder. Then as Tom and the priest look up they witness a dozen, jagged bolts of lightning streak over the horizon in a red blitz!

Suddenly, a lone bolt strikes upon the church spire and Father Conlon looks worryingly at Tom. 'So much for keeping this quiet my son?' Tom wipes his brow. 'Father I don't know what to say but we are burying a mermaid for heaven's sake. Maybe you should say a few words?' The crash of deafening thunder greets Tom's words. The priest nods. 'Maybe you're right, it can't do any harm in current circumstances.' Both men are afraid. The priest gazes towards the ocean which appears to be bracing itself for a gigantic storm. They drop their shovels and Father Conlon crosses himself.
…'Oh Lord, we deliver onto thee one of your children. Please welcome her into the kingdom of heaven and may almighty god have mercy on her soul. In the name of the father and of the son and of the holy spirit...'
'Amen,' finishes Tom.
'What will you do after tonight Tom, there's sure to be trouble with the others when they find out what you've done?'
'I'm leaving Ireland and going across the water. To be honest I should have done it years ago and got out of this place. I've cousins in Manchester in the building game. I'll find work with them. After tonight there's nothing left here for me Father.'

COLETTE

Earlier, back at The *Shark's Finn,* its interiors shuddered as the ferocious, clatter of thunder startled everybody! The lights dimmed and flickered, the jukebox shut down and drinks toppled off the table. A panic filled the air! Brendan and Fergal Finn headed outside and across the road to stare at the raging ocean and the monstrous storm gathering on the horizon. Yet as lightning bolts crashed down onto the sea there was still no rain?
'It looks like Armageddon,' said Brendan, 'The end of the world.'
'My god Brendan, what have you and your boys done?'
'Ah Fergal, don't be making such a scene out of all this, it's just a storm man, stop your crazy talk.' Just as Brendan finished speaking another bolt careered down and smashed into the *Madam Marie* moored at the pier's end! This enough to send the two scuttling back inside the pub.
  Elsewhere in the village at the Rogan home, 9 year-old Colette is stood in a white nightgown watching through a bedroom window this strange storm heading towards Drunamere. Her mother Brigitte walks into the room and crouches down. 'Don't worry my love, you're safe here with me, the storm can't hurt you.'
Colette continues to stare out of the window onto the beach. Through the darkness, lit up sporadically by the lightning she spots a figure emerging from the sea. A tall man with a long beard in a white flowing gown and carrying a spear. He's walking up the beach.
'Mummy look!' Colette points but Brigitte sees nothing.
  'There's nobody there Colette, your eyes are tired and playing tricks on you. Now back to bed my girl.' Brigitte closes the curtains as her daughter jumps back under the sheets. She straightens Colette's pillow covers and kisses her on the forehead.
  'Goodnight my sweet angel, go to sleep and no more silly talk. School in the morning.' Brigitte leaves the room and Colette clutches tight of her favourite doll. Still convinced what she saw was real. The

little girl closes her eyes and is soon fast asleep. Wholly unaware of the tall figure that has appeared at the bottom of the bed.

ACT TWO

THE FAMOUS BROTHER

The next day. It's a bitterly cold morning on the Drunamere front. The night's weird, rainless storm has cleared and once more calm seas have returned. A Land Rover appears from a winding ribbon road heading down from a mountain peak into Drunamere. Inside is William Finn and his long-time personal cameraman, Shay Cosgrove. Finn is a famed, Irish television personality. A world renowned news reporter and documentary maker. This is the first time he's been back to Drunamere in twenty years and his mind fills with childhood memories, though few happy ones.

'So, this is where the great William Finn was born?' asks Cosgrove. 'How come you've not been back for so long Bill?'

'Look around you Shay? You know me better than most. Am I really the kind of character to spend every night on board a broken down old fishing boat hauling in stinking fish? Then when not on board that piece of junk, sat inside my brother's pub until either my liver or brain explodes? I think not. Either the booze or boredom would've killed me. Probably both.'

'Isn't the pub both of yours Bill, off your ma and pa?'

'No, I signed it over to Fergal a long time ago. I needed to cut all ties with this place. To be honest Shay, me and Fergal don't really get on. We don't like each other much. Never have. No one is more surprised than me I'm here, but that crazy phone call off him last night? It can only be something really important for him to ring me. Also the fact we're in dire need of a good story lately means it's worth a few hours' drive from civilisation back to this hovel.'

'Did yer man give a hint of what it's all about?'
'Nothing. Fergal is a man of very few words but whatever it is has truly shocked him, take it from me that takes some doing for my brother.'
Waiting to greet them outside The *Shark's Finn* stands Fergal and a hungover Brendan Rogan, Sean Clancy, Donal Malone and Patrick Kelly. The two step out of the Land Rover and Fergal walks across to shakes his brother's hand.
'How are you keeping Bill?'
'I'm good, it's grand to see you Fergal.'
There's a coldness in the air that isn't just the weather and it's hard to ignore. 'This is my cameramen Shay Cosgrove, Fergal,' continues William. The two shake hands. 'Pleased to meet you at last Fergal,' smiles Cosgrove. 'Likewise,' he replies, hardly meaning it. William looks around the harbour and towards the fishing boat at the pier's end. 'The old place hasn't changed much,' he sighs. 'The last hole on god's forsaken earth.' These words shake the fishermen, but they still continue to stare in awe at a man they've grown used to seeing so often on their televisions.
'Let me do the introductions,' says Fergal.
'Bill, Shay, these are four good friends of mine. Brendan Rogan, Sean Clancy, Donal Malone and Patrick Kelly.' Everybody exchanges handshakes. On finishing William smiles wide and rubs his hands together. He stares towards the fishermen. 'All right lads, now all that's out of the way what have you got for me?'
'Sean go and fetch the sack,' replies Brendan. Let's show our two fine guests from Dublin our prized catch from last night.'
'Will do Brendan.' Clancy heads back around The *Shark's Finn* and returns dragging the sack, clearly struggling. Malone and Kelly go to help him carry it, as William Finn watches on.
'What on earth have you got in that thing?'
'Bill,' replies Brendan. 'What you're about to see here has never been witnessed before.' Shay Cosgrove is pointing a hand-held camera at Brendan. 'Brendan, look at the camera please!

'Just relax Brendan,' says William. 'Go and rip open the sack but look towards the camera whilst talking to me.' Brendan goes across and urges his fellow three fishermen and Fergal Finn towards him so they're also on camera. All four stand next to Brendan as he stands proudly with the sack. 'A few words to the camera please Brendan,' asks William. He coughs to clear his throat as this is to be Brendan's grand performance! The start of a new life.
'On the night of September 23, 1973, we the fishermen of the *Madame Marie* caught what's in this sack here.' He points to it just as Fergal Finn coughs loud. Brendan suddenly realising he's left him out! 'And of course Fergal here helped tremendously.'
Fergal smiles. Happy his part in the saga has also now been documented!
'I shall now empty the sack!' declares Brendan. He does so and out falls the previous evening washing and items stuffed in there by Tom! It sits lying in a dishevelled mess on the road. A stunned silence descends and Fergal Finn and the other fisherman look on aghast.
'What the hell's going on here Fergal?' asks a seething William.
'Is this some kind of joke lads? You mean to say you've brought us all the way from Dublin for this?' Brendan fiddles with the sack frantically turning it inside out. 'I don't understand!' he exclaims. 'It was in here, the thing was in here!'
'What was in there Brendan?' asks William trying hard to stay calm.
'The mermaid Bill, we caught a mermaid!' Already busy loading the filming equipment back into the Land Rover, Cosgrove hears this.
'Ah Brendan, at least you lot are original. It beats the usual Leprechaun tales. A mermaid eh? My god no wonder you got out of this place Bill. They're a strange breed around here.'
A furious Brendan launches himself at Cosgrove and has to be pulled back by the others. He drags himself from their arms and finds himself facing William. 'We're not crazy Bill, I know what's gone on here, it's my brother Tom.' The other fishermen nod their heads in agreement. 'He changed the sacks over last night. Tom had a guilty conscience. Let me speak to him and sort this out? I'll bring you that mermaid!'

'I don't think so. I've heard and seen enough already Brendan,' replies William. 'You've had your joke.' William looks towards Fergal. 'Please god tell me you weren't part of this childish charade?'
'I know what I saw Bill. It was a mermaid. True as I'm stood here.' William shakes his head. 'Unbelievable! Come on Shay we're going home.' Before they set off William winds down his window.
 'I thought more of you than this Fergal. I really did.' The Land Rover drives off and a stern faced Fergal watches it go.
'Good riddance,' he murmurs, almost to himself. 'I never liked the bastard anyway!'
A fuming Brendan goes to storm off. 'Brendan where are you going?' shouts Fergal. 'Where do you think?' he replies.
  'To sort out my damn little brother, that's where I'm going!'

A CHILD'S DOLL

Tom is at home packing a suitcase for England, when there's a loud banging on the front door. He looks down from the bedroom window and sees Brendan.
'Thomas Rogan you get yourself out here now or so help me!'
Tom sighs. 'Oh Brendan,' he says quietly before heading downstairs to open up, only to suddenly finding himself being grabbed by the collar! 'Where is it Tom what have you done with it?'
'I'm sorry Brendan I had no choice.'
Brendan pins him up against a wall. 'Why Tom, why do we have to pay the price for your conscience? Now I'll ask you one more time what have you done with the mermaid?'
'I threw her back in the sea where she belonged.'
A wild eyed Brendan lets go of Tom and steps back unable to believe what he's just heard. Then as Tom thinks the worst is over Brendan punches him and he crumples in a heap to the floor!
'Oh god what have I done?' mumbles Brendan, before offering a helping hand to Tom who shrugs it off. 'Tom, I'm so sorry.'
 'Get your hands off me!' he rages. Suddenly, both their attention is distracted by seeing their Mother running towards them.
 'I can't find her!' she's screaming.
Brendan grabs hold of her. 'Ma, calm down, what's happened?'
'It's Colette she's gone missing. I went to wake her for school and she was gone!'
'Maybe she got up early and went down to the pier?' says Tom, whilst holding his bloodied nose. 'You know what Col is like ma, whenever there's a storm she always heads straight for the beach to see if anything has been washed up. Come on, let's go take a look.'
The three head down to the front, but there's no sign of Colette. Tom and Brendan are searching the beach and Brigitte is at the pier's edge.

She's looking out and spots something floating on the water that appears to be a child's doll. It's Colette's, Brigitte covers her mouth in horror before screaming out loud!

    Later that day the brothers are at the family house which is a hive of activity. They're being questioned by the Garda. The two officers sympathetic in manner, but also suspicious for Brendan and Tom appear nervous in explaining their whereabouts the previous night. The oldest officer, a Sergeant Pat O'Hare watches them closely. Something doesn't feel right.

'So, lads, let me get this straight. Brendan, you were in the pub all night with the other fishing boys, and you Tom, you were with Father Conlon before returning home around four in the morning? Am I right?' They both nod. Sergeant O'Hare is again staring hard at the brothers. Both are clearly devastated. 'Tom is sporting a black eye. 'How'd you get the eye Tom?' he asks.

'On the boat during the storm. The net hit me in the face as we lowered it.'

'You can't honestly think myself or Tom had anything to do with Colette's disappearance Sergeant?' says Brendan. 'She was our little sister for Christ sakes!'

'Just doing my job Brendan, calm down son. Rest assured we'll do everything we can to find her but have to eliminate all possibilities. And I mean all possibilities. Is that understood lads?'

Neither of the brothers speak.

    'Look,' continues Sergeant O'Hare, 'I've known you boys since you were both knee high to a pint of Guinness and I sincerely believe you've done nothing wrong, but something is definitely bothering you, I can see it, I can feel it. What's going on here?' Still the two say nothing. They daren't.

BARE NETS AND BROKEN HEARTS

Manchester. 1982.
　In the *Peveril and Peak* Tom finishes telling his story.
'And that's it. We never found her.' Brendan puts an arm around Tom. He looks across to Archer and Conwell. 'The Garda's investigation swiftly concluded that Colette had been caught up in a freak wave and washed away. Case closed, end of story.'
'I'm so very sorry,' says Archer. The brutal reality of the so called fairytale hitting home after hearing it from the other brother's lips.
'After Colette went missing and Tom left for across the water we tried in vain to carry on with some semblance of normality, but life could simply never be the same again. There was just too much sadness in the air, plus something else had turned dreadfully wrong. The fish in our waters had disappeared. We were fishermen and that was our trade, the village's entire lifeblood but we had no fish.

　Drunamere. 1973.
　The *Madame Marie* sits quietly bobbing on the water below miserable, black skies. On board Brendan Rogan, Sean Clancy, Donal Malone and Patrick Kelly stand idly around. The nets are bare. Astonishingly, the sea appears bereft of all life. Brendan leans over and gazes hard at the water. There's no sound, not a ripple of the waves. It's as if the sea has been poisoned and all life drained out of it. He turns to the other fishermen and shakes his head in total dismay.
'Let's go home, there's nothing here for us.'
It's the mermaid Brendan,' replies Clancy.' A mermaid's curse that's what it is.'
'Sean's right,' adds Malone. 'This is payback time for us.'
It's definitely a curse Brendan,' says Kelly. 'We should never have gone along with you, Tom was right. He was right after all!' Brendan

listens on unable to argue against any of it. The price of his greed has been unbearable. Colette had vanished and their lives changed forever. They all should've listened to Tom and not him, he thinks. Tom's big heart should've ruled the day. The fishermen prepared the *Madam Marie* for a return to shore with bare nets and broken hearts.

Manchester. 1983.
'And that was it,' sighs Brendan. 'For a year, the sea was dead and the fish had gone. Soon people started packing up and going. Some for the big city, others like Tom to England. Or America. There was nothing left. Drunamere became a ghost town. The pub shut down and Fergal god bless him passed away with a heart attack. Father Conlon too. He was a good man, a good priest and a friend to our family. We buried him up in the church cemetery in view of the ocean. He would've loved that.'

Drunamere. 1975.
An ailing Father Michael Conlon lies clutching a crucifix on his deathbed. He's not long for this world. At his side are Father Eamon Quinn and Sister Teresa Cosgrove from the nearby neighbouring village of Tralee. Father Conlon tries hard to speak but is struggling badly and out of breath.
'What is it Father?' asks a tearful Sister Teresa.
'What are you trying to say?' The priest gently grabs the nun's hand and brings her head lower. He whispers, then with a last gasp of breath Father Michael Conlon passes away. Father Quinn closes his eyes. He makes the sign of the cross over the lifeless body and takes the crucifix from his chest before softly pulling up the bed sheets to cover the dead priest's face. Father Quinn then turns to Sister Teresa.
'What did he say to you?'
A crying Sister Teresa blows her nose on a handkerchief. She's confused and doesn't understand Father Conlon's last words on his dying breath.
'He said Mermaid.'

Manchester. 1983.
'Brendan do you remember the day Colette went missing?' asks Tom.
'I told you I'd thrown the mermaid's body into the sea?'
Brendan nods. 'Of course I do what about it?'
'Well I lied.'
'I know you did you dumb ox!'
'What?' replies a startled Tom.
'That's why I punched you in the face! I knew you were lying. That morning after the television guys had gone and I went gunning for you, I suddenly realised what a selfish idiot I'd been in not listening to you on the boat. When you left I went to see Father Conlon and although he never let on it was obvious by his demeanour that you two had buried her somewhere in the cemetery. He never liked me the old bugger even when I was a kid.'
Tom shakes his head and is clearly confused. 'Then what was all that nonsense you said about paying the price for my conscience?'
'Ah, I was just a little annoyed,' smiled Brendan. 'You made us look like a right bunch of clowns. I still had leprechauns on my mind.'
'It would have been good to have a leprechaun!' laughs Conwell. 'That's really all this story is missing.' Tom and Brendan stare daggers towards Conwell who knows he's just well overstepped the mark with the comment. Archer too glares towards his cowering researcher. 'I apologise that was a crass and stupid remark,' he says with a look of huge remorse on his face.
'That's your one chance,' warns Brendan. 'The next time I'll knock your block off!' Fearing Conwell is close to getting a beating Archer decides best to call time on the meeting. 'Gentlemen, I think that is enough for tonight.'
'One last thing Archer,' asks Brendan. 'There's something you've never told me, just how the hell did you ever come to first hear about this?'
'Would you believe off an old man in a Dublin pub?'
'What was his name?'

'I never found out because I never got the chance to ask him. It was all quite remarkable really. He was the real old sailor type. A huge man, tall as a house with grey, scraggly hair and a long, white bushy beard. You would have sworn he'd stepped right out of the sea. He told me about this strange rumour of a mermaid buried on the West coast, and of how the fish dried up. A dead sea. Of a young girl missing presumed dead. All taking place in a ghost town called Drunamere. He also gave me these.'

Archer goes into his pocket and produces a small vial containing two tiny speckles of water. 'He claimed these were real mermaid tears and possessed the power to bring the creatures back to life.'

Brendan is intrigued. 'And, you kept them, why?'

'For good luck really. Anyway, I started researching first for a novel but as I dug for information. As is always the case fact becomes stranger than fiction. And gentlemen, here we are all here today.'

Tom puts out his hand. 'Can I have a look at them?'

Archer passes the vial over and Tom handles them with great care before giving back. 'You be real careful with those Mr Archer.'

"THE OLD COUNTRY"

Later that evening at Tom's apartment the brothers are busy finishing off a bottle of whiskey. There are beer cans also scattered around. 'Do you think often of that night?' asks Tom.

'Every day. It's the first thing that comes to mind when I open my eyes.'

Tom has to ask but is dreading the answers. He takes a deep breath. 'When are you going to tell me what happened to the others?'

Brendan leans down looking for a still unopened can of beer. He finds one and takes a huge gulp.

'They all met with some almighty bad luck Tom.'

'Go on.'

'For a start they're all dead.'

An ashen faced Tom suddenly sobers up. 'Tell me what happened to them?'

'Well,' sighs Brendan. 'After the incident Patrick Kelly packed up and went off to America. I later heard he got himself a job as a New York City cab driver.'

Brendan smiles. 'Apparently for extra tips he used to ply customers with strange tales of adventures back in the "old country" with a real life mermaid. Can you believe that? Anyway, one night he picked up a wrong un who tried to rob him at gunpoint. Pat put up a fight but was shot and killed.'

'And Sean?' Brendan takes another large swig of his beer.

'Sean went a little crazy. He marched himself off to Dublin and mixed with the wrong crowd. He started using.'

'What, drugs?'

Brendan nods. 'Sean ended up overdosing on heroin. They found him dead down a back alley His body so full of holes the only place he hadn't injected was his eyes. I got a phone call. Apparently mine

was the only phone number on him. That and a piece of paper with a word written on it.'
'What word?'
Brendan takes another drink. 'He'd wrote down mermaid.'
'Jesus!' mouths Tom. 'And Donal?'
'It was tragic,' sighs Brendan. 'Six months after Donal became terribly sick. He took to his bed one night and just never woke up. His wife Noreen told me at the funeral that he'd confided in her about what happened. She claimed he died of a broken heart. He simply couldn't live with himself. It's been brutal Tom. That night wrecked all our lives. But you, you haven't deserved to suffer. You didn't kill her we did.'
'No I was as much at fault. We all caught her Brendan in our nets, we all made her cry. We caused the tears and we killed her.'
'Please don't torture yourself Tom, you forget you were out-voted 4-1.'
'You really think that makes me feel better? I should have picked her up and threw her back in myself. But what did I do? I did nothing. Instead I was a coward. What we did was evil beyond words. Against nature. You were my older brother and you should have looked after me. You should have listened to me!'
Brendan looks upset. 'That's not fair.'
   Tom is furious and appears in no mood to ease up. 'But you'd rather take the money. The fame. See your name in the newspapers. Your face on the television. Go on Wogan. "Ladies and gentlemen. Here is Brendan Rogan and his boys. The mermaid killers!"
We could have told them all about how we made her cry. She begged us with those eyes Brendan. Begged us to put her back in the water. But oh no, not the grand old fishing boys from Drunamere. What we did was wicked and we'll be damned for it!'
   Brendan himself is close to tears. 'Do you feel better now you've cleansed your soul? I'm going to bed and if you can still stand the sight of me I'll see you in the morning!
He walks into the bedroom and slams the door behind him!

An ashen faced Tom feels sick to the stomach and fears he has gone way too far.

The next morning Tom is fast asleep on his sofa when the smell of bacon and Brendan singing from the kitchen wakes him up. He yawns and stirs. Brendan's head pops through the door.

He's smiling wide. 'Good morning misery guts! I took the liberty to knock us up some breakfast. I hope you don't mind?'

Tom rubs his eyes. 'Brendan, about last night...'

'You mention last night one more time and I will straighten back that broken nose I gave you in 1973. Have we got a deal?'

'We have a deal!' laughs Tom.

Brendan enters with a plate of bacon sandwiches and a mug of coffee for Tom. 'Best cure for a hangover brother.'

ACT THREE

DUBLIN'S FAIR CITY

Tom, Brendan, Archer and Conwell are at O'Neill's wine bar on Suffolk Street Dublin. Conwell is eager to improve relations with the brothers after his unfortunate comment back in Manchester.

'Look, Tom, Brendan, I know you think I am an idiot after the other night with my crass, unthinking remark about the leprechaun. I just want to say again I am truly sorry for any offence caused. With your sister and all. I was a bloody idiot and I profusely apologise.'

'You're right Conwell,' replies Brendan. 'You're truly a bloody idiot.' Conwell appears crushed as he plays with his near empty beer glass. 'But if you were to buy the next two rounds then no longer an idiot would you be!' Conwell's mood suddenly becomes buoyant and he's now beaming from ear to ear. He stands to go to the bar, 'Thanks Brendan, you too Tom.' Tom winks in recognition. Conwell heads off and Brendan leans across to Archer. 'It still stands though Paul, he remains one sarcastic comment away from having his teeth knocked out!'

Archer can't help but smile. 'Absolutely! Tomorrow we all travel to Drunamere, is that okay with you two?' Both Tom and Brendan nod.

'Agreed,' replies Tom.' We dig her up and she goes back into the sea. You have your book and myself and Brendan have some closure of kind?' Archer reaches into his jacket pocket and hands Tom the vial containing the alleged mermaid's tears.

'For good luck.'

Brendan smiles. 'You're a good man Paul Archer.'

Tom puts the vial in his pocket. 'Thank you Mr Archer.'

At that moment Conwell returns with the drinks. Brendan takes a huge swig of his. 'Aah, it's good to be home. But only one more after this then I have to make a move. I've to pick some stuff up for my son's forthcoming wedding. Which I might add you're all invited too.

Even you Conwell.'

At first Conwell appears shocked before smiling wide. Happy to be back in the fold. 'Likewise,' says Archer. 'I've a meeting with my American publishers on the phone later today. Should be an interesting conversation when I tell them the storyline of my next book. Especially when I explain its non-fiction! Which is why I will need you next to me Liam. Just to prove I haven't gone completely mad.'

Tom laughs. 'So then you're all leaving me alone in Dublin's fair city?'

A smiling Brendan ruffles his brother's hair. 'Don't you go talking to strangers now!'

THE OLD MAN OF THE SEA

Two hours pass by and Tom is now sat alone in O'Neill's. He's happy enough in his own company enjoying a pint, a cigarette and reading his newspaper. Suddenly a very tall, imposing old man with grey, scraggly hair, piercing eyes and a long, white bushy beard approaches him. 'Would you mind if I sit down?'

Tom is intrigued and remembers Archer's description of the old man who gave him the mermaid's tears. He smiles. 'Be my guest.'

The old man sits next to Tom. He stares at him, 'Thank you. You look like a man with a lot on his mind. How are you Tom?'

'Excuse me but how do you know my name?'

The old man smiles wide. 'A mutual acquaintance you might say. A very dear friend of mine helped out your Grandfather once.'

Tom puts out his cigarette in the ash tray. 'Who are you?'

'Oh, I think you may know me best as the old man of the sea.'

Tom laughs. 'That's ridiculous. The old man of the sea eh? Aren't you supposed to carry a sea spear and wear a white flowing gown?'

The old man laughs. 'Now who is being ridiculous?'

'Prove it old man of the sea,' demands Tom.

'Very well then.' The old man puts his hand over Tom's pint glass then moves it away. 'Look into your drink?'

'I'm sorry?'

'Look into your drink Tom,' insists the old man. 'Go on do it.'

Tom smiles and looks into his pint glass. He blinks and can't believe it for there's a scene of the Titanic slowly sinking and his Grandfather and the mermaid watching from the water as it slips under the waves. Then we see the mermaid whisper into his ear before hoisting him next to a lifeboat and vanishing back beneath the sea.

Tom rubs his eyes looks again and the scene has vanished. He glances up at the old man. 'Like I said Tom. A mutual acquaintance.' Suddenly, Tom feels scared. 'What do you want from me?'

'You have something of mine and I want it back.'

'Tomorrow,' replies Tom. 'You can have her tomorrow.'

The old man nods his head in satisfaction at Tom's answer, 'You're a good man Tom, just like your Grandfather. He understood. He knew that we always win. One day, all of this. This city, this island. This continent. The sea will take it back. But until then.'

He stands up. 'Oh, and tomorrow bring your Mother.'

'Why? She's done nothing wrong. My Mother has suffered enough.'

'She's in no harm. Besides, I have something of hers.'

Then as Tom blinks the old man vanishes into thin air! He looks around at the packed pub but no one appears to have even noticed his strange encounter. Tom decides to go leaving the pub in a state of shock. What did the old man mean? Surely it couldn't have been? He heads outside and steps into the nearest telephone box to ring Brendan's house. Tom needs to speak to his Mother, Brigitte.

'Hello, is that you Ma?'

'My god Tom! It's been so long?'

'Ma, listen, I've something really important to ask you. I need you to come with me to Drunamere tomorrow. I've a feeling something might happen. I can't tell you what because I'm not sure myself but I do know you need to be there.'

'Tom, I don't understand. I haven't been back to that place since Colette went missing. Why are you asking me to do this?'

'Ma, please don't argue I can't tell you. All I know is you have to be there. Will you come, please?'

'Okay, okay, I'll come!'

'Ma, that's grand. I love you.'

Tom puts the phone down.

'Tom are you there. Tom?' A confused Brigitte replaces the hanger. She sighs. 'I love you too son.'

THE SEA ALWAYS WINS

The next day the car carrying Tom Rogan, Brendan Rogan, Brigitte Rogan, Liam Conwell and Paul Archer, turns the final bend on the mountain. Drunamere comes into view. All are quiet, only Brigitte who sits in the back with her two sons has attempted conversation. But even she so full of questions finds neither Tom nor Brendan are in the mood to tell her what's about to happen. On seeing Drunamere again after so long Brigitte suddenly panics. 'Please god no!' she shouts out. 'I can't do it!'

'Ma, calm down,' says Tom. 'Please trust me, we have to do this.'

'Do what?' screams Brigitte. 'For heaven's sake Tom what's going on?'

'We're all going to dig up a mermaid Ma,' says Brendan.

'Then put her back in the sea where she belongs.'

'Brendan son, have you been drinking?'

'You did ask Ma!' he replies smiling wide.

'Brendan is telling the truth Ma,' adds Tom. 'And you do have to be here. The old man of the sea insisted after he shown me the Titanic sinking and Grandfather William being saved by a mermaid in my pint glass!'

Brendan glares at Tom. 'What did you just say?'

Tom laughs. 'I'll explain later.'

'My good god!' says Brigitte. 'I've raised two lunatics.'

The car arrives in a deserted Drunamere main street and the passengers step out. It's a ghost town. Archer goes to the boot and grabs two shovels, whilst Tom and Brendan stare out across the ocean and over to the beach where the rotting remains of the *Madame Marie* still lie. Archer walks over to the brothers handing each a shovel.

'Shall we go then gentlemen?' All five head off towards the cemetery. Tom and Brendan take the lead as they enter through the gates.

Brendan taps Tom on the shoulder. 'I hope you remember where you buried her.'

'Not the type of thing you forget Brendan.'

'What was all that about with Ma and the old man of the sea stuff?'

'Well it turns out that the Titanic was sunk because it's propellers trapped a mermaid and killed her. Grandfather witnessed it and I saw it all happen in a pint glass.'

Brendan sighs deeply then smiles. 'I suppose I did ask. But how mad does that make me when I believe you?'

Tom points towards a spot of land beneath the church spire. 'She's over there.'

They all gather around the unmarked grave. 'Tom, Brendan, are you really both okay to do this?' asks Archer.

'Let's just get it over with,' replies Brendan. He looks across to Tom. 'Are you ready?' Tom nods his head and the two start digging. Brigitte crosses herself whilst Archer and Conwell stand aside, nervously watching. In no time they reach the sack containing the mermaid's body. The brothers lay down their spades and gently lift the sack onto the surface. Brigitte appears close to a nervous breakdown. 'Are you seriously telling me inside that sack is a mermaid?'

Before anyone can answer her the winter blue skies above suddenly go a fearful black, and a lone, lightning bolt strikes the top of Saint Malachy's church spire!

'Oh, not again!' says Tom. 'Brendan hurry we need to get her down to the pier!' Fiddling furiously with a camera Conwell pushes Brigitte out of the way to take a picture. 'No, wait!' he shouts. 'Not until I document the body! Empty the sack now.' This is the final straw for Brendan who motions across to Archer to hold the sack with Tom. Brendan then walks across to Conwell and delivers a right hook that sends him crashing to the floor!

'You were warned lad,' insists Brendan stroking his fist. 'Now Mr Archer, if you don't mind can I have my mermaid back?'

Under newly arrived, eerie black skies, Tom and Brendan carry the mermaid's body down to the seafront whilst Brigitte and Archer follow close behind. The four stand at the pier's edge. Tom takes out the mermaid's tears from his jacket. He remembers Archer's comments and opens the vial to let the tiny speckles of water dissolve into the sack. Tom looks at Brendan. 'Are you ready? On the count of three she goes in. As far as we can throw.'

'I've never been more ready in my life little brother!' say Brendan.

'Okay big brother, I'll count down, one, two…three!'

The sack is thrown long and lands with a huge splash on the ocean! As it hits the water the black clouds above immediately clear and blue skies once more cover the heavens. Also the sea appears to come back to life as the swish of the waves return. All eyes are on the sack now lying flat on the surface. The body has emptied and slipped beneath. Brendan puts his arm around Tom's shoulders.

'Come on, it's over.'

Tom smiles. 'Brendan, it hasn't even begun!'

'Look!' shouts out Brigitte.

Tom and Brendan turn and watch on in disbelief as they see the mermaid swimming with great joy and jumping over waves! Her fins clearly visible as she surfaces then dips under. Her blond hair like gold in the winter sun. On seeing this astonishing sight Archer is both crying and laughing. 'I don't believe it, I don't believe it!'

Brigitte also is in tears. 'Oh my god!' she repeats over and over.

The brothers stand transfixed as the mermaid is joined by huge shoals of fish swimming alongside her. Momentarily she vanishes and Tom and Brendan struggle to locate her. Only then to be shocked to the core as the mermaid resurfaces only yards from them leaping high in the air. As she comes down the brothers can clearly see her smiling towards them! Then, she's gone.

'Looks like the show's over,' says Brendan.

As they all head back down the pier Liam Conwell is running towards them from the shore. He's nursing a tissue over his nose where Brendan punched him. Conwell is waving animatedly.

'What the hell is wrong with him?' says Tom? Conwell races towards them. 'Look behind you!' he screams out. The four hear him and turn around. There standing at the end of the pier is the old man of the sea. Dressed in white flowing robes and carrying a huge sea pike, he has his arm around a young girl about 9 years-old. Colette Rogan. Colette has remained the same age.

Brendan begins to cry. 'It can't be!'

Brigitte runs towards Colette who races into her arms and they come together! 'My love, my love, my love!' she sobs wildly.

'I'm okay Mummy,' replies a smiling Colette. 'I'm okay.'

Archer smiles at seeing the old man of the sea in full regalia.

'I've seen you somewhere before sir!' he says quietly to himself.

Tom approaches the old man. 'You look ridiculous!'

The old man laughs. 'Needs must I'm afraid. Working hours!'

'So, what happens now?' asks Tom.

The old man shrugs his shoulders. 'The world goes on Tom. Your people keep polluting my oceans and we shall keep striking back. Until humans learn their lesson that the sea always wins, nothing will ever change. We just ask to be left alone but I'm afraid it just isn't in human nature to let us live peacefully. But let us see what the future holds. Nothing is ever written.'

Tom puts out his hand and the two shake. 'Look after yourself Tom Rogan.'

The old man vanishes. 'I wish he'd stop doing that,' sighs Tom.

He goes across to Brendan, Brigitte and Colette and the four embrace. Tom picks Colette up and hugs her tightly.

'No more hide and seek please sister!'

She smiles and places her hand on Tom's face to whisper into his ear. 'I have so much to tell you!' Though smiling Tom has tears streaming down his cheeks. Together, the Rogan's make their way back off the pier. Watching on Conwell and Archer are dumbstruck.

Conwell shakes his head. 'The non-fiction section?

'No one is ever going to believe this.'

Archer smiles wide. 'Who cares, I have my happy ending after all!'

"Breaking on RTE news now are reports of strange, atmospheric conditions off Ireland's West coast. Unconfirmed stories tell of a fish like, half-human creature moving swiftly through the water heading out into the ocean. But I must stress these reports are unconfirmed. Because as we all know there are no such thing as mermaids!''

WITH TREMBLING HANDS AND A BROKEN HEART

A young sailor sits crouched on the deck of the RMS Carpathia. The first ship to arrive in the aftermath of the horror that befell RMS Titanic. He's a survivor of the greatest Maritime disaster of all time. The sailor is scribbling a few notes. Trying to make sense of what has just occurred.

"It is the date of our Lord, April 15, 1912.

I write these words with trembling hands and a broken heart. My name is William Rogan. I am 17 years-old and an able seaman off the RMS Titanic. Just hours ago I watched hopelessly from a lifeboat as she not so much slipped beneath the waves but vanished before our eyes with such terrible force.

How many poor souls lost I dare not even to think. I so wish to share with someone, anyone what happened to me whilst I was in the water but I do believe they would consider me insane. Driven mad with the cold and shock. So I think best to stay quiet. Also around me on the deck of the Carpathia, amid such grief and tragedy I fear my tale of being plucked from the ocean by a mermaid may well not be appreciated by those whom have lost everything they treasured dear. Therefore I intend to say nothing, nothing at all."

'You're right not to say anything William. Now is not the time.'

Stood above him is a tall old man with grey, scraggly hair and a long beard. He's smiling dressed in naval attire and has in his hand a steaming hot mug of coffee. The old man passes it down to William, who simply stares at the kindly stranger. 'Drink this I've put a little rum in it to warm you up,' he says smiling.

William takes a sip. 'Who are you sir and how did you...'

'How did I know about the mermaid?'

He crouches down low next to William. 'What was it she whispered to you as the ship went down? Ah, yes. ''The sea always wins.'' You were saved William because you have a good heart. We were watching two nights ago when you said a prayer for our sister who got caught in the propellers.' William simply stares at the old man. He's speechless. He has no words. Maybe he's hallucinating?
'Oh, I'm real enough, but not in a way you could ever understand.' He looks around on the deck at the scattered bunch of survivors crying over lost ones. Others sleeping or simply exhausted. The old man sighs. 'So much sadness.'

He fixes William with a fearful stare. 'Never forget William Rogan the tears of a mermaid are a terrible thing and the consequences of such are beyond human comprehension. For out here beneath the waves we look after our own. Now drink your coffee boy, come on.' The old man wraps a blanket around William's shoulders and gently strokes his hair.

And then…

Then he was gone.

GOOD AFTERNOON MR TURING

"Those whom imagine anything, can create the impossible."
        Alan Turing

ACT ONE

CIRCUMSTANCES

On the last day before his death Alan Turing takes a walk in his local park, and comes face to face with the Tall Man.
  The ghost of his life.
  The date is Monday 6th June 1954, just nine years after World War two ended, and a dark-suited, solemn faced, 41 year-old Alan Turing is sat on a Wilmslow park bench. He appears nervous and upset. A Tall Man in a similar dark suit, wearing a trilby low down on his face, and clutching a small brief case approaches him.
 He's smiling. 'Mr Turing sir, I do believe you have been expecting me. We have been in much correspondence recently.'
Alan sighs and ushers him forward. 'Yes. Yes, please, sit down.'
  The Tall Man does so.

His eyes darting around. He takes off the trilby and places it alongside him on the bench. 'May I, may I please call you Alan?'
'Of course. Feel free. That is after all my name.'
'Thank you, such a beautiful day don't you think Alan? I really love this time of year. The smells, the sounds. Even a place like Manchester appears to take on a more sunny disposition. I've never been here before when it hasn't been raining.'
The Tall Man wipes the sweat of his brow with a handkerchief, and stares at Alan. His eyes trying to lock onto his, but a clearly nervous Alan appears reluctant to do similar.
'Yes, yes, I agree, I really do. A beautiful day. I appear to appreciate them much more lately. Although I don't mind the rain also. I feel it cleans the air around me. Please, will you stop staring at me. I find it frightfully rude.'
'I'm sorry, I do apologise. You have no need to be nervous Alan, I don't bite! I really don't! I'm here to make everything right. I'm sure you remember the contents of our recent correspondence?'
'Yes, you're here to put everything right? You really do have a perverse sense of making everything right. Tell me stranger, do you have a name?'
'Yes. Don't we all?'
'Well, what is it?'
'I'm not sure I'm at liberty to digress.'
'Why not, does it embarrass you? Surely it doesn't matter after tomorrow? Nothing does.'
'I understand that,' replies the Tall Man. 'I just feel people like me in my line of work should stay rather impersonal in matters of business. Polite, friendly, but nothing more. It doesn't help, when, well...'
'I understand. A smiling assassin, the man with no name,' replies Alan.
'Fair enough. So, what shall I call you then?'
'Call me today, call me tomorrow,' smiles the Tall Man. 'But don't call me the day after that! It's far too late then.'
'So, it appears now. Do you know something. You're not really what I expected.'

'No, what did you expect Alan? I'm curious.'
'I suppose someone a little more sombre. Despite our situation you do appear to be quite a jovial chap. Maybe you enjoy this kind of thing?'
'No, I don't enjoy it Alan. I hate it.'
'Nice to hear.'
'Thank you.'
'That's quite all right stranger.'
'I really can't believe I'm sat here in your esteemed company. Someone like me should be bowing at your feet. And, yet, here I am, an absolute nobody in this world sat next to you, a man who has changed the course of history, and saved millions of lives. We do owe you our world Alan, quite literally. We really do.'
'Yet you have come here today with the sole intention to crucify me?'
'No, I have come to settle all debts. And to thank you for your integral role in cracking the ENIGMA code, and everything since.'
'Thank you, but what you speak of is all rather classified as they say. Actually, I shouldn't be talking about this, I don't think you should be either. I'm surprised. You really should know better,'
'I will consider myself duly chastised, but it's quite all right old chap. Here Alan, let me show you something.'
  The Tall man goes into his pocket and hands Alan a piece of paper. On it is written a message from the British Prime Minister,
  Sir Winston Churchill.
Alan stares at it for a moment then starts to read out loud.
  ''My Dear Mr Turing.
  The man before you speaks for myself and the British Government. His actions are my actions. His words are my words. On behalf of myself, and all the people of this land, we would like to thank you for all you have done. Now, please, I must implore you to think of the greater good.
Yours's sincerely,
  Prime Minister Sir Winston Churchill.''
  A shocked Alan hands the note back over to the Tall Man.
'Thank you. I accept this letter as being the nails for your cross. Suddenly, it all feels much more real.'

'It is very real Alan, I'm afraid. Can I assume now that we're both clearly on the same page. That there can be no misunderstanding of what's at stake here?'

'When you receive and read a death warrant for yourself off the Prime Minister, I think any understandings of a happy ending swiftly eviscerates.'

The Tall Man puts the note back in his pocket. 'Ultimately, there's no such thing as a happy ending Alan. We all die.'

'All this being true, you must believe me when I say I've never breathed a word about ENIGMA or anything else to anyone. I am a true patriot? I love my country.'

'Your loyalty has never been of doubt Alan. It has never been questioned. Not by me, my superiors or as you've just read, the Prime Minister himself. These are all just an extraordinary sad set of circumstances.'

'There's no such thing as circumstances.'

THE BIGGER PICTURE

I am a mathematician don't forget. Everything happens for a reason. All acts, whether miniscule or astronomical have their basis in mathematical equations. There's a reason behind them. So, tell me the truth. Why is this happening to me?'

'It's because of the bigger picture I'm afraid. The playing field has changed out there considerably since the war, you know this. It's gone cold, our said, true enemy now exists beyond the Iron Curtain, in the East. This being the case, you've made certain friends of ours extremely nervous. Paranoid, even.'

Alan shakes his head. 'That's just simply ridiculous. Look at me, I'm a broken man. You've destroyed my body because of who I chose to love. It was inhuman what I was subjected to. Take a close look, Mr, whoever you are. How on earth can I make anybody nervous? Let alone paranoid?'

'No Alan, it's what people can't see. It's the genius. It's what exists in your head. Your brain functions unlike anyone else's. It has monstrous capacity to shape the future faster and easier than normal human beings make cups of tea, or bake cakes.'

'These certain friends of ours you speak of?'

'The Yankee Doodle dandies!' replies a smiling Tall Man.

'The Americans?'

'You could say that its them, me? I couldn't possibly comment.'

'Their paranoia exists because of my holidays in Greece and Norway doesn't it? The bastards have been watching me with my friends. They think I've slept with communist spies and passed on secrets. I would never do such a thing. I'm a proud Englishman, I love my country. I'm no traitor!'

'Our friends believe you are a huge a security risk. There has been good, reliable information which I have seen personally of you being targeted by Soviet spies. Blackmailed, you wouldn't be the first Alan. You definitely won't be the last.'

'Information, by who? What, the Americans? Oh, please…It's all to suit their paranoid ends.'

'You could even have been drugged, talked, told all and simply don't remember.'

'That's utter nonsense. I am no weak minded fool.'

'You're human Alan, the KGB could have kidnapped you, taken you to the Soviet Union, returned you to where they found you, and you would never had known anything about. What if I was to tell you I've seen pictures of you in Moscow.'

'I have never been to Moscow.'

'See what I mean!' smiles the Tall Man.

'Nonsense…this is all hysterical nonsense.'

'No, this is all reality Alan, as we were saying, it's where we are at now.'

'A necessary sacrifice to our friend, is this what you're saying to me stranger?'

'Yes. For the greater good old chum.'

'This is sheer madness. Surely you can see?'

'It's the way of this new world. The new order Alan.'

'If as you have already stated, if my loyalty is beyond doubt, why doesn't someone on our side stand up for me?'

'Some have tried, believe me, powerful people. But there appears a cruel insistence even by those pulling the strings here, that this has to happen.'

'Who is pulling my strings?'

The Tall Man shrugs his shoulders. 'Obviously, you know I can't tell you that Alan.'

'Can't you have a word? You say I can shape the future with my mind, then why not use me for that? I have ideas in my head. I know I could end the cold war in ten years without a drop of blood being spilt if, if I was allowed the opportunity to carry on my work. Despite what's been done to me, I still love my country, I want to serve, and I want to live.'

'You are preaching to the converted Alan, but let me be honest here as to whom I'm talking about, as if you didn't know. To our friends across the ocean, you are a terror? The Rosenbergs whom the Americans executed truly spooked them. It heightened their paranoia beyond all reason. You're Joseph McCarthy's worst nightmare, and the Soviet Union's wet dream. An explosive concoction, what with your genius, and shall we say, somewhat erratic, colourful lifestyle.'

'You are talking about my homosexuality I presume? Me being a queer, a poof, a Nancy boy? I suppose there's more, fairies, faggots.'

'Calm down Alan. I'm not judging, I'm simply stating the facts as they stand.' The Tall Man shakes his head, produces a small silver box from his suit jacket and lights up a cigarette. He inhales, takes in the greenery around him, and then turns to face Alan.

'Personally, Alan, I couldn't care less who you fuck. Half of our secret service are Homosexuals, and god knows how many Politicians who sit in the House of Commons or the House of Lords. Let me tell you, the bars and side-rooms are full of young boys and special friends, shall we say. Not known to their wives or families. The difference being we can control these people, use them for our advantage when, and if necessary.

You see, peace today is so very fragile, the bomb has made both sides believe victory can be achieved and worthwhile, even if only your fucking flag is left standing. It's infected normal human thinking. This madness is only kept at bay these days by what happens in the shadows. A secret war fought not by guns and ships, but by deception and blackmail. And you, you terrify. To some you represent a bigger threat than the Atomic bomb, because possibly in that computer head of yours, you possess the capability to make the so-called ultimate weapon, null, void and ultimately fucking useless.'

'And that stranger, you are telling me is the case for the prosecution?'

The Tall Man nods. 'Yes.'

'Nonsense,' replies Alan. 'You give me far more credence as to my importance in the way of things than I deserve. I am simply a scientist. I am neither a Prophet, nor am I looking to change the status quo. So, what if I did find a way to make both side's bombs tick out like children's alarm clocks, instead of blowing up? Surely that has to be celebrated by all men of sound mind?'

'Alas, where and when it truly matters, men of sound mind are in short supply these days Alan. As for far more credence than you deserve, you have no idea the esteem you're held in, and the fear you install in the cold hearts of powerful men.'

'Strange, I don't see myself that way at all. I never have.'

'Sadly Alan, I see you as others do.'

'Really?'

GHOST OF MY LIFE

'Really. In fact, I've known you from the cradle to the grave.'
'You sound like the ghost of my life?'
'Yes,' smiles the Tall Man. 'Yes, I suppose you could say that.'
'Explain yourself please?'
'Alan. It has been my job, more a privilege really to be selected to look after you.'
'Spy on me you mean?'
'I really don't like that word Alan.'
'Oh, excuse me, I do apologise for upsetting your fragile nature Mr whoever you are.'
'That's quite alright, but I really do know everything about you. You were born 23rd June 1912, in Maida Vale, London. It was clear from your early school days that here was a boy of exceptional intelligence. A one of his generation. At 9 years-old, your headmistress from Saint Michael's Primary school said "I have taught clever boys and hardworking boys, but Alan is a genius."
In 1922, you moved to Hazlehurst Preparatory School, where you became interested in chess. You would spend hours working out complex chess problems on your own. For you was a loner, Alan. The world that existed inside your head, was far more exhilarating and exotic than the one outside it.'
'Enough!' snaps an angry Alan.
'Please forgive me, I was showing off. An irritating habit I'm afraid.'
'This choice I have been given, and the decision I came to.'
'What about it Alan?'
'Well, I maybe having some doubts.'
'Your decision is non-negotiable I'm afraid. This was explained to you at the time.'
'Yes, but what if I were to run away and disappear?'

'Where would you run to Alan? You are being watched as we speak now.'

'I could run, and you would never catch me. I came close to making the British Olympic squad twice. I could run away and just keep running…Run forever!'

'There are some things you can just never outrun Alan, and we are one of them. I'm sure I don't have to draw you a picture?'

The Tall Man point out three distant fingers stood around the park.

'They even have people watching me, look.'

Alan does so and can clearly see them. 'Are you telling me they don't even trust you?'

'What do you think?' smiles the Tall Man.

'So, in a small sense I know how you must be feeling.'

'No, you don't, you can't that's impossible. I'm sat next to my Grim Reaper.'

'I'm trying to make this as easy as I can for you. I, we owe you that much Alan.'

'Yes, you do, I've been treated with nothing short of middle-aged bestiality. You castrated me? If that wasn't enough you took my security clearance barring me from continuing my work. My life is my work. Wasn't castration enough for you people?'

'You need to look elsewhere, don't blame us for that. Blame Arnold fucking Murray. That little bastard was the one who screwed you over. If it wasn't for him, none of this would probably have occurred. He put you in the limelight and caused fucking heart attacks amongst the people I work for.'

'Maybe so, but it wasn't Arnold who performed chemical castration on me.'

'Forgive me, but wasn't you given a choice if I recall. Castration or jail? You chose the castration.'

'Gross Indecency was the charge? The indecency was the choice I was given.'

'It was the law of the land Alan.'

'Some law of the land. I find it hard to stomach that we here in Great Britain, who defeated the monstrous tyranny of fascism. We whom are supposed to be a civilised society can still inflict such cruelty onto our own people. What was done to me was the reason we fought the Nazis. To prevent such, and yet...'

'I don't make the laws Alan. As I said, you were handed a choice.'

'You do know I'm impotent now? Your type took away not just my pride, but my manhood, the ability to make love.'

'I'm so very sorry, if it had been my call, I would have made everything go away. The burglary inquiry, Murray, the letters, all of it. Sadly, I was overruled.'

'Overruled, by who?'

'By men who simply didn't recognise your genius Alan. I argued your case, so much that I was reprimanded and shipped off to Berlin. They told me I had grown too close to you. It had become unhealthy and was clouding my judgement.'

'If all this you say is true, then why are you here today?'

'Because I asked to be.'

'Oh, I see, so you can prove worthy once more to those who doubted you. Get yourself back in the good books. Deal with Turing and receive a slap on the back, and a medal. It all makes perfectly good sense now.'

'No, nothing like that. It was because I felt I owed you. If it had to be anybody, then, then it should be me.'

'I am honoured. My very own Brutus. Et tu, Brute?'

The Tall Man smiles. 'Te gratissimum, you're welcome!'

ACT TWO

AN OCEAN OF CANDLES

Alan points at the briefcase.
'Tell me then Brutus, what is in the briefcase?'
'Not just yet Alan. I'm not ready.'
The two men go quiet for the moment. Around them children are playing, and young couples are walking past hand in hand.
'All these people around us Alan, it's quite possible many would not be here if it were not for you. You will have a million epitaphs, and they will have children, and you'll have another million. An ocean of candles lit to your magnificent deeds.'
'No one will ever know what I did. Especially now. It will all be buried, ripped out of the history books.'
'That you shortened the war by at least two years by cracking the ENIGMA code. Such astonishing achievements cannot stay secret forever. They will know one day. The world will know, times will change. The Cold war will thaw, there will be warmer days ahead.'
'Is it strange for you, is it ironic when you look at me that the supposed good guys won? Also, the people who chased Hitler and his henchmen all the way back from Russia to his bunker in Berlin are now our sworn enemy. It is all so fucking twisted.'
'None of that changes the fact ours was a savage battle for survival, and without you it's possible we wouldn't have survived Alan. The country was on the brink of starvation, the U Boats were winning. If not for you…'
'If not for me, yes. And your visit today. This is how I am to be repaid?'

'If it were down to me you would be a national hero with your face on the front pages of children's science schoolbooks everywhere. An example to young boys and girls, that, as you famously said. "Sometimes, it is the people no one imagines anything of, who do the things that no one can imagine."'

'And when these same people you talk of have done these extraordinary things?'

'The times dictate Alan. History has always been thus.'

'Yes, I agree. History has always enjoyed a forte for violence. Especially the winners, whom have tended to write it in their own voice and image.'

The Tall Man looks at his watch.

'Am I keeping you from something?' asks Alan. 'God forbid its important.'

'No, please excuse me,' says the Tall Man with an apologetic smile. 'I'm terribly bad mannered. Another bad habit I'm afraid. It's a legacy from the war. I spent a lot of time behind enemy lines, France, Holland, Italy, Germany, Russia, waiting for contacts etc. I swore blind that after it was all over, I would never wear a watch again. Sadly, events proved otherwise, and I'm still wearing, and looking. Just a lot closer to home these days.'

'Let me tell you something stranger. The paranoia with the Americans we spoke about earlier, it has drifted here. You and your kind see traitors where they don't exist these days. The McCarthy witch hunts carried out by those maniacs over there have infected your thinking. You, those you work for need an enemy, someone for us to despise, so they can continue to divide, conquer and rule. Most importantly, to crucify once in a while, a scapegoat, and now it's my turn. Why can't they understand, my natural tendencies for love, does not make me love my country any less. My god, what is going on here? Just because I'm a Homosexual does not make me a fucking Communist spy? The two don't naturally go together.'

'I have no love for my job Alan. I justify what I do by thinking there are those out there who would wish us harm, and I, and people like

me act as buffers. I do as I'm told to keep the big, bad, red wolf from the door.'
Alan smiles. 'You're only following orders? Sounds very familiar.'
'You can't possibly draw that comparison?'
'I can't can I, then just why are you here today? You may be and indeed do appear like a good fellow, but you come with grim tidings for my soul.'
'I'm the last good Nazi Alan, is that what you're implying?'
'If the cap fits…'

PATRON SAINT OF LOST CAUSES

Again, the two men go quiet. An uneasy silence. There is the sound of an ice cream van nearby. Finally...
The Tall Man smiles. 'Can I buy you an ice cream Alan?'
'No thank you. This really is all quite surreal. I'm sat here with a man who's name I don't know, who claims to be the ghost of my life, and who has arrived bearing for me the ultimate gift. Though I'm not sure that's the correct word to describe it.'
'My name is Christopher.'
'Do not mock me,' snaps Alan. 'That's just beyond cruel. You owe me that much.'
'I'm serious, my name is Christopher Marshall. I'm 31years-old. My wife is called Lucy, and I have two children, twins Michael and Thomas. We live in a tiny village called Dearth Moor in Surrey. Our house is by a river, and the few times I'm home, I love nothing better than to take my two boys fishing. I love books, specifically reading about ancient Rome. Playing cricket and watching sunsets with my Lucy. Oh, and the village we live in has a pub, a post office and a Catholic Church named Saint Jude's.'
'The Patron Saint of lost causes,' replies a smiling Alan.
'Prominently, Policemen and spies,' adds the Tall Man. 'I heard a very interesting story regarding Saint Jude. Would you like to hear it?'
'Yes please, why not? I have a little time left.'
'We have time Alan. 'Well, it was claimed that few Christians dared to invoke Saint Jude for help, in a misplaced fear of praying indirectly to Christ's betrayer, Judas Iscariot. Thus, the ignored Saint Jude tended to be quite affable to assist any who sought his help. Beggars can't be choosers sort of thing. Even to the extent of many times interceding in the neediest of circumstances.'

'Maybe I should have a word with him, what do you say, get me off your hook? There's a couple of churches nearby.'
'I think not Alan. That time has passed. It's far too late now.
'I suppose so, for death does come to us all. When my Christopher died, the world for me changed forever. I did years later seriously consider through science whether it would be possible for me to make contact. Grief and blind faith powered me forward in the belief that one day, through some miraculous scientific breakthrough we would meet again, wherever death had taken him. Alas, it was never to be.'
A distraught Alan has tears falling down his cheeks. The Tall Man passes him a handkerchief. 'Thank you, I did promise myself I wasn't going to cry.'
'Maybe it's time, and we should move on now to the business in hand?'
'The choice?'
'No Alan, you have made your choice, I'm here because of the decision you came to.'
'Remind me Christopher, the choice, I would like to hear it one last time, but this time from your lips.'
'Very well, forgive me Alan, but the choice is this. The people I represent consider you a serious threat to the security of her Majesty's Government. An enemy of the realm. Therefore, you were given a choice. You can face the wrath and fury of the entire British establishment and be vanquished in a firestorm of slurs and innuendos, with names and faces to back everything up. Young boys prepared to destroy you. You can go to jail for life, ostracized. Maybe even worse, if it is proven treason has been committed, then the gallows possibly await you. Your family name disgraced. Your Mother left to live her remaining days in the dark shade of your wicked, disgusting misdemeanours. Not forgetting your lifetime work in the fields of science gravely tainted. Your genius mocked, belittled. The defining memory of your name in history, that of whatever the powers that be chose to destroy you with. In short, we could throw enough mud at you so that it sticks so hard you won't be able to fucking breathe.

Or, the other option. The one you ultimately have chosen.'

The Tall Man goes into his briefcase and takes out a single red apple. He shows it to Alan. 'One bite. It's the Roman way Alan. Tam honestem.'

'Tam honestem,' replies Alan. 'The honourable way.'

'The only way,' replies the Tall Man.

Alan stares at the apple then takes it off the Tall Man, and puts it in his pocket.

'You won't feel a thing Alan. It will all be over in seconds.'

'Well, I best be off. I need to start making arrangement. Putting my affairs in order.'

Alan stands and the Tall Man follows him. He offers his hand.

'Goodbye old chap. It's been a pleasure to finally make your acquaintance. Such a terrible shame about the circumstances.'

The two men shake hands.

'So long Christopher, if it had to be anyone, as you said, I'm glad it was you.'

'One day Alan, this will seem like fucking madness, and the country will feel totally ashamed as to what we are doing to you.'

Alan smiles. 'When that day arrives, I hope you are still around to tell them of me.'

'I shall shout it from the rooftops. Goodbye Alan.'

Alan walks off down the pathway. He's watched by the Tall Man until out of sight.

'My god,' he says quietly to himself.

'What the fuck have we done?'

ACT THREE

Tuesday 7th June, 1954.
Alan Turing was found dead by a cleaner at his Wilmslow home of 43 Adlington Road. He was just 41 years-old. The bitten apple laced with cyanide sat at the side of his bed. That very same evening, a post mortem was performed, and the inquest two days later ruled suicide.
With an almost unholy haste, Alan's body was cremated in Woking cemetery the following Saturday. His ashes scattered.
Fifty-nine years later on Christmas Eve, 2013, Alan Turing received a posthumous royal pardon by the Queen. Finally, a small semblance of justice had seemed to be served.
On the 23rd June, 2001,
Alan's birthday, the Alan Turing Memorial in Sackville Street Manchester was unveiled. Alan is shown sitting, holding an apple. Twelve years later, once the Queen's pardon had been given, that same Christmas Eve, as snow fell heavy, a tearful old man sat himself down next to the statue.
'Hello again Alan.'
Now the grand age of 89 years-old, Christopher Marshall has decided to keep a promise made many years ago.
'Well, it took them long enough to do the right thing, but its finally happened. After our meeting I returned to London and tried to resign my commission, but in my job, old chum, its once in, never out. When I got the news of your death, it literally did break my heart. Ultimum Proditione. Yes, it really was the ultimate betrayal.
I see you're still holding that damn apple. Me, I've not been able to touch one since. The Tall Man puts out his hand to touch the ice-cold snow. He smiles. 'A little different to the last time we met. A beautiful June afternoon, I seem to recall. I remember also telling you about my family. Well, they've all gone now Alan. I've outlived

them. Maybe that's my punishment for what I did to you? But I'm not here today to talk about my sadness, it is to celebrate your life. For I believe Professor Alan Turing, that in what you achieved in the scientific field, you will now rightly stand alongside Darwin and Newton. Far more importantly, I hope and pray you've finally found peace in death by being reunited with the one true love of your life. Christopher.'

The Tall Man smiles and whilst putting an arm around Alan's statue, for the first time in fifty-nine years, he feels at peace.

As the snow continues to fall…

"Finding such a person like Christopher makes everyone else appear so ordinary, and if anything happens to him, you've got nothing left but to return to the ordinary world, and a kind of isolation that never existed before."

Alan Turing

JFK: GRANADA CALLING

...How Granada Television broke the news of President John F. Kennedy's assassination back on Friday 22nd November 1963...

"President Kennedy was shot at today while riding in a motor convoy. A photographer reported seeing blood on the President's head." Reuters

"I think that what Manchester sees today, London will see eventually." Sidney Bernstein

ACT ONE

SIDNEY

Sidney Bernstein's Jewish roots can be traced back to a small, Russian village from where his family escaped the terrifying pogroms of the Tsars by emigrating to England. Shortly after settling in Ilford, Essex, Alexander Bernstein married a local girl, Jane Lazarus, and together they went on to have eight children. To support such a large family, Alexander was constantly looking for new ideas. His business interest were wide, diverse, innovative and fascinating. The chosen profession which he loved was the leather trade, but such being Alexander's style of having his hand in several business pies at the same time, he also owned a part interest in a slate quarry in Wales, as well as acquiring local properties around Essex at auctions. Not least of which a run-down housing estate in a place called Manor Park, that he paid only a paltry £270 for. A gamble, as originally Alexander had never even set eyes on the place!

While most investors may have been content to simply add the odd lick of paint here, a bit of wallpaper there to cover gaping gaps and damp, not Alexander Bernstein. For he had far greater plans in mind for the estate. Those building with sound foundations become fully renovated and modernised. Gas was installed into them, and splendid Venetian blinds fitted on the windows. A high level of security was guaranteed for the properties by handing out a number of free houses to policemen and firemen. Tough well-known characters and not to be messed with. The local villains wouldn't even dare for fear of a good hiding and much worse if caught! Two of the roads were named after leading judges of the that period to give the area a proper air of respectability. To keep the money coming in Alexander's residents were also encouraged to not fall behind with their rent by being promised a free sack of coal at Christmas!

A keen eye for a bargain in the property market and producing money from dust saw him enter into the entertainment industry. He did a similar deal like Manor Park for a plot of land in Edmonton. The plan being to build a grand array of shops and a theatre. One would run alongside the other. Knowing nothing about running a theatre he employed an impresario, but this partnership proved disastrous. So much that Alexander sacked him and planned to take over the job himself. Instead, having second thoughts, he employed the impresario's assistant. A man called Harry Bawn to work for him. This coming together proved far healthier and the two went on to build their theatre and shops. When done Alexander offered Bawn the ownership/running of the theatre at a cost of £900 a year rent, which he duly accepted.

Boxing Day. 1908.
the Edmonton Empire opened with a special invitation to every local child in the area to attend. A circus act featuring clowns, acrobats and a troupe of performing elephants paraded for the grand opening ceremony, and bags of sweets were given to each child entering the theatre. Among those handing out the treats to the excited children, Alexander's 9 year-old son, Sidney. The heady magic dust of showbusiness sprinkling over young Bernstein for the first time.
In 1922, Alexander sadly passed leaving behind eight Bernstein theatres.
The Edmonton Empire.
The Electrodome Bow.
The Lyric Cinema, Guernsey.
Plus, the Empire group of Ilford, Plumstead, East Ham, West Ham and Willesden.
It appeared on the surface as if Sidney Bernstein's future had been clearly mapped out. Young Sidney had been given a "silver spoon" upbringing, but the truth was far from that. After finishing Highlands School, Ilford, Alexander sent his son out into the world to learn the hard ways of business elsewhere in different companies, harsh environments, and not from the comfort of his own families' ever-growing empire. It was only with the tragic death of Alexander's eldest son, 21 year-old Selim, on the slaughterhouse, battlefield of Suvla Bay, Gallipoli, on 8th September 1915, that 16 year-old Sidney became next in line to take over from his father. Sidney's first act on doing so was to buy back the lease of the Edmonton Empire theatre from Harry Bawn. Times had grown hard and Bawn had not been able to keep the business going. The building became badly run down, left to rot almost and close to ruin. Being the son of his father, Sidney immediately saw gold in dirt and set about its renovation. He contacted one of his father's former business partners Maurice King, proposing they ran it together.

It took five years of hard work but the two ultimately succeeded in once more lighting up the Empire. The period's leading acts in music-hall entertainment all performed there to full houses and cheering crowds. These included Will Hay, Harry Champion, and a promising young Lancashire lass from Rochdale, who could carry a note or two called Gracie Fields. The most famous of all music-hall stars, Marie-Lloyd of "My Old Man (Said Follow the Van)" fame gave one of her final performances at the Empire. Later, in 1933, the theatre became the early beating heart of the Bernstein dynasty, after being converted into a cinema. By this time all the Bernstein brothers had entered into the family business, but it was Sidney's vision for the future that saw their empire keep expanding, making them all fortunes in doing so. With younger brother Cyril alongside him they created *Granada Theatres*. Named after the Spanish city which Sidney once visited on holiday while cycling around Spain. On travelling to America, and being impressed by New York's famous Roxy cinemas, with their fabulous decor and value for money customer comforts, he vowed to bring such style back to England. Sidney promptly set about turning the family chain of cinemas into picture palaces worthy of the name. He also introduced the original first cut-price children's matinees. This in no time became a highly, successful portfolio of sixty cinemas and theatres. Alexander would have been a proud father. Sidney did not stop there, he became involved in publishing, real estate, retail shops and bowling alleys, as well as the hugely profitable television-rental business. All with huge success.
In 1925, Sidney also co-founded the London Film Society, where he met and got to know well a brilliant young movie-maker from Leytonstone, called Alfred Hitchcock. They became lifelong friends. Bernstein adored movies and was behind the idea to bring the classic Sergei Eisenstein's and Grigori Aleksandrov's, *October: Ten Days That Shook the World* to London.

Sidney Bernstein was also before many others an ardent and active anti-fascist. In 1933, he helped German actors, such as Peter Lorre, plus directors, cameramen and other Jewish and anti-Nazi filmmakers to escape Adolf Hitler's Germany. Bernstein travelled again to America frequently during the 1930s, where he met with Hollywood studio executives attempting to persuade them to support the anti-fascist cause against the Nazis on the big screen.

Between 1939-1941, Bernstein joined in producing and bringing anti-Nazi and pro-British films to American audiences during those critical two years, when the United States remained neutral and Britain fought on alone under a constant Luftwaffe air blitz, and the threat of imminent invasion. Then came the Japanese sneak attack on Pearl Harbour, and the United States finally took sides.
 Bernstein had by then begun working on films to help the new allies understand each other and rally to the cause. He advised greatly on early drafts of *Mrs. Miniver*. Bernstein talked MGM into making this after meeting their executives in Hollywood. His sheer passion overwhelmed them into agreeing. This was a classic war story set on the home front starring Greer Garson, as the heroic mother of a British family. It turned out to be a huge critical and commercial success, becoming the highest-grossing film of 1942, winning six Academy Awards, including Best Picture, Best Director, Best Actress for Garson, and Best Supporting Actress for Teresa Wright. It was also the first film centred on World War Two to win Best Picture, and the first to receive five acting nominations.
1944. As the invasion of France, D Day, loomed large, Bernstein brought his old friend and movie director Alfred Hitchcock back from Hollywood, to help him work on two short doc-films specifically for the post-invasion French audience. Then, through a nightmarish tunnel shone a dark light as the grim reality of the Holocaust began unveiling to disbelieving eyes. Bernstein heard the first reports of extermination camps and took it upon on himself to visit Belsen. Horrified beyond belief, he became determined to create a film that would be seen by both German and English-speaking audiences, so that they would all be able to bear witness to the true extent of the barbaric atrocities committed, and the mass murders carried out with such frightful efficiency in the camps. Factory style. A conveyor belt

from hell. Bernstein spoke to Hitchcock on making such a document for the ages, and the director began to oversee the work of US and British Army cameramen documenting the horrors of the newly liberated camps, under the working title of...
German Concentration Camps Factual Survey.
But then to Bernstein and Hitchcock's anger, their film of the camps was suddenly scrapped in July 1945, with the British Foreign Office claiming the material far too "incendiary". The reason put forward for cancelling the release, being the need for co-operation from a defeated, devastated and broken German population. By this period Hitchcock had already begun to screen and edit the astonishing 800,000 feet of film taken from Allied cameramen and confiscated German footage, when the project became shelved and placed under number F-3080, in the Imperial War Museum archives. Not to be released to the general public until discovered once more on a dusty shelf in 1984 and shown on the BBC. In originally documenting the concentration camps, Hitchcock suggested to his cameramen they film the longest takes possible, giving the audience a true feel of the stark, brutal reality of what occurred in those planted Nazi hellholes on earth. Hitchcock would in time become the grand master of using such long, uncut sequences in his own greatest movies. Such as *Rope* starring James Stewart. On which, incidentally, Sidney Bernstein was an uncredited producer.

GRANADALAND

Post War Britain.
In 1948,
Sidney Bernstein lobbied the British government to give the cinema industry the right to produce and transmit television programmes, not to individual homes, as the BBC did at the time, but to audiences gathered in cinemas and theatres. Many his! Six years later, he won a franchise licence to broadcast commercial television to the North of England, including Manchester, Liverpool, Leeds and Sheffield. Bernstein's thinking being this would not have any detrimental effect on his cinemas, as most are largely based in the South. More so he strongly believed the North possessed a cultural population with no real voice. Here was a region teeming with a reservoir of untapped talent. A deep oasis of creative, broadcasting potential just waiting to be realised and given an opportunity to shine.
It was not the metropolis of London.
The South spoke a different language. The North might as well have been from another planet in regard to the capital. With Manchester at its very hub, Bernstein made his plans and bankrolled the building of the United Kingdom's first purpose-built television studios. The construction of "Granada" Studios began in 1954. The architect Ralph Tubbs, designed the site on Quay Street, purchased from the city council for the sum of £82,000. Tubbs had previously designed Charing Cross Hospital, in Hammersmith, London.
Manchester was still recovering from the blitz. Huge parts of the city remained a scarred landscape of fallen, burnt-out warehouses, decrepit landscapes and wrecked factories. There was no shortage of space. Instead though Bernstein decided to build from scratch. Make his own castle on the hill. A brave new world for brave new ideas. Despite objections to a commercial franchise being awarded to a company with overtly "left-wing" leanings, "Granadaland" was born of and "From the North". The TV transmitter at Winter Hill, Chorley,

Lancashire went live and Granada began broadcasting in the North of England at 7.30.pm, on Thursday 3rd May 1956.

Its logo the letter G forming an arrow pointing North. The tagline: "Granada: from the North".

The opening announcement...

"From the North, this is Granada on Channel 9. A year ago, Granada was a blue-print, a promise. Tonight, the North has a new television service created by the devotion and hard work of thousands of Northerners and friends from all over the world. Come with us now to meet the people."

The opening night's show *Meet The People* was hosted by American journalist and World War Two war correspondent, Quentin Reynolds and comedian Arthur Askey. To add to pre-broadcasting nerves, Reynolds got himself blind drunk just hours before transmission and had to be sobered up with a cold shower and copious amounts of strong black coffee! *Meet The People* featured a generously filmed tribute to the BBC, introduced on camera by Sidney Bernstein, though he was also quick to claim that the new kid on the block would break their monopoly! "Granada's will outdo their programming, not running as simply the voice of the nation, but as a new voice. Innovative, adventurous".

Quentin Reynolds was known to millions in Britain for his wartime broadcasts. He introduced some of the people who had worked tirelessly behind the scenes to put Granada on the air. The building foreman, the architect Ralph Tubbs, a telephone operator and an engineer. Reynolds then brought on the Lord Mayor of Manchester (Alderman) Tom Regan, and the Chairman of the Independent Television Authority, Sir Kenneth Clark. Gracie Fields was also brought to the party. A classy beginning, one impressing the following day's newspapers who reported wholeheartedly on its down to earth roots, much surely to Sidney Bernstein's delight. Viewers interviewed claimed: "It's so slick, a wonderful reception and superb entertainment." Another said: "It's better than the BBC!" At the time no higher praise. Granada presented that night what was to be a typical evening's schedule, so an audience could see what lay in wait in terms of their nightly entertainment after a hard day's working slog. Bernstein was not playing games by promising them the strange, weird and wonderful eight wonders and more of the broadcasting world. The theatrical extravagance of dear old London town would not be found on tuning into Channel 9. The night's line-up amongst other local-based stories included boxing from Liverpool and a variety programme. But one quite simply turned on its head featuring comedians Arthur Askey, Bob Monkhouse, writer and actor Dennis Goodwin, and actresses and singers Pat Kirkwood and Lena Horne, called "London salutes Lancashire!"

The journalists, writers, editors and producers employed by Granada Television all shared a desire to bring a new harder, realistic style to broadcasting. They wanted to light a fire and bring to the screen their own particular Northern brand of realism to the network. A "Social realism" that would come to characterise the station. Make it not just the passionate heartbeat of the North but one laced with sheer quality. The writing, the acting, the reporting, the ideas, new and raw simply made Granada an exploding grenade in the world of broadcasting. They took chances, went where none had previously feared to tread. Although born in Essex, Bernstein swiftly became an adopted Northerner. He led from the top demanding always to go further. He lived and breathed the North. Indeed, he refused to employ anyone, no matter how talented who was not prepared to live in or travel to Manchester. The actor Jeremy Isaacs famously labelled him a "genial giant". More importantly Sidney Bernstein was Manchester genial giant!

As early as January 1957, Granada was moving mountains and responsible for the top ten programmes in the region. With Bernstein's guidance they already had become regarded as one of the most progressive and innovative operators amongst the independent television companies. There was one programme though that when put before Bernstein did not exactly fill him with confidence. It was called Florizel Street, scripted by an exceptionally, talented local writer called Tony Warren. A back-street soap drama set on the cobbles of the rainy city. Bernstein simply at first could not see the potential, claiming "Warren has picked up all the boring bits and strung them together one after another". Nevertheless, there followed a name change, and Coronation Street was given a chance to blossom. From small acorns, so began one of the most loved and enduring television programmes ever made that is still going strong today. Granada also earned a reputation for producing quality current affairs and documentary programmes, such as the barnstorming *World in Action, Disappearing World* and *What the Papers Say*. All of which Bernstein had in mind when beginning the company. Undoubtedly, as the years moved forward everything that came from the studio had his Granada Television's, founding Father's hallmark of class written all over them.

A triumph of broadcasting.

Sidney Lewis Bernstein.

30th January 1899 - 5th February 1993.

TIMELINE:

1954: The Company is set up by Sidney Bernstein and listed on the Stock Exchange.

1954: The Independent Television Authority (ITA) awards Granada the franchise for the North of England.

1954: Construction begins on Granada studios.

1956: Sidney and Cecil Bernstein become the first two directors of the Granada TV Network.

1956: Granada's first broadcast.

1957: "What the Papers Say" is first broadcast presented by Brian Inglis.

1957: The First live football on independent television with Manchester United v Real Madrid, European Cup semi-final broadcast as a live outside broadcast.

1958: "Death of a Salesman". A drama described by critic Bernard Levin as "the best (production of a) play since ITV began".

1958: The First by-election result coverage at Rochdale by-election.

1959: Marathon – general election coverage.

1961: The first episode of "Coronation Street" is broadcast.

1961: Granada's Annual Report states that the region has the largest number of ITV homes. Three million.

1962: The "Younger Generation" Eleven new plays about, written and acted by young people.

1962: Granada building opened, designed by Ralph Tubbs. The first commercial building to be built in Manchester after World War Two.

1962: "You In Your Small Corner". Play of the Week. This is believed to include the first televised interracial kiss on British television.

1962: The First episode of "University Challenge" is broadcast.

1963: The Beatles make their television debut on "People and Places" from Studio Four.

1963: Friday 22nd November. 6-30.pm…

ACT TWO

THE FALL OF CAMELOT

29th November 1963.
Four days after her husband's burial, Jackie Kennedy, now a widowed mother of two small children invited Life Magazine journalist, Theodore H. White, to the family home in Hyannis Port, Massachusetts. "Don't let it be forgot," she told White.
"That for one brief, shining moment there was a Camelot in the White House." This originally associated with the legendary King Arthur. In English legend, Arthur and his knights of the round table lived in Camelot, a gleaming white castle built onto a mountainside, or at least they rested there in between great adventures. The word itself evokes romantic ideals of chivalry, courage and high hopes. All qualities associated with the 35th President of the United States.

Friday 25th October 1963.
Adlai Stevenson, the American Ambassador to the United Nations, spoke in Dallas, Texas, where he was heckled and spat upon by protestors at a Convention. All because he was a Democrat and an ally of President Kennedy. At one point a woman hit Stevenson on the head with a sign. Unable to continue his speech because of the barracking and boos, Stevenson was then subjected to a barrage of hate and spitting contempt. On returning to Washington, he warned President Kennedy's advisers about the "ugly and frightening" mood he discovered in Dallas, but Stevenson never discussed his concerns face to face with Kennedy, before the President's visit there the following month.

Friday 22nd November 1963.
Early morning in Fort Worth, Texas.
A light rain falling. A huge crowd in their thousands had gathered on the parking lot outside the Texas Hotel where President Kennedy and his First Lady were staying in suite 250. A platform was put up and to huge applause. the President appeared.
 "There are no faint hearts in Fort Worth. I appreciate your being here this morning. Mrs Kennedy is organising herself. It takes longer, but, of course, she looks better than we do when she does it!"
 The crowd roared with laughter! Amidst a sea of smiling faces the warmth can almost be felt as the President reached out to shake Texan hands. It appeared the hearts and minds of this supposedly hostile territory for the king of Camelot had already been conquered.
So began the last day of John Fitzgerald Kennedy's life.

11.38.am. The sun had shown, and it was now a beautiful, late morning in Texas. Touchdown. CST, (Central Standard Time).
 President John F. Kennedy, his wife Jackie, and the rest of their Presidential entourage arrived at Love Field airport in north-west Dallas, aboard Air Force One, after just a short, thirteen-minute flight from the nearby Carswell Air Force Base. Mrs Kennedy was accompanying her husband on a public engagement for the first time since the tragic loss of their baby, Patrick, the previous August. On disembarking the aircraft, both immediately walked towards a fence where a large crowd of well-wishers had gathered, and they spent several minutes talking and shaking hands. The first lady was gifted a bouquet of red roses, which she carried with her to their waiting limousine. A midnight blue 1961 Lincoln Continental open convertible. The Governor of Texas John Connally and his wife, Nellie, were already seated as the Kennedys entered and sat behind them in the rear.
 Earlier that morning Kennedy had picked up *The Dallas Morning News* to see the infamous "black border" ad accusing him of treason. He also read a prediction from his great nemesis Richard Nixon that

"Kennedy will be dropping his Vice-President Lyndon B Johnson from the ticket for the forthcoming 1964 election."

Despite concerns expressed by the Dallas based Special Agent in charge of the Secret Service, Forrest Sorrels, the President made it clear that he wanted to be as accessible as possible to the Dallas crowds lying in wait for him. This was deeply concerning for them due to recent incidents. Just three weeks earlier on 2nd November, a motorcade taking the President from Chicago O'Hare Airport to Soldier Field, to watch the Army-Air Force football game was abruptly cancelled after the FB1 informed the Secret Service of a plot to shoot Kennedy in his motorcade with high-power rifles before he reached his destination. The event was cancelled at the last minute. Also, later that month another plot to kill him was discovered by law enforcement officers in Tampa, where Kennedy had been scheduled to ride in a lengthy motorcade from Macdill Air Force Base, to deliver a speech at the National Guard Armoury, and then a second at the International Inn. There surely had to be something brewing for it appeared like the President was being hunted.

On 9th November 1963, in a Miami hotel room. A Kennedy hater and racist agitator, Joseph Adams Milteer was having a no-holds barred conversation with a supposed man of similar virtues called Willie Somersett. In the course of which Milteer told Somersett about a plot in place to assassinate the President. Unknown to Milteer, Somersett was actually a police informer secretly tape-recording. The transcript of the tape revealed Milteer informing Somersett that the killing of Kennedy "was in the working." That the president could be killed from an office building with a "high-powered rifle."

That the rifle could be "disassembled" to get it into the building, and that they will pick up somebody within hours afterwards.

Somersett passed on the recording to local Miami police, who immediately forwarded it to both the Secret Service and the FBI. After a hurried, seemingly rushed investigation that astonishingly did not include interviewing Milteer, the Miami field office of the Secret Service prepared a file on Milteer entitled...

"Alleged Possible Threat Against the President."

Beginning late on the afternoon of Monday 18th November, the Monday before the Friday, Dallas visit, President Kennedy carried on with his trip to Miami, Florida. The information gained by Somersett meant extra precautions were taken to protect the President. JFK travelled mostly through the Miami area in a helicopter, instead of the normal motorcade, and during the one that did occur in his open limousine, they drove at forty to fifty mile per hour the entire route. There was attempts to dissuade Kennedy from going to Miami by his inner circle, but he refused to listen. The President even stood up in the motorcade waving to the adoring crowds, much to the distress of his Secret Service entourage led by Ray Kellerman, and other Tampa police officers designated to protect him. So soon after cancelling in Chicago, Kennedy was determined to go ahead despite the dangers expressed to him of an assassination attempt. He understood the electoral importance of Florida in the upcoming 1964 Presidential election. Both plots claimed to involve amongst other Kennedy haters, exiled Cubans fuming at JFK'S refusal to send in US troops and planes during the disastrous Bay of Pigs, CIA backed invasion. So, it was with good reason, the Secret Service remained extremely edgy on that sunny Texas late morning. With Chicago and Miami still fresh in their minds, the next order to remove the bubbletop off the Presidential limousine due to the expected, even warmer weather later that afternoon was doubly troubling.

The President's younger brother and Attorney General, Bobby Kennedy, (RFK) was fully aware of the Chicago and Tampa plots. He in particular worried about the Cuban exile-world and their hatred towards the President. Bobby knew they were not the type to make idle threats. These were dangerous times. The Bay of Pigs would never be forgiven. Bobby viewed himself as his brother's protector, but he was also his go to man on politics. It was the two of them together against the world. He like JFK, understood the importance of travelling to Texas in relation to the 1964 election. Bobby could not have dared asked Jack to cancel the trip to Dallas, for it would have been seen by their many enemies both in sight and hidden as a sign of

weakness. The Kennedys could never afford to be seen in such a cowardice light. Yet, something truly irked Bobby about the upcoming 22nd November trip and planned motorcade through downtown Dallas. Such was the concern he did actually feel strong enough later to approach Jack about whether it was worth the risk going to a place where there was more than few who wished them both dead. "Maybe you should stay home and not go on these political missions Jack? You're the President and those duties are enough."
"Ah, Bobby, politics is a noble adventure," replied a smiling JFK. He then slapped Bobby on the back and walked out the door.
This was the last time Bobby ever saw his brother alive.

"It's Kennedy weather," sighed a Secret Service agent, as if to suggest the sun always shines brightest for the President and his First Lady. Kennedy's insistence also that he did not want agents riding on the back of his limousine, simply another headache for them to deal with. The King of Camelot unknowingly riding headfirst without the round table knights surrounding him to his own *Camlann*. The ancient Welsh village being the setting of a legendary battle, where King Arthur perished.
The plan was for the President's party to travel from the airport through downtown Dallas, before arriving at the Trade Mart building. There, Kennedy was scheduled to deliver a speech and share a lunch with local government, business and religious leaders. Following this the Kennedy's would then travel to Lyndon Johnson's ranch for a weekend of rest and recuperation.
The motorcade departed Love Field approximately at 11.40.am, fifteen-minutes after Air Force One first touched down.

The first car. An unmarked white Ford (hardtop) carried Dallas Police Chief Jesse Curry, Secret Service Agent Win Lawson, Sheriff Bill Decker and leading Dallas Field Agent Forrest Sorrels.

The second car. A 1961 Lincoln Continental convertible, was occupied by driver Agent Bill Greer, Secret Agent in Charge Roy Kellerman, Governor John Connally, Nellie Connally, President Kennedy, and Jackie Kennedy.

The third car. A 1955 Cadillac convertible code-named 'Halfback" contained driver Agent Sam Kinney, Assistant to the Special Agent-in-Charge Emory Roberts, Presidential aides Ken O'Donnell and Dave Powers, driver Agent George Hickey and PRS agent Glen Bennett. Secret Service agents Clint Hill, Jack Ready, Tim McIntyre and Paul Landis were riding on the running boards.

The ten-mile route would take the motorcade from the South end of Love Field to West Mockingbird Lane and continue through to central Dallas. It progressed down Main Street.

12.29.pm. The motorcade turned right, (westbound) into Houston Street, before entering Dealey Plaza. The crowds along the way filled the roadsides and pavements ten to twelve deep. The motorcade made its winding way through the Dallas streets without any incident whatsoever. Indeed, stopping twice so that the President could shake hands with some Catholic nuns and schoolchildren. There appeared nothing but an outpouring of love for the visiting President. Nellie Connally, turned to Kennedy, saying "Mr. President, you can't say Dallas doesn't love you!"
"No, you certainly can't!" he replied. These were claimed later to be President John F. Kennedy's last words…The motorcade then continued on approaching the Texas School Book Depository, before making a sharp 135-degree left turn onto Elm Street, a downward-sloping road extending through the plaza and under a railroad bridge at a location known as the "Triple underpass". The giant Hertz Rent-a-Car clock on top of the School Book Depository building changed from 12:29 to 12:30, as the limousine turned into Elm Street. Surprisingly, there was no television or radio stations broadcasting live, instead, the vast majority of media lay in wait at the Dallas Trade

Mart in anticipation of President Kennedy's arrival. The few members of the media with the motorcade were riding at the rear of the procession taking little notice.
And then...
12.30.pm. Camelot fell.

On Monday 10th June 1963,
President Kennedy had spoken at the American University in Washington, D.C.
...."I speak of peace because of the new face of war. In an age when a singular nuclear weapon contains ten times the explosive force delivered by all the allied forces in the Second World War, an age when the deadly poisons produced by a nuclear exchange would be carried by wind and air and soil and seed to the far corners of the globe and to generations yet unborn.
I speak of peace,
therefore, as the necessary rational end of rational men, world peace, like community peace, does not require that each man love his neighbour. It requires only that they live together in mutual tolerance. Our problems are man-made therefore they can be solved by man. And man can be as big as he wants..."

"They have killed my husband! I have his brains in my hand! All the ride to the hospital I kept bending over him saying "Jack, Jack, can you hear me? I love you, Jack!" I kept holding the top of his head down...trying to keep the brains in."
Jackie Kennedy

OSWALD: A DARK FAIRYTALE: TIMELINE 1963

Born Wednesday 18th October 1939.
Lee Harvey Oswald is amongst the most controversial figures in United States history. Condemned to burn in American hellfire for eternity as the treacherous Marine veteran who betrayed the nation in the most foul way by killing the President and his own Commander in Chief, JFK. Though many now claim as Oswald did himself…
"I'm just a patsy!"
The name Oswald alone screams assassin, lone gunman and the sixth floor of the Texas Book Story Depository. Countless conspiracy theories that have since been proved as fact regarding Kennedy's killing, duly now rage against this. But not back in the early afternoon of Friday 22nd November 1963, where the truth of the conspiracy lay hidden behind a grassy knoll.

28th January 1962. Oswald ordered a 38 calibre Smith and Wesson revolver by mail.

10th March 1963. Oswald took photographs of the home of General Edwin Walker, a right-wing activist.

12th March 1963. Oswald ordered a rifle from Klein's Sporting Goods in Chicago.

20th March 1963. The rifle and the revolver were shipped.

25th March 1963. Oswald picked up the weapons.

31ˢᵗ March 1963. Oswald's Russian wife Marina took the infamous backyard Photos of Oswald with the rifle.

10ᵗʰ April 1963. Oswald fired a single shot at General Walker but misses him.

14ᵗʰ April 1963. Oswald retrieved the rifle which he hid near the shooting site.

3ʳᵈ June 1963. Oswald rented a new PO box, using A.J. Hidell as one of the people that would receive mail there.

17ᵗʰ September 1963. Oswald obtained a tourist card viable for one visit to Mexico City from the Mexican consulate in New Orleans.

26ᵗʰ September 1963. Early in the morning, Oswald boarded a bus for Laredo, Texas. He crossed the border into Mexico in the early afternoon.

27ᵗʰ September 1963. Oswald arrived in Mexico City and registered at the Hotel del Comercio. He later went to the Cuban Embassy and filled out the application for a visa to Cuba. In the afternoon, Oswald returned with passport photographs he had obtained. When told that the visa could take up to four months and not possible without a Russian visa as well, a seething Oswald walked the short distance to the Russian Embassy, to inquire about a visa to Russia, and was put off until the next day.

28ᵗʰ September 1963. Oswald returned to both the Cuban and the Russian Embassies with no success.

30ᵗʰ September 1963. Oswald phoned the Russian Embassy one last time again with no success. He gave up and later bought a bus ticket from Mexico City to Laredo, Texas.

2nd October 1963. Oswald departed on bus number 332 for Texas.

3rd October 1963. Oswald crossed back into the United States and Dallas.

16th October 1963. Oswald started at the Texas Book Depositary. He rented a room in Dallas near work, while a pregnant Marina and his young daughter remained at the home of a friend called Ruth Paine, where they had all been living.

29th October 1963. FBI agent James Hosty made inquiries regarding Oswald in the Paine's neighbourhood.

1st November 1963. Hosty interviewed Ruth and Marina at the Paine home.

2nd November 1963. Oswald instructed Marina that if Hosty returned, she should get his plate number.

12th November 1963. Oswald delivered a note to the FBI building addressed to Hosty, warning him to leave his family alone.

19th November 1963. The Dallas Times Herald detailed the exact route of the presidential motorcade.

22nd November 1963. 6.30.pm. A new day dawned in Dallas. After a restless night, Lee Harvey Oswald slid out of bed and started to get ready for work. Unusually, he stayed with his family on a weekday. Before leaving he took off his wedding ring and left it in a cup on the top of his wife Marina's dresser. Oswald then pulled $170 out of his wallet and placed it alongside the cup.
It was time to go. He later hitched a lift to the Texas Book Depositary with a man called Wesley Buell Frazier. The two had become friends

since Frazier also began working at the Depositary two months previous. That morning Oswald carried with him a long bag which when asked by Frazier what was inside, he replied, "Curtain rods".

12.05.pm. Fellow Depositary co-workers saw Oswald eating his lunch, just as the Presidential motorcade left Love Field Airport to begin the parade through downtown Texas.

12.30.pm. Shots rang out in Dealey Plaza at the President's limousine and all hell broke loose! According to the official investigation, after shooting Kennedy from the sixth floor of the Depositary, Lee Harvey Oswald covered his rifle with boxes and ran down the building's rear stairwell. About ninety-seconds after the shots were fired, he encountered in the second-floor lunchroom, a Dallas police officer called Marrion L. Baker, stood alongside Oswald's supervisor, Roy Truly. Baker pointed his gun but let Oswald pass by after Truly identifies him as a company employee.
 Mrs Robert A Reid, a clerical supervisor who worked at the Depository had returned to her office within two minutes of the shooting, and said she saw Oswald looking "very calm" on the second floor holding a Coca-Cola bottle. As they walked past each other, Mrs Reid spoke to Oswald saying: "The President has been shot," to which he mumbled something in reply, but she couldn't understand him.

12.33. Following this, Oswald was believed to have left the Depository through the front entrance just before the police sealed it off. Once outside in the ensuing mayhem he calmly walked past a frantic NBC correspondent Robert MacNeil, desperately looking for a phone to call in the shooting. A story existed McNeill actually asked Oswald, but this like so much of that day is covered in myth, mistruths and dark legend. He did finally find one, only for an NBC employee who answered to hang up! The next day NBC officials tracked down the man responsible and fired him.

12.40.pm. Ten minutes after the shooting, Oswald boarded a bus. With the entire Dallas surrounding area in meltdown, the bus became trapped in huge traffic jams, and he exited just two blocks later, choosing instead to hail a taxi. Oswald asked the cab driver, William H. Whaley, to stop several blocks past his boarding house at 1026 North Beckley Ave, then he walked back.

1.00.pm. Oswald arrived at the house. According to his housekeeper Earlene Roberts, he immediately went to his bedroom, but left after only a few minutes, zipping up a jacket not previously worn on entering.

1.15.pm. After being told to patrol the Oak Cliff section of Dallas, Police Officer J.D. Tippit pulled up in his patrol car alongside Oswald. He resembled the description being broadcasted over the radio of a suspect seen by a witness called Howard Brennan. Minutes after the assassination, Brennan had spoken to Dallas County Sheriff's Deputies, saying he was sat across from the School Book Depository, seven stories high, waiting for the parade to come past, when spotting a man at the east end of the building, one story from the top. He was simply sitting in the window and looking down at the parade route. Brennan's description was of a white man in his early thirties, slender, weighing about 165 to 175 pounds.
Meanwhile,
Officer Tippit encountered Oswald near the corner of East 10th Street and North Patton Avenue. A mile and a quarter from Oswald's boarding house. Tippit exchanged words with him through the car window, then stepped out and Oswald immediately fired four shots, three times in Tippit's chest and one in the temple killing him instantly. Shortly after, there was chatter picked up on Tippit's car radio back at Dallas Police Station.
"It's a police officer! Someone shot him!"
Numerous other witnesses present heard the shots being fired and also saw Oswald flee the scene on foot carrying a revolver. Four spent

cartridge cases were later found at the scene and identified by experts as having been fired from the revolver found in Oswald's possession. The bullets however taken from Tippit's body were never positively identified as having been fired from Oswald's revolver, because they were far too damaged to be properly identified.

1.22.pm. On the sixth floor of the Book Depositary, Police found a rifle behind a stack of books in the room from which the alleged assassin fired.

1.35.pm. Following Tippit's murder, the manager of Hardy's shoe store, Johnny Calvin Brewer, on West Jefferson Blvd, watched from inside as Oswald ducked into the entrance alcove of the shop, after turning his face away from the street. Suspicious of this, when Oswald left the entrance, Brewer followed and watched him slip without paying or being seen into the Texas Theatre cinema, showing the film *War Is Hell*. Brewer told the ticket attendant, Julie Postal, who immediately then telephoned the police.

1.40.pm. Two dozen policemen, sheriffs and detectives in several patrol cars arrived with sirens blazing and race inside the theatre. The lights are raised, and Brewer pointed out Oswald to Police Officer Nick McDonald, that he was sat in the rear seats. McDonald headed over towards him. Oswald looked up and greeted the officer by saying "Well, it's all over now," before pulling out his revolver. McDonald duly leapt on him and managed to get his finger in front of the pistol's hammer, so the gun did not fire. Oswald tried to resist, punching and kicking out, but the former Navy and Air Force man was far too strong wrestling and disarming him to the floor, giving Oswald a black eye in doing so. Swiftly, more officers jumped in to help and once handcuffed and being led from the cinema, Oswald shouted out "I'm a victim of police brutality!"

The following day, Police Officer McDonald became an ordinary Joe cop again, arresting two local youths for stealing hubcaps. For his bravery in arresting the soon to be charged Oswald with killing the President, McDonald was swiftly promoted to the Special Services Bureau, and then assigned to the Secret Service protection of...
Lee Harvey Oswald's widow, Marina, and her two small children.

2.07.pm. Shortly after being apprehended, Oswald arrived at the Homicide and Robbery office, on the third floor of Dallas City Hall. A Detective asked him if he wanted to hide his face from reporters who were prowling all over the building?
"Why should I?" he replied.
"I haven't done anything to be ashamed of."
It was pandemonium in the building. The corridor outside the Homicide and Robbery Bureau lay jammed with reporters, cameramen and police of various sorts, many not sure what the hell to do. Plain clothes Detectives in business suits and broad-brimmed hats, city police in flat caps and state-troopers in enamelled helmets and despatch-riders' boots, all were desperate to just catch a glimpse of Oswald. This being living history breaking now before their very eyes.

3.00.pm. The first interrogation of Lee Harvey Oswald got underway. Confronted with photos of himself holding a rifle in his backyard, a sneering Oswald claimed they are "fake" taken by the police, and "superimposed" upon the photographs are the rifle. He eventually stopped answering their questions shutting down. Oswald displayed a strange kind of calm demeanour, this despite his seemingly, hopeless situation. Next, paraffin tests were carried out on his hands and face to check if Oswald had actually fired a gun, and they returned positive.

4.00.pm. Oswald took part in a line-up for a lady called Helene Markham, who witnessed Tippit's murder.

6.20.pm. The second interrogation took place in Captain William Fritz's office. The head of the Homicide and Robbery Bureau of the Dallas Police Department. This was considered the elite unit of the Dallas Police, it's Detectives wore distinct Stetson hats. The 67 year-old veteran, Texas law officer, Fritz joined the force in 1921, and swiftly rose through the police ranks to Detective. In the early 1930s, he was involved in the hunt for Bonnie and Clyde. Fritz thought he had witnessed everything until that November, Texas day. Throughout the afternoon, the Captain had been the primary interrogator of Oswald. A skilled operator. Feared and respected in equal measure, Fitz ran the bureau like his personal fiefdom He had earlier led the search of the Texas School Book Depository building where a bolt action rifle and three empty rifle cartridges were discovered on the building's sixth floor by his Detectives.
It was after Oswald's apprehension as a suspect in the killing of officer Tippit, that Fritz connected him to the Kennedy assassination. FBI agents sat in on the interrogations watching Oswald like a stalking leopard with eyes on an unsuspecting deer. Just looking for one sign, anything, a single word or look that signified a crack in his defences.

7.10.pm. Upon Oswald's arrest and during subsequent questionings by police, he continued to deny any involvement in Tippit's murder. However, based on eyewitness statements and the gun found in his possession at the time of the arrest, Lee Harvey Oswald was formally charged with the murder of Police Officer J. D. Tippit. "Murder with malice". When being moved from the interrogation room Oswald encountered reporters in the hallway. He declared to them "I didn't shoot anybody! They've taken me in because of the fact that I lived in the Soviet Union. I'm just a patsy!"

7.50.pm. Oswald was interrogated for the third time. A fake draft card in the name of "Alek James Hidell" found on Oswald when he was arrested. A. Hidell turned out to be the name used on both the envelope and order slip to buy the alleged murder weapon that killed the President, and also the pistol in Oswald's possession when arrested at the cinema. Both had earlier been shipped at separate times to Oswald's Dallas P.O. Box 2915, as ordered by the same A. Hidell. Oswald was then taken for a third line-up where he was identified by witness J.D. Davies in regarding the Tippit shooting. Immediately following, Oswald's finger and palm prints were taken.

Later, at an arranged press meeting, a reporter asked Oswald outright "Did you kill the President?"
"No," he replied. "I have not been charged with that. In fact, nobody has said that to me yet. The first thing I heard about it was when the newspaper reporters in the hall asked me that question."
On being led from the room more questions in machine-gun tatter were hurled towards him...
"What did you do in Russia?"
"How did you hurt your eye?"
To the second Oswald answered "A policeman hit me."

9.00.pm. Wesley Buell Frazier came to the homicide and robbery office to say he saw Oswald carrying a package with him to the Texas School Book Depository that same morning.

1.26.am. After Captain Fritz signed the complaint charging Oswald with the murder of Kennedy, Judge David Johnson ruled that Lee Harvey Oswald "voluntarily and with malice of forethought killed John F. Kennedy by shooting him with a gun."

1.30.am. Lee Harvey Oswald found himself charged with the assassination of President John F. Kennedy. Oswald was interrogated several more times during the next two days. He eventually admitted that he went to his boarding house after leaving the Book Depository, changed his clothes and armed himself with a 38-calibre revolver, before leaving for the cinema. However, Oswald still vehemently

denied killing the President and Tippit, he denied owning a rifle, and continued to claim photographs of him holding a rifle are fakes. Oswald also denied carrying a long, bulky package to work on the morning of the assassination and knowing anyone by the name of A. J. Hidell. He was then shown the forged draft card bearing his photograph and the alias of Alek James Hidell in his possession at the time of being arrested. A smiling Lee Harvey Oswald refused to answer any questions concerning the card, as if resigned to the fact, all would soon be over. One way or the other.
"You have the card yourself," he said.
"You know as much about it as I do"

Two days later on Sunday 24th November 1963, Captain Fritz's Detectives were escorting Lee Harvey Oswald through the basement of Dallas Police Headquarters toward an armoured car taking him to the nearby County jail. Suddenly, Dallas nightclub operator Jack Ruby approached Oswald from the side of the crowd and shot him once in the abdomen at close range.
"Jack you sonofabitch!" screamed one of the Detectives who knew Ruby, as they jumped to apprehend and disarm him. A network television pool camera were broadcasting live to cover Oswald's transfer, and millions watching on NBC saw the shooting as it happened, and on other networks within minutes afterwards.
On hearing of what occurred the crowds outside the station headquarters applauded. An unconscious Oswald was taken by ambulance to Parkland Memorial Hospital.

1.07.pm. Dallas Police Chief Jesse Curry announced Lee Harvey Oswald's had died on a television broadcast.

Oswald's family struggled finding a cemetery willing to accept his disgraced remains. Finally, Rose Hill Cemetery in Fort Worth reluctantly agreed. A Lutheran Reverend was arranged to do the service but failed to appear at the burial. In his place a Reverend Louis Saunders of the Fort Worth Council of Churches volunteered, claiming "Someone has to help this family". He performed a brief graveside service surrounded by a small army of police officers on 25th November 1963. Reporters covering the burial were asked to act as pallbearers. Some did so under duress and Lee Harvey Oswald was put into the earth. The secret of his involvement in the assassination of President John F. Kennedy dying with him.

INTERRUPT

12.38.pm. In Dallas, the Rex Jones Show on music station KLIF was interrupted by the first news bulletin. A "bulletin alert" came in during the song *I Have a Boyfriend* by the Chiffons. The newscaster Gary DeLaune made the announcement...
"This is a KLIF bulletin from Dallas. Three shots reportedly were fired at the motorcade of President Kennedy today near the downtown section. KLIF News is checking out the report. We will have further reports. Stay tuned."

12.45.pm. Dallas' ABC television affiliate WFAA were airing *The Julie Benell Show*. The screen suddenly turned fuzzy like interference, only then to news director Jay Watson, who had been present at Dealey Plaza, heard three shots and raced back to the station...
"Good afternoon, ladies and gentlemen. You'll excuse the fact that I am out of breath, but about ten or fifteen minutes ago, a tragic thing, from all indications at this point, has happened in the city of Dallas. Let me quote to you this." Watson then looks down at a bulletin sheet in his left hand. "And I'll, you'll excuse me if I am out of breath. A bulletin, this is from the United Press from Dallas...
"President Kennedy and Governor John Connally have been cut down by assassins' bullets in downtown Dallas. They were riding in an open automobile when the shots were fired. The president, his limp body carried in the arms of his wife Jacqueline, has rushed to Parkland Hospital."

12.36.pm. Nationally, the first news bulletins of the shooting were transmitted over the ABC Radio Network. The network was airing *The Music in the Afternoon* program hosted by Dirk Fredericks and

Joel Crager. Doris Day's recording of *Hooray for Hollywood* was playing when newscaster Don Gardiner came on air...
"We interrupt this program to bring you a special bulletin from ABC Radio. Here is a special bulletin from Dallas, Texas. Three shots were fired at President Kennedy's motorcade today in downtown Dallas, Texas. This is ABC Radio. To repeat, in Dallas, Texas, three shots were fired at President Kennedy's motorcade today, the President, now making a two-day speaking tour of Texas. We're going to stand by for more details on the incident in Dallas. Stay tuned to your ABC station for further details. Now we return you to your regular program."

12.40.pm. CBS were the first television network to report, breaking into its live broadcast of the soap opera *As the World Turns*. A CBS News Bulletin slide appeared while Walter Cronkite, broadcasted an audio-only report. Cronkite could not immediately appear on the air because in that era there were no active and ready cameras in the CBS newsroom. This because television cameras used image orthicon tubes, requiring twenty minutes warm up before use. Cronkite announced...
"Here is a bulletin from CBS News. In Dallas, Texas, three shots were fired at President Kennedy's motorcade in downtown Dallas. The first reports say that President Kennedy has been seriously wounded by this shooting. More details just arrived. These details about the same as previously: President Kennedy shot today just as his motorcade left downtown Dallas. Mrs. Kennedy jumped up and grabbed Mr. Kennedy. She called out: "Oh, no!" The motorcade sped on. United Press says that the wounds for President Kennedy perhaps could be fatal. Repeating, a bulletin from CBS News: President Kennedy has been shot by a would-be assassin in Dallas, Texas. Stay tuned to CBS News for further details."

CBS then aired a Nescafé commercial, a NuSoft promotional spot and a Route 66 promo before Cronkite's second audio-only bulletin aired with new details. Oblivious to the tragic events occurring, the

live broadcast of *As the World Turns* continued, with the actors totally unaware of the carnage that had occurred in Dallas.
Cronkite filed one final audio-only bulletin, interrupting a Friskies dog-food commercial. The bulletin remained on screen until a television camera finally became available at 2.00.pm. Following the tumultuous day's events, CBS instituted a policy whereby a broadcast-ready to go camera would always be available to the newsroom.

ABC and NBC were not broadcasting nationally at the time of the CBS bulletins, and their affiliate stations aired their own content.
1.42.pm. In New York, WABC-TV's first bulletin came from Ed Silverman, interrupting *The Ann Sothern Show*.

1.45.pm. Don Pardo interrupted WNBC-TV's local rerun of *Bachelor Father* with the news, announcing...
"President Kennedy was shot today just as his motorcade left downtown Dallas. Mrs. Kennedy jumped up and grabbed Mr Kennedy. She cried: "Oh no!" The motorcade sped on."

1.53.pm. NBC broke into programming with an NBC Network bumper slide followed by coverage anchored by Chet Huntley and Bill Ryan. However, NBC's camera, like CBS's were not ready and it's coverage was also limited to audio-only reports.

2.00.pm. CBS's main anchor-man Walter Cronkite, appeared on camera for the first time that day.

2.11.pm. CBS News correspondent Dan Rather was able to confirm that Kennedy had died.

2.25.pm. ABC Radio broadcasted President Kennedy was dead, but then stressed unconfirmed. Upon reporting the news, their anchor Don Gardiner solemnly declared...

"Ladies and gentlemen, this is a moment trying for all of us. Let us pause and let us all pray."
The station then stopped coverage to broadcast only orchestral music.

2.27.pm. At CBS, the decision was taken to give Rather's report to Cronkite, who relayed this to his viewers…
"We just have a report from our correspondent Dan Rather in Dallas that he has confirmed that President Kennedy is dead. There is still no official confirmation of this. However, it's a report from our correspondent, Dan Rather, in Dallas, Texas."
Five minutes later one of the newsroom staff members rushed to Cronkite's desk with another bulletin. As Cronkite started to read it, he became visibly upset…
"The priests who were with Kennedy…the two priests who were with Kennedy say that he is dead of his bullet wounds. That seems to be about as close to official as we can get at this time."
Although Cronkite continued to stress that there was no official confirmation, the tone of his words clearly indicated just a matter of time before the worst of the worst became official. Three minutes later, he received such grim news.
"And now, from Washington, government sources say that President Kennedy is dead. Those are government sources, still not an official announcement."
Watching a clearly distraught Cronkite felt like death by a thousand cuts. Still no official confirmation, but he knew, they all knew. Just two minutes previously at the Parkland hospital press conference, they had indeed confirmed Kennedy's passing. But this had yet to reach the press wires, before erupting like a blazing forest fire across the world.

2.33.pm. The ABC Television anchorman Ron Cochran reported a priest called into the hospital to administer the last rites to the President, had said that he died from his wounds. Although still an unconfirmed report. ABC, rather prematurely with the fact not fully

known put up a photograph on the screen of their President with the words...JOHN F. KENNEDY 1917–1963.
Shortly after Cochran had it confirmed that Kennedy was gone and relayed the following statement...
'Government sources now confirm, we have this from Washington. Government sources now confirm that President Kennedy is dead. So that, apparently, is the final word and an incredible event that I am sure no one except the assassin himself could have possibly imagined would occur on this day."

Back on ABC Radio, Don Gardiner reported the news, but not whether it was official. ABC then switched to their reporter Pete Clapper on Washington's Capitol Hill for an interview with the Senate's press liaison officer Richard Reidel. Moments later, the interview was abruptly interrupted by Gardiner...
"Ladies and gentlemen, the President of the United States, John Fitzgerald Kennedy, is dead. The President is dead. Let us pray."
ABC Radio then returned to its orchestral music.

2.38.pm. A CBS News employee was seen in the background ripping a sheet off from the AP News ticker. He quickly relayed it off camera to Cronkite, who puts on his glasses, took a few seconds to compose himself, then made the historic announcement...
"From Dallas, Texas, the flash, apparently official. President Kennedy died at 1.pm, (CST), 2:00.pm, Eastern Standard Time, some thirty-eight minutes ago."
After reading the flash, Cronkite took off his glasses and stared up at the studio clock as if in a state of incredulity. He paused for a moment then replaced his glasses...
"Vice President Johnson...". Cronkite cleared his throat; he was clearly struggling. "Has left the hospital in Dallas, but we do not know to where he has proceeded. Presumably, he will be taking the oath of office shortly and become the thirty-sixth president of the United States."

ACT THREE

GRANADA CALLING

"AND NOW. FROM THE NORTH…GRANADA"
England.

6.42.pm. GMT. A Reuters tickertape machine reported news of the assassination twelve minutes after the event.
…."President Kennedy was shot at today while riding in a motor convoy. A photographer reported seeing blood on the President's head"….

4607 miles away in Manchester, Northern England.
On the Granada television channel, The show *Scene at 6.30*, was in its early moments. The evening had been quiet, nothing truly newsworthy. The presenter Mike Scott had just started his opening lines, while the programme's news-editor Terry Dobson was looking through all the programme stories for a silly pun or some daft line to end the news, because this had already become a *Scene at 6-30* tradition. Finish the show with a smile to cheer up their viewers. *Scene at 6-30* had only come on air that same year, launched on Monday 21st January 1963. The entire Granada newsroom moved lock stock and barrel to the fifth floor of the building on Quay Street. On exiting the lifts, you turned right and there it was. The entire floor! In no time it became a hive of journalistic activity. A constant ringing of phones, the clatter of typewriters. The shouts of "Copy!"
It was exciting.
It was pulsating.

It was Granada Television, who in just a few moments were set to conquer the world with a sensational scoop in a manner few could ever have dreamt of. Tragically, regarding the macabre contents, more so their worst nightmares.

The still blossoming, thirty-minute, daily regional magazine programme consisted of news, current affair, music and topical Features. It had proved extremely popular with viewers. Each night there were special featured guests. Already ahead of the times in terms of presentation and format, amongst the presenters, some were set to become all-time broadcasting legends in the industry. Peter Eckersley, James Murray, Brian Trueman, Bill Grundy, Michael Parkinson, Bob Greaves, Chris Kelly and that fateful Friday night's host, Mike Scott. Here was a show where anyone at Granada who could write, and present were given an opportunity. Including Michael Parkinson. Parkinson first went live with the great Bill Grundy who informed the nervous Yorkshireman just beforehand "Lean forward as if engaging the viewer in conversation." Also, if anything went wrong. "Look pleadingly in my direction!" Grundy also reminded Parkinson, that come the end of the show he should always thank all in the studio who helped to put it out. Quite simple, but huge tips for a young man starting off in television and something Michael Parkinson never forgot. *Scene at 6.30* was produced by Granada in Manchester, specifically with the thinking being for the people of the North. Let the South take care of its own. It was irreverent, it possessed pure Northern attitude and it was live!

Scene at 6-30 was also able to attract the best new bands into the studio before their records had even hit the charts, none more so than The Beatles, when earlier that month on Friday 18th October, they travelled to Manchester to perform *She Loves You* in the *Scene at 6-30* studio. Their third appearance on the show. Many other artists had performed on *Scene at 6.30*, including Lulu, Cilla Black, the Searchers, Howlin' Wolf, Bo Diddley, Duke Ellington and countless other stars of the day. Eventually the format became one of the longest-running magazine and ten years later, on 1st October 1973, became *Granada Reports*.

Back to the night of 22nd November. The programme had been on the air for just five minutes when the telephone rang in the newsroom opposite the studio. Terry Dobson received a phone call from a Press Association sub-editor called Stan Kirby, who Granada had in place a special arrangement that any major news breaking between 6.pm and 7.pm, was phoned through to them on a reserved number. Kirby informed Dobson of the extraordinary, frightful news that the 35th President of the United States, John F. Kennedy had been shot in Dallas. The story was being reported by United Press International, White House reporter Merriman Smith, who actually fought with a rival AP reporter Jack Bell for a radiophone in their wire services limo, so that he could be first to report that the President's motorcade had taken fire. This story easily the biggest breaking news story in America, since the Japanese attacked Pearl Harbour.

"As soon as the news came from Dallas," recalled Kirby. "I dialled Granada's number and was through in seconds. They reacted without delay and was the first in Britain to tell viewers the news."

In the background while speaking to Kirby, Dobson could make out the first news reports being received in the PA newsroom on Smith's live radio link from Dallas. Dobson later spoke of those truly historic moments. "Because it was a live programme, Granada had arranged a "priority newsflash" arrangement with PA to ensure we received major news."

Now, at that time there existed an unwritten rule amongst independent broadcasters that if such a huge story broke none would go with it, but instead wait for ITN to lead. On the scene when the call came through was Granada's Scottish executive, Denis Forman. One of the founders of the company along with Sidney Bernstein. A formidable character, Forman had a distinguished military career. During World War Two he was wounded at Monte Cassino. A smoke canister fired by a supporting gun battery hit Forman's leg causing him to lose it. He later in his career presided over the creation of acclaimed series such as The *Jewel in the Crown* and ground-breaking programmes, *World in Action, University Challenge* and *Family at War*. Forman contacted ITN, but was informed they were not prepared to break into their schedules and go live with the story until it had been officially confirmed from their own people on the ground in the United States. This did not sit right with Forman, who with typical Granada fearlessness and determination to not let such a moment in history pass them by, decided Granada themselves should go ahead and break the news. A full half-hour before the rest of the country was informed of the assassination attempt on the American President, an ashen faced Scott received the message from Dobson.

Around eight minutes in Granada pulled off the greatest television scoop so far that century.

"Citing press wire sources, we are getting reports that shots have been fired at President Kennedy's motorcade in Dallas."

Dobson kept an open line to the *PA* for the rest of the programme as the dramatic events in downtown Dallas unfolded.

One lady present that evening was a copytaker and Secretary Joan Riley. "Mike had been on air about seven or eight minutes, it was normal chatty stuff. Then the phone went in the office, and it was answered by Terry Dobson. Terry picked the phone up and he whispered to me "Paper and typewriter quick!" This when I knew a late story was coming in. Moments after, he drew across his throat and whispered into my ear "Kennedy has been shot". Terry then dialled the programme's producer Barry Heads in the control room saying to him "There's been shots fired at Kennedy." And asking if Mike Scott could go live on air with the dreadful news?"

Heads was in fact a huge supporter of Scott and the two became lifelong friends. "When I was producing *Scene at 6-30* in the mid-Sixties, I remember that I would groan with frustration if Mike was having the day off, even though the team included such luminaries as Bill Grundy and Michael Parkinson. Mike was the essential presence. Quick-footed for the lighter items, sharp and probing for the more serious ones." So, at least Heads knew the story, if permission was granted to go ahead would be in safe hands.

"You better be right about this?" he replied to Dobson.

Dobson rang Kirby back to double check and when he had it confirmed beyond any doubt contacted Heads once more.

"It is true," he told him. "Shots have been fired, we think an aide has been shot, but the President is all right."
After speaking with Denis Forman, the word returned back to Dobson "Go ahead".
Mike Scott went on to update the viewers as the news came through on the wires, continuously updating, until eventually announcing the grave news…
"The President is dead."
"I haven't forgotten any of it," recalled Joan. "I was in shock, but the story was so big my typewriter had sparks coming off it!"

In Manchester city centre opposite Lewis's store, there stood an electronic ticker tape that screamed out in bright lights the dreadful news. Mancunians looking up in sheer disbelief. Young lads and ladies on their way for a Friday night out, couples meeting up to go to the cinema or dancing. Suddenly, the evening had turned from one of joyful expectation to sadness and despair. Back in November 1963, Great Britain's Prime Ministers were the ageing, ailing Harold Macmillan, just replaced by Alec Douglas-Home, both viewed by young people as relics of the past. Whereas Kennedy, he offered them something else. His speeches were inspirational, he was a symbol of hope for their futures. That they would have one. Coming off the back of a Cold War almost boiling over with the Cuban Missile Crisis, brought to a peaceful conclusion with America's young President, this king of Camelot negotiating with the Soviet Union and bringing the world back from the brink of a nuclear apocalypse. That Manchester night, as the grim tidings from Dallas, Texas, hit home, a grim silence not felt in this city since the Munich Air Disaster, five years previous took hold. Tears fell aplenty for Camelot's finest son who lay slain.

Back at Granada, Joan remained on the phone taking calls and keeping an eye on the PA wires for stories and tributes to Kennedy. For the station was planning an eleven o'clock programme dedicated to the dead President, but there was a terrible problem first to resolve. This was an obituary that could never have been foresaw. Who in their right minds would assassinate the President of the United States, especially one such as this? With Kennedy being so young, just 46 years-old, nobody at Granada had pre-prepared anything serious regarding footage, copy or pictures to deal with such an awful scenario. So, it was that soon as Joan discovers something useful, researchers rushed to rip it off her typewriter or the wires and raced away taking it to be used later. The programme did eventually go out, but little else as the network all but closed down in grief. Although congratulated by other news agencies on what was truly a monumental scoop, the feeling of complete shock and sadness at Kennedy's brutal killing remained the overwhelming memory of that bleak midwinter's night under Northern stars, for all involved with Granada Television.

"When you walked through the door into Granada Television, on Cross Street, Manchester, you felt the place was special. In every office hung a portrait of P.J. Barnum, the American circus-owner, as a reminder that we might be journalists, but never forget the razzle-dazzle."
Michael Parkinson

CATCHING UP

The BBC.
Mr Roberts.
7.05.pm. On the other channel, the BBC broke the news between *Points of View* and their current-affairs programme *Tonight*. A newsflash appeared on screen to show an unknown presenter staring grimly into the camera. The senior colleagues Richard Baker, Robert Dougal and Kenneth Kendall were enjoying themselves at the Dorchester hotel, for the annual dinner and ball of the Guild of Television Producers and Directors. It fell to Wellington, New Zealand born John Roberts, a young staff newsman to fill in, who had only been with the BBC since the previous June.
After Roberts first appearance, *Tonight* returned but was then pulled off air nineteen minutes short. Roberts came back reporting, telling his audience the President had been shot in the head and his condition critical, when suddenly the telephone beside him started to ring live on air. It turned out the BBC's Monitoring Service had picked up a monumental bulletin from the *Voice of America*. Robert's face turned ashen grey as he took the message, and announced back into the camera…
"We regret to announce that President Kennedy is dead."
With that said John Roberts bowed his head solemnly. He would be seen on air throughout that dark evening. Roberts later received much deserved acclaim from both colleagues and viewers for the calm manner he handled such a historic and deeply distressing announcement on behalf of the corporation. Such as the following letter from BBC TV news editor Waldo Maguire, dated Tuesday 26th November 1963…Four days on from the assassination.

"Dear John,
May I offer my sincere thanks and congratulations on the magnificent way you read the news of Kennedy's death on Friday

night. Viewers rang to say how much they had appreciated the calm and dignified announcement, thrust on you at such short notice. May I also say that I thought your reading of the 9 o'clock News and News Extra was excellent, and that your unflappability was a considerable comfort to the harassed editorial and production staff. Many thanks and best wishes.
Waldo."

By 11.pm, four hours after the news first broke on the BBC, they broadcasted a tribute to President Kennedy, featuring heads of all three major parties. The Liberal Leader Jo Grimond, had been driven to Broadcasting House from Oxford by undergraduates. The Leader of the Opposition Harold Wilson arrived by fast car from North Wales to the BBC's Manchester studio, and the recently appointed Prime minister Sir Alec Douglas-Home, spoke of a "young man, a brave statesman killed in the full vigour of his manhood".

The BBC's Peter Watson was reporting from the United Nations in New York when news first broke of President John F. Kennedy's assassination.
Within hours Watson was broadcasting from Dallas.
"President Kennedy was shot at 12.35 local time from the fifth floor of a state book warehouse as he drove by on his tour of Dallas. The murder weapon, a 6.5.mm Italian rifle with a telescopic sight was found in the warehouse. Two miles away and forty-five minutes later, after a description of the suspected killer had been broadcast, Police Officer Tippit was shot dead as he went to question a man. This man was Lee Harvey Oswald, who has now been charged with both the murder of Tippit and the President. This much is known about him: He is 24 year-old, slim, dark, married, was employed at the book warehouse and had a curious background of connection with the Soviet Union and Cuba. He is a Texan from Fort worth, went to Russia four years ago and returned to this country eighteen months later at United States Government expense. When his wife visited police headquarters, she was accompanied by a Russian speaking

interpreter. In Cuban affairs he is reported to have claimed to be pro-Castro".

Walker then filed another report entitled...
Dallas. The Day After.
"In a city of a million people there can be few outward signs, even of the death of a President. The sun shines out of a clear blue sky onto the pale brown, brick warehouse from which the assassin's bullets were fired. Only a couple of police cars nearby mark the difference between this and any other commercial building. There are no crowds, but from every car and bus that passes eyes turn upwards towards that fatal fifth floor window. There are no crowds either outside police headquarters where Lee Harvey Oswald spent the night after being charged with the murder of President Kennedy. Outwardly there are few signs in the chilly windswept streets of the city known as "the big D". But inwardly there is only one word to describe the feelings of Dallas and all Texas. It is Shame, shame not only at the crime, but shame that Texas hospitality could have been breached. In the city itself, the Dallas Morning News talks of "a cruel, shameful mark in this city's history". From the place where President Kennedy made his last speech and which is Oswald's home, the Fort Worth Star Telegram says: "There arose a sense of outrage and, especially for those who live in Texas, shame. The shock was all the greater for Texans because this unspeakable thing happened in their midst in a state known for its goodwill and hospitality to all. What is quite remarkable here is that, although Oswald had a known communist record, and that his lodgings were full of Communist literature, no-one is talking about a communist plot; no-one is trying to shift the blame or shuffle off the burden of shame.
As for Dallas, the brightly lit streets are rather empty but still brightly lit, except for one shop full of children's toys which is dark and bears a neatly printed notice.
"Closed in memory of John F. Kennedy".
"The people, many of whom were not so long ago blushing at the undignified treatment accorded to Mr Adlai Stevenson, what do they

think? One man with whom I flew from New York said: "I come from Dallas…and I guess I am not proud of that just now."

The BBC Television schedule on 22nd November 1963.
18.00: News
18.30: Weather
18.34: Trailer: Here's Harry
18.35: Look: Fish Families
19.00: Trailer: Britten At Fifty
19.01: Points Of View
19.04: News Flash - President Kennedy Wounded (John Roberts)
19.06: Tonight
19.26: News Flash - Death of President Kennedy (John Roberts)
19.28: BBC Graphic/Silence
19.32: News Flash - Death of President Kennedy (John Roberts)
19.33: Graphic/Music
19.41.04: News Flash (John Roberts)
19.41.24: Graphic/Music
19.47: News Flash (John Roberts). Live Washington insert by Leonard Parkin
19.49: Graphic/Clock/Announcement
19.50: Here's Harry: The Musician
20.14: Graphic/Special Announcement
20.15: News Flash (John Roberts). Live Washington insert by Leonard Parkin
20.19: Dr. Finlay's Casebook: The Face Saver
20.59: Graphic/Special Announcement
21.00: Dr. Finlay's Casebook (cont.)
21.09: News (John Roberts) Leonard Parkin Washington Report and Joseph Harsch on what death means to Americans
21.26: Weather
21.27: Special announcement
21.27: Filler - Recital - Andor Foldes
21.34.39: Blank screen
21.34.42: clock announcement

21.35: Britten At Fifty
22.43: Clock/Special announcement
22.44: Filler: Vienna Soloists
22.59: Clock
23.00: Tribute to President Kennedy. Intro and links by Ian Threthowan and included tributes by Sir Alec Douglas-Home, Harold Wilson and Joe Grimmond
23.30: Graphic
23.31: News Extra (John Roberts)
23.55.10: Graphic
23.55.21: Epilogue read by Father Agnellus Andrew
23.59: H.M Queen caption and National Anthem
00.00.38: Close down

Whereas on ITV,
despite Granada in the North having already broken the news, elsewhere, audiences remained totally unaware of events happening in Dallas. And then...
7.00.pm. The ITV network joined up for the game show *Take Your Pick*.
7.10.pm. ITN's first newsflash appeared on screen. *Take Your Pick* then returned to air.
7.30.pm. The scheduled continued on with the poignantly named, now looking back, *Emergency Ward 10*.
7.50.pm. Ten minutes in it was pulled for another newsflash confirming: "President Kennedy is dead." No commercials were then broadcasted for ninety minutes.
8.00.pm. The network started to play solemn music performed by the Halle Orchestra.
8.55.pm. A further news bulletin followed, then ITV returned to its advertised schedule showing a play by the great playwright Jack Rosenthal.

ITV'S "original" scheduled line up for 22nd November 1963.
17.55: News
18.15: The Weekend Weather Forecast

19.00: Take Your Pick
19.30: Emergency-Ward 10
20.00: Route 66
20.55: News from ITN
21.10: Friday Night presents
22.05: Boyd Q.C.
22.35: News Headlines
22.37: Roving Report
23.02: Dateline Westminster
23.20: The Weather Forecast
23.50: The Epilogue

Read all about it!
The Manchester Guardian.

5.30.pm. The Guardian newspaper late-shift clocked in on Cross Street. That Friday evening, they could never have dreamt what lay in wait for them. For in just an hour's time they would all be playing a part in producing a truly historic edition of their newspaper. News begun to filter though from different sources that something huge had happened in America. At first no one knew what was actually going on, but then the shout went out that shocked all to their core.
"Kennedy has been shot!"
Even the most hardened of journalists found themselves struggling as this unprecedented news story unfolded in deadly quick time, especially when it became confirmed Kennedy was dead. Killed by an assassin's bullet. With a 9.30 deadline looming for the first edition, emotions had to be put aside to get the stories to print.
However, in every part of the building, a sombre mood prevailed, from the newsroom to those in the composing department, to the men working the printing presses and proofing section. Everyone was deeply affected. This the first time that The Guardian had gone with a banner headline, and not their usual single columns style. The opening edition contained an astonishing four-thousand-word obituary,

Kennedy's inaugural address, a piece on the new President, Lyndon B Johnson, and emerging background stories on the lone assassin arrested for JFK's killing.
A man being named as Lee Harvey Oswald.

CALLING CAMBRIDGE

During his highly controversial 2016 presidential campaign, Donald Trump seemingly became obsessed with a conspiracy theory that the father of one of his Republican opponents, Senator Ted Cruz of Texas, was somehow involved with the assassination of President John F. Kennedy. This a claim vehemently denied by the Cruz family. Trump's only evidence for his theory was based on a grainy old ripping photograph from 1963, showing Cruz standing next to a man resembling Lee Harvey Oswald. Both were handing out fliers supporting the then Cuban leader, Fidel Castro. Once President, Trump did allow the National Archives to post 2,800 other pages online, but he waived on a promise to release them all, holding back an unspecific number of documents at the request of the FBI and CIA, due to national security concerns. But one document did slip through and told a quite extraordinary tale. A storyline out of the most fantastic, ridiculous spy movie. But could it have been true? A British local newspaper, The *Cambridge News* received an anonymous telephone call about some "some big news" set to happen shortly in the United States. The caller said only that the *Cambridge News* reporter should call the American Embassy in London for some big news, and then he hung up. This information came from a CIA memo released by the American National Archives, but one hardly noticed. Simply just another tiny piece in a never-to-be-finished jigsaw puzzle on the most controversial murder in United States history. An overseas call was made from America to England at 18.05, GMT time, on Friday 22nd November 1963. A full twenty-five minutes before President John F. Kennedy was assassinated in Dallas, Texas. The document belonged to the Deputy Director of the CIA, James Angleton, to the FBI Director, J Edgar Hoover. It claimed that the British Security Service, MI5, had reported the call was made to the senior reporter of The *Cambridge Times*. It read "The caller said only that the Cambridge News reporter should call the American Embassy in London for some big news and then hung up. After the word of the President's death was received the reporter informed the Cambridge police of the anonymous call and the police informed MI5. The important point is that the call was made, according to MI5 calculations, about twenty-five minutes before the President was shot. The Cambridge reporter had never received a call of this kind before, and MI5 state that he is known to them as a sound and loyal person with no security record." The memo goes on to state that similar anonymous phone calls "of a strangely coincidental nature" had been received by people in the UK over the past year. "Particularly in connection with the case of Dr Ward". A reference to Doctor Stephen Ward, one of the central and tragic figures involved in the Profumo affair. Ward ultimately committed suicide because of the stress and embarrassment this caused him.

Back to 2017, once the story broke, the current staff at The *Cambridge News* claimed they had no idea who took the alleged call. One reporter, Anna Savva said hearing about it was "completely jaw-dropping. It would have been common knowledge in the office who took the call, but we have nothing in our archive, we have nobody here who knows the name of the person who took the call".

Of those who worked at The *Cambridge News*, back then, one senior reporter, Jock Gillespie remained highly sceptical that anything actually happened. Indeed, the first Jock heard of it came in 2017, when the file was released. "There is no way in hell that would have happened without being talked about," he claimed. "There are three or four of us that still get together, the old farts, and there is no way that wouldn't have been talked about. That would have never ever have got past us. People I knew at that time would not have shut up about it. It would have been published as well. A windup, are you sure it wasn't Cambridge Massachusetts they were talking about?"

This actually wasn't the first time the story had appeared. Back during the eighties, a London solicitor by the name of Michael Eddowes, started to investigate a document he had come across, claiming it to be CIA based. In the document it mentioned a call had been made to the Cambridge News warning that something big was going to happen...The mystery goes on.

Printed in Great Britain
by Amazon